"Why are you not sleeping, *niña?* It is very late." Rafael's eyes raked her boldly.

Sara felt almost naked in her thin gown. She wished now that she had slipped on her robe. "It was hot . . . but perhaps I should try to go back to sleep," she said, and pushed away from the wheel. In trying to turn away without brushing against him, she stepped on her gown and tripped.

His arm flashed out to catch her, and he hauled her against his hard chest. "Careful, *niña,*" he warned in a seductive voice. Instead of releasing her when she regained her footing, he held fast.

Sara squirmed in the circle of his arm, her hands fluttering against his chest. "Thank you, señor, you can let go now," she whispered, as something intense flared between them. She was powerless to resist, when he bent his head to claim her lips.

"Impossible," he breathed. His mouth covered hers hungrily. Sara's senses spun out of control. Her knees weakened, as shivers of desire raced through her.

Rafael groaned. His heart pounded, and the blood raced hotly through his veins. He wanted her so much, it was like a physical pain . . .

SANDRA DONOVAN

SILVER SEDUCTION

ZEBRA BOOKS
KENSINGTON PUBLISHING CORP.

*This book is dedicated to two people
who have been very dear to me through the years:
my cousin, Marilyn Barton,
and my sister-in-law, Violet DeSha.*

Chapter 1

St. Louis, Missouri
June 28, 1831

"You needn't concern yourself with my wife and six children, Sara. That part of my life will be separate from the time I spend with you," Farber pointed out impatiently in answer to her question. He shifted his large bulk on the settee in her drawing room, trying to ease the ache in his loins. He wanted this young woman more than he cared to admit— even to himself.

Sara Anne Clayton stared aghast at the man. A feeling of revulsion washed over her, as he licked his thick lips and eyed her as if she were the main course at dinner. His bulbous nose dominated meaty features, and was growing redder as his temper rose. Sara opened her mouth to decline his preposterous proposal, but nothing came out. She was shocked that this man who was now her legal guardian—who had been her father's trusted banker and financial advisor for several years—could so degrade her with the suggestion that she become his mistress! Finding her voice at last, she gasped, "I can hardly believe you're saying these things to me, Mr. Farber. My father trusted you to see to my welfare, not to . . . to prostitute me." Her soft protest ended in a shaky whisper. In all her sheltered eighteen years, she'd never had to face an indelicate situation such as this . . . and she was alone.

Farber watched her twisting a handkerchief in her hands in agitation. She was trying valiantly to blink away the tears that filled her large eyes. Her beauty was different from that of any other woman he'd known, and since the first time he'd laid eyes on her, he had become obsessed with her. She was petite and perfect in every respect. She had a most unusual shade of silver hair, and dark, thick lashes surrounded those beautiful, cornflower blue eyes that gazed at the world with innocence. And that innocence excited him more each time he saw her. His obsession began when William Clayton moved all his assets to Farber's bank five years before, bringing his daughter, Sara Anne, with him. Even at thirteen, she was a beauty. From that day on, he had ingratiated himself with Clayton, in hopes of seeing Sara occasionally.

Abruptly returning to the business at hand, he said briskly, "I choose not to think of it in those terms, my dear. Rather, consider me your protector . . . someone who will cherish and love you." His voice dropped to a husky note then. "I will give you the world, if you'll but cooperate."

Standing, Sara straightened her shoulders. "I

think you should leave, Mr. Farber. I will never agree to such a thing."

Even though she was withholding what he wanted most, he grudgingly admired her dignity. He stood as well and nodded. "I will leave you for now, but I insist that you think about this before you make up your mind. I'm not a man who takes no for an answer, Sara, and if you deny me, I won't feel obliged to keep your family secrets, as I've done in the past."

Sara's head snapped up at his veiled threat. "Secrets? What secrets do you speak of?"

His mouth twisted into a sneer. "Your father's business practices were sometimes, shall we say, shady. Not strictly illegal, but borderline. And then there are those quaint little stories your father told me in confidence about how your mother, uh, entertained—yes, that's a good word for it—some high-ranking politicians, to gain government contracts for his lumber." He paused and let his words sink in, before he continued, "I can't be concerned with your family's reputation without some incentive. Do you see what I mean?"

Sara felt a raging anger suffuse her whole being at his vindictiveness, but she hardly knew how to vent it, given her gentle nature. Sputtering, she said, "That's not true and you know it! Please . . . just leave."

He made his way to the door, but turned to speak again. "I will give you until Friday to see reason, Sara. That's five days. Friday night at eight sharp, I'll return for your answer." He smiled smugly, as if he already knew what her answer would be.

"Remember also that I have control of your money. A young woman without reputation or money cannot go very far in this city." He left her alone then, closing the door behind him.

For a moment, or perhaps much longer, Sara didn't know, she stared at the closed door, replaying the whole conversation in her head. She grew pale, and then flushed in anger by turns, thinking about the outrageous plan he'd put to her. He was completely mad to think she'd agree to it. Her stomach constricted, however, at his threat to ruin her family's reputation. She knew in her heart that his ugly accusations were false, but society, being what it was, would not be so fair-minded. Many people would believe his lies or, at the very least, would insure that she was shunned.

Sinking back down on her chair, she dropped her head in her hands, and gave way to the tears that had been threatening. Her whole world was crumbling around her, and she hadn't the vaguest notion of what to do or where to turn. Her parents' families lived in Savannah, Georgia, but did not care about her. There had been a rift between both her parents and their people when her parents married, which was why William and Melanie had moved to St. Louis. Not one word had passed between the estranged branches in nineteen years. If Sara had not read her mother's journals a week ago, she wouldn't have known of these relatives at all, for they had never been spoken of openly in the Clayton household.

It had only been a month since the freak carriage accident had claimed her parents' lives, and now

Jonas Farber was trying to take away her innocence, and withhold her funds as well. Moreover, this new grief had dredged up the terrible hurt she felt over the loss of her beloved older brother, Maxwell, two years ago.

Sara blew her nose and wiped her eyes as a discreet knock sounded at the door. She called permission to enter and was relieved to find it was Fillette, her personal maid.

"Cook send me to fin' out if you be wantin' tea, but I see yo' visitor done gone, Missy." The black girl, a few years Sara's senior, spoke as she crossed the large room. When she came close, she frowned. "Sweet chile, why is you upset? I ain't seen you cry since de funeral."

Sara's face crumpled and the tears started again. "Oh, Fillette . . . it was awful," she whispered brokenly.

The girl stooped down and wrapped an arm around Sara's trembling shoulders. "What, Missy? Did dat man bring you mo' bad news?" she asked in alarm.

Sara wiped at her wet cheeks and nodded. "In a way, yes." She told Fillette what had transpired with Jonas Farber, and ended with a soft wail, "What am I to do?"

Fillette shook her head in disgust. There was more knowledge in her young soul of the vile ways of men than she cared to think about. The black girl felt as protective of Sara as she might have a child of her own, despite the few years that separated them, and so this situation distressed her sorely. "What 'bout dos fine Creole friends of yo mama and papa, chile?

11

Can you git help from one o' dem?"

"They were more or less social friends, Fillette, not close friends. I'm sure that's why Father left his banker in charge of me and everything else. Besides, I don't think any of them would want to get involved in scandalous gossip," Sara said quietly, her tears under control now.

Fillette clenched her jaw resolutely. "Twixt the two of us, Missy, we think of sompin', 'cause you ain't gonna be dat old bastard's whore!"

Sara felt better just knowing she had an ally, even if the girl was a slave and even more helpless than herself. She gave Fillette a watery smile. "We have until Friday to think of something."

"Don' you worry none, chile. Dat be long enough," the black girl promised with more confidence than she felt.

Rafael Esteban Delgado looked out the open, second-story window of the Southern Hotel on Broadway Street at the late afternoon traffic moving apace. The occasional shouts of the wagon drivers reminded him of the muleskinners on the streets of Sante Fe. Aside from that, there was no comparison between Santa Fe and this busy, bustling city of St. Louis. Life in New Mexico was geared to a slower pace, and the colors of the landscape easier on the eyes than this crowded, brick metropolis.

Behind him, his companion's voice broke into his thoughts, and he turned. "Forgive me, Pedro, I was not listening."

Pedro Pino was of medium height, with steel gray

hair and a wiry frame. He was dressed in tan trousers, white shirt, and a matching silver-trimmed, short coat, but felt more at home in the working clothes of the *rancho*. He had been born on Hacienda Delgado sixty-two years ago, and had worked his way up to the favored position of overseer at a young age. For the last ten years, he had been teaching Rafael all that he knew of the workings of the vast estate. Now, he looked at his friend and protégée, and smiled. "I merely asked if you wanted to take a walk along the river, before we dine."

"*Sí,* it is too hot to stay inside." Rafael reached for his black coat.

The two men drew much attention as they passed through the lobby of the plush hotel. Not only because they were both finely dressed in the Spanish style with braid and silver trim on their suits, but more for the old-world dignity they exuded.

Rafael nodded politely as two female guests passed them. He missed their sighs and breathless comments, as he stepped out onto the boardwalk. He would have been surprised to learn that he had been the major topic of discussion among the female guests, since he had arrived ten days ago.

His face was strong with a square jaw, high cheekbones, and large, dark brown eyes. His black hair brushed his collar, longish by American standards, and it parted naturally on the side. Standing six feet tall with broad shoulders, he was well muscled, but moved with an easy grace. Not only did his handsome appearance draw attention, but he exuded an air of great power, barely contained. These qualities all combined to make him irresistible to the fairer sex wherever he traveled.

The two men walked to the levee and gazed at the wide expanse of the Mississippi. A breeze blew off the water, making it somewhat cooler than was the case in the confines of the hotel, and Rafael breathed deeply of the fresh air. He smiled for the first time that day, and commented, "The *Río del Norte* would be jealous of this mighty waterway, eh, Pedro?"

The older man chuckled. "*Sí*, my friend. Even in the spring, her banks do not stretch this far." Glancing at the barges, side-wheelers, and stern-wheelers that plied the river, he added, "If we had navigable rivers at home, there would be no need to travel to places like this for goods and such. They would come to us."

Rafael sighed. "I, too, grow weary of this trip, Pedro. Speaking of our mission, in two days we will have contracted for the silks from New Orleans. After that, I say we leave."

Pedro's eyebrows raised in question. "But what of the teacher your grandfather ordered us to bring back? We haven't yet found the right person."

Rafael gave an impatient snort. "There have been several suitable applicants who answered the advertisement, and you found something wrong with each one. What sort of paragon are you looking for, Pedro?"

Pedro's expression was bland. "Don Vicente had certain requirements in mind, and so far I haven't found a woman who meets them. I cannot fail my patron, Rafael—I owe everything to him."

Rafael decided not to argue with Pedro. He understood that his friend was caught in the middle of the animosity between grandfather and grandson. He nodded. "One more week and no more, Pedro, no matter what Don Vicente wants. We must get back before winter."

Meekly, Pedro agreed. The older man wished for the thousandth time that these two proud men he loved could forget their differences and become a real family, but he didn't hold out any hope. Don Vicente Martin Delgado was a proud Spaniard, and stubborn to a fault. He had done his duty by raising his daughter's son, but could not accept the fact that the boy was half-Comanche. Nor could he bring himself to show Rafael any love. Rafael had felt the slight at a very early age, and had grown bitter over the years, building a hard shell around his heart. Pedro sighed and prayed God would send the right woman for the post of teacher. Perhaps Don Vicente's plan of finding a wife for Rafael was an indication that he did care for the boy. And then again, Pedro thought, it could mean that the old Don merely wanted to control another aspect of Rafael's life.

Neither Sara nor Fillette had found a solution to Sara's problem by Wednesday. And although she had practiced her meditations each day, Sara was growing more nervous by the moment. For a brief time, she reconsidered trying to contact family members in Savannah, but discarded that notion as it would take too long. She had gone to the bank and tried to quietly draw some money on her father's account, but was told that his assets were frozen by order of Mr. Farber. All of her mother's jewels were locked away in Jonas Farber's care, so she could not even sell those to get money to escape. By evening, she had a throbbing headache, and refused dinner when Fillette came upstairs to fetch her.

"I bring you some tea, chile, an' some headache powders. Mebe some fresh baked bread, too. You got to eat sompin', Missy. You ain't eat since Monday!" Fillette left her lying on the bed and went to fetch these things. When she returned, she had the *St. Louis Beacon* folded on the tray. "De paper done come, Missy. Mebe you could read a while, an' take yo' mind off yo' troubles."

Sara thanked her in a listless tone and sat up, placing the tray over her lap. She stirred the powders into her tea, and sipped absently as she scanned the headlines. There was an article about the summer storm that destroyed a farmer's barn in Frenchtown a few days before, and one about Mayor Page's new plan to improve the streets of St. Louis. Turning the page, she glanced at the newest fashions in ladies-wear, but cared little that the merchants were now carrying reticules with embroidery done in ribbon, chenille, and tiny white fish scales.

She finished her tea and felt somewhat better, as the powders seemed to ease her headache. Then, as she flipped through the remaining pages, her eye caught an ad that read, Help Wanted—Female. Her lethargy disappeared as she read on: "Young woman, single, willing to emigrate to the province of New Mexico to act as teacher on large estate. Apply

16

to Señor Pino at the Southern Hotel for an appointment."

Sara's hands were shaking as she read the advertisement twice more. Her heart pounded and life surged back into her body, as she flung the paper aside and scrambled out of bed. The province of New Mexico! That was where Maxwell had gone to live. Her brother had written to her of the beauty of the country, the warmth of the people, and how he had loved Sante Fe. Sara had longed to go live with him, but her parents had scoffed at the idea. She was a wealthy young lady and must marry well and take her place in society, they had said. And then, two years ago, word had reached them of Max's death. He had had a partner in a silver mine, and the man had written to her, sending his condolences and telling her how much Max had talked of her the three years he had known him.

The desire to go to Santa Fe was reignited in Sara. She wanted to see the town and her brother's final resting place. The move would solve her immediate problem as well. If only the post wasn't filled yet—if only she could convince them she was the person for the job! Dread and anticipation warred within her breast, as she rang for Fillette.

When Fillette entered the room, Sara was buried in the wardrobe, pulling out one dress after another in a frenzy.

The change in her mistress astounded Fillette. "Have you done gone mad, Missy?"

Sara looked around the closet door to smile at the maid. "Oh, Fillette, I may be saved yet! Help me find a conservative gown that will make me look a bit older. I may have a job interview as soon as tomorrow."

"Praise de Lord!" the maid breathed, moving to Sara's side. "I been prayin' sompin' would happen. Here, let me look, chile. You is makin' a mess of dis wardrobe, and I knows better than you what's here. Stan' back an' tell me all 'bout dis job you foun'."

From the moment Sara left the house on Carondolet Road in her carriage Thursday morning, until she arrived at the Southern Hotel on Broadway, she wavered between doubt and hope. Over and over, she practiced in her head what she would say to this Señor Pino, regarding her qualifications. Her education had been better than average, thanks to her dear friend and tutor, Master Filbert. He had taught her right along with Maxwell, when she should have been in the nursery playing with her toys. He had opened up the world of math, science, languages, and philosophy to her, and found her an apt pupil. Even if she didn't speak Spanish fluently, she was sure she could learn quickly.

Her driver stopped at the front door and helped her alight. "I don't know how long I'll be, Joseph," she told him nervously.

"I watch for you to come out, Missy. Don' you worry none," he said kindly. The servants at the Clayton house adored their young mistress, and had always pitied the lonely child, knowing her parents had little time for her or her brother.

Once inside the lobby, Sara crossed to a wall mirror and reassured herself that she looked presentable. She had decided on a dark blue muslin day dress with short puffed sleeves. Her wide-brimmed bonnet matched the color of the dress, and was free of any decoration excepting the cream-colored ribbon that secured it at her chin. A cream-colored muslin pelerine draped her shoulders, despite the warm day, and completed her sedate outfit. She was sure it added a few years to her age, and hoped Señor Pino would not take a good look at her and pronounce her too young.

Glancing at the watch pinned to her bodice, she turned toward the stairs. She had sent a note to the señor last evening asking for an appointment; a return reply had invited her to appear at Suite 202 at ten o'clock this morning. Her relief that the post had not been filled as yet was short-lived, and she worried the night through about how her interviewer would receive someone as young and inexperienced as she.

Resolutely, she made her way to the second floor and found the correct suite. Knocking, she took a deep breath and waited to be admitted.

When the door opened, Sara found herself staring at a man's wide, muscled chest, visible where his white shirt lay open to his lean waist. His skin was the color of polished bronze. She blushed and started to back away. Surely, she had knocked at the wrong door. No decent man would answer the door thus. "I . . . I'm sorry. I must have the wro—"

"Señorita Clayton?" he inquired softly in a deep voice. "Excuse my appearance, *por favor*. I thought you were the maid with our refreshments. You are early, you know."

Sara dragged her gaze away from his chest to look into the man's face, and found it equally disturbing. He had a square jaw, high cheekbones, and large brown eyes with lashes as long as her own. Her tongue felt thick, and her mind refused to think coherently. "I . . . perhaps I should come back later," she stammered, and started to turn away. His steady regard made her feel like a mouse cornered by a snake.

He smiled, showing white, even teeth that sparkled against his darkly tanned face. It caused the most alarming flutters in her stomach.

"No need to run away, señorita. I will not bite you . . . I promise," he said with amusement, as if he had read her mind.

Just then, an older man stepped to the door. "Ah, I see you have arrived, Señorita Clayton." The younger man turned and disappeared back into the room. Sara let out the breath she'd been holding.

"Señor Pino?" Sara asked, her voice shaky. He was more what she'd been expecting, and was suitably dressed in a black coat and trousers trimmed with silver braid.

He bowed slightly from the waist and smiled. "*Sí.* Please come in." He stepped back to allow her entry, and noticed the uncertain look in her eyes. "Do not be offended by Rafael's appearance. He was not expecting you as yet, and finds the humidity in your fair city quite uncomfortable."

Sara plucked up her courage and stepped through the door. Out of the corner of her eye, she saw the younger man donning his coat. Just then, a maid arrived with a tray. Señor Pino directed her to place it on the low table in front of the settee.

"I thought you might like some lemonade, while we discuss the post," he explained.

Sara sat down, murmuring her thanks. When the younger man disappeared into a room off the sitting room, Sara began to feel more comfortable. Señor Pino asked her some general questions about her family and education, and Sara found it easy to talk to this charming man. He, in turn, told her something of the Hacienda Delgado, explaining that Don Vicente wanted his workers' children given some basic education, and that the priest in Santa Fe was growing too old to teach the young ones.

"Also, when the children get old enough, they work on the hacienda along with their parents. If we had a resident teacher, they could spend a few hours in the morning at their lessons, and then the remainder of the day doing their chores."

"Don Vicente must be a generous man to hire a teacher for these children, when he does not have to," she commented shyly.

Hearing a rude snort, she glanced up and found the younger man standing in the doorway of the sitting room watching them. He was more presentable now with his shirt fastened and a coat on. Nevertheless, the butterflies returned to her stomach.

"His workers adore him, señorita. He is very good to them," Rafael said with a hint of sarcasm. He walked over to stand beside Señor Pino's chair, casually leaning against the high back.

Once again, Sara felt smothered by his presence, and asked nervously, "Do you also work for Don Vicente?"

His sensuous lips twisted into a cynical smile. *"Sí,* but with less devotion perhaps."

Señor Pino looked up at the younger man and frowned slightly. "I did not realize Rafael had not introduced himself to you. This is Don Vicente's grandson, Don Rafael Esteban Delgado."

Sara nodded and wondered at the younger man's tone, but did not dwell on it, for he was looking at her in a way that made her tingle all over. He made her feel so strange, she was not sure that she wanted this post after all. The only thing that stayed her tongue was the knowledge that Jonas Farber awaited.

Señor Pino returned to the business at hand. "If we should decide to offer you this post, señorita, how soon could you be ready to travel?"

Without hesitation, she said, "Tomorrow."

Señor Pino's eyebrows rose, but he said blandly, "Very well. We will send a messenger to your home by three this afternoon with our answer."

Señor Pino rose and fetched a pen and paper, asking her to write down her address. Once that was done, Sara thanked him as he walked her to the door. She could feel the younger man's dark eyes burning her back.

Rafael and Pedro sat across from each other in the hotel dining room at lunch. Each man was lost in his own thoughts, while partaking of the beef steak and vegetables.

Rafael couldn't get Señorita Clayton out of his mind, and it irritated him. He had felt a stirring of something inside that he thought long dead. She was so young and beautiful, with her perfect face and blue eyes the color of the summer sky back home. He supposed her ivory skin fascinated him, because the women of his country were dark. Her slender body was gracefully rounded in the right places, and he had ached to take her in his arms. *Por Dios!* It had been a while since he'd bedded a woman, and he was getting overly sentimental about this girl—this stranger. But there had been something about her that made him want to protect her. There had been an innocence . . . a vulnerability. He scowled and attacked his steak with a vengeance.

Pedro's thoughts were on Sara as well. She was exactly what Don Vicente had asked him to find: beautiful, intelligent, of good family. No matter what the old man's reasons, Sara would make a perfect wife for Rafael, and an exquisite mistress for Hacienda Delgado. He glanced up at Rafael. "I think Señorita Clayton is a good choice, don't you?"

Rafael continued eating and shrugged. "She is perhaps too young."

"We need someone young to make the journey, my friend. And to keep up with her young charges. Since she has no family, she will not be pining to come home," he pointed out. "I think it is very sad about her brother dying in that mineshaft. I remember the incident."

Rafael nodded, but refused to be drawn in by pity. "She speaks very little Spanish, Pedro. How will she teach the children anything?"

"I can tell she is bright and will learn quickly. I will teach her on the trip. By the time we reach Santa Fe,

23

she will be fairly fluent." Pedro was puzzled by Rafael's behavior. Just the day before, he had complained that Pedro was being too critical of the candidates.

"Do what you will. It makes no difference to me," Rafael said. "Don Vicente gave you charge of that mission, not me."

Pedro smiled placatingly. "He knew you would have your hands full with the cargo, Rafael, and would not wish to be bothered. It is settled then. I will send a messenger to the señorita's house this afternoon, and request that she be ready to depart tomorrow at noon."

Chapter 2

When the messenger arrived at the Clayton house, Sara felt as if the weight of the world had been lifted from her shoulders. She and Fillette began immediately to plan what she would take. Joseph and one of the younger boys hauled a traveling trunk up to her room, and the two young women began packing.

She remembered Max had written that the winters were very cold in the high plains, so she chose several soft wool day dresses, as well as silk and satin gowns for evening wear. Her two new riding costumes, one blue and the other green, would be essential, she decided, along with a pair of sturdy riding boots.

After a while, she left Fillette and another maid to continue packing, and wandered about the red-brick mansion that had been home to her for as long as she could remember. The only happy memories she had were tied to Maxwell. Her parents had always been busy with each other or with their social life, leaving little time to spend with her. But Max had played childish games with her, taken her to the park, read stories to her of knights, castles, and kings.

She'd been thirteen when he left, and it had broken her heart. Walking about the schoolroom, she touched familiar books on a shelf, and traced the initials Max had carved on the tabletop where he sat for so many years. The pain of losing him still cut deeply. Gathering several school books, she added two books of the romantic Arthurian tales to take with her. She would read to her students, as Max had read to her.

When she left the schoolroom, she went to her parents' bedroom and retrieved her mother's journals, along with her father's small derringer from the wardrobe. She slipped both in her pocket. They would be the only momentos of her parents she would take to her new home. She had no need for anything else.

"There's a small town up ahead where we will stay the night," Rafael informed the man and woman in the carriage.

He had ridden ahead on his stallion and returned with the welcome news. Sara was relieved, for she and Señor Pino had been bouncing along on the rough road for eight hours, with only two stops to rest and water the horses.

Rafael moved alongside the carriage at a walk to cool his animal. Through the windowless openings in the side, he fixed Sara with a concerned look. "Are you all right, Señorita Clayton? You look weary."

She tried to smile. "Just a little, señor. I will be fine, once we've rested and had something to eat."

Rafael frowned. She seemed so fragile, and there were bluish spots under her eyes. *Por Dios!* The trip had barely begun, and she looked exhausted already. "We are in the easy stages now. I hope you will be able to bear up when we get to the plains," he said, impatient all of a sudden.

At his tone, Sara sat up a little straighter and unconsciously pushed out her chin. "I may be city born and bred, Señor Rafael, but I am very strong."

When she'd arrived at the hotel that day, that peculiar feeling had assailed him again, making him want to put as much distance as he could between them. The effect she had on him was irritating, and his good manners seemed to have vanished. He scowled. "You look as if a good puff of wind would blow you away. Are you sure you won't change your mind and return home? We could hire a carriage in town to take you back."

Pedro had been watching the two of them, and listening to their exchange with great interest. He'd never seen Rafael treat a woman with so little courtesy before, and the young señorita had such a sweet nature! She had touched Rafael in a way that made him wary, Pedro thought with a flash of insight. He barely suppressed a smile as he said, "The *niña* will be fine, I'm sure. The first leg of a journey is always the hardest, as we accustom ourselves to the pace." Turning to Sara, he explained, "Rafael always worries about those smaller and weaker than himself."

Sara took little comfort from the older man's

explanation, but was glad of his intervention. Rafael made her nervous, with his dark looks and sharp words.

Shrugging, Rafael said in a clipped tone, "I will ride ahead to secure lodging for the night." With that, he spurred his stallion and was gone in a cloud of dust.

Sara lay in her bed at the small boardinghouse that night, and thought about how angry Jonas Farber must have been when he arrived and found her gone. She had told Fillette to inform him that she had gone to visit friends in the country for the weekend, and would return Sunday evening. Fillette, she knew, would play her part well, and tell him that a hired carriage had whisked her mistress away and that the young mistress had not told the servants where she was going.

Sara was sure she could depend on the rest of the staff to play as dumb as Fillette about the whole situation. They were like family, and would not betray her. It would give her some time before he started looking for her. She sighed and kicked the sheet off in the hot room. It had been hard to leave them behind, especially Fillette, but there was no help for it. Fillette's two brothers were owned by another family in St. Louis, and she didn't wish to leave them. And Sara knew the bank would take care of the servants . . . if for no other reason than the fact that slaves were valuable property. Someday, she promised herself, when she was settled in Sante Fe and she felt safe, she would write to the president of the bank and inquire about the servants and the property.

Her thoughts drifted to Rafael and, involuntarily, she shivered. He had all but ignored her at dinner, talking to Señor Pino about the cargo they purchased in St. Louis. It was a relief not to have his piercing eyes cut through her, yet somehow she felt dissatisfied. He tied her feelings in such knots, that she wished he had stayed behind to ride with the cargo wagons.

The next two weeks went by swiftly, as they traveled across Missouri. The only break in the routine had occurred on their second day on the road, when they'd encountered a Fourth of July celebration in the small town they'd stopped at for the night. The sounds of fireworks and a street celebration had gone on long into the night.

They stopped at noon each day for a rest and some food, and then again at night at a hotel or boardinghouse or even a farm, wherever they could find lodging.

Señor Pino and Sara rode in the dearborn which was large and roomy, easily seating four. With the sides open for fresh air and a roof to keep off the sun, they were relatively comfortable. Rafael rode his stallion, usually up ahead of them. Sara accepted the older man's suggestion that he teach her Spanish on the trip, and they spent many hours thus engaged.

Sara was so tired at night, she barely minded that Rafael ignored her. She didn't have the energy to spar with him. What she did find unsettling, were the times she caught him staring at her in a strange fashion. When it happened, he would turn away, seemingly annoyed with her. It was puzzling.

When they reached the bustling town of Independence, Missouri, Sara breathed a sigh of relief. All along the way, she had expected Jonas Farber to appear and drag her back to St. Louis.

The main street of town boasted every convenience imaginable, as far as Sara could see. There were two general stores, a barber shop, several hotels, saloons, a bank, and three livery stables. It was not all brick and stone like St. Louis, but seemed more alive— more exciting.

Carlos, their driver, pulled the horses to a halt in front of the Merchant's Hotel. Señor Pino instructed him to carry in their bags, and then take the carriage and horses to a livery stable. The old gentleman helped Sara down, while Rafael was tying his stallion to the back of the carriage and admonishing Carlos to see that the animal got extra oats.

As the three moved into the lobby of the hotel, Sara asked Señor Pino, "How long will we be here, señor?"

"Possibly two days, while the cargo wagons catch up. It will give you time to rest, while we see to our supplies for the trip across the plains," he replied with a smile.

Rafael arranged for their rooms. Turning, he handed a key to Sara. "If you need anything, señorita, we will be down the hall from you," he said stiffly.

She dropped her eyes and murmured her thanks, as his fingers brushed hers. His touch made her pulse race, and she felt breathless all of a sudden. Señor Pino offered his arm to her. She took it gratefully, as they ascended the stairs.

"We are dining with friends from home tonight, señorita. Rafael met them quite by accident at the general store this afternoon," Señor Pino told Sara, as he escorted her through the lobby and into the dining room.

"How nice," Sara said, after a quick glance around the room. She sighed with relief to find that Rafael was nowhere in sight. It was a small reprieve, but a reprieve nonetheless. Sara was glad she'd hung up several gowns so the wrinkles could fall out, since there were to be guests at their table. The one she wore was lilac and white striped, with a dainty floral print. White kid slippers peeked beneath the full hemline as she walked.

They were barely seated when Sara spied Rafael in the company of two women moving in their direction. Both wore lace mantillas draped over high combs on their heads. The older woman was in black silk, and the younger in primrose yellow.

Señor Pino rose and seated the matron, while Rafael held a chair for the young woman. They looked curiously at Sara as Rafael made the introductions.

"Don Rafael tells us you are to be teacher to the children of Hacienda Delgado," the older woman commented, after the waitress took their orders and departed. "You seem little more than a child yourself."

Sara nodded respectfully. "I realize that eighteen is not a great age, Doña Josefina, but I was educated along with my older brother by a very learned tutor."

The older woman eyed her critically for a moment. "I find it curious that your family would let you travel to such a faraway place without so much as a chaperone. In my country, such a thing is not done."

Sara cheeks flushed at the censure in her tone, but she managed to reply evenly. "I have no family left, Doña Josefina. My brother was killed in an accident outside of Santa Fe two years ago, and I lost my parents recently. There is no one to object to anything I do anymore."

Señora Perez had the grace to look somewhat ashamed, and said stiffly, "I am sorry for your losses, señorita. However, you should not be without a duenna. Estella and I will be traveling with your caravan back to Santa Fe, and I will chaperone the both of you."

Señorita Estella gave Sara a warm smile. "I shall be very happy to have you along on this tedious trip, Señorita Clayton. Madre does not enjoy riding, but perhaps the two of us could ride together."

"I would love to, Señorita Estella, except that I don't have a horse," Sara said.

Rafael spoke up. "We will be taking several mounts, Señorita Clayton, and you may have use of one."

Estella turned to him. "Rafael, how kind you are! We can always count on him to find a solution to any problem, eh, Madre?"

The older woman ignored her daughter's question and frowned slightly. "We will talk more of our traveling arrangements later, Estella. For now, our dinner is here."

Sara was relieved the conversation did not revolve around her as they ate. From beneath her dark lashes, she watched her companions quietly, and noticed how Señorita Estella's coutenance brightened each time Rafael addressed her. He, in turn, smiled at the young señorita and spoke in the gentlest of tones when conversing with her. Sara noticed also that the girl's mother kept a wary eye on the two of them.

Sara sighed. Just that morning, she had been looking forward to the remainder of the journey, but now it appeared that Señora Perez as well as Rafael would see to it that the time would not be so pleasant.

The following morning, Rafael rode out of town a mile or so, to where the bulk of his freight wagons were parked, and made sure all was well with his men and merchandise. He had left these men in Independence, while he made the trip to St. Louis. The six Mexican teamsters had been passing the time playing at dice and cards. Rafael informed them that the remainder of the wagons should arrive by evening, and the following day, they would depart.

Riding back into town, Rafael's thoughts drifted to dinner the night before. He had felt nearly suffocated sitting across the table from Sara. His first glimpse of her as he crossed the dining room had affected him almost like a punch in the stomach. He wasn't prepared for the thick cascade of silver hair that floated about her slim shoulders, or the delicate beauty of her face. During the time he'd known her, she had hidden her beauty with hats and sedate traveling dresses.

The flawless ivory shoulders and swell of rounded breasts above her bodice made his mouth go dry. He'd had to force his attention away. Consequently, he'd spent the evening talking to Estella. Her hard-eyed mother had not been happy with his attentions, but he didn't care. He and Estella had been friends for a long time, and he had no designs in that direction.

At one time, his grandfather had spoken to him of a possible match between him and Señorita Estella, but the Perez family had declined as tactfully as possible. Don Vicente had heard indirectly that Dona Josefina had set her sights higher than a half-breed for her daughter. Rafael had not wanted the marriage anyway, and resented his grandfather even more for putting him in that position.

Rafael shrugged off his disquieting thoughts, as he entered the town. Leaving his horse at the livery, he made his way to the general store to secure the remainder of their supplies for the trip.

When he entered the dim building, he heard a commotion at the back of the room, but couldn't see anyone. He assumed it was the shopkeeper, until a feminine protest caught his attention. A thud and a crash sent him in the direction of the scuffle. Looking behind a stack of barrels, he saw an unkempt man in dirty buckskins pulling Sara hard against his chest, while she fought with all her strength.

A white-hot anger boiled up in him as he moved forward, lifted the man off his feet, and tossed him in the corner. Rafael's piercing gaze then raked over Sara to make sure she was all right. He saw fear in her large blue eyes that maddened him further. "Señorita?" he breathed in a deep voice.

Her eyes darted to something behind him and then she screamed, alerting him to danger. Turning, he met her attacker, and feigned to the right as a sharp knife arced in the air where his mid-section had been a moment before.

Rafael crouched in a wide stance and warily watched the man retreat a step. They sized each other up in the small space, as Rafael slipped his knife from his waistband, making the fight equal. "I saw 'er first—she's mine," the man muttered in a harsh tone, eyeing the slender blade Rafael held poised.

"The señorita is not up for grabs. She's a lady," Rafael said with deadly calm.

The man glanced at Sara and licked his lips. For a moment, he contemplated fighting for her, but then reason asserted itself and he backed away, dropping the knife to his side. "Don't need no trouble . . . plenty of willin' women," he said finally.

Rafael straightened and sheathed his knife, keeping his eyes on the trapper. "A wise decision— now apologize to the señorita, and you can be on your way."

The man saw something in Rafael's eyes that sent

a chill through him. "Right sorry, ma'am," he muttered and backed away, leaving them alone.

Rafael turned to Sara then and she flew into his arms. He was caught off guard by her action, but instinctively, his arms closed around her. A faint scent of lavender filled his nostrils as she sobbed into his chest. He stroked her back as he would a child. Whispering soothing words, he held her until she calmed and began to sniffle. Finally, she leaned back and looked up at him with a tear-streaked face. "Thank you, Señor Rafael. I don't know what I would have done, if you hadn't come along when you did. He was a horrid man," she said in a shaky voice.

Rafael tenderly wiped at the wetness on her cheeks. "I'm thankful that I happened to be here, but I thought Doña Josefina was going to chaperone you along with Estella?"

Sara looked contrite and dropped her gaze guiltily. "She was taking a nap, and I wanted to get some things before we left. I shouldn't have, but I slipped away on my own."

He tipped her chin up and his eyes lit with amusement. "It was a brave thing to do, considering what a dragon she is."

She gave him a tremulous smile and conceded tactfully, "She is a bit formidable."

Rafael chuckled. "What nice manners you have. But enough of this—did you get what you came for here? Where is the proprietor?" He led her around the barrels, his hand riding at the small of her back.

She explained, "He went upstairs to the storeroom to find a hat for me. That's when that man came in the store and began bothering me." Opening her reticule, she pulled out a derringer and waved it in his direction. "If I'd had time, I would have frightened him away with my gun."

Rafael sucked in his breath and extracted the small weapon from her hand. She gave him a startled look. "This is not a toy, Señorita Clayton," he admonished firmly. "Do you know how to use it?"

She shook her head. "No, but having it in my reticule made me feel safer. I was going to buy some ammunition and ask the storekeeper to load it for me."

He broke open the barrel. "That won't be necessary, *niña*. It's already loaded."

Sara glanced at the gun and her eyes widened. "Oh my . . . I didn't know. It was my father's, and I thought perhaps it might prove useful someday."

He slipped the gun into the pocket of his buckskin trousers, and led her to the long counter. "It will be when you learn how to use it properly. I will teach you later. For now, we will purchase some ammunition and I will hold it for you."

Sara thought his attitude was a bit high-handed, but since he'd just saved her from that ruffian, she didn't say so. And besides, she did want to learn to use the gun. The shopkeeper's boots sounded on the wooden steps at the back of the store, and he soon came into view.

Smiling, he held out a brown, wide-brimmed hat with a black band around the flat crown. "This should work, missy. It's for a boy, but darned if your head ain't small enough to fit it."

Sara tried it on and found it perfect. She drew the chin strings up and smiled at the balding man. "Thank you. I'll take it. I'd also like to see some denim skirts and some blouses for day wear."

The man nodded and turned to Rafael, "I'll be with you in a jiffy, sir. Just let me show the little lady where I keep the dry goods."

He moved away, and Rafael touched Sara's arm. "Once I make my selections, I will escort you back to the hotel, señorita." Sara's answering smile caused him to catch his breath.

For the next half-hour, Sara was busy choosing several skirts and calico blouses. While she was engaged, Rafael went over his list with the shopkeeper: beans, rice, coffee, sugar, bacon, flour, cornmeal, salt, and dried fruits for the caravan. When they finished, Rafael made arrangements to have her things delivered to the hotel, and the food supplies delivered to their wagons outside of town.

Leaving the store, he said, "I'm famished. Would you have lunch with me?"

She nodded, "I feel quite hungry myself."

"*Bueno.* There's a restaurant down the street where the food is excellent. Once we move out, our menu will have little variety, so we might as well enjoy ourselves now."

Sara hadn't realized how hungry she was until their steaks arrived. The restaurant was small, but every table was occupied, and the smells coming from the kitchen made her mouth water. While they ate, Rafael talked easily of Hacienda Delgado and some of the people they employed there, but Sara couldn't quite get over her nervousness of him. She tried to listen to what he was saying, but each time she looked at him, she found herself taking inventory of his handsome features.

Today, he had been gentle and solicitous with her, but she never knew when he might turn stern and forbidding. His moods seemed to swing abruptly, and she had become wary.

They finished the meal with apple pie and coffee, and he changed the subject suddenly. "I know you said that after your parents died you had to find work, but I have to admit I don't quite believe that, señorita."

Startled by his abrupt statement, Sara concentrated on her dessert for a moment, chewing and swallowing slowly. Her mind raced for an answer. Finally, she took a sip of her coffee and said quietly, "It's true, Señor Rafael. I have very little I can call my own." And it was true, she thought. Jonas Farber had control of everything, except a small amount of cash she had found in her father's safe at home.

He lounged back in his chair and eyed her thoughtfully. "Out of curiosity, I rode by your house the morning after our interview, and it was not the home of a pauper," he persisted, watching her expression.

Sara nervously fidgeted with her napkin and lied. "There were debts to be paid, and when all was said and done, nothing would have been left." She hoped she sounded convincing, for even at this late date, she feared he would send her back.

He could tell there was something more; she seemed almost frightened, and that caused his protective instincts to rise up. His eyes caressed her bowed silver head, and he relented. "Forgive me for prying. It is none of my business. If you are finished, we should get back before Doña Josefina finds you gone."

Sara breathed a sigh of relief as they left the restaurant.

Chapter 3

"I sent Estella to fetch you for lunch today, señorita, and you were nowhere to be found." Doña Josefina's voice had an accusatory tone as she seated herself at the dinner table.

Sara glanced up at Señor Pino, who was holding her chair. He lifted his eyes heavenward as if to say, "The woman misses nothing."

Sara cleared her throat. "I didn't wish to disturb you—"

Rafael, who had been helping Estella with her chair, interrupted her smoothly, "So I offered to escort Señorita Clayton to the general store, where she purchased some items she needs for the trip."

Sara's surprised gaze swung to Rafael as he sat down and carefully placed his napkin on his lap. Doña Josefina eyed the two of them suspiciously before turning her attention to her daughter.

A small smile touched Sara's lips as she caught Rafael's eye. He gave her a wink and turned to his menu, feeling vaguely disturbed at the ache of

41

longing that filled him. This young woman was beginning to awaken the places in his heart he had thought dead forever. They were the places Tuwikaa, his Indian wife, had occupied.

Señor Pino asked, "Did you find some sturdy clothing for the trail, señorita?"

"*Sí,* and it was a *bueno* idea that you suggested it. The things I packed have not been *apropiados,*" Sara said with a mischievous grin.

The older man chuckled and looked at her fondly. "Your Spanish is improving daily, and I'm happy to hear you use it."

Estella offered, "I will be happy to help you as well, Señorita Clayton, as I'm hoping we will be spending much time together."

Sara gave her a warm smile. "*Gracias.* I'm looking forward to it." She liked Estella very much, and pitied her for the fact that her mother constantly found fault with every little thing she did. Doña Josefina practically smothered her daughter, and Sara did not know which was worse—being smothered or ignored, as she had been as a child.

As the dinner progressed, Rafael grew more withdrawn and let the others carry the conversation. Sara stole several looks at him from beneath her dark lashes, and wondered at his mood. He was an enigmatic man, and her curiosity drew her to him like a magnet. From several cryptic remarks he'd made, she guessed that he and his grandfather were not on the best of terms; however, she didn't have the nerve to question him on the subject.

Before they were finished, a swarthy *vaquero* entered the dining room and made his way to their table. He pulled his sombrero off respectfully, and spoke quietly with Rafael. When he departed, Rafael announced to the group, "Our wagons have arrived from St. Louis and we will depart tomorrow, if you are ready," he added to Señora Perez.

The older woman nodded. "*Si.* I am anxious to return home."

Sara was relieved. The more distance she put between herself and Jonas Farber, the better.

Even Doña Josefina's incessant complaining of the heat did not dampen Sara's spirits that first day out. She, the older woman, and Estella rode in the carriage, while Señor Pino and Rafael rode horseback with the other *vaqueros*. There were twenty wagons; most carried merchandise, while the others were sleeping wagons for the women. One additional wagon was for the cook and his supplies. Rafael had purchased a small herd of cattle; they trailed behind the caravan, to keep down dust.

The early morning hours had been spent securing the merchandise, and tightly covering the wagons with Osnaburg sheets, to protect them from the elements. Sara had been delighted to find that she had a sleeping wagon of her own provided by Rafael. Señora Perez had protested and insisted that Sara sleep in their wagon, but Rafael deferred to Sara, when she said that she would not hear of crowding the two other women.

Secretly, Sara didn't think she could bear Doña Josefina's company twenty-four hours a day.

By the following evening, they reached a place

called Round Grove. There was a creek near the campsite, and Sara wished she could bathe in it; however, there was little privacy. She made do with a pan of cold water in her covered wagon, washing the dust from her face and hands.

Brushing her hair, she secured it with a ribbon and made her way to the cook's wagon. A large kettle of beans was hanging on a tripod over the fire, and the cook was busily stirring corn bread batter in a bowl. "*Hola,* Juan," she said with a smile for the swarthy little man. The night before, he had carried a plate of food to her at dinnertime, and was so kind, she had developed an instant liking for him.

He smiled in return. "*Buenas noches,* señorita. Soon we will eat, eh . . . when the bread is brown."

Sara watched as he poured the batter into a long pan and placed it on an iron rack near the fire. "My mouth is watering already," she confessed, leaning against the back of his wagon. "I don't know how you feed this many people, and make it look so simple."

He chuckled. "Because I have done it many times. I am the cook when we round up the cattle on Hacienda Delgado every spring. As many as fifty *vaqueros* are needed to do the work, and I feed them all."

Sara's eyes grew rounder as she asked, "What do you do with them, once they're gathered up?"

He didn't laugh at her naive question as another might have done, but patiently explained, "There are new calves to be branded, and then there are the older ones to be butchered for food for the hacienda." He grinned then and added, "We also have a rodeo when the work is done, and there is another before winter begins as well."

Her eyes lit up at that. "My brother took me to a rodeo once. It was exciting. Do you think we will reach Santa Fe in time?" She smiled to herself when she thought of the time Max had taken her to see the rodeo out in the country. Their parents had been on one of their numerous trips to New Orleans, and he had snuck her out after dark, beneath the nose of her prim governess.

Juan smiled at her enthusiasm. *"Sí,* señorita. They could not do without Don Rafael. He is braver than all the rest put together. You should see him ride the wild mustangs!" He rolled his eyes for emphasis. "Don Rafael has a way with horses that can be matched by no other," he said.

Sara felt a tingle of anticipation at the thought of seeing Rafael atop a wild horse. She could easily imagine him mastering any beast, for he seemed in control of every situation.

The object of her thoughts came walking up just then, and nodded politely to her before having a brief conference with Juan. Sara turned to the open end of the wagon and busied herself getting out a stack of tin plates and silverware to place on one end of the tailgate. At Rafael's appearance, her composure fled, and in her nervousness, she dropped the wooden box that held the silverware. It spilled open and a few pieces fell into the dirt. "Oh my!" she exclaimed, bending to retrieve it.

A strong hand on her arm lifted her up, and she looked into Rafael's dark eyes for a moment. The touch of his hand as well as his warm gaze made her pulse skitter.

"That is too heavy for you, *niña*. I'll get it," was all he said as he bent to pick up the box, but he was disturbed by the contact as well.

Sara murmured her thanks and hurriedly excused herself, "I should get back to my wagon."

Rafael watched her walk away, and felt a hunger gnawing at him that had nothing to do with food.

"I cannot understand why we must get out and walk! Our carriage is not that heavy," Doña Josefina complained to Sara and Estella, after a young *vaquero* stopped long enough to pass on the instructions from Rafael.

The two young women climbed down and gave a helping hand to the frowning matron. "It will not be for a very long way, madre," Estella said soothingly. "The rain this morning has mired this ridge, making it hard for the animals to pull their load."

The older woman snapped, "I heard the man, daughter. I am not deaf! They should have made an exception for us, however."

Over the mother's bent head, Sara gave the daughter a sympathetic smile. "We'll help you, Doña Josefina, for it is rather slippery," Sara offered.

Señora Perez sniffed disdainfully as she looked at the mud that covered her shoes, and then straightened her shoulders. "I am not a doddering old woman, señorita. I will manage alone, *gracias.*" And with that, she left them behind.

She hadn't gone five yards when her foot sank deep in the spongy, oozing mud, causing her to turn her ankle and then fall. Estella gasped and hurried to her mother's side, calling for one of the *vaqueros* to help.

Rafael had been riding down the line, seeing to snags in the progress of the wagons, when he spotted the mishap. He rode up, quickly instructing the *vaquero* to help the señora back into the carriage, and to hitch another horse to help pull the load. He apologized. "I did not mean for you ladies to walk, but I did not make this clear to my messenger. Forgive me, *por favor*." He bade Estella to ride with her mother and then turned to Sara. "I will take you up on my horse to make the carriage lighter," he suggested, easing back in his saddle to make room and holding out his hand.

Sara gazed up at him dubiously, and then placed her hand in his. He removed his booted foot from the stirrup, and she used it to step up. Without effort, he lifted her up to sit in front of him, then closed his arms about her to hold the reins.

She could feel his strong heartbeat against her arm, as she was forced to lean against him. It did strange things to her senses being this near, their bodies touching. As they moved away, Sara said, "I wouldn't hold out much hope that she will forgive you, Don Rafael."

That drew a chuckle from him. "I think you are right, *niña*. Doña Josefina does not care for me in any case."

Since he had opened the subject, Sara's curiosity got the better of her. "Why is that, Don Rafael?

47

Estella seems quite fond of you."

Rafael glanced down on the top of her silver head, and wondered what her reaction would be to the fact that he was a half-breed. After a moment's hesitation, he decided to find out. "I am half-Indian, señorita. Señora Perez does not approve of the circumstances of my birth."

Startled by his blunt reply, Sara turned her face up to his. "Forgive me for prying, señor. I shouldn't have asked such a personal question."

Seeing her genuine dismay, he felt sorry that he had caused it, and his tone softened. "It is common knowledge, and besides, it is not something of which I am ashamed. The Comanche are a proud people, and I am proud to call them relatives. Sometime I will tell you the story, but for now, we are on higher ground, and you can return to the carriage."

He pulled his horse to a stop and helped her down. She turned to look up at him with a timid smile. *"Gracias* . . . and sometime, I would like to hear your story."

The *vaquero* driving their carriage stopped to help her aboard. Rafael moved on, regretting the fact that he could not hold her longer.

"There is no relief from this sticky heat in this godforsaken country, even at night," Doña Josefina complained for the tenth time that morning. She fanned herself vigorously, a scowl on her face.

Sara offered encouragingly, "We will be stopping for a rest and the noon meal soon, señora, and you can bathe your face with cool water."

"Little help that will be," the older woman grumbled, determined to hang on to her negative attitude.

Sara sighed and stole a glance at Estella, sitting quietly beside her mother and doing her needlework. Sara was beginning to realize that the other girl retreated at times into a little world of her own to escape her mother's nagging. Wishing for some escape of her own, Sara glanced up ahead and saw Rafael riding toward them on his black stallion. As usual, her heart raced at the sight of him.

When he came abreast of them, he wheeled about and slowed his pace to match theirs. Nodding politely, he suggested, "After our meal, would you ladies like to ride for a time? It will break the monotony."

Estella's hands had stilled, and her gaze rested on Rafael with undisguised warmth. "Oh, *sí!* I could use the exercise, Don Rafael."

Sara nodded her agreement as well, while Doña Josefina sighed painfully.

"Very well. We will be stopping shortly," he said, and rode back to the head of the column.

Awhile later, as they ate the cold beans and bread Juan provided, Sara felt as if a heavy load had been lifted from her shoulders. Estella had talked incessantly after Rafael's offer, until her mother admonished her sharply to stop chattering. Both girls finished the meal in silence, but with light hearts.

Sara went to fetch a pan of water from the small creek close by, and retired to her wagon to freshen up and change into her riding clothes. She chose the soft blue, but omitted the fitted jacket, wearing a simple white blouse with a full skirt, because of the heat. At home, it would have been terribly unfashionable to be seen without the entire ensemble, but she decided wryly that here on the plains it didn't matter. It was more important to avoid heat prostration.

She brushed her hair and tied it at the nape of her neck with a blue ribbon, and then donned the tophat that matched. It would keep the sun from giving her heatstroke, she decided.

When she emerged from her wagon, she spied Estella once again sitting in the carriage with her mother. Walking over, she said brightly, "You haven't changed, Estella. Better hurry!"

The Spanish girl glanced up with a dismal expression in her brown eyes. "I will not be riding today, señorita. Madre has a headache, and needs my companionship."

Sara caught the older woman's haughty look and wished she had the courage to reprimand her for her selfishness. Instead, she nodded. "I'm disappointed, Estella, but perhaps tomorrow."

She turned and made her way to the place, outside the circle of wagons, where the horses were staked. Rafael was holding a pair of sorrel mares, waiting for them.

"Estella will not be joining me, señor. Her mother is taken with a sudden headache," she said shortly, her cheeks pink in anger.

Rafael's eyebrows lifted at her tone. He had never seen her display any temper before, and found it interesting. "I am not surprised," he said mildly. "Doña Josefina is afraid her daughter will compromise her reputation with me, before they can marry her to someone more suitable."

Sara studied him intently for a moment, and quickly asked before she lost her nerve, "Are you in love with Estella? Is that why the señora is afraid?"

His dark eyes held hers without wavering. "I love Estella as a sister, *niña*. We have been friends since we were children, and I would never do anything to hurt her."

Sara expelled the breath she'd been holding, and felt a lightening of her spirit. She wasn't quite sure why his answer pleased her, but it did.

He helped her to mount one of the horses, and passed the reins of the other mare to a *vaquero* he motioned over. Climbing astride his own black horse, he turned to her. "Stay close to me, Señorita Clayton. There are hostile Pawnee in this area from time to time."

For most of the afternoon, they rode at the head of the two lines of wagons. The sun beat down fiercely, and the heat caused rivulets of perspiration to run between Sara's breasts and down her back, but it was the most pleasant day she'd spent since leaving St. Louis. She no longer worried that Jonas Farber was going to find her, and even though Rafael intimidated her at times, she felt strangely safe and content with him.

Just before sundown, Señor Pino rode up, giving Rafael the chance to ride back down the column. "Your face has grown very pink, señorita. A wide-brimmed hat would protect you a little better," he said with concern.

She smiled ruefully. "Vanity, señor. This hat

matches my outfit. However, I think you are right."

"I have something you can apply to your face tonight that will help with the burning," he offered.

"Thank you . . . and I shall remember to wear my other hat from now on," she promised.

"Perhaps after dinner we could have a Spanish lesson, and I will bring it then?" he suggested.

She smiled again. *"Sí, señor, muchas gracias."*

Juan made fresh corn cakes each night at dinner and heated beans. While the caravan was on the move, some of the *vaqueros* ventured out during the day to hunt deer and rabbit, so that they could have fresh meat. By day's end, Sara was ravenous, and the simple fare tasted better to her than the elaborate cuisine served at Clayton House.

She usually ate with the Perez women at a small table with low stools, while the men sat on the ground around the cook wagon, seemingly oblivious to the lack of comforts. That evening, two of Juan's helpers delivered plates of food to the women. Sara thanked them and asked to be remembered to Juan.

Doña Josefina chided her with a frown. "If you are too familiar with the servants, Señorita Clayton, they will forget their place."

Estella looked up from her plate and protested. "She is merely being kind, Madre, and that is an admirable quality."

Señora Perez fixed her daughter with a firm eye. "Hush, Estella. You will take your place as wife to a *haciendado* some day soon, and should learn the correct way to deal with servants. They will become lazy and disrespectful, if you are not careful."

Sara felt stung by the reprimand and was still angry that the older woman had taken away Estella's pleasure that afternoon. "I beg to differ, señora. We had fifteen servants in our home, and not one was lazy due to good treatment. They are human beings and should be treated with dignity," she said firmly.

Doña Josefina's face grew red with anger as she glared at Sara. "Perhaps it will not matter in your case, Señorita Clayton. In your position, you may not have any servants to worry about."

Sara had meant what she said and did not intend to recant, but neither did she wish to be on unfriendly terms with the woman for the next few weeks. In a calm tone, she replied, "That could very well be the case, señora."

They finished the meal in an uncomfortable silence; once Estella gave Sara an apologetic look. When the señora rose to retire to her wagon, Sara gathered the plates to take to Juan.

Sara found the slightest movement caused her muscles to protest. It had been a good while since she'd ridden a horse, and she had never ridden for several hours at a time. By the time she reached the cook wagon, she was in pain. Everything hurt, from her arms to her toes.

Juan glanced at her as she put the plates on the tailgate, and a frown of concern creased his brow. "Señorita, what is it? You don't look so good."

Rafael and Señor Pino walked up just then, and Pino made a similar comment.

Sara blushed. She was afraid if she complained, Rafael wouldn't let her ride anymore. "I am just a little tired. A good night's sleep will do wonders for me," she assured them. Turning to the older man, she asked, "Could we have a lesson tomorrow night, Señor Pino? I fear I couldn't concentrate tonight."

"Of course, but I will bring the salve for your face later. I'm afraid your skin is worse than I thought earlier."

She tried to smile, but it was painful when the skin on her face stretched. "Thank you. I will most assuredly wear my other hat from now on."

Rafael, who had been silently watching her, spoke up. "I will have one of the men bring your bathing water from the creek, señorita. I know you've been doing it yourself, but you are not a servant. From now on, Carlos will do it for you."

Sara supposed the easy rapport of their peaceful afternoon together had come to an end. "I didn't want to be any trouble, señor." Sighing, she turned and made her way slowly to her sleeping wagon.

Carlos had been assigned to drive her wagon, and he was nearby to help her up. Sara collapsed on her cot for a moment, as beads of perspiration popped out on her brow. Her muscles screamed, her bottom was sore, and her skin felt like it was on fire. It had been over a week since she'd been able to wash her hair, and she felt grimy from cold water sponge baths. A lone tear trickled down her sunburned cheek and then another, until a torrent was loosened. Turning her face into the pillow, she allowed the tears to flow. She didn't hear her name called, or the discreet tapping on the side of the wagon.

"Come *niña* . . . it cannot be that bad," Rafael's deep voice said soothingly.

Sara's head jerked around. He was standing

beside her cot with a bucket of water in one hand, and a tin in the other. He put them on the floor and sat down beside her, gently taking her in his arms. For once, she lost her shyness and drew comfort from his embrace. Not since the day Max had left, had she felt so secure.

Rafael felt the warm stirrings of tenderness within his breast as he held her. He had tried to stay away from her, but as the days went by, he found one excuse after another to seek her out. Like now, he thought ruefully. Instead of sending one of his men with the water, he had gotten it himself. He could feel his resolve slipping where she was concerned.

Finally, he pulled back and tipped up her chin with his finger. "Tell Rafael what is troubling you, eh? I will try to help," he said, gazing into her eyes.

She took a handkerchief from her pocket, dabbed at her eyes, and then blew her nose. "It's silly, and you will laugh at me, señor," she said, her voice shaky.

The corner of his mouth curved up with gentle amusement at her childish tone. "I promise, *niña,* I will not laugh."

She blurted out, "I hate being dirty! If I could have a real bath, I would feel so much better."

When he'd first entered the wagon, he had been afraid that she was ill; to find her problem no more serious than this was a great relief. He smiled. "Father Mendoza always says that cleanliness is next to godliness. That is no small thing, señorita."

She studied his expression suspiciously. "You are laughing at me," she accused. She was feeling better, even without the longed-for bath. Her skin was beginning to tingle through her sleeves, where his hands held her arms lightly. She suddenly became aware of the fact that they were alone, sitting on her bed.

Rafael sensed a change in her expression. Her eyes seemed to beckon to him seductively. When her lips parted and her breathing became shallow, he lowered his head to taste the sweetness of her inviting mouth.

Sara closed her eyes, and her whole being tingled with expectation. She had never been kissed before, and her heart fluttered wildly at the pleasurable feeling it evoked. A delicious shudder raced over her body as he moved one hand to the back of her neck to hold her more firmly and deepen the kiss.

Rafael's loins tightened at the exquisite pleasure he found in the kiss. For a moment, the mere touch of her lips was enough, but soon, unble to resist, he invaded her mouth with his tongue, exploring gently and then with more passion. His other hand found its way to her tiny waist, where he caressed a path to the swell of her hip.

Sara moaned with pleasure as her untried senses came to life. Her emotional response was as erratic as a summer storm, as he awakened desires in her.

Rafael trembled with a violent need as he pushed her back against the pillow and covered her body with his own. Her gasp of pain, however, cooled his passion, and he drew back to gaze into her face. "*Amante* . . . forgive me. Did I hurt you?" he questioned in a husky voice.

Sara gazed at his dark-skinned face in wonder, her breathing rapid. She was loath to give up the strange new feelings that had invaded her body, but they were also frightening. "It's just that I am sore . . . from the ride today," she said, her voice not quite steady.

Rafael leaned forward and touched her lips ever so gently with his own, and then he rose from the cot. "It is for the best, *niña*. I had better leave . . . before it is too late," he said, stifling the desire he felt.

Sara felt her cheeks flame at his candid reply. She was not sure exactly what happened between a man and a woman in the bedroom, but she knew it should be sanctioned by marriage vows. Turning her face away in embarrassment, she said in a small voice, "Yes, perhaps you should."

In the dim light of the wagon, he pulled his gaze away from her lovely form, but it was an effort. His emotions were mixed. On the one hand, he wanted to make love to her passionately and completely, and on the other, he was loath to let her into his heart. She was not like the prostitutes he paid to ease his basic needs.

Walking away from Sara's wagon across the grassy plain, he was so deep in thought, he did not see Doña Josefina sitting under her canopy, observing his movements.

The following afternoon a summer storm brought driving rain to the caravan. The *vaqueros* and wagon drivers donned waterproof ground sheets and they moved on, heedless of the downpour. Sara and the other two women had a roof on their carriage, but the wind whipped the rain through the sides of the vehicle. Before long they were all soaked.

Doña Josefina, of course, moaned and complained from the first drop. Rafael, riding by, saw their plight, and rode off to return a little later with mackinaw blankets for them. Sara refused to look at him, but took her blanket and wrapped it around herself gratefully. The only good thing about the storm, she decided dismally, was that they could not converse above the noise. The entire morning, Doña Josefina had talked about the Delgado family, mentioning Rafael's name repeatedly. Sara noticed the older woman giving her sly looks, as if she knew a secret that delighted her. However, Sara didn't know what that could be. In any case, the afternoon storm was preferable to listening to that woman.

By the time they stopped to make camp, the rain had ceased, and everyone welcomed a warm meal and a dry bed. Sara spent an hour after dinner with Señor Pino, conversing in Spanish before retiring. Curled up on her cot, she felt alone in the world once again. Rafael had avoided her as much as she had him that day. She regretted the loss of a budding friendship.

She tried to sort through her jumbled feelings, but had no basis for comparison. Before his death, her father had been in the process of choosing someone suitable for her to marry, but she had never really been courted. And since her mother had never spoken to her of such things, Sara was woefully ignorant of the most basic facts. The only education she had, had come from a chance encounter in the stable one day. One of their gardeners and Lizzie, the cook's helper, were kissing in a deserted stall, when she had happened upon them. For a moment, she had frozen, not knowing what to do. Lizzie had been moaning while her lover stroked her bare buttocks, her skirt pulled up around her waist. They had broken the kiss, and Lizzie had put her hands on the front of his pants, rubbing and whispering to him.

At that point, Sara had turned and fled, her face flaming in embarrassment. That night when Fillette had helped her with her toilet, Sara told her what she'd seen. The black girl chuckled. "Deys in love, chile. Dat Lizzie cain't keep her hands offen dat boy. Yas, ma'am, dey sure do enjoy makin' love. Someday, Missy Sara, when yore papa fin' you a husband, you'll see." Sara was too shy to ask the girl what actually happened, but now she wished she had. When Rafael had kissed her and touched her body, it had felt wonderful, but was that love? She hardly knew him, and he was certainly not her husband. Sara fell asleep trying to sort it all out.

A second, and more violent, storm hit the caravan in the middle of the night, and it brought Sara awake with a startled gasp. The thunder fairly rocked her wagon, and great flashes of lightning seemed close enough to touch. She sat bolt upright and then regretted the sudden movement, for every muscle in her body still ached. Drawing her blanket up under her chin, she wished she were not alone. Storms had always frightened her, particularly at night.

For a time, she huddled against the wagon's side and waited for the worst to pass, knowing there was no hope of going back to sleep. She tried to meditate and fill her being with peace and tranquility, but her concentration was lagging. During one flash of lightning, she glimpsed the dark shape of a man at the back opening of her wagon, and an involuntary scream escaped her. Before the sound died in her throat, he was climbing inside. "Who is it?" she gasped in fear. "What do you want?"

"Don't be afraid, *niña*. It's Rafael," he replied, and pushed back the dark hood that covered his head. Another flash of lightning revealed his wet face.

Her relief was so great, Sara felt her whole body go weak. "You frightened me nearly to death," she managed in a shaky voice.

He squatted beside her cot. "Forgive me, *niña,* but I was just going to look in on you, when you screamed," he explained patiently. "I was on watch, and thought perhaps the storm might make you uneasy."

A brittle laugh escaped her as she moved away from the wagon's side to sit up straighter. "He who overcomes others is strong—he who overcomes himself is mighty," she quoted, and then added with a sigh, "I shall never be mighty, I fear."

He smiled to himself. "The teachings of Tao are wise, but not always easy to follow."

Pleased at his knowledge on the subject, she asked, "You have studied the Tao, señor?"

"*Sí,* I had a very enlightened priest for a teacher. As a young man, Father Mendoza studied a great deal of philosophy before entering the priesthood." He paused for a moment, and then said, "I suppose your Master Filbert is responsible for your knowledge, eh?"

"Yes, but I've found that applying the things I've learned is sometimes difficult," she admitted.

"You are human, *niña,* and none of us can master every emotion." He was thinking of the attraction she held for him. Being this close to her was growing more difficult minute by minute. With each flash of lightning, his gaze hungrily took in her soft form, outlined in the blanket she was hugging close to her bosom. His hands itched to caress the thick mass of silver hair flowing about her shoulders. Abruptly, he added, "I must get back to my post, señorita. Will you be all right?"

"Yes. Please don't worry about me," she assured him, and watched as he turned and climbed back out. Sara wondered how he could be so warm one minute, and so withdrawn the next. It was a puzzle to her.

Chapter 4

Eleven days after leaving Independence, Sara was once again on horseback, having recovered from her soreness and sunburn. Her wide-brimmed hat sat securely on her head, and she wore one of her denim skirts and calico blouses.

Riding alongside Señor Pino and Estella, she gazed in fascination at the wide strip of timber in the delightful valley. There was a stream in the distance that looked cool and inviting. "I haven't seen timber this thick since we left Missouri," she said.

The older man took his hat off and wiped his brow with a kerchief. "*Sí*, Council Grove is an unusual sight after the sparce plains, señorita. There is a rich variety of trees also—the oak, walnut, hickory—and a few more besides. It is here we will procure timber for axle-trees and other wagon repairs."

Estella asked, "How long will we be here, Señor Pino?"

"Two to three days, Señorita Estella," he said and smiled at the young women. "It will be a good time to get some laundry done."

Estella grimaced. "Madre will no doubt have poor Felipe scrubbing at the creek like a serving girl. She is still in a bad humor over Marta leaving us when we got to Independence."

The overseer shook his head regretfully. "Marta's family will be *muy* sad that she has run away with a peddler."

Estella turned to Sara. "Marta was the maid we brought with us on the journey. I think she found the trip not as exciting as she had hoped, and when we reached Independence, she took up with a traveling peddler. She left word for us with the hotel clerk. I hope the man is good to her, for Marta is not a bad girl, just impetuous."

Sara didn't say anything, but guessed that the poor girl had probably been driven to running away by Doña Josefina's constant nagging and criticism. She was eternally grateful it was not the Perez family *she* would be working for.

Señor Pino chuckled. "I have noticed Felipe's sulks and pouts. I am sure he feels it is beneath a *vaquero* to be a lady's maid."

The two girls tried to look sympathetic for Felipe's sake, but laughed in spite of themselves.

Up ahead, Sara saw Rafael directing the forming of the circle of wagons, and her heartbeat quickened. He was so handsome, it took her breath away sometimes. The hot sun had turned his face the color of polished bronze, as he never wore a hat. Abruptly, Sara reined in her wandering thoughts to attend what Señor Pino was saying.

"—Will be having company on the trip after all."

Sara glanced to the right, and in the distance, she saw another small caravan camped. Spirals of smoke were drifting up from several campfires inside their circle.

"Is it not unusual for the traders to be traveling to Santa Fe at this time of year, señor?" Estella asked.

"*Sí,*" he replied. "Perhaps they are going home, just as we are, and not merely taking trade goods."

The three of them rode past their own wagons to where a young *vaquero* was already setting stakes in the ground to hold the saddle horses. Sara offered to brush her horse, but Jose waved her away. "No, no, señorita. I am happy to do this for you."

Señor Pino went to speak to Rafael, and the two women strolled back toward their wagons. Estella smiled. "Jose is *infatuado* with you, Sara. He gets so nervous when you are around."

Sara turned surprised eyes on her friend. "Oh, Estella, I'm sure you're mistaken. He's just shy."

The Spanish girl laughed softly. "You truly don't realize what your beauty does to men, do you, *amiga?* Every man on this caravan follows you with his eyes . . . even Rafael," she added after a pause. "He has not shown an interest in anyone since . . . well, for a long time," she finished, her mood having turned solemn.

Filled with dismay, Sara protested. "I don't mean to be contrary, but that can't be so. If they do look at me, it is probably because the color of my hair is unusual. Why, look at me, Estella—my eyes are too large for my face, and my nose is too small and straight! I bear no resemblance to the tall, beautiful women in the fashion plates."

They had arrived at Sara's sleeping wagon, and Estella turned to her. "You are very pretty, Sara, whether you know it or not, but forgive me for embarrassing you." In the next wagon, Doña Josefina's strident voice could be heard reprimanding poor Felipe, and Estella's eyes lifted heavenward. "I must go," she said. "I will see you later."

Sara climbed into her own wagon to rest before Carlos brought her wash water. She puzzled over Estella's compliments, and also over her comments about Rafael. Was he interested in her, or had he kissed her merely because of the particular situation? Fillette had once told her that a man did not have to be in love with a woman to want her. Sara had been disturbed over the fact that her father was going to choose a complete stranger to be her husband, and had voiced her concerns to her maid. Fillette, although very knowledgable about the relationship between a man and a woman, had not enlightened her further.

It was frustrating, and she had no one to ask. Doña Josefina was the only woman who would know the answers. But, Sara had no desire to confide in her.

A discreet tapping on the side of the wagon signaled Carlos's return with the water. She looked out, and to her astonishment, a new brass bathing tub sat on the ground. "What?" she muttered and climbed out. Carlos stepped into view and smiled broadly. "For you, señorita."

She stared at him in amazement. "Where did it come from, Carlos? And who—"

He shook his head regretfully and moved to lift it

up into her wagon. "It is a gift, and the giver wishes to remain unknown."

He disappeared inside, and then stepped back out to lift in two buckets of cold water. "Juan is heating water for you, señorita. I will bring it." With that, he strode off in the direction of the cook's wagon.

Sara was more pleased than she could say, and didn't waste any time climbing back inside to inspect her new treasure. Of course, Rafael had sent it—it had to be him, she thought. Hadn't she been whining to him about needing a real bath? But where did he get it?

Happily, she ran her hands over the polished rim, and thought rapturously of soaking in warm water. It would be heaven! She laid out clean clothes on the cot and dug in her trunk, until she found the fragrant bath salts she had packed.

Carlos returned with another *vaquero* and four buckets of hot water, and Sara thanked them profusely.

When she finally sank into the warm water, she gave a deep sigh of satisfaction. Sara was appalled at the things she had taken for granted all her life. Living in wealth and comfort had not prepared her for life on the trail, and she now appreciated the simplest things.

She scrubbed until her skin was a healthy pink, and then washed her thick hair. Having reserved half a bucket of the warm water, she used it to rinse the soap away.

After dressing in the clean skirt and blouse, she opened the back flap and let in a breeze to help dry her hair as she combed it. Deftly, she braided it in one long braid to hang down her back, and then left the wagon. It was time to eat, and she was ravenous.

Doña Josefina and Estella were already seated at their table with steaming plates of beans, rice, and venison. They looked up as she approached, and the older woman's eyes narrowed. "Have you been bathing in the creek, señorita? Your hair is damp," she said in an accusing tone.

Sara's face flushed with irritation as she sat down. Did nothing escape the woman's eagle eye? She kept her voice casual. "No, Señora Perez. I had a bath in my own tub."

Estella's eyes brightened. "I did not know you had a tub, Sara! We didn't have room for one in our wagon, and I would give everything I own for a real bath!"

Sara smiled at her. "You're welcome to use it anytime," she offered. Remembering her manners, she added, "And you also, señora."

Senora Perez eyed her coldly. "I've seen the inside of your wagon, señorita, and I do not remember a tub. How is it an article that large could escape my attention?"

Sara wondered angrily when the woman had seen the inside of her wagon. She had never invited her. Keeping her temper in check, however, she replied coolly, "It was a recent gift. And before you ask, I do not know from whom."

Sara had a strong feeling that the tub had come from Rafael, but wasn't positive, so it wasn't a lie. Just then, one of Juan's helpers arrived with a plate of food for Sara. She thanked him, and began eating as if the subject was closed.

Señora Perez stared intently at Sara's bowed head with a calculating gleam in her eyes, and then went back to her own meal without another word. Estella, however, pushed her plate away and rose. "Excuse me, *por favor,* I am not hungry," she said in a tremulous whisper. She was gone before an astonished Sara could speak. Only moments before, Estella had seemed in high spirits. Finishing her meal in silence, Sara decided that later she would find out if she'd done something to upset her new friend.

After dinner, Sara took a stroll around the camp to exercise her legs. She stopped for a chat in Spanish with Señor Pino, and casually asked where Rafael could be found. The señor informed her that he had gone to talk to the captain of the other caravan, and would be back later. She was disappointed, for she intended to speak to him about the bath tub. Instead, she mentioned it to Señor Pino, but he shrugged. "I know nothing about it, señorita." After she walked away, however, his eyes twinkled knowingly.

Sara stopped by the Perez wagon, where Doña Josefina was sitting outside doing needlework. The older woman informed her that Estella was resting, and could not be disturbed. After that, Sara wandered over to Juan's cook-wagon and offered to help him make the corn cakes for breakfast. He smiled indulgently and gave her the ingredients and a bowl.

He began talking of Hacienda Delgado, and Sara

asked, "Are there any women in the household? I know Don Rafael lives with his grandfather, but is there a grandmother?"

Juan was stirring the kettle of beans and glanced up at her. "She died before he was born. I was just a little *niño* and do not remember her, but the older ones say she was a saint. There is Don Vicente's widowed sister who runs the household, Doña Ines."

Sara continued to stir the batter, wanting to ask more questions, but shy about doing so. She decided she would ask Rafael himself—if he ever returned to camp.

Two hours after dark descended on the prairie, Sara tired of waiting for Rafael and went to bed. She was exhausted from a full day in the saddle, but pleasantly so. Her muscles had become accustomed to riding now, but hours in the fresh air and sun demanded an early bed.

Rafael, on the other hand, was restless, and had accepted an invitation to dine with Sam Drake, the captain of the other caravan. He sat around a campfire after the meal with the members of that group, telling himself it was necessary to know what kind of men they were, since they might depend on each other for support at some point. The truth was, however, he was avoiding Sara. The more time he spent with her, the more he wanted her. At times, he could feel his hands tremble with the need to touch her.

When he observed that the campfires and lamps had all been doused in his own caravan, he took his leave. He found Señor Pino sitting outside their wagon smoking a cheroot. "Will our friends be joining up with us?" he asked, stubbing out the cigar in the dirt.

Rafael leaned on the side of the wagon and nodded, "*Sí*. I told them we would be departing the day after tomorrow."

Pedro rose and pulled his bedroll out of the wagon, spreading it on the ground. "Why do they leave so late in the year?" he asked.

"The captain—a man called Sam Drake—is going out to look for his brother in Taos Valley. He and the brother are partners in the fur business; he selling the furs in St. Louis, and his brother trapping them in the mountains." Rafael paused as he lit a cheroot. "It seems the brother was due in St. Louis by midsummer but never arrived, and Señor Drake is worried. The others are going along for various reasons. One is an artist who wishes to sketch some Indians; one is a merchant from Boston who thinks the trip will restore his health, and then there is a gambler. He gave no reason for traveling."

Pedro eyed him thoughtfully. "What did you think of them?"

Rafael shrugged and drew on his cigar. "I believe Señor Drake can be trusted and relied upon . . . time will tell about the others."

Pedro nodded, turning toward his blanket, and then he abruptly turned back. "I nearly forgot, Rafael. Señorita Clayton was looking for you earlier, and she acted as if it was quite important."

At this, Rafael straightened, his brows drawing together. "Did she tell you what it was about?"

Pedro shrugged. "No. I offered my help, but she wished only to speak to you."

"I will check on her," Rafael said and added, *"Buenas noches,* Pedro."

A smile curved the older man's lips, as he watched Rafael walk away.

For several minutes, Rafael stood outside Sara's wagon, debating about whether to disturb her or wait until morning. If it had been urgent, she would surely have told Pedro, he reasoned. And besides, he thought with irritation, he didn't know if he could hold his desires in check.

Deciding abruptly, he turned away and went to his pallet, to sleep until it was his turn to stand guard duty.

Sara awoke in the middle of the night, her gown soaked with sweat, her throat parched. She rose and got a drink of water from her pitcher. Taking off her gown, she groped in her trunk, looking for another. Finally, she lit the lamp and found one at the bottom. Before she put it on, she poured some water in her bowl and sponged her face and body to cool off. The July heat was excruciating, and she knew August could be worse.

Even after donning a clean cotton gown, the heat still felt oppressive, so she climbed out of the wagon to see if it was any cooler outside. A slight breeze caught her loose hair, and she sighed with relief. It wasn't much, but it was better than nothing. Leaning against one of the large wagon wheels, she gazed across the open space to where the creek wound its way into the heavy woods. She could see a faint shimmer of moonlight on the water, and longed to take a dip in its coolness; however, she knew it would be folly to wander away from the encampment in the middle of the night. Instead, she contented herself with lifting her hair off her neck to catch the breeze.

In the distance, she heard the howl of a wolf, and was doubly glad she was not out there alone. That thought reminded her suddenly of Rafael's promise to teach her to shoot. Until now, she'd quite forgotten about that.

It was strange, she mused to herself, that her parents' death had affected her heart so little. She felt guilty, but they had been more like acquaintances than family. The pain of losing Maxwell and Master Filbert, on the other hand, had been sharp and lasting. Even now, tears threatened if she dwelled on the memories too long.

Her thoughts were cut short by an unexpected hand touching her shoulder. Startled, she gasped and flinched away. A low, deep voice spoke, even as she turned to glimpse the intruder. "It's Rafael—do not scream."

Sagging back against the wheel, her hand went to her heart, and she whispered shakily, "Must you do that, señor? A few more times and my hair will be snow white from fright."

He smiled, unrepentant, and said, "Ah, that would be a shame, *niña*. It is so beautiful as it is."

Sara looked away from his intense dark gaze and ignored his compliment. "I wanted to thank you for the bath tub, señor, but you were gone all evening," she said, a little breathless.

He leaned a shoulder against the wheel, just a hair's breath away from her. "What makes you think it was me?"

She glanced quickly at him and noted a glimmer of amusement in his eyes. "Well, I didn't think Juan had an extra tub lying around in his wagon, and he was the only other person I complained to about the bathing facilities on the trail," she said, a slow smile curving her lips. He was so close, she could feel his body heat, and smell a faint scent of tobacco on him. Her heart began to beat a little faster.

He shrugged. "I purchased three of them from Don Vicente's store, and did not see why you should not have use of one." Changing the subject, he asked, "Why are you not sleeping, *niña?* It is very late."

His eyes had raked her boldly as he talked, and Sara felt almost naked in the thin gown. She wished now she had slipped on her robe. "It was hot . . . but perhaps I should try to go back to sleep," she said, and pushed away from the wheel. In trying to turn away without brushing against him she stepped on her gown and tripped.

His arm flashed out to catch her, and he hauled her against his hard chest. "Careful, *niña,*" he warned in a seductive voice. Instead of releasing her when she regained her footing, he held fast.

Sara squirmed in the circle of his arm, her hands fluttering against his chest. "Thank you, señor, you can let go now," she whispered, as something intense flared between them. She was extremely conscious of his virile appeal, and powerless to resist when he bent his head to claim her lips.

"Impossible," he breathed in a husky whisper, before his mouth covered hers hungrily.

Sara's senses spun out of control as his mouth moved over hers, devouring its softness. When his tongue pressed for entry, she willingly allowed it, and her knees weakened as shivers of desire raced through her.

Rafael groaned. His heart pounded and the blood raced hotly through his veins. He wanted her so much, it was like a physical pain. Yet, a small voice of reason bade caution. She was like a rosebud, opening up to him, new and innocent, and it would be dishonorable to take advantage of that. He groaned with frustration as his lips left hers to nibble at her earlobe. *"Niña,* why do you torture me so?" he breathed, his hands caressing her back.

Sara slid her hands up to encircle his neck, as she unconsciously pressed her body closer to his. "Oh, Rafael . . . I've never felt like this. Is it wrong?" she breathed in confusion.

With an iron will, he struck down his desire and held her gently, kissing her hair. "No, *niña.* What you feel is a natural thing, but it is wrong of me to encourage such desires. Someday, you will have a husband, and that right will be his," he said in a husky voice. Setting her away from him, he felt a stab of jealousy. He realized he didn't want another man to have her.

Sara knew in her heart that he was right, but she wanted nothing more at this moment than to be in his arms. She yearned to explore the passions between a man and a woman, for she felt instinctively that there was something even more wonderful than Rafael's kiss. She gazed up at him with wide innocent eyes. "I may not marry, señor," she said, thinking that she no longer had a dowry or an inheritance.

His smile was grim. "You were made for love, *niña*. The only question will be which man you will choose. And there will be many vying for your affection."

Sara's expression was doubtful. She wondered why he did not include himself. After all, he seemed to enjoy kissing her a great deal. Perhaps it was as she suspected; he would require a dowry. She was puzzled and a little hurt.

Extricating herself from his arms, she turned. "I shall be too busy with my new post to worry about such things," she predicted in a level tone. She accepted his help up into the wagon.

"I'm glad you're feeling better this morning, Estella," Sara said, as they walked toward the creek with Felipe in the lead. Doña Josefina had instructed him to do their laundry, and Estella had promptly offered to supervise. Truthfully, she wanted a respite from her mother. Sara had joined them with her own basket.

The Spanish girl nodded. *"Gracias.* It was nothing—a slight headache. I get them sometimes."

"Wait, señorita!" a voice behind them called out. Both girls turned to see one of Juan's helpers approaching at a trot. When he got to them, he nodded politely and offered, "I will carry that load for you, señorita. Juan says you should not be lifting such heavy things."

Sara smiled in bemusement and turned the basket over to him. *"Gracias,* Alonzo."

He hurried ahead to catch up with Felipe. Estella

gave Sara a significant look and chuckled. "See what I mean?"

"Nonsense. He was just being po—"

"Polite, I know," Estella finished. They laughed together, and then began discussing what they were going to do with their time until the caravan moved on.

"I promised Juan I would pick some blackberries this afternoon. One of the men found some growing just across the creek. Would you like to come with me?" Sara asked.

They had just reached the creek and Sara thanked Alonzo once again for his help. He dropped his head shyly and headed back to camp. Estella frowned. "I would like to, but Madre would be upset if I stained my fingers. She is very particular."

Sara thought for a moment and then suggested, "You could carry the bucket, and I will do the picking."

Estella brightened. *"Sí,* we could do that! You are so kind, Sara. I am very glad Señor Pino found you."

Sara smiled and began taking the clothes from her basket. Felipe looked up from his work and said, "I will do yours also, señorita. You must not ruin your delicate hands with such scrubbing."

Sara sighed. It seemed that Juan was the only person who would let her do anything, and that was not much. *"Gracias,* Felipe, but I will do the rinsing, since you do the hard work." Her tone was adamant and he nodded.

Estella found a soft spot of grass beneath a tree near the bank, and she kept Sara company until the work was finished. As they walked back to camp for lunch, Sara felt exhilarated. It felt good to be productive rather than an ornament in the parlor. Her new life, she thought suddenly, was going to be very satisfying. The only doubt that crept in concerned Rafael and her feelings for him. Although she wasn't quite sure what she felt, he definitely disturbed her peace of mind.

The noon meal was almost like a feast, compared to their regular fare on the trail. Juan had made a spicy stew with venison and canned vegetables, and there were little apple cakes for dessert. Two of the *vaqueros* brought out guitars and played after the meal, while everyone rested in the shade and enjoyed the music.

Sara shared a canvas lean-to with the two other women, and she could see Rafael and Señor Pino across the camp relaxing and smoking. Rafael looked more masculine than any man she'd ever seen. His fawn-colored buckskins molded his body like a second skin, and his dark hair, worn longish on his neck, caught the rays of the sun like the wings of a black bird. From time to time, his eyes rested on her, and she felt delicious little shivers run up and down her spine.

After a short siesta, Sara and Estella set out to pick blackberries. Doña Josefina was still resting, and Sara guessed that Estella had slipped out without explanation. Until she met the Spanish girl, Sara had thought her own life was confining, bordered by strict convention. But Estella could barely breathe without permission from her mother, and Sara felt sorry for her.

They found a place in the creek where a tree trunk had fallen across, affording them a way to reach the other side without getting wet.

Finding the berry vines without too much trouble, Sara began picking the luscious fruit, her bucket in hand. Estella wandered along a path of sorts deeper into the woods, picking wildflowers to take back.

Sara pushed her hat back several times to wipe the perspiration from her brow. After a while, her bucket half full, she glanced around, wondering why Estella had not returned. A sudden explosion near her feet caused her to drop the bucket and jump with fright. She whirled about and saw a man standing just a few feet away, his gun still in hand. Her fear intensified as she stared at the stranger. "Who-o-o are you?" she stammered, her heart thumping wildly.

In an unhurried movement, he slipped the pistol inside his belt and removed his hat with a flourish. "Garth Prescott, ma'am, at your service," he said in a pleasant voice and gave a little bow. "I'm sorry I scared you."

Sara had recovered herself somewhat, and no longer felt threatened. "Why did you shoot at me?" she asked in a puzzled tone. Glancing down, she saw the bucket on its side and her berries spilled. "Look what you did!" she gasped, bending to pick them up.

He walked over and knelt down to help her. "I suppose I didn't consider your berries when I saw that copperhead. I just shot," he said casually, scooping up the fruit with both hands and refilling the bucket.

Sara's hands stilled, and she glanced quickly to

her left. Lying in two pieces at the base of the vines was a deadly-looking snake. The color drained from her face, and she felt light-headed for a moment.

Garth, noting her sudden pallor, reached for her hands to steady her. "Are you okay, ma'am?" he asked, his blue eyes filled with sudden concern.

Sara swallowed hard. She had never seen anything bigger than a garden snake, and *they* gave her the shivers. This reptile was at least four feet long—or had been when it was in one piece—and had a wicked-looking head. "Oh my," she gasped softly, unable to take her eyes from the dead snake.

He helped her to her feet and urged her toward the creek. Pulling out a linen handkerchief, he wet it in the water and squeezed it out. She took it and wiped her face, her hand shaking. "Thank you, Mr.— I'm sorry, I've forgotten your name already," she said softly.

He smiled—a warm, infectious smile—and supplied, "Garth, ma'am. Garth Prescott."

Sara couldn't help returning his smile, as she held out her hand. "I'm Sara Clayton. And I do sincerely thank you."

"You are most welcome, Miss Clayton, and I'm happy to meet you. I'm traveling on the other carav—"

At that moment, Estella appeared from the woods, and Señor Pino came running in their direction. Sara called out, "I'm fine, Señor Pino. Estella, it's all right, don't look so worried," she added to the Spanish girl. "This is Mr. Garth Prescott, and he saved me from a nasty encounter with a copperhead."

"Garth!" Estella gasped, when she came face to face with him. She looked as if she'd seen a ghost.

Sara looked from one to the other with great curiosity. His expression was nearly as shocked as hers. "Estella . . . how are you?" he asked, his voice barely audible.

"I take it you know each other," Sara said, trying to smooth the awkward moment. Estella dropped her gaze finally and mumbled, "*Sí*, Sara. We've met before."

Señor Pino reached them, and Sara made the introductions and repeated the story of the rescue. "We are in your debt, Señor Prescott," Pedro said. "If there is ever anything we can do for you, we would be most happy."

His handsome face was enigmatic. "I would accept a dinner invitation tonight at your camp, if one was offered. You could then consider the debt paid." His gaze touched all of them, but lingered on Estella.

The Spanish girl refused to meet his eyes, as Señor Pino graciously extended the invitation. The two men walked away to inspect the dead snake and retrieve Sara's berries. Sara turned to watch them. "He seems a nice sort. Do you know him well?"

Estella's eyes were following the men as well, and she sighed. "*Sí*, Sara, we met two years ago when Madre and I were traveling down the Mississippi to visit her sister in Natchez. He is a gambler, and Madre will be very upset to find him here."

"Why would she care? He is traveling with the other caravan," Sara pointed out reasonably.

"He is not suitable—just as most men are not

80

suitable. I have no say in the matter of a husband. It is no better than being a cow that can be bought and sold!" Her voice had grown bitter, and Sara noticed a suspicious moisture in her eyes.

The forlorn slump of Estella's shoulders and what she had not said told Sara more than words could have done. Sara had also seen the look that had passed between her friend and Garth. Gently, she asked, "Were you in love with him?"

"What does it matter?" Estella said in a husky whisper and walked away toward camp. Sara let her go and then followed more slowly, not wanting to intrude on Estella's privacy.

Chapter 5

Two small tables had been put together, and Juan had produced a clean cloth to cover them, making an effective dining table for six. Juan's helpers served the food as if their patron and his guests were dining formally at Hacienda Delgado. Rafael sat at the head of the table, Garth Prescott at the other end, and Señor Pino, Sara, Doña Josefina, and Estella on the sides.

Sara thought Garth Prescott was a handsome man. He looked especially striking in his black trousers, black coat, and a white ruffled shirt. She had noted the diamond ring on his finger, and a diamond stickpin on his lapel. He carried himself with an air of confidence, and his manners were impeccable. When he arrived for dinner, he kissed her hand and complimented her on the blue silk dress she was wearing. Sara could see why the shy Estella was enamored.

Doña Josefina, on the other hand, was coldly polite to the man when he turned to speak to her.

As they sat around the table, Rafael and Pedro kept the conversation going, mostly with Garth. Over dessert, their guest addressed Sara. "This pie is delectable, however, if you ever decide to go berry picking again, Miss Clayton, allow me to offer my services as escort."

Sara laughed, her blue eyes dancing. "Thank you, Mr. Prescott, but I won't be wandering around in the woods anymore."

"Had I known the two of you were leaving camp, I would have sent Carlos or Alonzo with you. It is dangerous to go about alone," Rafael said, his expression stern.

Sara's smile faded at the obvious reprimand. He seemed angry, and, for some reason, she felt it was directed more toward her than Estella. "I'm sorry if I caused a problem."

Pedro frowned at Rafael, but hastened to say, "He just does not want anything to happen to you, señorita. Other than that, everything turned out fine—thanks to Señor Prescott." Changing the subject, Pedro turned to Doña Josefina, "Our guest tells me you met during a trip you took a few years ago."

The older woman sniffed disdainfully. "We were traveling on the same riverboat, Señor Pino." Rising, she said, "If you will excuse me, I will retire now. Come along, Estella."

The men rose hastily, and Sara watched her friend nod politely before following her mother. She did not understand why the older woman was so intent on making her daughter's life miserable. Sara's own good spirits had been effectively dampened by

Rafael's tone, and she also asked to be excused.

"Would you take a walk with me, Miss Clayton? After a dinner like that, I need the exercise," Garth pleaded with a smile.

Sara returned his smile. "That would be lovely."

He tucked her hand in the crook of his arm as they strolled toward the creek. A cooling breeze had lifted the heat of the day, and it felt wonderful to Sara. She was glad she had this time alone with Garth, for she intended to ask him about Estella when the chance presented itself.

"If you don't mind my asking, why are you going to Santa Fe, Miss Clayton?" he asked casually.

She turned her head up to smile at him. "I'll tell you, if you'll call me Sara. I don't think we need be so formal, especially since you saved my life."

He chuckled. "All right, Sara, but you must return the favor—it's Garth."

She nodded. "Señor Rafael's grandfather hired me to teach the children on his hacienda."

"What does your family think of your going that far away?"

They had reached the edge of the water, and Garth bent to pick up a stone. He sent it skipping across the top of the water, and Sara smiled. "My brother used to do that at the pond down the road from our house. I tried to learn, but never managed it."

He picked up another stone and did it again. "It's all in the wrist motion," he explained.

"I have no family now," she said quietly, and picked up her own stone.

"I'm sorry, Sara." He glanced at her delicate profile, seeing strength and character there. Always having been a loner, he was surprised that he felt a sudden urge to protect her from the cruelties of the world.

She gave him a smile. "I miss them, especially my brother Max, but as my tutor always said, 'Death is no cause for sorrow; sorrow is that one dies without benefit to the world.' My parents meant everything to each other, so it was good that they went together. And Max, well, he saved me from a lonely childhood and taught me many things."

Garth felt his estimation of her growing by leaps and bounds. "Except how to skip rocks?"

She chuckled. "Yes, except for that." They began to walk again, following the creek and moving away from the caravan, and Sara asked, "And why are you going to Santa Fe?"

He shrugged and pushed his hat back from his forehead a bit. "Oh, the adventure, I suppose. Never having been any farther west than Independence, I had an urge to see some unexplored territory." He grinned down at her. "I've spent most of my life in gambling saloons, and lately I've felt cooped up."

"I suppose you've been to a lot of places though. It must be an exciting life—traveling. Master Filbert used to talk to Max and me about all the countries he had visited when he was a young man, and it made me want to see those places," she told him wistfully.

Garth gave her hand a pat. "Perhaps this trip will be the first of many," he said encouragingly.

She nodded solemnly. "If it's my karma. And speaking of fate, meeting Estella and her mother again like this surely was meant to be, don't you think?" Glancing up at his expression, she saw that she'd caught him off guard.

His brows drew together in a frown. "I suppose so. I never thought I would see Estella again after we docked in Natchez."

"I think the two of you were more than mere acquaintances," Sara said, as the woods thickened in front of them. They turned in silent agreement to walk back.

Garth smiled, his thoughts faraway. "Much more. I was in love for the first time in my life." He fell silent, and after a few moments, he glanced at her. "I was standing at the rail when they boarded the boat at St. Louis. I was fascinated by her dark, exotic looks. It was plain though, that her mother guarded her like a hen with only one chick, immediately whisking her below to their cabin."

Sara smiled. "Knowing Doña Josefina as I do, I'm surprised you ever got close enough to say hello."

He chuckled. "It was coincidence, I suppose . . ."

"Or fate," Sara supplied.

"Or fate," he conceded, "that brought us together. That first night out, I was taking some air on the promenade deck around midnight, and literally ran into her. She had slipped out after her mother was asleep, to look at the stars. We didn't see each other coming around a corner, and ran into each other head on."

Sara's blue eyes sparkled with excitement. "Oh, Garth, how romantic! What happened then?"

He laughed. "Well, that would be telling now, wouldn't it? Suffice it to say, we met secretly every chance we got until we neared Natchez." His expression sobered as he finished the story. "I wanted to elope, but Estella wanted her mother's blessing, so she told her, thinking the old woman would come around when she realized how much in love we were."

Sara sighed. "Señora Perez did not come around, did she?"

He shook his head. "No. She locked Estella in her cabin until we docked, and then took her ashore before we could even say goodbye. At the time, I was furious with Estella for not standing up to her mother, but I've since come to realize that her upbringing would not allow her to do that."

Sara gave him a slow smile. "You and Estella have a second chance now. What do you intend to do with it?"

He looked startled for a moment, and then thoughtful. "I don't know, Sara, but you're right."

They had arrived at her wagon, and dusk was descending on the prairie. All around them, camp fires were being lit, and the sound of a lone guitar vied with the music of crickets and tree frogs. Impulsively, Garth bent to kiss her cheek. "Thank you, Sara," he said softly.

She glanced up. "For what?"

He smiled. "For being so wise." He strode off whistling softly.

Sara watched him until he was out of sight. She didn't realize Rafael was standing across the camp, taking in the scene with narrowed eyes.

Amid shouts of "All's set!" from the teamsters and

the rattle of harnesses the following morning, the two caravans set off, running parallel, leaving Council Grove behind. Everyone was rested and anxious to continue the journey. Sara chose to ride her horse that morning, rather than ride in the carriage. She didn't want her excitement spoiled by the señora. Estella, however, had not the luxury of choosing, and was forced to keep her mother company. Sara was frustrated over this development, for she had been anxious to speak to the Spanish girl about Garth.

Señor Pino rode beside Sara, while Rafael galloped back and forth alongside the wagons, helping with problems. The wide prairie stretched out like an endless sea of waving grass, wild and awe-inspiring.

"We will stop to load fresh water at Big John's Spring, just two miles from here," Señor Pino told her as they rode along.

"Oh. I thought we would have done that at the creek we just left," she answered, puzzled.

He shrugged. "The water at the spring is far superior, and it will not take long." He gave her a sidelong glance, and then asked, "What did you think of Señor Prescott?"

She smiled. "Aside from the fact that I'm grateful to him for saving my life, I like him. And you, Señor Pino, did you find him *simpatico?*"

"*Sí,*" he said cautiously. "However, we do not know him very well, and should reserve judgment until we do, eh?"

She made a face at him. "I realize I have no experience of the world, but I think he has a good heart. My instincts cannot be so bad. After all, you and Señor Rafael were strangers to me, and I trusted you both."

He chuckled at her good-natured jibe. *"Sí, sí—* you are right, but I worry about you as I would about one of my own daughters." He had grown to like the silver-haired señorita very much, and felt protective. He also thought she would be the perfect wife for Rafael, and did not want another man whisking her away before the two of them had a chance to fall in love.

They fell to discussing his six offspring, all grown and married now with children of their own. Sara would be teaching his grandchildren, and wanted to know everything about them.

Their conversation halted as they reached the spring. It lay at the foot of a steep hill where the road wound up and around. Not more than a foot deep, the crystal clear water sparkled in the sun, with vegetation thick and wild growing along its banks. The men descended with their barrels and buckets. Sara shivered with the sudden thought that a hungry wolf or a wild savage could be lurking in the thick grapevines, ready to pounce. Thoughts like that were occurring more often to her. Soon, however, they were on their way once more, and she forgot her fear.

The scenery was truly magnificent, with lofty hills stretching before them, green meadows, and giant trees along the creeks. Before noon, Sara saw one of the men from the other caravan riding on the top of a cargo wagon with a sketchpad on his lap. She watched him for a long while, and he seemed deeply engrossed in the picture he was drawing. Curious to see what his subject might be, she felt the surrounding countryside offered any number of beautiful scenes for his pen.

When they stopped to eat, Sara mulled over the fact that Rafael was avoiding her again, having barely spoken to her that morning. She had contented herself with Señor Pino's company, but felt the sting of disappointment all the same. She rested under the canvas lean-to, set up at the Perez wagon, with the señora and Estella. Her friend was more quiet than usual, and declined Sara's suggestion that she ride her horse in the afternoon.

In mid-afternoon, a band of Pawnee was sighted in the distance, and Rafael rode up to alert Señor Pino. "I have ordered everyone to keep their guns ready just in case," he said, and then glanced at Sara. "I think you should return to the carriage, señorita. It affords more protection."

Sara's eyes widened. "Do you think they will attack?"

Rafael shrugged. "Probably not, but it is best to take precautions."

Sara nodded and turned her mount toward the carriage. For the remainder of the day, a wary eye was kept on the uninvited guests. Doña Josefina bemoaned the fact that they would probably be murdered, and she would never see her homeland again. Estella and Sara had their hands full consoling her.

When they stopped for the night, extra guards were placed around the caravan to insure safety, but still a general feeling of unease prevailed.

After dinner, Sara offered her services to Juan for the clean-up, to get her mind off the tense situation. She was wiping plates when Garth Prescott found her.

"I hope you don't mind. I find your company so much brighter than that of my fellow travelers," he said with a grin.

Sara smiled in return. "I'm glad you came over, Garth. My nerves have been stretched to the limit today, and I could use the diversion."

He picked up a cloth and began helping her dry dishes. "Don't let those Indians upset you. I'm told they rarely attack, especially when they know they're outnumbered."

Sara handed him another plate to dry and wrinkled her nose. "I wasn't talking about them—Doña Josefina's hysteria was just about more than I could bear."

He let out a great peal of laughter. "I, too, am more wary of her than the savages."

Sara finished the last plate and placed her cloth over the end of the tailgate to dry. "I suppose we should pity rather than berate her; she's so miserable."

"True, but her misery is of her own making, remember that," he pointed out, handing her his cloth. "I brought a deck of cards. Would you like to pass the time with a game or two?"

Sara brightened. "Oh, yes. But, I don't know how. You would have to teach me."

He grinned. "My pleasure."

Juan offered the use of his work table to them, and they happily settled down to play.

Garth chose poker, and began showing her the basic strategy of the game. Sara caught on and found herself enjoying it immensely. He interspersed the play with amusing anecdotes from his days on the riverboats. The time passed quickly, and at dusk, Garth pulled out his pocket watch and sighed. "I'm on for guard duty in a short time, so I'd better get back." He gathered up the cards and gave her a smile. "If you ever tire of being a teacher, you'd make an excellent gambler, as fast as you're catching on."

"I'll remember that," she promised with mock-seriousness. "Thank you for an enjoyable evening. I was so engrossed, I didn't think of the Pawnee once."

He offered to walk her back to her wagon, but she declined, saying good night there. Juan returned from his stint at guard duty and began stirring the cornmeal mixture for the breakfast bread. Pouring a cup of coffee for herself, Sara said good night to him and started for her own wagon.

Halfway there, she met Rafael crossing the enclosure. He fell into step beside her. "Did you and Señor Prescott have a pleasant evening?"

His question contained a strong suggestion of reproach, and she glanced up at him with puzzlement. "Yes, it was quite nice. Is there something wrong, señor?"

He shrugged. "He is a gambler by trade, and they are not considered a respectable lot. I just don't wish to see you make a mistake, señorita. People are not always what they seem."

Sara smiled. "Señor Pino has already given me

this fatherly advice, Don Rafael, but I don't think either of you need worry. Garth has no dishonorable intentions, I'm sure."

Rafael cringed a little, hearing her use the man's first name in such a familiar way. In his mind, she was sweet and naive, and had no way of knowing that some men used silken words and beautiful manners to ensnare their victims. Aside from forbidding her to see Prescott again, however, he was powerless to prevent their friendship. "I hope you are right, *niña*. I would like to avoid trouble."

Sara's smile faded at his cold words, and an angry flush colored her cheeks. "You are my employer, not my father. I see no reason for you to choose my friends."

It was rare that she was roused to anger, much less to angry speech, and it struck dread in his heart. Did she care about this Garth Prescott so much already? He gave her a brief nod. "I have no right to interfere, as you say," he said stiffly.

Sara felt an unexpected stab of disappointment that he gave in so easily. For a moment, she had hoped he was jealous, but she now realized he was just being bossy. He apparently did not care about her except as an employee. Turning to him as they reached her wagon, she touched his arm. "No. I'm sorry, señor. You have my best interest at heart, and I was rude."

Her soft voice caused something to twist in his heart, while her touch burned like a brand on his arm. Unconsciously, he reached out to caress her face with his thumb, following the delicate line of her jaw. "I feared that you were being far too trusting, *niña,* for your spirit is pure. Just be careful, eh?" His voice grew husky as he leaned forward; but then he checked himself and straightened. Dropping his hand, he said, "Secure the flap on your wagon tonight, señorita, with the Pawnee about. It will be safer." With that, he turned and strode away.

Sara stared at his retreating back and wondered, was she mistaken or had he almost kissed her again?

The caravans reached Cottonwood Fork the following evening. Sara had spent a restless night thinking about Rafael, and was also uneasy over the Indian situation. Her shoulders drooped, and her face was pale from fatigue, as she stepped down from the carriage to stretch her legs. Estella and her mother followed with Felipe's help.

"Another dreary camp," Doña Josefina complained as she looked around.

Sara silently disagreed, but refrained from saying so. The prairie had its own kind of beauty, if one looked—the soft billowing grass, wild roses, and there were always streams meandering through valleys dotted with trees.

"At least those Pawnees are gone today, Madre," Estella said.

"Come along, Estella, you must help me walk away the stiffness," the older woman commanded, ignoring her daughter's bit of good news.

Seeing Alonzo across the circle with buckets in hand, Sara ran to catch up with him. "I'll help you with the water, Alonzo," she offered, as they walked toward the creek.

He smiled, now accustomed to her presence around the cook-wagon. *"Sí,* señorita. You can carry the canteen back, but not a full bucket," he admonished.

One thin brow rose skeptically, as she asked, "Are you sure that won't be too much for me?"

He smiled. "I think you tease me, eh?"

Sara laughed. *"Sí.* Everyone treats me like a hothouse flower, but I'm very strong—really."

Alonzo stooped down at the water's edge to dip the first bucket. "Don Rafael does not want you to get hurt, *niña.* He gave orders that you were not to do heavy work."

Sara blinked. Rafael? He interfered in even the smallest things she did around camp, she thought irritably. Didn't he give her credit for having any common sense? Returning to the chore at hand, she gave the second bucket to Alonzo. "I see. Well, I wouldn't want you to get into trouble because of me, so I'll behave," she promised.

He took the canteen strap from around his neck and filled it for her. They were soon trudging back up the steep bank of the creek. When they reached the level plain, Sara gasped and pointed to the west. "What is that?"

He squinted at the dark object in the distance for a moment, and then grinned. "Buffalo, señorita! This is *muy bueno*—there will be meat for our table!"

His excitement was infectious, especially when Sara envisioned a change in their dull diet. "Do you think there are more, Alonzo? Perhaps this one will get away," she said, suddenly anxious over the prospect of a good meal.

"We must let Don Rafael know."

They hurried back to camp, and Sara offered to find Rafael. "*Sí,* and I will pass the word to the others," Alonzo agreed as they separated. Sara found Rafael with his small herd of cattle, talking to the *vaquero* in charge of them. They were out beyond the caravan, and Sara was out of breath when she reached him.

Rafael glanced up at the sound of his name and saw her running toward him. Her cheeks were rosy, and tendrils of hair had escaped the long braid down her back. Fearing something was wrong, he hurried to meet her. "What is it, *niña?* Are you all right?" he asked anxiously, taking her hands in his.

Sara nodded, catching her breath. "We spotted a buffalo, señor, beyond the creek! Alonzo is passing the word, but I came to find you."

He smiled then at her enthusiasm, and also with relief that there was nothing wrong. "That is good news, *sí!* I think by the look of you that you are tired of beans, eh?"

She laughed and agreed, "Very."

He took her arm, and they started back to the caravan. "Before darkness falls, perhaps we will have fresh meat."

"I'll help Juan prepare a celebration," Sara said, her blue eyes sparkling. "We'll have music and dancing as well."

He glanced down at the animation in her face, and found himself extremely conscious of her appeal. The thought of holding her close as they danced sent a spreading warmth through him. A slow smile curved his lips. "And will you save most of your dances for me, *niña?*"

Sara flushed as her heartbeat quickened. His dark gaze was devouring her, and she felt out of her depth. Dropping her eyes, she murmured, "I'll be happy to señor."

They had reached the horses, and Rafael assured her, "It is buffalo." He mounted the stallion Jose was holding for him, and without looking back, he called for the *vaqueros* to follow.

Sara felt a lurch of excitement as she watched the men ride away to the hunt. There was a secret smile on her face as she headed for the cook-wagon.

Estella and Sara moved along together in the food line, as Juan and his helpers filled their plates with buffalo steaks, corn cakes, beans, rice, and gooseberries. It was a meal fit for a queen, Sara laughingly stated. The hunters had returned triumphant well after dark. Three buffalo had been killed, skinned, and butchered.

After helping Juan with some of the preparation earlier, Sara had retired to her wagon for a warm bath and had washed the trail dust from her hair. She had donned a blue taffeta dress and splashed herself liberally with lavender cologne. Her long silver hair was held away from her face with a blue ribbon, but left to hang loose down her back.

Sara had asked for more hot water for Estella, and then had fetched the Spanish girl for a leisurely bath also. Her offer had not been merely kind, however, for she had some matchmaking in mind. Her next chore was given to Jose: instructions to ride over and invite the members of the other caravan to the party.

Makeshift tables had been set up inside the circle of wagons, and the two young women made their way to one already occupied by Doña Josefina. The older woman was eating her food with relish, and glanced up as they seated themselves. "This steak is tough. It must have been an old buffalo," she commented between bites.

Estella and Sara smiled at each other across the table. Señor Pino and Rafael had just joined them with full plates, when Sara saw the men from their neighbor caravan arrive in camp. She excused herself and hurried over to greet them, while Rafael eyed her gesture with a frown. After speaking with them for a moment, she returned to take her place.

"I hope you don't mind, Don Rafael, but I invited Garth and the others to share our dinner," she said quickly, noting the grim set of his mouth.

Before he had a chance, Doña Josefina spoke up. "You have overstepped your bounds, young woman. Your position is that of a servant in the Delgado household, and as such you had no right."

Rafael's eyes narrowed. "At the risk of being rude, Señora Perez, I must correct you. Sara is not a servant, nor will I allow you to treat her as such."

Sara had been about to speak for herself when Rafael defended her. It gave her a warm feeling, and eased her anger at the older woman's sharp words.

Doña Josefina's mouth thinned with displeasure. "What is her position, may I ask?"

Rafael's gaze rested on Sara for a moment. "She is a valued employee."

Sara looked from Rafael to Doña Josefina. "I

98

don't appreciate being talked about as if I'm not present."

Her quiet dignity prompted Señor Pino to intervene. "The invitation was a generous gesture on the señorita's part. Let us just enjoy this celebration, eh? There won't be many chances on the trail for such a party."

His conciliatory tone diffused the tense situation. Doña Josefina sniffed and returned to her meal without another word. For Sara, though, the evening had lost its sparkle. As soon as she finished eating, she excused herself and returned to her wagon for a brief respite.

Rafael followed her and found her standing on the far side of her wagon, staring out into the shadows of the prairie. He dropped a hand awkwardly on her shoulder. "I am sorry about what Señora Perez said," he apologized.

Sara tensed at his touch. "I don't care what she thinks. But I could tell that *you* didn't like the fact that I had invited the others," she said.

He turned her to face him, tipping her chin with his finger to look into her eyes. "It wasn't that . . . I just wanted you to myself," he admitted in a husky voice.

Sara's expression softened, and she moved closer to lay her hand on his chest. "Is that true? I wanted this party to be special . . . for everyone," she added wistfully, thinking of Garth and Estella as well.

Rafael's arms automatically went around her, and he felt a tightening in his loins. Her beauty was intoxicating and her nature so gentle, he longed to protect her from anything hurtful. Ruefully, he realized that sometimes it was *he* who caused her pain. He didn't want to hurt her; it was just that he didn't wish to get involved emotionally with another woman. Rational reasons were fine, but standing here in the dark with this warm, seductive woman in his arms was playing havoc with his senses. "Any time I spend with you, *niña,* is special," he breathed softly, his hands caressing her back in slow circles, while the heady smell of her lavender perfume filled his nostrils.

His sweet, tender words were like a balm to her soul, while the feel of his hands on her sent warm shivers of pleasure up and down her spine. Even though she didn't understand much about man-woman relationships, she knew she belonged in Rafael's arms on this warm, star-filled night. He made her feel like a desirable woman, and she longed for more of his lovemaking—whether it be right or wrong.

His strong hands moved to cup her face and turn it up for his kiss. His mouth covered hers hungrily, and his tongue slipped between her parted lips.

Her heart thundered in response as her arms tightened around his waist. He moved seductively against her, and a raw passion burned within her that she did not yet understand.

"Mi alma, I want you," he rasped in his throat, as he trailed hot kisses down her neck.

Sara's hands slid up to bury themselves in his thick, dark hair, as his lips reached the swell of her breast above her bodice. She gasped in delight as he lifted her off the ground and buried his face in her fragrant skin. "Oh, Rafael," she breathed, "I want you, too."

The sound of laughter and deep voices on the other side of her wagon brought him to his senses. The world around them had been forgotten for a few moments in the throes of passion, but his ardor began to cool as he realized anyone could have come upon them. Letting her slide back to the ground, he touched her face lightly and gave her a twisted smile. "You make me forget myself, *niña.*"

Sara searched his face, looking for his true feelings, but his enigmatic mask was back in place. "I, too, am guilty of that," she admitted softly. "But, Rafael, I am confused about—"

He placed a finger on her lips to stop her words. "Sometime we will talk, but not now. We have guests, remember?" The truth was, he didn't have answers for her at the moment. His feelings were new and raw, and he didn't know how he felt. How could he explain anything to her?

He smoothed her hair back and took her hand. "Come, I hear the guitars tuning up. You and I will have the first dance, eh?"

She nodded and let him lead her back to the festivities. The tables had been moved back to provide room to dance. Sara saw Doña Josefina and Estella sitting in chairs on the sidelines. The older woman's eye caught them, and she watched like a vigilant hawk as Sara and Rafael made their way through the crowd of people hand in hand to a table where drinks had been set up.

Sara ignored the ruthless stare of the older woman. She accepted a glass of wine from Juan, who presided over the table. *"Gracias,* Juan. I didn't

101

realize there would be fine wine to go with our feast," she teased, sipping recklessly.

He grinned. "Señor Pino ordered a small barrel opened for the occasion."

Rafael said in an undertone, "See that no one has too much, Juan. We must be watchful, in case the Pawnee come back."

Juan nodded. "*Sí,* Señor Pino cautioned me on this already," he said, and refilled Sara's glass before they moved away.

The two guitar players began a ballad, and Sara let the sad music surround her as they moved through the crowd, stopping to say a few words to this one and that one. Rafael's steadying hand at her elbow was reassuring, and she began to feel mellow and happy, forgetting about the old dragon who watched her.

Before they could dance, Garth Prescott, along with a short, balding man, approached them. The gambler was impeccably dressed as usual in black pants, a white shirt, and a brocade vest. "Good evening, Sara, Don Rafael. Thank you for inviting us to share your party." He turned to his companion. "This is Matt Harrigan. He's an artist."

Sara smiled at both men. "I'm happy to meet you, Mr. Harrigan. I saw you sketching the other day, and wondered what your subject might be."

The man's brown pants and white shirt were clean, but wrinkled, as if they'd been wadded in a ball before he donned them. His wire-rimmed spectacles rested down on the bridge of his nose, as he stared intently at her. "I'd like to paint *you* before we get to Santa Fe, young woman, or at least get some good preliminary sketches done," he said.

Sara blinked at his abrupt statement. "Well . . . I suppose so," she stammered.

Garth laughed. "You'll get used to him. The man has only one thing on his mind—pictures. He sees nothing but subjects."

Rafael's dark eyebrows rose. "I understood you wished to paint the Indians?"

Harrigan nodded eagerly. "Oh, yes, that's my main ambition, but I like unusual subjects, and the young lady here is so beautiful, and that silver hair— well, it's magnificent!"

Sara blushed at his extravagant compliment. "I'm flattered, Mr. Harrigan, and, yes, I think that would be fun," she agreed with a smile.

"I want that exact smile when I sketch you," he said quickly, becoming even more animated. "There's a quality about your face that's a mixture of innocent child and sensuous woman. I must capture that!"

Rafael frowned and Garth laughed again. "Don't mind him, Sara. He's looking at you with an artist's eye."

Matt Harrigan looked confused for a moment, and then frowned. "Of course, I am, Prescott! How else would I look at her?"

Sara laughed then, forgetting her embarrassment. He seemed harmless. He began badgering her about the first available time she could spare for a sitting, when Alonzo approached Rafael and spoke quietly to him. Rafael told her, "I must see to something, but will return shortly."

Sara nodded and continued to talk to the artist.

103

When Rafael was out of earshot, she leaned closer to Garth and whispered, "Have you talked to Estella yet?"

He shook his head. "Her bodyguard won't leave her side, and I doubt she would be allowed to dance with me."

Sara took another sip of her wine and gave him a thoughtful look. "There must be a way, but I don't know what."

He chuckled. "You invited me so you could matchmake, didn't you?"

Her eyebrows rose innocently. "Whatever gave you that idea?" she asked.

"Just a hunch," he said dryly.

Harrigan, not interested in the mundane conversation, took his leave of them. The musicians began a ballad, and Sara finished off her wine in one gulp. She handed the empty glass to Jose, who was passing, and asked him to dispose of it. Turning to Garth, she had a glint of mischief in her blue eyes. "We must lull her suspicions first, I think. Dance with me," she ordered.

He asked no questions, but smiled and complied. As they moved in time to the rhythm, Sara explained. "If she thinks you're interested in me, she won't hover over Estella all the time. Then you'll have a chance to talk to her."

Garth laughed at her lopsided smile. "Maybe, Sara, but I think the wine is going to your head."

Sara gave him a sidelong glance. "Where did you get that silly notion?" Her head did feel a bit fuzzy, but she felt so good, it didn't matter. She searched the crowd for Rafael, wondering suddenly why he hadn't returned. She finally saw him standing next to Estella's chair, talking to her. When the Spanish girl stood up to dance with him, Sara felt a stab of jealousy. Rafael was supposed to dance the first dance with her! She watched the other couple over Garth's shoulder, but Rafael was not even looking her way.

By the time the song ended, her spirits had plummeted. She suggested to Garth that they have another glass of wine. "It's so very hot," she complained.

His eyebrows rose at her request, but he led her to the refreshment table. She sipped the Madeira slowly, as she watched Rafael lead Estella through a flamenco. The men on the sidelines clapped and shouted encouragement to the dancing couple. They looked as if they belonged together, Sara thought, their steps matching almost perfectly. Garth and Sara were both scowling by the time the music stopped.

Jose made his way to Sara, hat in hand, and asked if she would dance with him. Without hesitation, she nodded. "Why yes, I believe I will. But I'm not as accomplished as Dona Estella."

He grinned broadly. "I will be happy to teach you some of the steps, señorita."

They moved to the middle of the circle, and the musicians began another flamenco. Patiently, Jose led her through some steps, and soon, Sara began to learn and keep up. Carlos stepped up next and then the others followed, wanting a dance with her. They were unfailingly courteous, but after several dances, she laughingly begged off for a rest.

Garth handed her another glass of wine and grinned. "You're the belle of the ball, Sara. If you continue to be this accommodating, the men will arrange a fandango every night and dance your feet off."

Taking a handkerchief from her pocket, Sara dabbed at the perspiration on her face. "It's not that I'm so popular, but the only available female partner, Garth." She sipped her wine, adding, "Doña Josefina did not seem disposed to taking a turn."

Garth smiled at the thought. "True. And she would not allow Estella to dance with any of the *vaqueros*." He sounded pleased about that.

Sara's gaze drifted to the other girl, across the circle. Rafael was now seated beside her, making conversation. He seemed very attentive to the two women, and had not once approached Sara for a dance. Had she dreamed the intimate exchange they had shared earlier? The kiss? He had told her he wanted her all to himself this evening. Apparently that had been just empty words. She suddenly felt very tired, her pleasure in the evening tarnished. Placing her empty glass on the table beside her, she touched Garth on the arm. "Thank you for coming tonight, Garth. I think I'll go to bed—I'm not feeling too well."

Concern creased his brow. "Is there anything I can do?"

She shook her head and was immediately sorry, for she felt dizzy. "No, I just need some sleep."

He lifted her hand and kissed it. "I've had a very pleasant evening, even though your matchmaking plans didn't work out," he said and attempted a smile.

Sara made her way to her wagon and undressed without a light. Her world was spinning faster now, and a clammy sweat beaded her body. She couldn't imagine what the matter was, but felt the need to hold onto the edge of the bed when she lay down. She drifted off to sleep with disturbing thoughts of Rafael chasing around in her befuddled brain.

Chapter 6

From a long way off, Sara heard the sounds of whimpering. When she forced her eyes open, she realized *she* was making the sounds. Strange pains gripped her stomach, and a sickening dizziness made her head swim. Coming fully awake, she shot up from her cot and bolted from the wagon, just in time to throw up the bitter contents of her stomach.

When the retching subsided, she leaned wearily back against the wagon for support and took in great draughts of clean air.

"I was afraid this would happen, *niña,*" a deep voice said beside her, giving her a start.

"Rafael! I think I must be dying," she croaked, after looking up to find him at her elbow. "Where did you come from?"

He slipped an arm around her and asked, "I was on guard duty. Do you think there will be more?"

She shook her head and leaned into him. "No," she said dismally. "There couldn't possibly be more."

He helped her back into the wagon and said quietly, "I'll be back in a moment with something to help you."

Once he'd gone, Sara bathed her face and rinsed her mouth with water. She pulled a fresh gown from her trunk and changed. The effort made her tired, and she lay down to wait. She didn't know what medicine he could possibly find to help her sickness, but just the thought was comforting.

Before long, Rafael was climbing inside to sit by her bed. "Here, *niña*. Sit up and eat these slowly."

When she raised up, she found he had brought soda crackers. Pushing them away, she protested weakly, "I can't eat anything, Rafael! It will just come back up."

"Trust me, Sara. This is the cure for too much wine," he said with a smile in his voice.

"Oh, dear," she moaned. "Is that what's wrong with me?"

He chuckled then. "I'm afraid so. You will live through this, but you may wish you hadn't before it's over."

Sara groaned again and nibbled at a cracker, swallowing slowly. When it stayed down, she tried a little more, and then finished two crackers. Finally, she looked at him and defended herself, "I was thirsty, señor, and I really didn't have that much."

"I doubt you are accustomed to drinking wine, and then there is the fact that you ate no dinner. When the stomach is empty, the wine travels to the head much faster. Do you feel better now?"

She nodded and then screwed up her courage to ask, "Why didn't you dance with me tonight?"

He hesitated for a moment. "You were enjoying Señor Prescott's company, and I did not want to intrude."

"I was waiting for you to return! When you kissed me before, I thought . . . well, I thought that meant something," she said, able to voice her doubts in the dark.

Rafael had a sinking feeling in his stomach at her simple trust. He felt like a snake taking advantage of her naïveté, but found himself drawn to her constantly. And when she was near, he couldn't help touching her. He took one of her hands in both of his. "You are very desirable, Sara, and I'm a man who enjoys beauty. I'm sorry if I've led you to believe it's anything more serious. I'm to blame for the misunderstanding."

His explanation left her even more confused. She sighed. "Are you saying that kisses between a man and a woman mean nothing? Do you kiss every woman you find attractive, señor?"

He groaned inwardly. What was he to do? She needed someone to protect her, but he found the task impossible, since lately all he thought of was making love to her. "That's not exactly what I meant, and no I do not kiss every woman I find attractive," he explained patiently. "Sometimes there is a certain special feeling between a man and a woman, and they are drawn to each other."

The warmth of his hands covering hers was causing her pulse to race. "Like with us? When you kiss me, it feels wonderful. And I get butterflies in my stomach when you touch me, Rafael, like now. Is that what you mean?" she asked earnestly.

She struck a vibrant chord in him, but he quelled the urge to take her in his arms. Unless he intended to follow through with a commitment, he was loath to dally with her. She deserved better. Taking a deep breath, he said, *"Sí,* but we cannot continue with the touching and the kissing. It will lead to other things . . . and I cannot in good conscience make any promises to you."

In the thick darkness of the wagon, Sara couldn't see his expression, but in his voice she heard a hint of pain. "Why, Rafael? Is there someone else that you care about?"

He hesitated a moment. *"Sí,"* he said slowly, "I am not free." Abruptly letting go of her hand, he rose. "I must get back to my post now."

His answer hurt more than she could have imagined. Without her realizing it, her feelings for him had been growing stronger each day, and now she felt as if the wind had been knocked out of her. Who was this other woman? And how could he kiss *her,* if he cared so much about this other person?

"Gracias, señorita," Juan said, as Sara handed him the last of the strips of buffalo meat to be hung over the drying rack. The fires had been banked low, so that the meat could be cured slowly. The caravans had stayed over for a day to preserve the excess meat and to do some needed repairs.

Sara washed her hands and left the cook-wagon behind. She made her way to her friend's wagon, looking for company. Estella was sitting alone beneath the canvas shelter rigged up on the side of their sleeping wagon. She let her sewing project drop into her lap as Sara approached. "Come sit with me awhile, Sara," she encouraged.

"Is your mother sleeping?" Sara asked, glancing around.

"*Si,* she cannot do without her siesta, but I was not tired."

"Why don't we go for a walk? I could use the exercise," Sara suggested, adjusting the chin-string on her hat.

Estella readily agreed and spread her lace shawl over her head for protection from the sun. The air was still, thick, and hot as they walked toward the creek.

The Spanish girl applied her fan rapidly back and forth to create a breeze, then cleared her throat nervously. "Madre is very angry with you, Sara. I wanted to warn you of this before you see her again. She's angry with me also over Garth."

Sara nodded. "That doesn't surprise me, Estella. And I suppose I shouldn't have interfered, but the two of you seem so miserable. I just wanted to see you have a chance. Garth told me that you wanted to marry, but your mother forbade it."

The girl sighed. "It's true . . . we were very much in love. I did not realize how much I still cared, until I saw him again."

"I believe he's an honorable man. I saw genuine kindness in his eyes."

"His integrity is not the issue, Sara. My parents have chosen a man for me from our social class. It was arranged several years ago, and I am expected to marry shortly after we get back to Santa Fe," she explained with a faint tremor in her voice. "When I fell in love with Garth, I was fifteen and did not know about this betrothal. My parents had not thought it necessary to tell me until it was time to marry."

. Sara stopped her with a comforting hand on her arm. "I'm sorry, and I understand what you mean. My father was in the process of choosing a suitable husband for me when he died. I don't suppose I would have had too much say in the matter, come to think of it."

There were tears in Estella's eyes as she blurted out, "The worst part of it is that my future husband is old enough to be my grandfather!"

"Oh, dear! How can they do that to you?" Sara sympathized with her friend. She couldn't imagine this lovely young girl being given to an old man. It reminded her of Jonas Farber, and she shuddered involuntarily.

They had reached the top of the rise that led down to the creek. Sara saw a lone figure at the foot of the hill, standing beside a cottonwood tree. She felt a twinge of defiance as she recognized Garth Prescott. The other girl was trying to bring her emotions under control, and hadn't noticed.

Sara gave her arm a squeeze. "Have faith, Estella. Fate may yet have something better in store for you. After all, I don't believe your meeting Garth again like this is coincidence. It could be destiny." Gently, she pointed to where Garth stood. "Go talk to him. I'll come back later, so that we can walk back to camp together."

Estella dabbed at her eyes with a handkerchief

and smiled. *"Gracias,* my friend."

Sara made her way to the other caravan and found Matt Harrigan perched atop a cargo wagon, sketchbook in hand. "Am I interrupting you?" she called up to him, shading her eyes from the sun.

He grunted, made a few more strokes with his pen, and then looked down at her. "Yes. But it's all right, Miss Clayton. I've been anxious to begin on you." He scrambled down to her side and took her arm. "Come along to my wagon. I have a blue cloth to drape over your shoulders."

He pulled her along before she could answer. "After giving it some thought, I've decided to do you in blue—you do own a blue dress, don't you? I also want your hair down floating around your shoulders like a sea of silver, as it were."

Sara laughed at his preoccupied attitude, which all but excluded her. "You're a very decisive man, Mr. Harrigan. I hope the Indians go along with your plans as willingly as I."

He stopped and blinked at her through his spectacles. "I think you're teasing me, Miss Clayton," he said, a smile slowly curving his mouth.

She chuckled. "Just a little. However, I bow to your more learned opinion on the subject."

In no time at all, he had her seated on a stool with a cornflower blue cloth draped over her shoulders, and a black cloth tacked up behind her on the side of the wagon. He told her it was merely for effect just now, since he was sketching in pen first, and would not be using paint until later. For a half hour, his pen made bold strokes on the paper, as Sara sat perfectly still. Finally he stopped and nodded with satisfaction. "That's enough for today. I want to let this rest, and then study it before I go on."

Sara gave a sigh of relief. She was stiff from holding her position for even this short time. "I'll come back every chance I get," she promised, handing the cloth to him.

When she arrived back at the creek, Garth and Estella were talking earnestly beneath a cottonwood. Seeing her, they said their goodbyes. He kissed her cheek lightly before coming toward Sara. Grinning, he said as he passed, "You're an angel, Sara."

Sara shook her head with a smile, and hurried to Estella's side. "I assume all went well?"

The Spanish girl fairly glowed, her dark eyes sparkling. "Oh, Sara! I thought I'd never feel this happy again." Impulsively, she hugged Sara. *"Gracias.* If it wasn't for you, I don't think I would have had the courage to talk to him."

"I did very little, but you're welcome anyway. It's good to see you smiling again."

Estella bit her lip as her expression grew serious. "Could we sit and talk a moment, Sara? I have a confession to make."

"Of course," Sara replied, as they spread their skirts out on the grassy spot.

Glancing down at her folded hands, Estella said, "I am ashamed to say I've been jealous of you, and once I even wished you had not come along on this trip."

Sara's brows rose. "But whatever were you jealous of, Estella?"

"It's a long story, but I'll try to explain. When Madre and I returned home from Natchez two years ago, I was heartbroken over Garth. Rafael was very kind and understanding when I poured out my tale of woe, and I gradually transferred my feelings to him. One day, I realized I was in love with him—or I thought I was . . . until I saw Garth again. Now I know I was fooling myself," Estella said with a sigh. "When you arrived in Independence with Rafael, I saw his interest in you, and I was envious."

"Do you think Rafael knew how you felt about him?" Sara asked.

"If he guessed, he was too good a friend to say anything. Really, that is all we've ever been—good friends. I fear I was being childish for a time," Estella said with a wry smile. "Can you forgive me, Sara?"

"What you did was so horrible, I'll have to think about it," Sara teased. Estella laughed with relief and chattered on about Garth for a time, while Sara listened with half an ear. Thinking back, she realized that some of Estella's somber moods had been because of Rafael, and not due to a quiet, shy personality. Sara suspected that her friend knew nothing of Don Vicente's attempt to betroth his grandson to her. However, she was sure Doña Josefina had made it plain to her daughter that Rafael was not suitable.

Curiosity finally got the better of Sara, and she asked, "Is Rafael betrothed to anyone, Estella?"

The Spanish girl hesitated a moment. "No. Why do you ask?"

Sara shrugged and tried to look nonchalant. "Oh, it was just something he said to me yesterday, about not being free."

116

"I know it's none of my business, but are you falling in love with Rafael?"

Sara dropped her gaze and nodded. "I think so. He makes me feel so . . . so . . ."

"Wonderful?" Estella finished for her with a smile.

Sara glanced up and laughed. "That just about sums it up. I suppose that's the way you feel about Garth."

"*Sí*. About Rafael, though . . . he's a good man, but he's been hurt badly, Sara. Our families are neighbors as well as friends, and I've looked up to Rafael since I was a child, but he can be stubborn. I would tell you his story, except that many things he's told me have been in confidence, and I can't break that trust. This I know—you are the first woman he has been interested in for a long while, and I believe he cares for you. I can see it in his eyes. I will give you the same advice you gave me—talk to him."

Sara was growing more curious by the moment, but respected Estella's reticence. "Well, you've given me hope anyway. But I don't know how I could bring up the subject without being too forward. He's already said the kissing and touching will have to stop," she said innocently.

Estella rose to her feet, hiding a knowing look of faint amusement. "I am sure another opportunity will arise, my friend. Just be ready for it."

Three days later, the caravans arrived at the Little Arkansas. Rafael had sent a small crew of his men in advance to lay a bridgework of brush and long grass on the steep, miry banks, so the wagons could cross without difficulty. Sara climbed out of the carriage to stretch her legs while they were stopped to wait their turn, and she watched Rafael directing the crossings.

He sat ramrod straight in his saddle, and the bright sun glinted off his raven, black hair. Not once in the last three days had he sought her out, and she had begun to think he intended to ignore her for the remainder of the trip.

Although well-meaning, Estella had surely been wrong about his interest in her. Her spirits plummeted when she thought about it. Climbing back inside, Sara closed her eyes with a sigh as Doña Josefina cleared her throat. The gesture was always a prelude to a reprimand or something equally nasty. "You should wear your hat whether you're riding or not, Sara. Have you looked in a mirror lately? Your skin is turning as brown as an Indian's. If you ever hope to catch the attention of a *caballero,* you must see to your complexion," the older woman said flatly.

"I will try to remember," Sara said evenly, as she gazed out the open side of the carriage. It was better, she thought ruefully, when the señora was angry with her and refused to talk.

The dearborn was moving down the steep bank when something spooked the mules and they stumbled, causing the vehicle to lurch sideways. It tipped precariously, before landing back on its wheel. The women screamed and grabbed for any handhold they could find. Frightened by now, the mules bolted down the embankment toward the creek, ignoring the efforts of Felipe to halt them.

118

The carriage, so much lighter than the wagons, careened wildly while the occupants were tossed about. When the carriage hit the level creekbed, an axle broke, and sent the vehicle crashing to its side.

Although a strange darkness surrounded Sara, she could vaguely hear excited shouts in the distance. There was a heavy weight on her chest and a stinging pain in her right leg. She struggled to ascend from the dark place, but the noise receded, and total blackness enveloped her.

The feel of gentle hands stroking her brow was Sara's first indication that consciousness was returning. There were soft voices murmuring above her, but she couldn't quite hear what they were saying. The earth, however, was no longer moving beneath her, and that terrible weight was gone from her chest.

A cool, wet cloth bathing her face brought her back slowly, and she opened her eyes. Rafael was on his knees beside her, and his expression was grim. "*Por Dios, niña,* you gave me such a fright," he said in a husky voice.

"I'm sorry," Sara whispered, noticing the concern in his dark eyes. Memory of the accident was returning, and her brow creased in a worried frown. "Estella . . . Doña Josefina, are they all right?"

"Better than you, Sara. When I got to the carriage, they were both on top of you. I thought you were crushed," he said, his expression growing more grim.

She tried to raise up, but he gently took her shoulders and pushed her back down. "Not yet. Rest a few more minutes, before you try to get up. I've

119

checked for broken bones, but found none."

Sara glanced around and saw most of the men from their caravan standing a short distance away looking anxious. She also saw Garth stooped down beside a disheveled Estella, who was sitting on a stool. Her mother sat on another stool beside her, looking dazed.

Glancing back at Rafael, she realized what he'd just said. She blushed when she thought of him checking her body over for injuries.

He smiled then, as if reading her thoughts, and leaned close. "Do not worry, I did it discreetly. And the others did not stand and stare. They have too much respect for you, *niña*."

She closed her eyes and nodded with relief. "Thank you," she whispered. After a time, he helped her to stand, and Señor Pino stepped up to assist.

"I will personally chastise those stupid mules, señorita," the older man said as they started up the hill.

A tenderness in her right leg made her limp, but otherwise, she felt stable. She smiled tremulously. "Joseph, our coachman, used to say, 'A mule will be a mule any way you fix it.'"

Señor Pino chuckled. "A wise man. I am very glad none of you were hurt seriously."

Sara glanced up at Rafael. "So am I. I'm so looking forward to getting to Santa Fe."

He was looking down at her intently. "We will try to take better care of you in the future."

A blush rose in Sara's cheeks at his intimate tone. It had taken an accident to get his attention once more, and she was determined to keep it. "Do you

120

think we could try some shooting lessons when there's time, Don Rafael? I know you're very busy, but I would feel better if I had my gun back."

Señor Pino spoke before Rafael had a chance. "That is a very good idea, señorita. There are many dangers along the trail, and another gun hand would be welcome, eh Rafael?"

"*Sí*. After we strike camp, we will have our first lesson," Rafael agreed, glancing at Sara. "If you feel well enough, that is."

She nodded. "I'm fine, just a little shaken up."

True to his word, Rafael sought her out when the wagons had been formed in a circle and the animals unhitched. Sara had changed into a dry blouse and skirt, washed her face, and rebraided her hair. She was chatting with Juan at the cook wagon when Rafael found her.

He had his pistol strapped to his side, and a satchel slung over his shoulder. "We will practice down beside the creek, away from camp."

Her mouth quirked with humor. "Afraid I'll shoot somebody?"

His laugh was low and throaty. "You forget I've seen your aim, Señorita Clayton."

Juan urged them to remember dinner as they walked away. When they found a likely spot at the foot of the hill, Rafael retrieved a piece of tin from his satchel and nailed it to a cottonwood tree. They moved back a good distance, and he showed her how to load the small derringer he took from his pocket. "This weapon will not be effective at a great distance, but I want you to get the feel of it."

Sara nodded and took it in her right hand. He

stepped behind her and placed both arms around her, with one hand on hers to steady the weapon. His warm breath brushed her ear, as he leaned down and spoke in a low tone. "Hold it very steady and take aim, *niña*. When you feel you have your target in sight, pull the trigger gently, and try to keep your arm straight."

His nearness was intoxicating, and Sara felt herself tremble involuntarily. Her hand shook slightly even as she tried to hold it still. How could she ever hope to hit anything with his body touching hers? She jerked at the trigger, and the shot went to the far right of the tree.

"No, *niña* . . . squeeze gently next time," he coached softly. The fragrance of lavender filled his nostrils and clouded his brain, while her soft body touching his caused a tingling in the pit of his stomach. His hands itched to caress her curves, and he fought for control.

Several times, she shot at the target. Finally she hit the tree, if not the piece of tin. Rafael's concentration was sorely lacking when he stepped back to replace the small gun in his pocket. "We'll try with my pistol a few times before we finish for today," he suggested, his voice taking on a husky quality.

This exercise proved to be more arduous for both of them, for this weapon was heavier, and Rafael had to help her hold it steady each time. Finally he put the gun back in his holster and turned away for a moment. "That is not bad for a start. We will practice more another time," he said gruffly.

Even though Sara's leg was aching from standing

so long, her mood was light. Being alone with him was more intoxicating than drinking wine, and she felt intuitively that he was not unaffected.

After dinner, Sara settled down beside Estella and tried to concentrate on her needlepoint, but found her attention straying. Rafael was moving around the caravan, taking care of small details, and her eyes followed him.

Estella touched her arm. "We were very lucky today, eh, Sara?"

Bringing her attention back to her friend, Sara smiled. "Yes. It could have been far more serious."

Estella laughed softly. "I meant the attention we received from Garth and Rafael."

Sara's smile broadened. "Oh. Rafael gave me a shooting lesson before dinner."

"I know. I saw the two of you leaving camp. Did you get him to talk of his past?"

Sara shook her head. "There was no way to open the subject, but I'm hopeful. There'll be more lessons, because I'm such a bad shot."

Estella advised, "Do not learn too quickly, eh? Garth was very attentive to Madre after the accident, and I believe she has softened a little. Anyway, she did not growl at him."

"That is indeed a good sign," Sara agreed. "Is she still in bed?"

"*Sí*, but she's all right—just a bit shaken up. I sat with her for a long time. How is your leg?"

"A little sore. I can walk just fine," Sara replied. She glanced up as Garth came around the wagon into view.

He greeted them and inquired after Señora

123

Delgado. When Estella told him she was sleeping, his eyes brightened. "Would you ladies like to take a walk with me?"

Sara shook her head regretfully. "Thank you for the kind offer, but my leg is throbbing and I should rest it."

Estella glanced at her in surprise, and then smiled slowly. "I think that's a good idea, Sara. Don't try to overdo."

"You two go ahead. I'll stay here in case the señora needs anything," Sara said with a significant lifting of her brows. She watched them walk away with a feeling of satisfaction. Perhaps things would work out for her friend after all.

As darkness was descending, Felipe appeared with some brush and dry wood. He built a campfire outside the señora's wagon. Sara smiled her thanks, and listened to the old lady's snores compete with a *vaquero*'s guitar. The sky was a black velvet blanket studded with stars. Several campfires around the circle dispelled the darkness. It was strange, she thought, that she hadn't once been homesick. As a matter of fact, she felt more at home in the caravan than she'd ever felt in the mansion on Carondolet Road. Her biggest regret was that Max was not there to share it with her.

Rafael, coming back to camp from the creek, saw Sara sitting by herself. He deposited his dirty clothes inside his wagon and made his way to her side. *"Buenas noches,* señorita," he said quietly, glancing at the empty stool beside hers.

Sara's heart fluttered, and she quickly offered, "Please sit down."

He did so, and she caught the clean smell of soap as he passed. His hair was still wet, and shone as black as sin in the firelight. She searched for something to say to cover her nervousness. "Can the carriage be repaired, señor?"

His dark eyes raked her boldly, but his voice was casual. *"Sí.* Tomorrow my men will see to it. Another day will be lost, but Señora Delgado will be more comfortable in it than in a wagon."

Sara gave him a shy smile. "That's very thoughtful of you."

He shrugged. "I am the captain of this caravan, and obligated to see to everyone's needs."

"You do a very good job of it, señor. It seems you are everywhere at once," she said.

"When each person does his work, it's not so very hard," he replied matter-of-factly, brushing off her praise.

"Do you make the trip for supplies to Independence every year, Don Rafael?"

He shook his head. "No, not anymore. For a few years I did, but Don Vicente has more than he can handle with the rancho and the silver mines. My cousin, Manolo, is helping out while Pedro and I are gone this time."

Sara shifted her weight on the stool to rest her back against the wagon wheel. "You never say my grandfather; it's always Don Vicente."

Rafael glanced at her in the flickering firelight, and a scowl darkened his strong face. "He has never wanted me to be his grandson, and so I oblige him."

Taken aback, Sara blinked. "Has he said this?"

Rafael looked away, staring into the fire. "Not in

125

words, but in actions. I know his views on the subject of half-breeds. He has never forgiven my mother, and he will not forgive me for being one."

What sort of man was her employer, Sara wondered, if he blamed a person for what they could not help? This was a man who went out of his way to hire a teacher for the poor children on his *rancho*, and yet did not wish to claim his own flesh and blood. "I don't understand," Sara said.

Rafael was silent for a few moments before he finally spoke. "My mother was Don Vicente's only child, and according to Pedro, he adored her. The year she was sixteen, the Comanches were raiding frequently in the Santa Fe area. My mother was traveling to the settlement one day, and was captured by a Comanche brave. She had an armed escort, but Flying Hawk was a fierce warrior and killed her guards. He took her to his camp farther north, and kept her as a wife. A few months later, during his absence, she escaped and was found wandering around by some trappers. They returned her to Hacienda Delgado."

"Your grandfa—I mean Don Vicente—must have been glad to see her alive and well," Sara said, her eyes round with wonder.

Rafael scowled. "He was, until he found out she was carrying a child. From that day on, he never spoke to her again, pretending she did not exist. My grandmother, Pedro told me, did not feel the same way, but was shocked by the news. She died shortly before I was born, and my mother died giving birth to me."

"How terrible!" Sara whispered, trying to imagine

the pain the young girl felt. The shame she bore was not her fault—and then to lose the love and support of her father must have been a cruel blow! "Both you and your mother were innocent victims—how could he blame you?"

Rafael shrugged as if it didn't matter. "Don Vicente's blood is pure Castilian, and he was too proud to accept anything less. He felt duty-bound to raise me, but he did not have to like it."

Sara felt like weeping for the hurt child inside of him, but knew he would accept no pity. Her tender heart raged at the cold man who had caused such senseless pain. She could not stop herself from asking, "When you were older, why did you stay with him?"

"I didn't. I ran away when I was sixteen to find my father's people. For four years, I lived with them, and learned the ways of the Comanche. But when my aunt sent word that Don Vicente had fallen ill and needed my help with the *rancho,* I returned and have been there ever since," he said in a voice devoid of emotion.

"Duty without love, on both sides," Sara mused, and then glanced up at him. "Were you happy with your father's people?"

He hesitated a moment. "For a time . . . but I had lived in the white man's world too long to be truly satisfied."

"And what of your life on Hacienda Delgado? Is there any happiness there?" she asked.

He shrugged. "The old man and I are civil to each other. He runs the operations at the silver mines, and I run the *rancho*. I am content taking care of the land

127

and the people. I also have my own *rancho* in a mountain valley. I go there to find peace and solitude."

She studied his profile, dark against the moonlight, and felt a tug at her heart. "You said before that you weren't free . . . is there a woman you care about?"

It was a question Rafael had dreaded, but knew would come. If he had not let his passions rule with Sara, he could have kept a safe distance. Now, however, he knew she deserved an explanation. *"Sí,* Tuwikaa was my father's tribe, and I married her when I was seventeen. A year later our daughter, Kahuu, was born."

His quiet revelation stunned her for a moment. Married? She had not expected that. Surely Estella could have told her that he had a wife and child! Her heart and hopes sank, and then as realization set in, she began to feel anger growing inside her. He was no better than Jonas Farber! She stood up abruptly and faced him with angry tears in her eyes. "I don't think I will ever understand men, señor! Do you all think it's morally right to keep a paramour, while your poor wives and children stay at home and pretend all is well?" Her shaking voice was beginning to get louder with the emotions that shook her. "You kissed me . . . and touched me! How do you think that makes me feel?"

Rafael stood up and grasped her by the arms, shaking her a bit. "Stop this, Sara! And lower your voice. You do not know what you are saying!"

The harshness of his tone sliced through her feelings like a sharp knife, and the tears poured down her cheeks. "I know that you've hurt me," she said brokenly.

Rafael swore under his breath and pulled her to him. He had been careless and unfeeling with Sara's tender heart, and he deserved to be horsewhipped. How could he make her understand that he dared not love a woman again with his whole heart, and then lose her? It hurt too much. Stroking her hair, he sighed. "My wife is dead, Sara. She's been gone for eleven years."

Sara leaned back to look into his face, her eyes wide and tear-stained. "Oh dear . . . I thought you were—"

"An unfeeling monster?" he supplied grimly. "No, *niña,* I am not a philandering husband, but neither am I proud of my behavior with you. My only defense is that you are so desirable, I forgot myself," he said, his voice growing husky. Gently, he wiped the tears from her cheeks and kissed her brow.

Sara extracted herself from his arms and stepped back. Her gaze dropped and she sighed. "I've made a fool of myself."

His arms felt empty, but he refrained from pulling her back. Softly, he said, "You are not foolish, Sara, but innocent. There's nothing wrong with that. When you are young, love is given and accepted very easily. It is not until you are older that you realize the danger in this."

Sara pulled a handkerchief from her pocket and wiped at her eyes. "I suppose you loved her very much?"

"*Sí,*" he said quietly.

Sara's heart constricted. "And your daughter?"

129

"She is with The People," he answered without further explanation. Abruptly, he said, "There are things I need to check on before I retire, señorita. *Buenas noches.*"

Sara stared after him until the darkness swallowed him up. She had never felt more alone in her life than at that moment.

Life on the trail settled into a pattern over the next two weeks for Sara. More days than not, she rode horseback at the head of the line with Señor Pino, talking companionably and learning more Spanish. Evenings were spent either playing cards with Garth Prescott while there was light, or sitting for Matt Harrigan while he sketched. Since the carriage accident, Doña Josefina seemed a bit more mellow, and allowed Estella to at least talk to Garth during the frequent time he sat at their dinner table. Several times, Sara caught the older woman staring at her with a speculative gleam in her eyes and it made her uneasy, but the señora spoke of nothing unusual, so Sara dismissed it.

No buffalo had been spotted recently so their diet returned to beans, jerky, and corn cakes, with an occasional rabbit for a stew. Though city born and bred, Sara never complained of the hardships of trail life; rather she seemed to thrive. Her skin had turned golden, and the constant exercise of riding or walking had toned her muscles and given her more energy than she'd ever experienced in her life.

In the last few days, a new threat presented itself. They had been traveling up the course of the

Arkansas, over sandy hillocks where rattlesnakes were abundant. The sound of gunfire to kill the disagreeable reptiles was becoming so common, Sara barely flinched anymore. She kept a watchful eye, however, when riding her mare. They had lost one of the mules due to snakebite, even though Rafael had ordered a vanguard to clear the route.

By the end of the day, Sara was exhausted. The sun had beaten down on them relentlessly, and she was longing for a cool bath, clean clothes, and some sleep. The men had their chores and were just as tired as she, so she was loath to ask them to bring water. Waiting until dark, she gathered her clothes and a bar of soap, and made her way down to the river.

The moon was bright enough to see her way, but she felt a little nervous being alone. She also felt guilty. If Rafael knew she had left camp, he would be angry. Since the night she and Rafael had talked by the campfire, she felt awkward in his presence and was reluctant to discuss anything with him. She decided that she would hurry and never be missed.

When she reached a safe distance from camp, she began undressing. A bird squawked in a tree nearby, and a band of crickets serenaded the quiet night, as Sara waded into the river. The water felt deliciously cool to her fevered skin, as she dipped herself to her neck. Wetting her loose hair, she applied the soap until a rich lather formed. She then stood up and scubbed the dust and perspiration from her body. Throwing the soap up on the bank, she rinsed by dipping once more, and then set about scrubbing her hair and scalp. It felt wonderful to be truly clean again. As tired as she was, Sara longed to stay in the water for a while, but knew she should get back.

The sound of a snapping twig brought her head up sharply. She scanned the area along the bank where a few scraggly cottonwoods grew. There was no movement, no human shape that she could see, but her peace was destroyed all the same. Quickly, she rinsed her hair and stepped out onto the sandy bank. Taking one towel, she wrapped her hair. With the other, she began to dry herself vigorously. A skittering sound in the underbrush sent gooseflesh crawling over her, as she gripped the towel tightly to her bosom. Her heart turned over as she looked up and saw a glow of red light near a tree. It looked like a tiny fire, and she instinctively knew what it was—a cheroot. Several of the men in both caravans smoked them, and one of them was watching her.

Chapter 7

She was paralyzed for a moment, wondering what to do. She couldn't force a scream from a throat closed with fear, and her legs felt rooted to the sandy bank of the river. The decision was taken out of her hands as the man moved forward into the moonlight and spoke. "Since you've spotted me, *niña,* I thought I'd better show myself," Rafael said casually.

Sara sagged in relief for a moment, before she began to blush with embarrassment. Futilely, she tried to cover her entire body with the inadequate towel. "You frightened me, señor," she gasped.

"Just be glad it is me standing here rather than one of the others, señorita. Or it could have been a Pawnee," he pointed out, throwing the cheroot down in the sand.

Sara felt hot and cold at the same time, as he watched her boldly. She knew what he said was true, but at the moment, she couldn't think beyond their present situation. "You watched me bathe," she accused in a breathless voice.

He shrugged and moved toward her in an un-hurried manner. "I am a man, *niña*. I could no more resist than a starving man could turn away from a feast," he said, his voice growing husky. Stopping directly in front of her, he lifted his hand and caressed her face with his thumb. "So beautiful, Sara . . . but so innocent," he breathed in a raspy voice.

A tumble of confused thoughts and feelings assailed her at his nearness. He smelled faintly of strong soap and tobacco, and she could feel the warmth emanating from his body. She had resigned herself to the fact that Rafael did not care for her, and now . . . now he was here, touching her, looking at her with those dark, compelling eyes. "I'd better get dressed, señor," she said, her pulse spinning.

"*Sí*, you should," he agreed lazily, but did not move away. Instead, he placed his strong hands on her bare shoulders, and pulled her slowly toward him.

"Rafael? I don't think—" she began to protest softly as his mouth descended to hers. The moment their lips touched, she was lost. An intense excite-ment curled in her belly and fanned out, causing her heart to pound. The warm night air caressed her, yet she shivered. She could feel the heat of his body even through her towel. His hands stroked her back and slid down to cup her buttocks, pulling her closer to him, causing her to tremble.

Rafael's heartbeat pounded in his ears like the beat of a Comanche drum. His whole body was on fire with a passion he hadn't felt in years. He wanted Sara desperately . . . wanted to slide into her velvet warmth . . . wanted to feel his release mingling with hers. A haze of desire clouded his brain as he struggled to control himself, but her whimpers of pleasure undid his resolve. He knew in that moment that she was his for the taking, and he wanted her as he had never wanted another.

Forgetting the towel, Sara wound her arms around Rafael's neck and returned his kiss. The feel of his tongue caressing the inside of her mouth blotted out any thoughts of protest. She wanted him to love her. She wanted to know what it was to be a woman. When he slid a hand between them and urged her legs apart, she complied, moaning with desire as his fingers stroked her. Explosive currents raced through her at this unexpected pleasure, and she arched her back instinctively, giving him greater access.

Rafael's lips left hers to trail hot kisses down her neck to her breast. He suckled at a ripe nipple until it grew hard, then he took the other one in his warm mouth, while Sara whispered his name and raked her nails through his hair. White-hot desire raged inside of him to take her immediately and relieve himself of the passion that had been building for weeks, but he knew he couldn't. He wanted to give her pleasure. It would frighten her if he took what his passion demanded. Raising up, he put her a short space from him and looked into her passion-glazed eyes. *"Mi alma,* I want you . . . but you must decide," he said in a husky voice.

Sara was beyond coherent thought, wanting only his wild touch, his tender whisperings in her ear. She cupped his face with both her hands and nodded. "I want you, too, Rafael," she whispered.

His heart gave a lurch, and he turned his face to kiss her palm. Gritting his teeth, he said, "I cannot promise to love you as you deserve, *niña*. Do you understand that?"

Sara barely heard his words, as her hands slid boldly down to touch his chest. She only wanted him to finish what he had started. Her whole body throbbed with desire. "I'll take what you can give," she breathed.

Her caress and softly spoken acceptance snapped his wavering control, and he pulled the towel from between them, dropping it on the sand. Sara waited breathlessly, dropping her gaze shyly while he shed his garments. Gently pushing her down onto the warm sand, he covered her body with his own.

Sara sighed with pleasure at the sensations that raced through her, as he again kissed and caressed her. His mouth trailed hot kisses across her firm breasts, down her quivering belly, and back again. Parting her legs with his knee, he took her mouth in a fierce, hungry kiss that left both of them shaken. Trustingly, Sara wound her arms around his neck and let him love her. As his fingers once again stroked the satiny folds of her womanhood, she rose to meet them and moaned her pleasure.

When Rafael could stand it no longer, he guided the tip of his erection inside her and pushed gently, entering the moist opening. Sara stiffened for a moment, her eyes swerving to his in question. He smiled and kissed her mouth slowly, before whispering, "There will be just a little pain, *cara mia,* and then you will feel pleasure again. Don't be afraid."

Sara relaxed in his arms. "I want you to love me," she begged softly.

He took her mouth in a slow drugging kiss, while one hand moved down to caress her hip. Gently, he began to move, barely inside her and back out again, teasing the opening, building a sensual rhythm. When she began to rouse to passion once more, and instinctively moved her hips in an erotic motion, he gave a harder thrust and broke the thin barrier that had separated them. Sara cried out at the pain and tried to pull away, but he held her tightly, ending his thrust deep inside her, giving her time to adjust. His soothing voice whispered that the pain was over, until her sobs stopped. He kissed her face gently and began to move slowly, feeling her begin to respond.

As the sharp stab of pain subsided, Sara tingled from the contact of Rafael's body inside hers. She knew now that even if Fillette had explained lovemaking to her, she wouldn't have understood fully. It was more wonderful than she could have imagined, even with the brief pain. At the moment, she was not even concerned that what she was doing was wrong. She had been lonely and unloved for too long . . . she needed Rafael. Sara rose to meet each thrust of Rafael's body as her pleasure escalated. She was marginally aware of a strange new sensation building inside of her. Reaching for that elusive feeling, they spiraled upward until their passion exploded in a storm of lightning showers, giving them both a shuddering release.

Sara called his name hoarsely, as he whispered fierce endearments in her ear.

Their bodies remained joined while their breathing

slowed to a normal rhythm. Rafael dropped light kisses on her face, and wound his fingers in her long, damp hair.

"I hope I didn't cause you too much discomfort, *cara mia?*" he questioned softly.

Her blue eyes wide with wonder, Sara whispered, "It hurt a little, Rafael, but I didn't know lovemaking would be like this."

He smiled slightly. "It's not always like this, *niña.* It depends on who you are with."

She frowned, suddenly possessive and a little jealous. She couldn't bear to think he had shared this magnificent experience with another. "Have you ever felt this way . . . I mean, was there anyone—?" She broke off, embarrassed and confused. Of course, he must have felt this way with his wife; he mourned her yet. But Sara yearned for assurance.

No, he thought with a sudden dawning, he had never felt this exquisite pleasure with anyone, not even . . . Unexpected guilt stabbed at him as he remembered his wife. He had loved her, but it was not the same. Sara's youth and innocence assailed him once again, and he felt a sharp pang of remorse. This should never have happened, but *por Dios,* he thought raggedly, he had wanted her badly. "Except for one, it meant nothing," he said finally. The feelings of passion and protectiveness were there for this woman, just as they had been for Tuwikaa, yet he felt subtly different. The thought frightened him. He didn't want to feel that strongly about anyone ever again.

It was not the answer she craved, but she could be patient, Sara reasoned. His hurt would ease, and he would come to care in time, she was sure. Her voice was gentle. "You've made me happy, Rafael," she said simply, smoothing the lines on his strong face.

Her words twisted his heart. She was so trusting, and he shouldn't have taken her. He faced a true dilemma now. Rather than make any decisions at the moment, he kissed her soft mouth lightly and rose to his knees, pulling her up with him. "Why don't we cool off in the river, Sara. Then we had better get back to the wagons."

Sara nodded and followed him into the water. She wrapped her arms around his neck, and he held her for a time. Rafael found that he was becoming aroused again with her soft body touching his, and had to strike down the desire in his blood with an iron will. Finally, he mastered his lust and led her out to dry off. They dressed silently and walked back hand in hand. He saw her safely inside her wagon, and kissed her face lightly when she leaned out. With turbulent thoughts whirling in his brain, he did not see Doña Josefina watching them from the shadow of her wagon.

"The desert plain between the Arkansas and Cimarron Rivers is fifty miles wide without a trace of water, señorita," Señor Pino explained to Sara, as they rode along the next day. "That is why we took on more barrels of water to see us through."

Sara lifted her hand to shade her eyes, as she gazed across the arid land. "Will it be like this until we reach the Cimarron?" she asked, indicating the sandy hillocks.

"For about five miles, but then the plain levels out. That will not relieve the dryness or the heat unfortunately," he said with a shake of his head. "I always dread this stretch of the trip."

Sara let her eyes wander, looking for Rafael, but he was nowhere in sight. "What will it take—four or five days?" she asked, her mind not really on what they were talking about.

"*Sí,*" he replied, noticing her distracted attitude. He had also noticed how content she seemed this morning. There was a glow to her face and a spring in her step. She had the look of a woman in love, and a slight hope rose in him that the patron's plan would work out. Señor Pino truly cared about Rafael and this young woman.

Rafael came into view up ahead. Sara watched the effortless way he rode, as if he and the horse were one. His wide shoulders stretched the limits of his buckskin shirt, and the hot breeze ruffled his black hair. A thrill of pride and pleasure shot through her, and her cheeks warmed as she remembered the events of last night. She had yearned to be with him this morning, but was too shy to take the initiative. Breaking camp had been accomplished as usual, with Rafael seeing to many details, and there had been no time for even a word with him. Although disappointed, she tried to be patient, just as Master Filbert had taught her.

By that evening when the wagons were circling to make camp, Sara was chaffing over the fact that Rafael had not come near her all day. Her pride was bruised by the slight. If he had wanted to, he could have found a moment to seek her out. Leaving her mount with Jose, Sara went to her wagon to wash off the trail dust before dinner. Stripping down to her chemise, she sponged her face, arms, and legs with a small amount of water in her basin; they were on short rations until they reached the Cimarron. The minimal bath made her think of the night before at the river.

She relived each moment, each word, each touch, until the blood coursed hotly through her veins, leaving her weak. Was this love? she questioned silently. Rafael had said that all lovemaking did not make you feel as wonderful. Lost in her musings, she lay down on the cot and curled into a ball, hugging her knees.

When she closed her eyes, she could see Rafael's smiling face above her, and also the fierce expression he had worn when the world exploded for the two of them. It made her shiver with desire, and she felt shamed by her wantonness. He had not said how he felt about her, nor what their relationship would be in the future. As a matter of fact, he had said he could not promise her love. An uneasy feeling crept over her, as she looked at the situation realistically. She had given herself to a man who was not her husband, and he had made no commitments. He had not even spoken to her today. Perhaps he regrets our involvement already, she thought with a sinking heart. Another thought hit her, and she sat bold upright. What if he had made her pregnant? She had seen several servant girls' bellys' swell over the years, even the unmarried ones. Could it happen the first time? Why hadn't she thought of this?

She chewed nervously on her thumbnail, and

wished there was another woman she could talk to about this confusing situation. She doubted very much if Estella knew any more than she did of such matters, and she couldn't possibly ask Doña Josefina.

Sara heard the bell clanging for dinner, and wished she could stay in her wagon and bury her head beneath the pillow. But she knew someone would come to see about her, and she didn't want to have to answer any awkward questions. Dressing in a clean skirt and blouse, she left the wagon and joined the other two women beneath their canopy.

When she sat down, her gaze moved automatically across the circle to Rafael's wagon. He was seated next to Señor Pino, looking intently in her direction. Sara blushed and then paled, tearing her eyes away. Her gaze swerved and met Doña Josefina's knowing one. A slow smile curved the older woman's mouth, and Sara had the uneasy feeling the woman could read her mind. *"Buenas noches,* Señorita Clayton. You look a trifle peaked—is something the matter?"

Hastily, Sara looked away and stammered, "No, nothing. The heat I suppose."

"It is dreadful, is it not?" Estella said, fanning herself. "I thought we would die in that carriage today."

Felipe walked up with three full plates then and, after Sara thanked him, he left. She had composed herself somewhat. "At least, on horseback I can catch a breeze, even if it is a hot one," she agreed, and began to eat. The food tasted like sawdust, but she forced herself to swallow some.

"The climate around Santa Fe is more bearable.

142

The heat is dry. I think you will enjoy it . . . among other things," Doña Josefina said pointedly.

Sara glanced up, noting her smug expression. How could the woman possibly know anything? she thought in a panic. But it was there in her eyes; she was baiting Sara.

With a calmness she didn't feel, Sara replied evenly, "I'm sure I will." She forced down a few more bites, but mostly pushed her food around while Estella carried most of the conversation. She spoke of the coming roundups and rodeos, as well as holy day festivals at the end of the year. Sara barely heard a word she said, but tried to nod occasionally.

As they were finishing, a shadow fell across their table, and Sara looked up to find Rafael standing there. He greeted the two Spanish women courteously before turning to her. "I thought perhaps this evening would be a good time for another shooting lesson, señorita. Do you feel up to it?"

His low, deep voice sent shivers up and down her spine, and she felt breathless and awkward. She, however, managed to accept his offer without stuttering.

When he was out of earshot, Doña Josefina commented, "It is kind of Don Rafael to take such an interest in you. He has always been so reserved."

Estella jumped to his defense. "True enough, Madre, but not with his friends. He has been most kind and patient with me."

Her mother turned a disapproving eye on her. "And you mistook that for a different kind of affection, Daughter. It is a man's nature to take whatever a woman offers, and that is why your papa

143

and I guard you carefully, especially since you are to be married soon." Her gaze took Sara in as well for a moment.

Sara wondered if the look was meant as a warning, and a feeling of frustration rose in her. How was she to know about men and their intentions? She had never been courted, nor had her mother explained the facts of life to her.

Estella's chin lifted at her mother's reprimand. As she opened her mouth to protest, Sara hastily rose and excused herself. "I'd best be on my way, while the light holds. *Buenas noches.*"

Glad to be away from the cranky old woman, Sara retrieved her hat from her wagon and made her way to Rafael's.

He was waiting with a saddlebag slung over his shoulder, talking in a low tone to Señor Pino. When he saw her approach, he nodded briskly and took her arm. "We will ride out, away from the caravan. I have no wish to chase stampeding animals tonight."

Sara said nothing as she followed him to the two horses Jose had saddled. When Rafael helped her mount, Sara's skin tingled where he touched her.

Sara's mare followed Rafael's stallion without much guidance from her, and she thought wryly that it wasn't much different with her. Rafael's wish was her command. However, there was her pride to consider, and she had come to a decision. She wondered at his mood, for he was silent and sat stiffly in the saddle.

When they were well away from camp, he reined in and slid off the horse. When he turned to help her, Sara searched his face for a clue to his thoughts, but his expression was bland. She felt his hands tremble, however, before he released her waist. Though a small thing, it gave her needed courage, and she placed her hand on his arm. "Is something the matter, Rafael?" she asked, a frown of confusion on her face.

Her touch burned, her scent intoxicated, and Rafael's stern resolve slipped. He caressed her face with his thumb, and a deeper frown creased his brow. "I have much on my mind, Sara." She looked up at him with such trusting eyes, he felt a stab of guilt. He had brought her out here to talk over their situation, but found he couldn't be as objective as he had planned. He wanted to kiss her sensuous mouth instead.

Sara had to look away from the intensity in his dark gaze to catch her breath. "I have been thinking about what happened . . . last night," she whispered, and then cleared her throat to go on. "No matter how beautiful it was, I feel it was wrong." She clasped her hands together and stared at them, trying to find the courage to finish her speech. "You are still in love with your wife and I must make a new life for myself. It wouldn't be fair to either of us to continue . . . well, to be more than friends."

Instead of the relief he should have felt, Rafael's heart sank at her words. She was giving him the opportunity to bow out of this situation with his honor intact, and yet he found the idea very unappealing. He tipped her chin up with his finger and gazed into her wide blue eyes. "You can forget what happened between us?" he asked quietly.

Sara stepped away from him and gazed across the

uneven, sandy hills. She didn't wish him to see the pain or the lie she struggled with. "I truly think it's best. Your grandfather hired me to do a job, and I really am anxious to see if I can stand on my own two feet." She forced herself to look at him. "You see, all my life I've been taken care of by others and, though they were well meaning, I would like to do my own thinking for a change."

Rafael was shaken as he looked into her clear, unwavering blue eyes. He was momentarily speechless in his surprise. Obviously he'd been wrong, he thought with sudden irritation. She wasn't merely doing him a favor—she didn't want him! He covered his consternation with a brisk nod. "Of course, Sara. I will agree to whatever you say." Abruptly, he turned toward his saddlebag and extracted a piece of tin and her derringer.

Sara's heart sank at his easy compliance. Apparently last night meant nothing to him, and he was relieved. The thought hurt, but Sara vowed to be strong and not let it show. She took the weapon from him and broke it open as he had taught her, while he walked a distance away and anchored the piece of tin upright in the sand.

Sara loaded the gun under his watchful eye, and then practiced firing at the target for a while. This time, however, he didn't stand behind her with his hands on hers, helping her aim. Instead, he stood to her side and gave verbal instructions. It was certainly not the same, and Sara sorely missed his arms around her as she tried to concentrate. The air was thick with more than the heat of the day. There was tension, and a formality that had not existed between them since those first days on the trail.

Sara managed to hit her target twice, and Rafael finally called a halt to the practice. "You are improving, señorita." His voice was carefully polite, as he handed her into the saddle and then placed the derringer in her hand. "I think you should keep it now."

Trying to smile, but failing miserably, Sara said, "I will take that as a compliment to my ability."

They rode back to camp without another word. The time was bittersweet for Rafael. She was like a mirage—so close and tempting, yet unattainable.

Jose was waiting to take their mounts. Sara thanked Rafael quietly before she walked away.

"After Madre went to bed last night, I met Garth and we slipped away for an hour," Estella confessed to Sara as they rode side by side under the hot sun. "I know I am being disobedient and sinful, but I cannot seem to help myself."

Sara sighed. What could she say to her friend? If Sara knew what was best, her own life would not be in turmoil. In the beginning, she had thought Estella and Garth belonged together, and that their forbidden love was romantic, but with her newfound experience, she wasn't so sure anymore. Cautiously she asked, "You haven't let him . . . I mean, the two of you haven't . . ." She was worried about Estella, but stumbled over the question.

Puzzled, Estella frowned at Sara, and then a dawning light came into her dark eyes. Shaking her head vigorously, she said, *"Por Dios!* Oh no, Sara.

We did nothing but kiss!" The dark-haired girl averted her gaze, and then admitted, "Not that I did not want to, *amiga,* but Garth has much respect for me and is very strong. And besides, Papa would kill him if that happened."

Sara felt a sickening lurch in her stomach. Rafael had not been strong; he had taken what was offered in the blink of an eye. "I suppose a man has no respect for a woman who comes to him too easily," Sara mused.

Estella shrugged. "That is what Madre says. Spanish girls of good families are chaperoned so closely though, there is no chance of that happening. Once we reach home, it will be impossible for me to meet Garth secretly."

Sara glanced over at her friend. "What will you do then?"

"I do not know, but Garth has promised to take care of everything . . . and I trust him," Estella said with confidence. "And what of you and Rafael? I have not had a chance to ask how the shooting lesson went the other evening."

"I actually hit the target," Sara hedged.

"That is not what I wish to know, Sara. Has he confided in you?"

"He told me of his life with his grandfather. And he also told me about his wife and child. He's still in love with her, you know," Sara said, her tone resigned.

Estella gave an unladylike snort. "He thinks he is, but I have seen the way he looks at you!"

Sara nodded. "That may be true, but I'm beginning to find out that just because you're

148

attracted to someone, does not mean you're in love with them. I've told him I wish only to be friends," she said firmly. She couldn't bring herself to tell Estella that they'd been intimate. Especially now that she knew Rafael didn't love her. She felt foolish enough.

Estella seemed surprised. "So you are not in love with him?"

Sara forced herself to reply in a light tone. "No. For a while, I let Rafael's attentions go to my head. As my old tutor used to say, no one is safe from flattery. Really, I am more interested in taking up my post on Hacienda Delgado than anything else. This trip, being on my own, well, it's an adventure and I want to take care of myself for a change. My brother Max had an adventurous nature, and I think I always envied his freedom to follow it."

Estella smiled dubiously. "I think you are *loco, amiga,* but if you are happy, that is all that matters." In a more serious vein, she said, "You miss your brother very much, don't you?"

Sara nodded. "Every day."

They were riding midway between the two caravans, and glanced up at the sound of shouts. One of the scouts was riding down the line of wagons yelling, "Cimarron River!", and waving his wide-brimmed hat with excitement. It was as if the animals understood and smelled the water, for they picked up their tired feet and moved at a faster pace, anticipating a long, cool drink.

Sara began to notice a few scrubby bushes and some stunted trees dotting the sandy, rolling landscape. The thought of enough water for a real bath lightened her somber mood somewhat. Everything she had told Estella was the truth, except for the part about not caring for Rafael—and that was the part that hurt.

The two women kept pace with the wagons, as they topped a hill and began their descent into the valley of the Cimarron. Green grass glades spread out on either side of the wide ribbon of rushing river. The vivid color of the scene was so welcome, the men sent up a loud cheer. Their initial elation was barely spent, when another cry from those in the front arose—this time, one of alarm. Sara slowed her mount and gasped at the sight before her. A band of Indian warriors on horseback were pouring over the opposite ridge across the river. In the confusion that ensued, Sara heard Rafael's voice shouting to the drivers to circle the wagons. As awkward as it was on the side of the hill, they were soon formed into two irregular circles. Sara and Estella, safe inside the formation, quickly dismounted. Estella rushed to help her mother alight from the carriage, and assisted her into their sleeping wagon. Sara hurriedly climbed into her own wagon, but not to hide. Instead, she took her derringer from the trunk and loaded it with shaking hands. Hastily, she climbed out and crouched behind the wheel to await the attack.

Rafael had been shoring up their defenses, calling out orders, and frantically looking for Sara. He had seen the two women gallop into the circle, but after that his attention had been diverted elsewhere. When he again looked for her, she was nowhere in sight. Heading toward the Perez wagon, he had to make sure the women were safe before he could concentrate on the attack. As he darted around loose horses and running men, he spied a flash of silver at the wheel of Sara's wagon, and his heart nearly stopped. She was on her knees in the dirt, her gunhand braced on a spoke, ready to fight.

Despite the fear it struck him to see her in such a vulnerable position, he felt a rush of admiration for her bravery. He ran to her side and dropped to one knee, glancing quickly down the hill to gauge the advance of the Indians. *"Por Dios,* Sara! What are you doing out here? You should be inside with the other women," he said harshly.

"You taught me how to shoot, señor, and I can help," she countered, her voice shaking almost as much as her hands.

"Keep your head down and save your shots for a target up close," he growled, and then he was gone, shouting for all to wait until the warriors came near and then to shoot over their heads first.

The bloodcurdling cries of the savages sent a chill up and down Sara's spine, but she held her ground. As the band neared the wagons, they split into two groups and began to circle, shooting arrows that landed harmlessly in the center of the circle, while Rafael's men fired several rounds, aiming high as they'd been told. The hostile attitude and warlike cries of the savages frightened Sara more than anything she could have imagined. She felt as if she were frozen to the small square of earth where she knelt. She watched the warriors ride by, their painted faces glaring hideously in the bright sunshine.

Rafael made his way back to Sara's side, unable to leave her alone. "I am here, *niña,*" he whispered, to warn her just before he fired a warning shot high in the air.

Sara's rigid body relaxed visibly, but she kept her gaze on the unfolding tableau, mesmerized by the sight.

"Their intent is to frighten us and steal the animals," Rafael said after a time. "If they intended us harm, a few of our men would be dead by now, and the wagons would have been fired. The Comanche's aim is accurate and deadly."

Sara's startled gaze turned on him. "These are your people?" she yelled above the noise.

He shook his head. "Not my father's tribe. There are many tribes on the Comancheria." Afraid of leaving her by herself, he took her arm and commanded, "Come with me." Cautioning her to keep her head down, he lead her to the wagon at the top of the rise. Sara heard Rafael growl something under his breath, and was thankful she couldn't understand what it was. There was a black scowl on his face, as he watched his cattle being driven off by two of the braves.

The two *vaqueros* who tended the herd had taken shelter inside the circle and were firing at the thieves, but couldn't get clear shots. When they saw Rafael, they broke into frantic speech. He silenced them with an upraised hand. "We will go after them," he said, his sharp eyes following the direction they took. "There are only eight braves."

Fresh fear washed over her at his flat statement. When he caught up with them, she was sure, the

Indians would not give back the animals willingly. There would be a fight. She clutched his arm and closed her eyes, as a wave of dizziness swept over her.

Rafael caught her around the waist and pulled her close, turning her body toward the wagon for protection. "Don't faint now, *niña,* the fight's not over yet," he said in a low, bracing tone.

She drew from his strength and refrained from telling him that her fear was for his safety. "I've never swooned, Rafael, and don't intend to now," she whispered, rallying. It felt wonderful to be in his arms again, but he was needed in the present situation, and didn't have time for her weakness. She gently pushed him away. "Don't worry about me. I'll stay down."

He looked deep into her blue eyes for a split-second, and then nodded. "Take care of yourself," he commanded softly, and then turned to his men, giving them some hurried orders.

The remaining warriors circled several more times and then, at a shouted order from their leader, left the wagons behind and headed across the river and out of sight.

In a matter of minutes, Rafael had organized the men in the center of the circle, assigning duties and ordering extra guards. He also checked Jose's arm, where a stray arrow had pierced it. Señor Pino protested when Rafael ordered him to take charge of the caravan in his absence. "One of the others can do it, Rafael. I should go with you," Pedro insisted.

Rafael clapped his friend on the shoulder. "I need you here for my peace of mind, in case some of them return. We have the women to consider, *amigo*. I will be back soon with the cattle, never fear."

Pedro grumbled, but realized the others were not used to being in charge. "*Sí*, Rafael. I will stay and I will tend to Jose's wound.

Rafael asked for three volunteers to go with him, and got them immediately. The women were standing back, and Doña Josefina was weeping copiously. When she realized Rafael was leaving them, she cried out, "You would leave us unprotected to regain a few cows? Don Vicente will hear of this, you can be sure, señor!"

Sara and Estella tried to quiet her, but the older woman shook them off and retreated into her wagon, muttering more threats. Estella turned to Sara and burst into tears. "Why does she make everything so difficult! I was trying to be strong, but I was frightened. And all the while I was worried about Garth. Do you think he is all right?"

Sara held her friend, patting her shoulder. "I'm sure he's fine, but I will ask Rafael to find out for you."

Estella's head came up as she wiped at her eyes. "Would you?"

"I'm sure he'll go check on them anyway, before he goes after his cattle, but, yes, I'll ask him to send us word that all is well," she agreed in a comforting tone, and then suggested, "Why don't you see if Señor Pino could use some help with tending Jose's arm?"

The other girl nodded, and Sara gave her an encouraging smile. Sara intercepted Rafael as he was about to mount up. "May I ask a favor?"

154

"*Sí*. What is it?" His eyes rested warmly on her.

"We are worried about Garth and the others. Would you find out if they're all right and send us word?"

Rafael's mouth tightened a fraction, but he nodded and swung unto the saddle. "*Sí*. Do not leave the safety of the caravan without an armed escort while I am gone, *comprender?*"

Sara gave a nod of assent at his gruff command. He seemed distant and cold all of a sudden, and she dared not say what was in her heart. Instead, she swallowed a lump in her throat and whispered, "Please be careful."

He acknowledged her plea with another nod, and then guided his horse through a space betwen two wagons with his men trailing behind him. Sara moved to the opening and watched him ride into the other camp with dread knotting her stomach. Would he come back? she worried silently. Turning away, she walked to the cook-wagon, and began helping Juan with preparations for dinner.

Chapter 8

A short time later, Matt Harrigan found Sara stirring a pot of beans over the fire. Impulsively, she threw her arms around him. "I'm so glad you're all right, Matt! Were there any wounded in your camp?" As she released him, he blinked in bemusement.

"No, but that fool, Asher Selby, nearly shot his own foot off when the attack began. He was so excited, he didn't realize he had his finger on the trigger," Matt said, shaking his head in disgust.

Sara smiled at his ability to find humor in the dire situation. "Isn't he the merchant from Boston, who's taking this trip for his health?"

Matt leaned over to see what she was stirring in the pot and nodded. "Yeah, but he nearly had a heart attack. This was not exactly a healthy situation."

Sara laughed outright this time. "You must admit it was a frightening experience. Or were you busy sketching the whole scene?"

He snorted. "I may be absorbed in my work, but

I'm not stupid. I was under my wagon, hugging a loaded rifle."

"I'm surprised Garth didn't come over with you. What is he doing?" she asked.

Matt accepted a cup of coffee from Juan with a nod and turned back to Sara. "That was my reason for coming over here, Sara. Rafael asked me to let you know that we were all right. Garth went with him to track his cattle."

Sara groaned. Estella would be more upset than ever at this news. "I'm worried about them, Matt. I just know there will be another fight."

"Well, I heard Rafael tell Garth that he's half-Comanche, and that when the Indians found out they'd stolen the cattle from him, they would most likely return them. It seems the Comanche don't see anything wrong in stealing from strangers, but wouldn't dream of taking anything belonging to one of their own," he explained.

Sara felt her tension ease. "Then perhaps it won't be as dangerous as I thought."

Matt shrugged. "If they get close enough to talk first, I guess."

"Thank you for that reassurance," Sara said dryly. "Would you like to stay for supper?"

Matt wrinkled his nose. "Nope. I can't face beans one more day. I think I'll go fishing." He ambled off, leaving Sara shaking her head and smiling.

Over dinner, Sara told Estella that Garth had survived the Indian attack, but that he had gone with Rafael to retrieve the stolen cattle. The Spanish girl would have cried out in frustration, if her mother had not been within earshot in the wagon directly behind them. Doña Josefina was still prostrate, and refused to get up for the meal.

"Why must men do these dangerous things and leave us behind to worry?" Estella whispered fiercely, tears forming in her brown eyes.

Sara was just as exasperated. "It's been that way forever, I think. In the Arthurian tales, the knights went off to war, and their women stayed home to weep, worry, and do needlepoint." She gave the other girl's hand a squeeze. "Try not to worry. Matt said it's not as dangerous as we think, what with Rafael being half-Comanche. He'll know what to do."

They bolstered each other's courage throughout the evening, but neither of them really felt better deep down. After they retired, Sara lay awake most of the night, wondering what she would do if anything happened to Rafael.

The following day, a small hunting party went out after a herd of buffalo was spotted. Señor Pino decided that the wagons should move closer to the river, so both caravans broke camp and relocated. When that was finished, Sara and Estella, accompanied by Felipe and Carlos, took their laundry to the river. Estella, whose delicate hands had never done anything more strenuous than lift a teacup, decided that this time she was going to help wash clothes. The men did the scrubbing, and the women rinsed. They all talked of the Indian attack, and

Estella told them about the time a band of Comanche warriors had raided their hacienda and nearly killed her father. The next time they had shown up, her father had bravely ridden out with a white flag and negotiated a treaty with them, promising grain, beeves, and cloth every autumn, in exchange for peace. "We have never been attacked since that time," Estella said, finishing the story. "I was young, but I still remember being afraid. Yesterday's attack brought it all back." She gave a shudder and glanced around, as if suddenly remembering that they were still vulnerable.

Matt Harrigan brought his sketchbook over after dinner that evening, and Sara sat for him. While he sketched, Sara's mind raced with worrisome thoughts about Rafael's safety. Each time she reminded herself he was more than capable of taking care of himself, she saw the painted faces of the savages, and their terrifying warcries echoed in her ears. When the silent torture became too much, she abruptly came to her feet. "I'm sorry, Matt. I can't sit a moment longer."

He sighed and dropped the pad to his lap, pushing his spectacles up. "I could use a cup of coffee myself."

Sara went to fetch two cups, and when she returned, he asked, "Do you think your friend would allow me to sketch her?"

Sara pulled her stool close to his and sat down. "You mean Estella?"

He nodded. "I'd like to add her to my collection."

Sara pulled a face. "Her mother would have to give permission."

"Would you ask?" He grinned then. "Sometimes I don't make a very good impression on people."

Sara teased, "Perhaps a first impression, Matt, but I like you quite a lot, now that I've gotten to know you." They drank their coffee and talked for a while of Santa Fe. Matt was enthusiastic about sketching not only the local Indians, but the Spanish residents and the scenery.

After he left, Sara wandered over to Señor Pino's wagon. Darkness had fallen, and the campfire, although not needed for warmth, was comforting. The older man was leaning back against the wagon's wheel, smoking a cheroot. When he saw her approaching, he began to rise, but she waved him back down. "Don't move, Señor Pino, you look so comfortable." She sat down on a stool next to him, and leaned back also.

"How are the sketches coming?" he asked comfortably.

Sara shrugged. "I don't know. Matt won't let me see. For all I know, he may be attaching a second head to the picture."

Señor Pino chuckled. "I doubt that, señorita. The one you have is so lovely, it would outshine the other."

Sara dipped her head, warmed by the compliment. "You are the most gallant gentleman I know."

He smiled. "It is in my blood to be appreciative of feminine beauty."

Sara thought of Rafael, and how he had said she was beautiful . . . or was it desirable? Obviously, she had read too much into his interest, and encouraged him when she should have kept a proper distance. Sara's cheeks flamed at the memory, and she was glad of the darkness. "Do you think Rafael will be all right?" she asked after a moment.

The old man heard the anxiety in her voice, and noted the fact that she had only mentioned Rafael and not the other three men. It was telling, and he was pleased. "I am always concerned for his safety, but not because I doubt his ability. I am an old man and old men worry," he said, tossing the butt of his cheroot into the fire.

Sara brooded as she stared into the flames. There was nothing to do but wait, and she was finding that nervewracking. She changed the subject to take her mind from her worries. "Do you think Don Vicente will approve of me?"

Señor Pino smiled to himself, but kept his tone serious. "*Sí*, señorita. I believe he will be most happy with the choice I made."

"What if the children don't like me? I've never been a teacher before, and I know I led you to believe I would have no problem with the post, but the truth is, I'm a little unsure," she confessed.

He reached over and gave her shoulder a fatherly pat. "Do not worry, señorita. I have great faith in you, and so does Rafael."

Sara turned to face him. "Did he say so? I was under the impression that he doubted I could make the trip, much less do my job once I got there."

Señor Pino laughed. "That is just his way. He is stubborn like his grandfather, and broods about things." His tone became gentle. "His life has not been happy, but he's grown into a fine, strong man. I am very proud of him."

"He told me about his wife," she said quietly.

Pino was surprised, but didn't show it. Rafael was very reserved, and rarely discussed his private affairs with anyone. "He was heartbroken over her death, but that was eleven years ago. It is time to live again, and perhaps risk his heart. I have told him this," the older man said with a sigh.

"Maybe he doesn't want to fall in love again," Sara suggested.

"He needs someone to care for him, a woman he can care for as well. Rafael does not know this, but his grandfather has chosen such a woman for him. She is suitable in every way, and I believe she will make him happy. Rafael only needs time to accept this," Pedro said, his tone conspiratorial.

Sara felt as if the wind had been knocked out of her. In a shaky voice, she said, "From what Rafael has told me, I can't imagine him going along with anything Don Vicente has planned."

Señor Pino smiled. "Ah, *niña*—this will be different! I, too, am in favor of this match, and will do everything in my power to see them together.

Three days after Rafael had departed, he rode back into camp, slumped over in his saddle. One of his men held the reins of the black stallion, while another one helped him down. Sara had been helping Juan cut strips of buffalo meat for drying, when she heard the commotion.

With her heart in her throat, she wiped her hands on her apron as she ran to see why Rafael needed help. By the time she reached them, a crowd had

162

formed, and she could not get to Rafael's side without pushing her way through. Frustration sharpened her tongue. "Let me pass! Is he all right?"

The men made a path for her, and she gasped when she saw the gray color of Rafael's face. Señor Pino was ordering two of the *vaqueros* to help the injured man to his wagon, when he saw Sara's face. "Come along, señorita. I can use your help."

Sara grasped Pedro's arm as they followed. "What is it? What happened?" she asked in alarm. Rafael was barely moving his legs on his own, and she could tell he was not aware of his surroundings.

"He has a shoulder wound, *niña*. He took an arrow, but I think it will be fine. You can help me with the medicines, eh?"

His tone was light, but Sara detected a thread of worry. "Of course, I'll help, señor," she said.

Señor Pino did not allow her inside the wagon, until he had Rafael settled on his cot. He cut the shirt away and ordered one of the men to fetch some boiling water. By the time he called Sara in, Pedro had covered Rafael modestly with a quilt. The ugly red wound on his left shoulder gave her pause. The flesh around it was broken and jagged, and a small trickle of blood and puss oozed. It was the ashen color of his face that frightened her, though. "What can I do, Señor Pino?" she asked.

"There's a leather bag inside that trunk, *niña*. Get it out, *por favor*," he instructed, as he placed his ear on Rafael's chest to listen to his heartbeat.

Sara found it and knelt by his side, untying the strap that held it closed.

"The large tin of salve—*sí*, that is the one. We'll

need that . . . and the herbs in the small pouch." He raised up, a frown creasing his brow. "There are some clean strips of cloth in the trunk that we can use for bandages."

Sara fetched the cloth, and Alonzo appeared with hot water in a bowl. Pino instructed him to bring more periodically. "I want this wound as clean as possible before we wrap it." Turning to Sara, he frowned. "Now is when I need your help the most. I will hold him, while you bathe the wound. It will pain him, but it must be done."

Sara nodded, her eyes wide with anxiety. The anxious old man moved up to stand at Rafael's head, and leaned over to grip his arms. He nodded when he was ready. "The water will be hot. Do you think you can stand it?" he said, eyeing her for a moment.

"Yes," she breathed, determined to do the job without fainting. Testing the water, she dipped a clean cloth in it and cringed slightly at the discomfort, but continued.

At the first touch of the hot cloth on the wound, Rafael bucked like a wild horse. Pedro called on all his strength to hold him, and bade Sara to repeat the process. Over and over, Sara applied the cleansing cloths, and her hands became as red as blood. Rafael's groans were pain-filled, and it took all of Sara's willpower to do what had to be done. Silent tears rolled down her cheeks each time she hurt him, but Pedro encouraged her. "We must draw the infection out, *niña,* or he will die."

Twice, Alonzo brought fresh water and emptied the soiled bowl. When the water in the bowl became

164

clearer, just barely tinged a pink color, Señor Pino called a halt. He stood and stretched his tight muscles, then placed some of the leaves from the pouch in some clean water to soak. "Rafael carries all sorts of herbs and concoctions with him. He learned of these medicines when he lived with the Comanche. It is fitting, I think, that they will save his life from a Comanche arrow, eh?"

Sara gazed tiredly at him. "Promise me he won't die, Señor Pino."

He gave her a reassuring smile. "This one? He is destined to live to be an old man. Now, take that tin of salve and spread some over the wound. Then we will pack these leaves on it and wrap it."

Sara wanted to believe him, but she was afraid. Rafael had not regained consciousness, and his color was no better. The older man helped her wrap strips of clean cloth around Rafael's shoulder after she applied the medication. He gave her arm a comforting pat. "Get some rest now. I will sit with him," he urged.

Sara started to protest, but he shook his head. "He may not wake up for a long while, and there is no need for both of us to stay. You have helped a great deal already."

She gazed at Rafael's pale face for a moment. "Will you call me, if he wakes up?"

"Sí," he promised.

She nodded and climbed out of the wagon. Garth was waiting there to help her down. Estella rose from the tongue of the wagon where she'd been sitting, and grasped Sara's hand. "How is he?"

"Señor Pino says he'll be fine, but I'm worried. He

165

hasn't regained consciousness." Sara closed her eyes wearily for a moment and leaned on Garth's arm. "He looks so pale and . . . helpless."

Estella put her arm around Sara. "Don't torture yourself, *amiga*. Señor Pino knows what he is doing. We must have faith, eh?"

Sara let the soothing words flow over her. "Yes . . . you're right, I know, but . . ."

Estella clucked her tongue. "Come, Sara. I will help you to bed. You must be exhausted."

Sara was only half-listening to Garth's recounting of the fight with the Indians, as she let them help her to her wagon. She protested that she'd never be able to sleep, but when she closed her eyes, sleep immediately claimed her.

In the wee hours of the morning, Sara came awake with a start. She sat up on her cot and rubbed her eyes for a moment, trying to decide what exactly had disturbed her. The memory of Rafael lying wounded flashed through her mind, and she wondered anxiously if something was wrong. Scrambling up, she slipped her shoes on and climbed out the back of the wagon. Her clothes were wrinkled, and her hair was coming out of its braid, but she didn't care. She had to see for herself that Rafael was all right.

Nodding to Alonzo, who was on guard duty, she made her way to Rafael's wagon. Dawn was breaking on the horizon as she slipped inside to find Señor Pino slumped over in a chair, sleeping soundly. She glanced at Rafael's face, but couldn't tell much about his color in the dim light. Carefully, she moved to his side to touch his brow. He felt feverish, but not excessively so.

"Buenos dias, señorita. I knew you would not stay away long," Señor Pino said behind her. He yawned and then smiled.

Sara turned. "He has not been awake yet?"

The overseer shook his head. "No, but his condition is fair, and his fever is not too high. Did you sleep?"

"Yes." She turned back to look at Rafael, willing him to open his eyes.

Pedro stood up and stretched his cramped muscles. "I will fetch some hot water, and we can change his dressing."

"I could get it, Señor Pino."

"Gracias, but I need some fresh air," he said. "Perhaps you could get the bandages and medicines ready, eh?"

She was digging in the trunk for clean strips, when she heard a low moan. Whirling about, she saw Rafael open his eyes. She knelt beside him, taking his hand in hers. "Oh, Rafael!"

He turned his head and focused on her face. A ghost of a smile curved his lips. "Sara," he said, his voice scratchy and weak.

"How do you feel? Does it hurt? Should I call Señor Pino?" She felt giddy with relief.

"So many questions, *niña,"* he rasped, giving her hand a weak squeeze. His eyes traveled over her face, as a starving man might eye a feast.

Suddenly realizing how she must look, Sara lifted a hand to her hair self-consciously and dropped her eyes. "Señor Pino just went to fetch hot water. He sat with you through the night. Everyone's been worried," she finished lamely.

"Including you?" he asked.

Especially me, she cried softly as her heart turned over. To cover her feelings, she reached for the cup of water that sat on a low crate next to his cot. "Of course, Rafael. I was concerned for the *vaqueros* who went with you, as well. After witnessing the attack on the caravans, I was afraid we would never see any of you again."

His spirits sank at her impersonal reply. He allowed her to lift his head, and his hand covered hers as he took a sip. His eyes met hers above the rim, and she hastily looked away. An overwhelming urge possessed him to caress her delicate face, and free her hair from its bonds. It was like a physical pain that cut into him more sharply than the wound in his shoulder. As he lay back, he closed his eyes to hide the longing there. *"Gracias,* Sara. All that matters, I think, is that we returned safe, and managed to retrieve the cattle as well."

Sara replaced the cup. "I assume they didn't wish to give them up?"

"Unfortunately, no. When we caught up with them, I didn't have a chance to show a white flag, nor to have a peaceful talk. They attacked and we found cover, but I took an arrow before the fight ended."

"Garth told me some of what happened." She turned back to the trunk to hide the trembling in her limbs. He could have died, she thought, a tight knot in her stomach.

Pedro climbed through the back opening, and grinned when he saw that Rafael was awake.

"Amigo! You have had a good sleep, eh? How do you feel?"

Rafael grimaced. "As if I had been trampled by a mad bull."

The old man chuckled as he deposited the bucket on the floor. "As happy as I am to see you awake, I wish you had waited another hour. It is time to change the dressing."

Sara placed the strips of cloth and the salve on the crate. "I had better leave you to your work, Señor Pino." She glanced at Rafael and found him watching her intently. "I'm glad you're better," she said, her voice breathless all of a sudden.

"I'd rather you tended to the wound, señorita, as you did last night. Your touch is more gentle than mine," the overseer said as he reached for the bowl.

Rafael reached out and took her hand, his dark eyes still holding hers prisoner. "So you took care of me?"

She nodded slowly, feeling her heartbeat quicken at his touch.

"It would please me, if you would change the dressing," he said, his thumb stroking the back of her hand.

Rafael made her feel vibrantly alive with a mere touch. He made her feel like a woman. It was hard to refuse him anything he asked, especially when he looked at her the way he was looking now. "All right," she said, turning away from the intensity of his gaze. Deftly, she slipped her hand out of his and took the bowl of water Señor Pino was holding.

As she worked at removing the old dressing, she kept her eyes on her task. She could feel Rafael

169

staring at her, and was afraid she would hurt him in her nervousness.

Señor Pino brought Rafael up to date on the small happenings of the past few days, while Sara worked. His inconsequential conversation helped to soothe the tension in her body.

When she began to clean the wound gently with a hot cloth, Rafael gripped the side of the cot, but did not flinch. She glanced up at his face and saw sweat beginning to form on his brow. He smiled at her, as if to assure her that the pain was not too great. Quickly, she bent her head. Tears stung her eyes while she finished the task.

"It looks better, eh?" Pedro commented, as he leaned forward for a look.

There was still a trace of red around the jagged edges, but very little puss this time. "Yes," she managed. She applied the healing salve and packed on the fresh, water-soaked leaves that Pino handed to her.

After wrapping the wound with clean bandages, she stood up. "I'll let you rest now, señor," she murmured, picking up the bowl of soiled water to steady her hands.

"*Gracias,* Sara. Perhaps . . . you could come back later?" Rafael asked, his eyes following her movements.

"If you'd like . . ." she replied without looking at him. "If you need anything, Señor Pino, let me know."

"He is the most stubborn creature!" Sara said to

Señor Pino, as they rode between the columns of the two caravans the following day.

Pedro chuckled. *"Sí,* señorita. I most heartily agree with that. However, Rafael does seem much better today. At least, he is staying in his saddle."

Sara glanced up ahead, to where the object of their conversation rode in advance of the wagons. Rafael had insisted on not only getting out of bed this morning, but moving out as well. "If I didn't know better, I'd think his head was injured instead of his shoulder," she said with exasperation. "What if the wound opens, or the infection returns?"

Señor Pino shrugged. "There is no reasoning with him, *niña."* Changing the subject, he commented, "When you didn't return to see him yesterday, he was upset."

Sara refused to look in his direction, keeping her eyes straight ahead. "I was busy." It had taken great effort on her part to stay away, but she knew it was for the best. She was afraid of the feelings he evoked in her . . . afraid he would see the love in her eyes. It had to be love, she decided. An emotion that caused your heart to soar one moment, then ripped it sharply in pain, could be no less than love.

Señor Pino glanced at her tense shoulders out of the corner of his eye. "I told him that was probably the case, but he was not satisfied. His injury was making him ill-tempered."

"That was it, I'm sure," she agreed. How she wished he truly cared about her, though. Memories of the night they'd made love haunted her dreams. For some reason, she thought dismally, it didn't mean as much to him. He had readily accepted the way out she had provided. And when she thought of the woman his grandfather had chosen for him, jealousy ate at her soul. Suddenly she was impatient for the journey to end. "How much longer to Santa Fe?"

Pedro's brow wrinkled in concentration for a moment. "Two, perhaps three weeks. I will be most happy to get there, señorita. These old bones are tired."

"I, too, am anxious." Trouble was, she thought with frustration, Rafael would be there as well. However, there was no place else for her to go.

Sara kept herself busy on the last leg of the journey. She took walks with Estella, played cards with Garth, and sat for Matt. The artist promised to choose his favorite sketch of her once he got to Santa Fe, and paint a portrait from it. He finally let her see the sketches, and she was impressed with his talent for reproducing the human likeness with a few simple strokes of his pen.

Sara was relieved and disappointed at the same time, when Rafael did not seek her out. No matter how busy she was, there was a deep ache of loneliness inside that refused to be assuaged.

However, there were compensations. The country they now traveled through fired her spirit with its beauty and wildness. She wished she had an artist's talent so that she might capture the bold scenes that met her eyes. There were towering cliffs, craggy spurs, and deep-cut crevices that spoke of savage haunts. At the click of a pebble or the rebound of a twig, Sara often expected the *whoosh* of an arrow. Death was a constant threat, yet, Sara felt more alive than she'd ever felt in her life.

One morning Sara and Señor Pino observed a lone horseman approaching from the south, as they rode in front of the caravan. "I wonder if it's one of our runners returning," he said, squinting.

"It could be. They were sent out only last week. Perhaps they had trouble," Sara suggested, shading her eyes with her hand. She had helped Juan pack food for these agents to take with them. Rafael had sent the avant-couriers on to Santa Fe, to procure and send back a supply of fresh provisions. It would also be their job to begin negotiating prices for the Delgado merchandise with the officers of the custom house.

Rafael came up beside them just then. "We have company," he observed, following the direction of their eyes. "It looks like a *cibolero.*"

"Ah, I think you are right," Pino said. "A buffalo-hunter, señorita. They come from the southern villages, as well as from across the Sangre de Cristo Mountains, to hunt on the plains."

"Perhaps he will have news of Santa Fe," Rafael added.

Sara felt shy in Rafael's presence, and was silent as her companions greeted the man. He was certainly colorful, wearing leather trousers and jacket. A flat straw hat sat on his dark head at a jaunty angle, while a quiver of bow and arrows hung on his shoulder. A long-handled lance was suspended by a strap from the pommel of his saddle, with a tassel of gay particolored stuffs dangling at the tip of the scabbard. In like manner, the stopper in the muzzle of his gun was fantastically tasseled.

The teamsters halted the wagons, and everyone gathered around to ask questions and hear any news the *cibolero* might have. Sara dismounted to stretch her legs, and moved back to allow the men more space around the visitor. Garth came up beside her and; putting his arm around her waist, he squeezed her affectionately. "Feeling better today?" he asked.

Sara smiled. "I'm not sick, Garth. I've just been a little tired lately. Thank you for asking though."

His left eyebrow rose a fraction. "You've been losing to me far too much the past couple of weeks, honey. Now I know you play better, but your mind's just not on the game. If you need someone to talk to, I'm a very good listener."

Her smile slipped a little, but she shook her head. "There's nothing wrong, really. But I'll remember your offer." She thought she had been hiding her feelings very well, but obviously he saw through her facade. She turned her attention back to the group around the *cibolero,* and caught Rafael's eye. He was scowling, and she wondered if the buffalo-hunter was giving him bad news.

It was decided that they would stop early, so the talk could continue. Garth led Sara's horse to the back of her wagon and tied it. "I'd better get back. It's my turn to get the fire wood," he said, and went off whistling.

Sighing, Sara wished her existence was as carefree as his. She took a small amount of water from her barrel and washed her hands and face. After rebraiding her hair, she emerged from her wagon

174

and literally ran into Rafael, who was coming around the corner.

His arms automatically went around her to keep her from falling. An involuntary grunt passed his lips, when she bumped his shoulder. "Oh, Rafael . . . I'm sorry!" she said.

"Are you meeting Señor Prescott—is that what the great hurry is about?" he asked, a scowl on his face.

Sara blinked in confusion and extracted herself from his arms. "Why no . . . and I don't believe this collision was entirely *my* fault." Her chin came up defensively. "Were you looking for me?"

He leaned his hip against the wagon wheel, and folded his arms across his chest. "I was looking for Carlos, but I need to speak with you about something as well, so I will take advantage of this opportunity."

Even though they stood two feet apart, Sara felt suffocated by his nearness. Her body still tingled from the touch of his, and his masculine scent lingered in her nostrils. She clasped her hands behind her back to keep them from trembling. "What is it?"

"You have been in Señor Prescott's company much lately. Since you are in my employ, I thought it my duty to warn you about him. His interest lies elsewhere, Sara, and I would not like to see you get hurt."

Across her pale and beautiful face, a dim flush raced like a fever. His arrogance knew no bounds, she thought with sudden anger. "Your concern leaves me speechless, señor," she said, her eyes flashing blue fire. "However, I can take care of myself."

Rafael straightened. This small display of temper from her was appealing. He liked the way her intriguing face came to life when she was mad. "He is in love with Estella. He told me so himself."

"What did you do? Speak to him on my behalf? What gives you the right to meddle in my affairs? I'll thank you to mind your own business from now on," she said, her words tumbling out almost without volition. Her fit of temper surprised her almost as much as it did him. Never in her life had she spoken to anyone in this manner, or felt the depth of emotions that this man evoked. Feeling tears very near the surface, she turned her back on him and snapped, "Is that all you have to say, señor?"

Rafael felt an uneasy stirring in his midsection. She had not denied an interest in Prescott, which was what he craved. And her reaction to his revelation was more emotional than he had expected. Was she truly interested in Prescott? For the moment, he didn't know what to say. "I did not mean to offend you, Sara. And no, there is nothing else I wish to discuss."

She nodded and walked away, heading for a sandy hillock where she might find some solitude. Tears of shame ran unchecked down her cheeks, at how weak she became in his presence. She wanted nothing more than to throw herself into his arms and let him love her. Silently she berated herself. What sort of woman was she? Her thoughts and feelings about Rafael were so brazen that it frightened her.

She had reached the top of the hill, and walked

along the ridge toward some scattered boulders. Her mind was so occupied, that she didn't hear the deadly chorus of rattles until too late. She felt a sharp stinging sensation in the calf of her leg, at the same time her gaze fell on the nest of vipers. Some were stretched out on the hot sand; while the ones nearest her had coiled in defense against her intrusion. A scream rose in her throat to choke her as she stumbled back. She felt another strike on her right boot, but didn't know if it had penetrated the leather. At that moment, a deafening shot sounded so near, she thought she'd been hit by the bullet. A strong hand grasped her arm and yanked her out of harm's way, while the gun exploded again and again.

Sara's heart was racing madly as she watched Rafael empty his rifle. Her knees were weak, and she could feel her hold on consciousness beginning to slip.

Chapter 9

The fire all around her was terrifying. The flames licked at her skirts. She pulled away from them, but there was no escape. Just beyond the ring of fire, she saw a familiar bulky figure, the evil-looking face smiling as if he were enjoying the fact that she was entrapped. "Help me . . . please help me!" she cried piteously.

"I can save you . . ." he offered, leering at her. "You know the terms. Are you willing to submit?"

Sara, knowing what he meant, weighed her choices, agonizing over sure death versus the humiliating life Farber offered. "You have no right! It's my money . . . my father was not a criminal . . . I'm to be a wife, not a mistress!" As the intense heat began to radiate up her legs, she gave herself up to the only possible choice and waited for the inevitable.

Cool hands touched her face. A wet cloth dampened her dry, cracked lips. And yet she fought with all her might, for she was afraid it was Farber who gave her ease, and that, at the last moment, she had succumbed to his demands.

"Sara, *mi alma,* do not struggle so. You are safe. Drink this." The voice was deep and calming. It did not belong to Jonas Farber. There was a familiar quality to it that immediately soothed her fears, and she rested for a time.

The man who sat beside her cot touched her fevered face gently and frowned. Rafael had heard enough to make him furious. A terrible anger welled up within him at the man who had frightened her so severely. However, when Sara became restless again, he had reason to feel guilty himself.

Sara found herself deep within the bowels of the earth . . . a cave, she thought. It was dim, with only a lantern hanging on the wall to show the way. She didn't know how she'd gotten there or why, but she felt there was a good reason. Walking along the tunnel, she found flickering lamps at intervals, and was reassured. The path had to lead somewhere. After a time, she began to pick up faint sounds, like metal striking metal—a sharp pinging noise—and relief washed over her. She was not alone, as she had feared. Someone was up ahead. She followed the sound until it grew louder. In the distance, fuzzy shadows turned into the forms of men, bent forward, intent on striking the rock walls with hammers. She spoke to them, but they acted as if they hadn't heard. Touching one of them on the shoulder, she gave a sharp gasp when he turned. It was Max. His expression was so sad, Sara felt tears well up in her eyes. "Oh, my darling Max," she whispered, reaching to take him in her arms. He shook his head and backed away. Sara stepped

179

forward, but halted when she saw the stark fear in his eyes. "What is it, Max? Let me help you." He shook his head again, and continued his retreat until he disappeared into the rock wall. Sara stared helplessly. She had lost him again. Her grief was as intense as it had been the first time, and she began to shiver, her body shaking violently, as if an icy January wind blew over her. The shadowy men around her continued to work as if nothing had happened. She knew there would be no help from them. Turning away, she ran blindly toward the nearest tunnel. The walls were closing in on her, and pain squeezed her heart. She ran until her side hurt, until her heart pounded so hard it was like a drumbeat in her ears. And when she felt as if she would collapse, she saw Rafael in the distance. He was waiting and watching her patiently. But when she drew closer to him, he turned and vanished down another tunnel. "No! Rafael . . . please don't leave . . . don't you care?" Dropping to the hard-packed earth, she held her throbbing head in her hands. "Gone . . . they're all gone," she whispered.

Rafael sat beside Sara's cot, and his stomach lurched as he raised his eyes to her gray face. For the moment, she lay quiet, as quiet as death. To Rafael, it seemed more like days than hours since he'd carried her to the wagon. Darkness had fallen, and he thought back over the medical treatment he had administered. Had he done everything possible? He had been so fearful for her life that perhaps he'd missed something. Cutting into her soft flesh with

180

his razor-sharp knife, he had sucked out the poison as best he could. Pedro, under his direction, had mixed the herbs and roots Rafael had named to make a paste.

While Rafael worked over her, applying and reapplying the paste to draw the poison, her fever had risen alarmingly. He had mixed a potion for the fever, and forced a few drops down her throat. When chills had wracked her body, he had lain beside her, giving her his own warmth. Treat the symptoms, he reminded himself, while you work toward a cure for the illness. When the nightmare had taken hold of her and she began to babble deliriously, Rafael had sent Pedro out, while he held her in his arms and spoke soothingly to her.

Rafael raked his fingers through his hair for the hundredth time. He wished he could be calm in the face of Sara's illness. She believed in fate, and to a certain extent, so did he. However, the fear that invaded his mind destroyed his faith. He wanted her to live no matter what her karma might be. By turns, he prayed to God and to the Great Spirit of the Comanches for her recovery, but her condition worsened as the night went on.

Pedro came and went, helping where he could and carrying hot coffee to Rafael to sustain him. At dawn, the older man climbed into the wagon and squeezed Rafael's shoulder. "I will sit with her if you wish to get some rest, *amigo.*"

Rafael shook his head. "I cannot leave her, Pedro. She might . . . worsen . . ."

Pedro nodded. He had expected Rafael to refuse, but wanted to offer anyway. "I regret we have no lye

181

to make a paste. I have seen this treatment work."

"The Comanche potions have worked many times. Why not this time?" Rafael's voice was marked with anguish.

"There is a doctor in San Miguel," Pedro said quietly.

"We are a hundred miles from there," Rafael replied, bathing Sara's face with a cool cloth.

"If you took a strong, fast horse, you could make it in three days. It will take the caravan at least a week." Pedro had no false hopes. He was desperately worried about the señorita, knowing her chances were slim. His suggestion was more for Rafael's sake. The younger man needed to do something positive.

Rafael looked up at his friend for the first time, the light of hope flickering in his eyes. *"Sí . . .* I could take her there."

Pedro smiled. "I will have Carlos pack some provisions and ready two fast horses."

Once the word was spread, the people on both caravans gathered to see them off. The extra horse had been packed with provisions, and Garth Prescott had brought his wider, American saddle for Rafael's use, since he would be holding Sara in front of him as he rode. Estella, her eyes red from weeping, stepped forward when Rafael carried Sara from the wagon and kissed her cheek. She touched Rafael on the arm and whispered a broken encouragement to him before she turned away. Garth stepped up to take Sara from him while he mounted, and then handed the unconscious girl up to Rafael. "We'll all be prayin' for the two of you," Garth said firmly. Rafael nodded.

All the *vaqueros,* Juan, Matt, and even Asher Selby and Sam Drake—who didn't know Sara very well, but liked her—stood by, hats in hands, to wish them well. Pedro shook Rafael's hand. *"Vaya con Dios, amigo.* We will catch up with you both in San Miguel, eh?"

Rafael held his friend's eye for a long moment. *"Sí.* Take care of yourself and the others."

Rafael chaffed at the slow pace he was forced to maintain at first. The road was rough and rocky. The streams he crossed were bordered with fine sandstone, and he knew if the horses slipped, they would be in trouble.

He kept a blanket wrapped around Sara, for they were now in the high plains, where no humidity penetrated and the heat was not as great. Her fever rose occasionally, and during those times, she spoke in her delirium. Each time she mentioned his name, he felt a fresh stab of guilt. From what he could gather from her ramblings, she had been hurt deeply by his careless attitude. Yet she had given him the impression that she didn't care for him. Perhaps if he'd been quicker to give her a commitment, though, she wouldn't have felt the need to dissemble. Since Tuwikaa died, he had withdrawn to a safe place where nothing could touch his wounded heart again. And then he met Sara—a silver angel—and she had slipped beneath the walls he'd built around his heart.

He glanced down at her flushed face, and vowed to make up to her the hurt he'd inflicted . . . if she lived.

By nightfall, he had crossed the Río Colorado and made camp in the foothills, next to a fount of water that flowed out of a rock formation. As Sara's fever had risen again, he bathed her face and hands repeatedly with the cold water, after he laid a fire. Then he removed her bandage and cleaned the wound, reapplying fresh paste he'd brought along. Her leg was swollen twice its normal size, and there were angry red streaks around the wound. She tossed feverishly about while he ministered to her. When he finished, he smoothed her skirt down, wrapped her in the blanket once more, and held her close.

As tired as he was, he refused to close his eyes and sleep. A little rest was all he required, and besides, she might need him, might need some whispered words of comfort. For two hours, he let his aching muscles relax. Sara lay quiet for a time, but began to shiver as a hard chill suddenly took her. Rafael left her long enough to fetch another blanket for her from his saddle. When her shaking subsided, he doused the fire with water, and mounted the fresh horse. The moon was full and Rafael wanted to move on.

During the years he had spent with the Comanche, he had learned many things. Strength through self-denial was one of them. Many times he had ridden with his father on raids, or hunting, and Flying Hawk had expected him to keep up. There had been very little food and water, almost no rest, hot days under the burning sun, and cold nights on horseback.

At sixteen, Rafael thought, he'd been looking for acceptance and had had much to prove. It had been grueling, but had stood him in good stead many times since.

Rafael rode on into the night, letting his horse pick its own way along the road. He shifted Sara's weight now and then, and tried to ignore the dull pain in his shoulder from his own barely healed wound.

At dawn, Rafael stopped once more beside a small stream. He made a fire and set some coffee on to boil. He got Sara to swallow a few sips of water. He bathed her face and hands, after changing her dressing. When she was resting comfortably, he took some corn cakes and jerked beef from his pack, and ate to keep up his strength.

He gazed toward the snow-clad mountains to the west, and rubbed tiredly at the stubble on his chin. His eyes felt as gritty as the sand under his boots. Two nights without sleep was enough. It wouldn't do Sara any good if he passed out in the saddle. Sitting down beside her with his back to a pine tree, he placed his rifle within easy reach and closed his eyes. Two, maybe three hours, and he would be ready to move on.

The snap of a twig followed by a shout brought Rafael awake and to a standing position in the blink of an eye, gun in hand.

"*Hola!*" a man called out from across the creek.

Rafael felt the tension drain away as he recognized the uniform of a custom's official. The man was leading his horse toward the stream, and waved his wide-brimmed hat in greeting.

Rafael lowered his gun and returned the greeting. He then saw several more men emerging from the woods. He recognized one of his *vaqueros* among them. Turning to check on Sara, he found her breathing easily for the moment, her skin not excessively warm. Felix, his *vaquero,* waded across the stream and swept his hat off respectfully. "Don Rafael! I am surprised to see you here."

"Señorita Clayton was bitten by a rattler, and I am taking her to the doctor in San Miguel. Do you have news of there, Felix?"

"I heard nothing about the doctor when I passed through. We had no need of him, señor, but perhaps he is still there." The *vaquero* cast a wary glance at Sara, and stopped just short of crossing himself. His uncle had died of snakebite.

The other men had gathered around, and Rafael acknowledged the highest ranking official. "Señor Gomez," he said with a polite nod.

The short, rotund man shook his head sadly. "Poor *niña.* I saw the doctor of San Miguel in the cantina, señor. He was very drunk. I hope when you reach him, he will be in a better state."

Felix said, "I will fetch more provisions for you, Don Rafael, from the supply we were taking to the caravan. And if you want, I will accompany you to San Miguel."

"Sí, Felix," Rafael said. He spoke briefly with Señor Gomez about the state of affairs in Santa Fe, but his mind was not on business.

"I have seen your cousin several times, Don Rafael. He tells me the *rancho* is running very smoothly in your absence."

Rafael's brows rose slightly. "If Manolo is in town frequently, he cannot be too busy. Perhaps his Castilian blood makes him a more efficient manager."

The rotund little man ignored the sarcasm. "It is rumored he gambles heavily, and also has a favorite *prostituta* at LaFonda."

Rafael tucked this information away and nodded. "I will soon be home. For now, I must get the señorita to San Miguel. When you reach the caravan, tell Señor Pino she is still fighting for her life, *por favor*."

In less than an hour, Rafael, Felix, and Sara were on their way, while the customs men moved on toward the caravans.

Juliana leaned indolently on the bar in the LaFonda Inn, watching a handsome young man at a nearby table. Her eyes traveled possessively over his thick, brown hair, lightly tanned skin, slim build, and beautiful green eyes. He was an aristocrat, and he was in love with her, she thought with a thrill of excitement. She watched his strong hands deal the cards to his fellow-players. His fingers were long and sensual, and they seemed to caress the pasteboards with the same care they lavished on her body. She shivered, and felt her nipples rise and harden against the low-cut peasant blouse she wore. At that moment, he glanced in her direction; a slow smile curved his full lips when their eyes met.

Juliana winked at him, and slid her tongue slowly around her lips in a provocative gesture. She could feel his hot gaze boldly raking her body, and wondered impatiently when he would finish with his stupid cards and take her to bed. It was the only thing she was jealous of, for he gambled with the same passion he brought to lovemaking.

"Here are the drinks for the soldiers at the corner table, Juliana. If you can find the time, eh?" Bernadino the bartender said, cutting into her thoughts.

She turned reluctantly from her lover, and gave the big man a sour look. "One of these days, I will not need to serve drinks to filthy soldiers."

His dark coloring matched hers, marking them both as mestizos—half Pueblo Indian and half Mexican. But her face was a shade lighter, due to the flour paste she applied to it every morning to bleach the skin. Bernadino's droopy mustache wiggled as he snorted. "I suppose Don Manolo is taking you to live at the hacienda, eh?"

Tossing her head, she said, "It is not impossible. He is in love with me."

"Pah! He is in love with what lies beneath your skirts. High-born *caballeros* take their ease with women like you. They do not marry them, or even keep them as mistresses for long."

She flinched as if he had struck her. "Why do you say such a thing? I thought you were my *amigo.*"

His expression softened. "Because it is the truth, and I do not wish to see you hurt, *niña.*"

She blinked back the tears. "This time it is different. You will see." Taking the tray, she stalked away.

Bernadino shook his head sadly. Juliana had

worked for him for the past year, and she was like the daughter he'd never had. Her soldier father had been killed in a drunken brawl in Chihuahua two years past. Her mother, a Pueblo Indian, had died of a fever a year ago. Juliana had come looking for work, and he had given her a job serving drinks. He hadn't meant for her to prostitute herself, but her beauty had attracted men from the start. When she found she could earn far more with her body, she began accepting the more lucrative propositions. Bernadino had tried to arrange a marriage for her with a young Indian who owned a small *rancho* outside the village, but she refused. "I do not wish to scratch at the earth like a chicken, and grow old and bent in a few years," she had declared vehemently. "I will find a man of substance to take care of me." Bernadino knew her youthful dreams had very little chance of coming true, but he could not convince her. She now had her hopes pinned on Don Manolo Delgado, and he would break her heart. This Bernadino knew.

Siesta was over, and the inhabitants of Hacienda Delgado were beginning to stir. There were two enclosed courtyards within the large rectangular adobe structure. One was for the family, and the other for servants and ranch workers. The latter was more like a small village, with a store, a blacksmith, a laundry, a smokehouse, storage rooms, and living quarters for the house servants. The hacienda was self-contained, and well protected by four wooden towers topping each corner of the quadrangle.

Don Vicente Martin Delgado sat at the desk in his private office, reading over the latest report from his mine manager, Sancho Valdez. His normally stern expression had ripened into a scowl. It was the only outward sign that anything was wrong. He sat ramrod straight in the carved wooden chair, his muscled forearms resting on the wooden arms. Three more deaths, he thought, mine workers dead of some mysterious ailment. That brought the total to nine, and in just five months! This made him uneasy. The Pueblos were a superstitious lot, and since he had a great many of the Indians working for him, he could envision them reading something supernatural into these deaths. He reread the report, but knew he had missed nothing. Valdez wrote that these three, like the others, were workers they had purchased from the prison at Chihuahua. Perhaps that was the key, Don Vicente thought. They may all have been exposed to some disease *before* coming to his silver mine to work. He drummed his fingers absently on the edge of the desk, as he gazed out the window into the courtyard. He was only marginally aware of the working sounds of the *rancho,* as he made his decision to ride out to the Santa Pilar the next day.

A tremendous peal of thunder shook the adobe walls of the small house. Rafael flinched at the loudness, even though he was accustomed to these erratic storms. He walked to the open doorway and studied the murky clouds that were moving from behind the mountains. A jagged flash of lightning touched the ground of the public square, and he heard the frightened cries of animals and man alike. There was much scurrying to get the animals to shelter, while chickens ran about squawking, getting underfoot.

He turned to glance at the doorway across the room; the doctor was at this moment examining Sara. They had arrived in San Miguel a few hours ago, and Rafael had sent Felix to find the *médico,* while he secured a house for them. The owner of the cantina had obligingly given them his house, and moved his meager belongings to the cantina to sleep. Felix had finally found the doctor—sleeping off a drunken evening—in the bed of a prostitute.

A sulphurous stench drifted into the room, as the lightning continued to strike and the thunder rolled over the town. Rafael, curious as to what the doctor might be doing, pulled back the blanket that covered the doorway and stepped inside the small bedroom. The wooden shutters on the window had been thrown open, and a candle on a small bedside table threw off a weak light.

The *médico,* a slovenly, middle-aged man, was bent over Sara's leg when Rafael stepped up behind him. "What is your opinion—" Rafael began, before he saw the blood that poured from Sara's wound. The doctor had his knife poised to make another cut, as Rafael grabbed his arm and yanked the man away from her.

The doctor's bleary eyes widened as he gasped and stared into the younger man's fierce gaze. "Señor? Why do you stop me . . . she must be bled, if the infection—"

"No, you fool! I asked you to examine her, not start treatment without my approval. Now get out and pray that she does not die from your dirty knife!" Rafael's glare sent the man scurrying for the door. He then knelt down beside the bed and examined the damage. The blood flow was not as excessive as he had feared. Searching in his saddlebag, he took a clean shirt and pressed it to the wound, shouting for Felix as he did so.

When the *vaquero* came in, Rafael instructed him to boil some water. Checking Sara's pulse, he found it had weakened somewhat. For the next hour, he worked over her, cleaning her wound, making pastes to stop the blood flow, and finally applying the herbal medicine he had been using all along.

Sara developed a hard chill as the afternoon wore on, but the fever did not return, and for that he was thankful. It had been three days since the snake bit her, and she had survived. Even in her weakened condition, he knew that was a good sign. The señorita was stronger than she looked, he mused to himself, and then remembered with a wan smile that she had once told him that.

When her chill passed, he took a bowl of warm water and stripped the clothes from her body down to her chemise and bathed her. "You will be fine, *niña*," he said softly, covering her over again with the blanket. He sat down beside her, and took her hand in his. "Soon you will wake up and smile that angelic smile of yours, and I will take you to Hacienda Delgado. It is a beautiful place that you will fall in love with, *cara mia*. And I will take care of you. I know I have not done such a fine job of late,

TO GET YOUR
4 FREE BOOKS
MAIL THE COUPON BELOW.

FREE BOOK CERTIFICATE

GET 4 FREE BOOKS

Yes! I want to subscribe to Zebra's HEARTFIRE HOME SUBSCRIPTION SERVICE. Please send me my 4 FREE books. Then each month I'll receive the four newest Heartfire Romances as soon as they are published to preview Free for ten days. If I decide to keep them I'll pay the special discounted price of just $3.50 each; a total of $14.00. This is a savings of $3.00 off the regular publishers price. There are no shipping, handling or other hidden charges. There is no minimum number of books to buy and I may cancel this subscription at any time. In any case the 4 FREE Books are mine to keep regardless.

NAME

ADDRESS

CITY   STATE   ZIP

TELEPHONE

SIGNATURE   (If under 18 parent or guardian must sign)   ZH0793
Terms and prices subject to change.
Orders subject to acceptance.

Heartfire Romance

Heartfire Romance

GET 4 FREE BOOKS

HEARTFIRE HOME SUBSCRIPTION
SERVICE
120 BRIGHTON ROAD
P.O. BOX 5214
CLIFTON, NEW JERSEY 07015

AFFIX
STAMP
HERE

but in the future, I will do better. I will show you my *rancho* in the mountains, where wildflowers cover the hillsides, and the sunsets take your breath away."

As he spoke, he stared out the open window, seeing the things he described instead of the darkening clouds. The sound of his own voice, making plans, reassured him. "We will ride, you and I, to the ancient pueblo of Pecos, to see the sacred fire in the temple of the Aztec that has been kept burning for over five hundred years. Indian legend says that wishes are granted to those who are blessed in the temple."

"How many wishes?" Sara whispered, her eyes devouring his face. She loved the strength of his dark profile, and the sound of his deep-timbred voice.

Rafael swiftly turned to her. He felt a weight lift from his shoulders. A warm smile curved his mouth. "As many as you want, *niña*. How do you feel?"

"Tired," she replied, her voice weak. "My leg hurts."

His smile broadened. "To feel pain is good. It lets us know we are alive."

Her gaze left his face to glance around. "Where are we, Rafael? What happened to me?"

"We are in San Miguel. I brought you here on horseback, after you were bitten by a rattlesnake. Don't you remember?"

Her eyes closed for a moment. "Yes . . . I remember now. We argued and I ran away. The snakes . . . they were everywhere." She gave a delicate shudder as the whole picture returned.

He took her hand and brought it to his lips. "You were lucky, *niña*. Only one pierced your leg. I found marks on your boots where others struck, but did not penetrate."

She opened her eyes to look at him. "You were there, you pulled me away."

"Not quickly enough," he said, frowning. "And it was my fault you walked into that nest of vipers. If I hadn't made you angry . . ."

Sara gave him a weak smile. "But you saved my life, so it doesn't matter. Besides, we don't control our karma, as much as we might think. Most likely I was destined to suffer that fate."

He shook his head. "My little philosopher. The important thing is that you are all right. Would you like something to eat?"

At the mere thought, Sara found that she was ravenous. "Yes. But no beans, please. I don't think I can look at another bean for a while."

He chuckled. "Already complaining. That is a good sign also." He rose and went into the other room to speak to Felix.

Sara sighed. Rafael looked worse than she felt. His clothes were wrinkled and dirt smudged, as if he hadn't changed in days. And the look she had seen on his face when she opened her eyes spoke of genuine anxiety. The thought lifted her spirits considerably. She raised the quilt to have a look at her leg, and saw that she wore only her chemise. She blushed and immediately wondered why it bothered her. He had seen her naked before.

Rafael returned and noticed the bright spots of color in her cheeks. He searched his saddlebag and sifted some white powder into the cup of water he was holding. "This will help with the pain," he said, helping her to sit up.

Her hands trembled as she grasped the cup. She didn't know if the reaction was caused by weakness, or his strong arm bracing her shoulders. She sipped slowly, finding she was very thirsty.

"Felix will be back with some food soon. You will grow strong now."

Sara's brow creased with worry. "Do you think I will be fit by the time we reach Hacienda Delgado? I don't want your grandfather to be disappointed if I cannot open the school."

Rafael shook his head and took the empty cup from her, letting her fall back gently on the pillow. "Don Vicente is more than fair with his employees, Sara. He will most likely order you to rest past the time you are well. Do not worry yourself about the matter." He pulled up a stool and sat beside her.

A look of puzzlement settled on her features. "The way you described him, I was anxious."

"Our relationship is different, *niña*. He reserves his prejudice for me . . . and my mother, when she was alive."

His voice had taken on a brooding quality, and Sara intuitively recognized the pain beneath his hard surface. Hadn't she, herself, sought love and approval from her own parents? In her case, the love was not purposely withheld, but they had been indifferent to her, which hurt. "Perhaps he cares, but is too proud to show it," she suggested softly. The conversation she'd had with Señor Pino came back to her. If Don Vicente didn't care about his grandson, why was he interested in finding the right wife for him? That reminder sent her weakened

195

spirits plummeting.

"I think not. When I was a boy, I wanted very much for him to love me. I remember once, Pedro's son, Arturo, and I were kept after our lessons were done, because we had been very unruly that day. We were seven and full of life, and did not wish to be confined indoors with books. When the other boys arrived back at the hacienda and informed my grandfather of the delay, he rode into town to talk to Father Mendoza. After their discussion, Don Vicente ordered me to spend an hour in prayerful repentance and then walk home. He took Arturo home with him and left me there. It was well after dark when I arrived at the hacienda. He told me a Delgado had to learn discipline and self-control." Rafael rose abruptly and went to the window to stare out at the pelting rain.

Sara saw a hint of dejection in the droop of his shoulders, and her heart went out to him. Don Vicente's punishment seemed cruel, especially when the other boy had not received the same. Whether he realized it or not, Rafael still yearned for his grandfather's approval. Sara wanted to say something comforting, but knew he would bristle at pity. Felix, however, called out his arrival with the food and covered the awkward moment.

Rafael insisted on feeding her; Sara managed to have a little broth and part of a tortilla. She asked him to tell her more of the pueblo of Pecos that he had been speaking of when she had wakened. So he talked about the fortified town built upon a rock promontory. Sara ceased to listen to the words, and let his hypnotic voice flow over her. They were in a

196

small world all their own with the heavy rain keeping the villagers at bay. For the moment, Sara pretended that Rafael was hers and hers alone. Fate had given him to her for this brief interlude, and she pushed thoughts of the future out of her mind.

When she became drowsy, Rafael covered her with another blanket to keep out the damp chill, and kissed her cheek softly before leaving the room.

The sound of a rooster crowing at dawn awakened Sara. She blinked at the bright sunlight streaming through the window. This morning there was only a dull ache in her leg, and she felt a general sense of well-being. The sound of quiet conversation in the other room had her straining to hear Rafael's voice. She touched the tangled mass of hair on her head, longing for a brush to put it to rights before he saw her. Her eye fell on his saddlebags across the room. Slowly she swung her feet to the floor and tested her injured leg. When it didn't give way, she wrapped one of the blankets around her and stood up. She felt dizzy for a moment, but the room soon righted itself, so she gingerly started toward the table. Just before she reached it, however, her energy flagged. A pair of strong arms caught her. Looking up, she met Rafael's warm brown eyes with a smile. "I thought I could make it," she murmured.

His arm caught her under her knees, and he lifted her against the solid wall of his chest. "You should have called me, if you needed something, *niña*. As yet, you are too wobbly to be out of bed." His voice was stern, but there was a faint glint of laughter in his eyes.

The feel of his arms around her was doing strange things to her senses. She dipped her head so that he couldn't read the longing in her expression. "I . . . I wanted a brush for my hair," she explained, as he carried her back to the bed.

When he placed her in the middle of the bed, her blanket covering slipped to reveal the soft rise of one breast. He swallowed tightly as he straightened. "I have a comb. Will that do?" he asked, turning away.

"Yes," she managed, tugging at the errant blanket. His heated look had seared her skin, yet she shivered. He wanted her as much as she wanted him. That thought filled her with a hot and awful joy.

She took the comb he offered. Rafael then walked out of the room without another word.

Sara slept through most of that day, and by evening she felt stronger still. The swelling in her leg had gone down considerably, and the pain was almost gone. Rafael had looked in on her frequently, and when he found her awake, he smiled. "Could you eat something? I will have Felix fetch it."

She raised herself on her elbows and blinked sleepily. He was freshly shaven and wore clean clothes. It reminded Sara of her own unkempt appearance. "I would rather have a bath and my clothes first."

"Whatever you wish," he said and disappeared.

If you loved me, I would have my wish, she thought with a sigh, as she swung her legs over the side of the bed.

Before long, a young Indian woman entered the room, bearing a bucket of warm water and some linens. She filled a basin on the small table, and then fished a bar of soap from her pocket and placed it alongside. Sara thanked her and the girl smiled shyly and left, pulling the curtain at the doorway.

This time when Sara walked across the room, she felt somewhat stronger. Dropping the blanket, she pulled off her chemise and began to wash. When she finished, she felt tired, but pleasantly so. Climbing back into bed, she covered herself to her neck and wondered where her clothes were. A swift check around the small room indicated that they were not there.

A shy voice asked in Spanish for permission to enter, and Sara called out, *"Sí, entra."*

The Indian girl came in with another bucket of water and placed it on the floor, speaking rapidly and gesturing with her hands.

Sara understood most of her words, enough to know that she was asking if Sara wanted to wash her hair. Sara smiled and nodded happily. "Oh, *sí,"* she agreed readily.

After emptying the basin, the girl brought a dipper and motioned for Sara to lay on her stomach and hold her head over the side of the bed. For that, Sara was thankful. She didn't think she could stand at the table any longer. The task was soon accomplished, and the Indian girl left her once again.

Sara sat up with the comb, but in a short time, her arms grew so tired from working with the tangles, she had to rest.

"Are you covered?" Rafael called out from behind the curtain.

Sara hastily pulled the blanket higher and bade him enter.

Over his arm, Rafael carried some clothing. Sara looked at him questioningly, when she realized it was not hers.

"I sent Felix out to find some things for you. The clothes you had on are being cleaned. I hope these fit," he said placing his bundle on the end of the bed. "When you are dressed, would you rather eat in the other room than in bed?"

"Oh, yes! And thank you for the clothes. That was thoughtful of you." She gave him a brilliant smile, feeling lighthearted. She lifted a hand to her hair. "It may take a while though. I'm having an awful time with these tangles."

The seductive picture she presented caused his heart to thump rapidly in his chest. He knew she wore nothing beneath the blanket, for he'd seen her chemise on the floor. Unable to resist, he took the comb from her. "Let me help you."

As his steady gaze bore into her in silent expectation, she nodded. He sat down behind her and began to work gently at the snarls. She could feel the heat of his body next to hers, and her breath caught in her throat. Closing her eyes, she sighed in pure pleasure.

"Your hair is so beautiful, Sara. I have never seen this color before," Rafael breathed, feeling desire well up in him like hot liquid. "The Comanche would say you have been chosen as a guardian spirit of the Mother Moon." He leaned forward and kissed her bare shoulder, before he resumed his gentle task.

Her body felt heavy and warm as her pulse quickened. "Is that good?" she whispered.

"Very good, *cara mia*. A guardian spirit is blessed, and has the power of natural gifts." His free hand slid down her arm in a light caress.

Sara sucked in a swift breath at his touch. "I can't imagine any gifts I might possess," she countered, her voice barely audible.

Rafael let the comb fall to the bed and turned her to face him. Lifting her hair from her shoulders, he let it fall down her back. His dark eyes glowed with an inner fire, as they pinned her gaze. "You make my heart thunder and my blood quicken . . . and I forget the rest of the world when you are near. *Sí, mi alma,* you have powerful gifts," he said, his voice hoarse. He tipped her chin up, and his mouth covered hers hungrily.

The tight knot that had formed in her stomach burst, and spread liquid fire throughout her body. She had been waiting for his kiss, yearning for his touch, for a long time. Sliding her arms around his neck, she laced her fingers in his thick hair. He smelled of soap and tobacco and masculine heat.

Rafael's hard body throbbed at her passionate response. His tongue invaded her soft mouth, while his hands moved over her bare back where the blanket had slipped away. She was still very weak, his mind counseled sternly, even as desire roiled hotly in his loins. Before his passion became uncontrollable, he pulled back, his hands gripping her arms. His breath was coming in short gasps, as was hers. "Not now," he rasped.

Sara looked into his heavy-lidded gaze and saw a

savage longing that matched her own. "When?" she breathed.

That one word from her nearly undid his resolve. Shaking his head, he repeated, "Not now." Rising from the bed, he said hoarsely, "When you're dressed, we will dine."

Sara stared at the fluttering curtain in his wake. She clutched the blanket tightly to her breast, her chest rising and falling with effort. Why had he stopped? She wanted him to make love to her more than she wanted to breathe. And he wanted her—of that much she was sure. His kiss had left her in no doubt. Tears misted her eyes as she stood up and reached for the clothing he'd brought. Was it always to be this way for them . . . so many partings?

There was a full white blouse with short puffy sleeves and a gathered red skirt. When she was dressed, she looked down at the skirt in consternation. It only reached mid-calf, while the blouse dipped low, exposing the rise of her breasts. She felt almost naked with no underthings on. A shiver raced down her spine when she thought about Rafael's reaction to the way she looked. She put on the soft kid slippers he'd brought, and smoothed her hair back. It was nearly dry now and hung in soft waves. With her heart thumping in expectation, she pushed aside the curtain and entered the front room.

Rafael was standing in the doorway, looking out into the plaza. There was a candle burning on a small table and two places set, along with a bottle of wine. Sara's eyes swung back to Rafael, and she found he had turned. His gaze roamed over her figure, and a warm blush stained her cheeks at his bold perusal.

202

With an unhurried stride, he crossed the room to her side, his eyes never leaving her face. Taking one of her hands, he lifted it to his mouth for a kiss. "My eyes must surely deceive me, señorita. I have thought you beautiful in every other guise, but tonight . . . tonight, you surpass my fondest recollection."

Sara's blue eyes softened at his extravagant flattery. She fluttered her dark lashes and smiled in a beguiling fashion. "I'm afraid you've been on the trail too long, Rafael. However, my illness has left me weak of will, and I accept the compliment."

He gave her a rakish smile and held out his arm. She took it, feeling a jolt of excitement at his touch. He led her to the table and seated her in a formal fashion.

Taking his own seat, he opened the wine and poured for both of them. He held up his glass and she lifted hers, waiting expectantly. "To your recovery, *niña* . . . and to our stay in San Miguel."

Sara looked at him for a long moment, reading the silent message in his dark eyes. She gave a slow nod and touched her glass to his, as if to seal a bargain. As they drank, she wondered briefly at this madness she was embarking upon. It would surely lead to heartbreak for her, but somehow, she couldn't turn away from it.

Lifting the warming cloth from her plate, Sara sniffed appreciatively. There was stewed chicken with onions, corn, and tortillas. Sara smiled. "It looks very good."

"I think you will find it palatable," he said, taking up his fork to sample the fare. "At least it is not beans, eh?"

Sara's gentle laugh rippled through the air. *"Sí,* that *is* something to celebrate."

He very much enjoyed making her smile, he suddenly realized. His mood had been low for so long now, that he'd forgotten how to tease—how to have fun. Tuwikaa's gentle face flashed in his mind's eye, and he could still see her smile. He had loved her with a young man's mindless devotion, yet there had been something missing in their relationship. In Sara, he saw qualities he admired greatly—her gentle sense of humor, her independence of spirit, her determination. Pushing these unsettling thoughts aside, he warned, "We will be back to trail food for a few more days before we reach Santa Fe, so enjoy this respite."

Sara's eyes glinted with mischief, even as she sighed in mock-seriousness. "Nothing endures but change."

He smiled. "Master Filbert's wisdom?"

"Yes," she said, taking a sip of her wine. "I miss him almost as much as Max. As a matter of fact, if I hadn't had him for moral support when we received the bad news about Max, I don't know what I would have done. His kindness and wisdom helped me through that grievous time. And then *he* died, a year after my brother."

She spoke calmly, but he could feel the weight of her grief in her voice. He was reminded of the anguish she'd spilled out during her delirium. Reaching across the table, he covered her hand with his. "You have good and loving memories to sustain you, *niña.* That counts for much."

Sara felt comforted by his touch, his gently

204

spoken words. Raising her eyes to his, she also felt ashamed. Throughout his life, Rafael had been denied this kind of love. Her tight expression relaxed into a smile. "Thank you for reminding me, Rafael. Of course, you're right."

Reluctantly, he removed his hand and changed the subject. They spoke in generalities—of the weather, of Santa Fe, of the caravan—but between them there was a heightened awareness of a tenuous bond.

When they finished eating, Sara was loath to see the evening end. "Could we take a short walk?" she asked.

Rafael moved around the table to help her. "*Sí.* If your leg is not hurting, the exercise will do you good." His gaze fell on the creamy swell of her breasts where the blouse dipped in front. He swallowed tightly and forced his eyes away.

Sara breathed in the cool night air as she stepped outside. It smelled fresh after the cleansing rain. A blanket of stars covered the sky, and a yellow moon hung suspended over the mountains to the east. There were spots of light in windows and doorways around the public square, and a few fires flickered outside some of the adobes, where dark women hunched over their cook-pots. The strains of a guitar could be heard drifting on the breeze from the cantina. Sara turned to Rafael, and found him watching her with a brooding expression. He offered his arm, and she took it as they began to walk.

A feminine voice began to sing along with the guitar. "Why is it that Spanish music is either sad or intensely passionate? Are there no happy songs in your culture?" Sara remarked.

Rafael smiled to himself and tucked her arm closer against his side. *"Sí, niña.* We have happy songs at our fandangos and festivals. It's just that the Spanish people are very emotional. We are not afraid of showing our feelings."

Sara gave an unladylike snort. *"We,* Rafael? You include yourself in that statement? You are the most private, unemotional person I've ever met." She was thinking of his restraint earlier that evening, when he'd kissed her and then walked away. Their whole relationship, as a matter of fact, had been governed by his cool reserve.

Rafael glanced down at her upturned face, a slow smile curving his lips. "I have my moments. However, the strict discipline of my Comanche blood tempers the erratic Spaniard in me."

They were past the cantina, and Sara nodded politely to an Indian woman who was sitting in front of her house stirring her cook-pot. The woman stared curiously at the handsome couple, until they were swallowed up by shadows.

As he thought about her opinion, Rafael grew irritated. "I would say, señorita, that you have little room to accuse me of being detached."

Sara's brows rose at the challenge. "And what do you mean by that?"

Rafael stopped walking and turned to face her. "What about the things you said the day after we made love? Would you not call that unemotional?"

His accusing tone set off a spark of anger in her. "You treated me like a leper that day! I only told you what you wanted to hear."

The truth of her words pierced his guilty conscience. He had been battling his own devils that day, and had given little thought to her feelings. And when she'd released him from any responsibility, he'd been more confused than ever. He groaned as he gathered her into his arms. "Forgive me, Sara. What you say is true."

Sara's heart thumped madly, as his mouth slowly descended to hers. At the first touch of his lips, she succumbed to the passion she'd been holding at bay. Sliding one hand inside his open-necked shirt, she stroked his chest while he caressed the curve of her hips, pulling her closer to his heat.

His mouth left hers to trail hot kisses down her neck and across her bare shoulders. "Oh, Rafael," she gasped. "I thought you didn't care. That's why—"

"I was a fool," he rasped against her soft skin. "I will not make that mistake again."

Sara arched her back, as his lips moved to the sensitive rise of her breast. His hand slipped her blouse down, revealing a hardened nipple. When he took the orb into his mouth, Sara pushed at his shoulders. "No, Rafael . . . not here."

Her breathless protest penetrated his clouded mind. They were standing in the shadows of a darkened building; it was not the place for lovemaking. He grinned rakishly and straightened her blouse. *"Sí, cara mia.* I sometimes forget myself, when I am with you."

The moonlight smoldered in her blue eyes, as she steadied herself against his chest. "And I can barely think when you kiss me like that," she told him, her breath coming in short gasps.

"Are you ready to return?"

"More than ready," she said, with a promise in her voice.

He put his arm around her waist and guided her back the way they'd come. Once inside the house, he shut the door and placed a wooden bar across it, to lock out the world. Sara stood in the middle of the room, suddenly uncertain of her decision, but as he crossed to her side, a warm smile curved his mouth, and she forgot her fears.

He swept her up into his arms and carried her into the darkened bedroom, where only a shaft of moonlight from the open window lit his path. He let her slide down his body until her feet touched the floor, and then bent to brush her parted lips with his own. "If you are not strong enough yet, *cara mia,* say so now," he said, his voice husky. "I cannot control myself much longer."

Sara smiled and slid her tongue provocatively over his lips. "Perhaps I should retract what I said about you being unemotional," she whispered, pressing her body closer to his.

He groaned as hot flashes of desire seared his body. "You can make up your mind after I love you, *mi alma,*" he growled, hooking his fingers in the top of her blouse and pulling it down toward her waist. He cupped her breasts in his strong hands, and bent to take her lips in a hungry kiss.

Sara moaned her pleasure, but trembled with more intense excitement as his mouth left hers to suckle at her exposed breasts, loving each in turn. She raked his shoulders with her nails, and was

208

barely aware that his hands loosened her skirt until it fell to the floor. Deftly, he disposed of her blouse, and stepped back to gaze at her moon-drenched body.

She was lovely beyond words, her body softly rounded, her delicate face flushed with desire, and her flowing hair a silver cascade down her back. His breath was a hoarse rasp in his throat as he spoke, "Beautiful Sara . . . I am near blinded by the sight. Tell me you are real, *por favor,* and not some mirage to tease my tortured mind?"

Sara moved to stand a mere breath away from him. Her eyes were soft and caressing, as she lifted a hand to trace the line of his strong jaw. "For this moment, I'm real, Rafael . . . and deadly serious," she whispered, reaching to undo the buttons on his shirt.

He stood stock-still, savoring the brush of her fingers against his skin. When she slipped the shirt off his shoulders and began working at the buttons on his trousers, he could stand it no longer. Pushing her fingers aside, he divested himself of the offending garment and reached for her.

Sara went into his arms willingly, loving the feel of his hard body against her soft one. The evidence of his arousal sent a wave of liquid fire from her belly to the apex of her thighs. She moaned as his mouth took hers, and his hands found every spot that gave her pleasure.

Rafael's desire rose to a fever pitch, and when he could stand the waiting no longer, he lifted her in his arms and carried her to the bed. Following her onto the mattress, he rose above her and took his own weight on his arms, capturing her lips once more.

Sara luxuriated in the feel of the corded muscles of his arms and his slim hips, as her soft hands roamed freely.

"Oh, Sara . . . *mi alma*. I never thought to find someone like you," he breathed against her mouth.

Sara tenderly framed his handsome face with her hands and smiled. "I found you . . . remember?"

His smile flashed white, before he dipped his head to nuzzle her ear. "Fate brought us together, *niña,* I am sure of that. I need you more than I need food for my body or water for my thirst."

Rafael's words were like a soothing balm to her spirit. They filled her with joy. Sara arched her body as his tongue slowly circled her ear. Hoarsely, she commanded, "Show me how much, Rafael . . ."

Ever mindful of her delicate condition, Rafael caressed her with gentleness, yet the fire between them blazed all the same. He kissed her breasts, her flat belly, and tasted the tender skin of her inner thigh. When his mouth moved to the most intimate part of her, her reaction was swift and violent. She tried to pull away, even as his name slipped passionately between her lips. Raising his head, his fingers moved to the spot his mouth had just left. His dark eyes held her confused gaze, as he stroked the moist, velvet opening. "Let me love you as I want, Sara . . . you will not be sorry," he promised in a husky whisper.

Sara closed her eyes as her body opened up with his masterful persuasion. "Oh, Rafael . . . yes," she moaned, arching her hips.

His mouth replaced his fingers, and waves of ecstasy throbbed through her. In moments, she gasped in sweet agony, her body wracked with tremors.

Rafael moved up beside her and wrapped her in his arms. Sara held him fiercely, reveling in the touch of his body against hers. "Well, *cara mia?*" he murmured, burying his face in her sweet-scented hair.

Sara savored the feeling of satisfaction. "It was wonderful," she breathed, caressing his chest. "But what about the other?"

He raised his head to look into her eyes. "The other?"

Sara's gaze fell shyly, but her hand strayed down his taut belly to encircle his arousal.

Sucking in a swift breath, he gave a low growl. "I intended to give you a moment of rest, but if you are that eager . . ." He covered her hand with his own and closed his eyes tightly, as if in pain. "Do you know what that does to me, Sara?" he gasped as she moved her hand up and down in a sensual motion.

Sara felt her own desire quicken once again. "I want to make you as happy as you've made me," she said softly, pulling his head down with her other hand.

When their lips touched, a new fire ignited. After a brief moment, Rafael groaned and broke the kiss. He moved to tower over her, urging, "Spread your thighs for me, sweet vixen, and let's be about our business."

Guiding the shaft of his swollen manhood into her moist opening, he barely controlled his passion. His gentle thrusts nearly drove him crazy, yet he had no wish to hurt her. Sara's desire for him overrode everything else, and she eagerly met his thrusts, moaning aloud with erotic pleasure. "Please love me," she begged, hardly aware of what she was saying, needing all of him.

"I do, *mi alma,* I do," he growled hoarsely, as he drove into her fiercely, matching her rhythm. *And I always will,* he thought fleetingly, just before Sara cried out her passionate release. His followed in a shuddering explosion of uncontrollable joy.

Their world spun crazily for a few moments, before it slowly began to right itself. Rafael fell gasping to her side and Sara rolled against him weakly, her hand falling on his chest.

Rafael stroked her face tenderly with his thumb. "I did not hurt you, did I?"

Sara smiled lazily. "Quite the opposite, my love. I thought I would die, there was so much pleasure."

The cool night air from the open window drifted over their sweat-dampened bodies, and Rafael reached down and pulled the blanket over them. Sara snuggled against him, yawning delicately. "Sleep, *mi alma,*" he urged.

She wound one hand around his neck and murmured, "Will you stay with me?"

"*Sí,* Sara. I will stay with you always," he whispered, his lips brushing her hair. The howl of a coyote sounded in the distance, and it made the hair on his neck prickle. Although not overly superstitious, he felt it was a bad omen. The coyote, little brother to the great wolf, was the spoiler of good things. He brought hardship and travail to the lives of the Comanche. That was what he'd been taught, and in his years with the People, he'd seen mystic happenings to substantiate that belief. For three nights before Tuwikaa died, a coyote had howled in the hills just beyond their tipi.

Sara didn't respond to his whispered promise. Her even breathing told him she was asleep. Rafael lay awake, holding her, long into the night. Nothing would happen to her, he assured himself, but an uneasy feeling settled in the pit of his stomach.

Chapter 10

The sun had just begun its ascent when Rafael woke Sara with a kiss. Even before he had opened his eyes to see her lying in his arms, Rafael felt a warm contentment. She belonged with him, and he intended to tell her so.

The touch of his lips on hers was featherlike. Sara stirred and opened her eyes. He was smiling, and her lips curved in response. "Good morning," she murmured, her voice husky with sleep.

"Good? It's a beautiful morning. Almost as beautiful as you." His gaze was as soft as a caress.

Sara felt a well of happiness bubble up inside her. She loved this dark, enigmatic man, and to wake up in his arms gave her the greatest of pleasure. If only they could remain in this haven away from the world, she thought. Sara's eyes lit with mischief. "Are you trying to woo me with overstated flattery?" she asked archly, running her hand lightly over his chest.

He slipped his arm about her waist and pulled her

214

closer to him, letting her feel his arousal. "It's not flattery, *niña*. Nor is it overstated, but, *sí*, I am trying to woo you."

Sara's eyes widened at the intimate feel of his obvious desire pressing against her leg. Even as her breathing quickened, she realized it was broad daylight. The morning sounds from the public courtyard reached her ears. "We mustn't," she protested weakly.

Rafael grinned rakishly just before he claimed her lips. His kiss sent her stomach into a wild swirl, as her hands crept up to bury themselves in his thick hair. A low growl sounded deep in her, like the sound of a she-wolf calling to her mate, and all thoughts of protest were forgotten.

Without breaking the kiss, Rafael moved over her and spread her legs. His fingers stayed to stroke her softness, until she became hot and wet. Sara strained against his torturous ministrations, writhing beneath him.

His mouth left hers as he guided his hardened staff to the silky place he sought. "Sara, Sara," he rasped, pushing into her as her hips rose eagerly to meet him.

She gave a small cry of pleasure as he filled her again and again. She clung to him as the flames of their passion devoured them. His sinewy chest teased her nipples, sending wild shafts of desire spiraling through her.

Rafael's world reeled with Sara's heated response. She met him thrust for thrust, making mewling sounds in her throat, while his heart beat fiercely in his chest, near to exploding.

Closing her eyes tightly, Sara could feel the first

215

tremors of release, and then the rippling, molten waves flooded her with unbearable pleasure. As Rafael felt her tighten around him, his own surging release filled her, and they were caught together on the swelling tide of rapture.

Rafael rolled to her side, and the world righted itself. They lay quietly for a few moments, letting their harsh breathing slow to normal. Sara closed her eyes in contentment. Turning onto her side to stretch, she felt Rafael's arm come around her waist as he fitted his body, spoonlike, against her back.

Sara sighed, as he brushed her hair aside and gently nibbled on her shoulder. "You have bewitched me, lovely señorita. I am your slave to command," he whispered.

Sara smiled and reached back to caress his face. "Then I command you to repeat that performance," she teased.

He groaned and nipped her skin with his teeth. "I will be happy to, once I have rested."

She clucked her tongue. "One small request and you make excuses."

He chuckled as he propped himself up on one elbow and drew a teasing finger down her ribs. "The task will be odious, but if you insist . . ."

Sara giggled and squirmed as he tickled her, begging him to stop. He finally took pity on her and pulled her closer, brushing his lips across her hair. His tone had turned serious when he spoke again. "I have been thinking, Sara, that we should marry."

Sara stiffened and grew very still. For a brief moment, an intense joy filled her. She loved him with all her heart, and had wanted to hear those words for a long time. But, did he love her? He hadn't said so. He hadn't even said that he *wanted* to marry her, but that they *should* marry.

"Sara?"

"Is it because you've made love to me and feel an obligation?" she asked quietly.

Rafael had been delving into his reasons since the night before. It was the honorable thing to do, he had decided. And the physical attraction was powerful, more powerful than anything he had ever experienced. She was sweet and had an innate kindness. She would be a perfect mother for his daughter Kahuu. He wanted to bring the child to live at his *rancho* in the mountains, but had been loath to do so without a mother to look after her. Mentally, he ticked off all the reasons for asking her. "There is that, Sara, but I want you to be my wife. It is time I married again."

She took note of his guarded tone, and felt a sinking feeling in the pit of her stomach. It wasn't enough for her. She wanted his love, not what had been left over from his first wife. And then she remembered what Señor Pino had said. Don Vicente had chosen a wife for Rafael already. If she accepted this proposal, the breach between grandfather and grandson might never be healed. She knew that deep down Rafael wanted his grandfather's love, even if he would never admit it. A pain seared her heart, as she realized she had to give him up. Last night, she had promised herself that this time with him in San Miguel would be enough . . . but she'd been wrong. If she spent several lifetimes with him, it wouldn't be enough. She swallowed past the lump in her throat. "I'm not sure that's wise, Rafael. I think you are still in love with Tuwikaa."

Rafael turned her in his arms, so that he could look into her eyes. "It is true that I will never forget her . . . and she is Kahuu's mother, but it is time to put the past behind me." He knew he should be telling Sara how he felt about her, but the words stuck in his throat.

"This physical thing between us, it's strong, but perhaps not a good basis for marriage," she hedged, dropping her eyes. Again, he had not expressed deep feelings for her. However, it did not matter, she thought dismally. If she refused him, he would most likely look favorably on the woman his grandfather had chosen. After all, what he wanted was a wife, not someone to love.

Rafael frowned. He could have sworn she cared for him, yet something was wrong. "What are you afraid of, *niña?* You can tell me."

There was a gentle note of concern in his voice that nearly broke her heart. She closed her eyes and pressed her face into his shoulder. "I have nothing to bring to a marriage, Rafael, no dowry. What would people think of you marrying a poor employee of your grandfather's? It would be scandalous."

Rafael listened to her muffled protests, while a chilled finger brushed his spine. Was this truly why she objected, or did she have other reasons? The cultured ladies in his grandfather's world had always flirted with him shamelessly, but the circumstances of his birth had kept the relationships on a purely physical basis. Gently, he tipped her chin up so he could look into her tear-filled eyes. "Those who

218

would gossip are not my friends. And as for a dowry, it is not important to me, but if it is to you, I will provide you with one."

Fresh tears spilled down Sara's cheeks at his generosity. She pushed herself to a sitting position, and wiped at them with the edge of the blanket. His gentle kindness was almost more than she could bear, but she steeled herself against her traitorous feelings. "I cannot accept charity, but I appreciate your offer, Rafael. Besides, you would be better off with someone else," she whispered brokenly.

He stared at her rigid back as bitterness rose in him. Her excuses were weak. He knew she had another reason; he could feel it in his bones. And that other reason was the fact that he was a half-breed. What hurt him more than anything was that he thought Sara was above that. In his own way, he had trusted her. He was doubly glad now that he hadn't told her he loved her. It would have been humiliating. Swinging his legs over the side of the bed, he reached for his buckskin pants and donned them. "If you felt that way, why did you let me make love to you?" he questioned in a level tone.

Sara flinched at the question and at Rafael's conversational tone. It hurt to realize that she'd been correct in thinking he didn't love her. "I'll admit that I'm attracted to you, Rafael, but marriage is an important commitment. It should take place for the right reasons," she said in a tremulous whisper.

As he buttoned his shirt, Rafael's bitterness swelled to anger. "So I am good enough to share your bed, but not your life, eh?"

It took a moment for his harsh words to penetrate,

but when they did, Sara jerked her tear-stained face around and caught a look of contempt in his dark eyes. She immediately knew what he was implying. Flinging out an imploring hand, she gasped, "No, Rafael! That's not it—I—"

"Do not lie to me, Sara," he said coldly, turning on his heel to leave the room. "I will not trouble you again."

"Rafael, no," Sara cried, and watched helplessly as he passed through the blanketed doorway. Her mind reeled with confusion, and her heart felt near to bursting. He thought she was reluctant because he was a half-breed! She scrambled from the bed and found her clothes. She had to make him understand that she didn't feel that way. Feverishly she slipped on the blouse and pulled on the skirt, her fingers trembling as she tied the strings. She slid her feet into the soft kid slippers. Touching her hair, she grimaced at the mass of tangles, but decided it would have to wait. If she was going to catch up to Rafael, she didn't have time to put her hair in order.

The front room was empty. When she stepped outside and scanned the square, she could not find him. Felix was nowhere to be seen either. The women of the pueblo were already stirring in their cook-pots and fetching water from the well in the center of the square. As Sara advanced down the covered walk toward the cantina, several of the Indian women looked at her curiously. The Indian girl who had helped her wash her hair came out the open doorway of the cantina just as Sara reached it.

"Have you seen the señor? Señor Delgado?" Sara asked in Spanish, enunciating each word slowly in an effort to say it correctly.

The girl smiled shyly and shook her head. Sara sighed as she watched her walk toward the well with a wooden bucket. Glancing around, she saw the door of the church standing ajar and headed in that direction. It was dim and cool inside the thick-walled church. Two high windows on opposite walls cast a faint glow of early sunlight over the ornately painted altar screen and a small gilded statue of Saint Michael. The serene beauty of the sanctuary did nothing to soothe her anxiety. Rafael was not there. She saw a priest praying silently, and left without disturbing him.

As she stood on the stone step outside, she despaired of finding him. She turned to walk back to the house. What could she say to him anyway? she thought. She could deny his accusation, but if her other excuses had not convinced him, perhaps it was better to let him think what he wanted.

When she entered the bedroom, she found a bucket of fresh water. Stripping her clothes off, she bathed and then put them back on. Taking the comb, she worked the tangles from her hair, remembering how it had felt when Rafael had performed this task the night before. Suddenly, her bright future seemed to dissolve into ashes before her eyes.

The following morning, Sara awoke to sounds of a great commotion in the plaza. She hurriedly arose and dressed, leaving her hair in the single braid down her back that she had fixed the night before.

Splashing some water on her face, she dried it and went to see what the noise was about. The wagons of both caravans were parked on the other side of the square, and she saw Señor Pino talking to Rafael near the lead wagon. Her heart turned over at the sight of him, for he had barely spoken to her since he'd stalked out the morning before. She had taken a solitary walk around the plaza and watched from a chair at her front door, while the inhabitants of the village went about their daily chores.

Having plenty of time in the last twenty-four hours to agonize over her problem, she had decided to let Rafael believe the worst of her. In this way, he could move forward with his life and his grandfather's plans.

Sara started across the square when she saw Doña Josefina and Estella being helped from their carriage. She waved to her friend, and Estella hurried forward to meet her halfway. The two friends embraced. "It is so good to see you well, *amiga!*" Estella said, laughing.

"And I'm just as happy to see you," Sara told her, drawing comfort from her friend's presence.

Garth and Matt walked up, along with several of the *vaqueros*. "My subject lives," Matt quipped irreverently, but in his gaze she saw relief. Sara laughed and hugged him.

Garth gave her a mock frown. "I should tan your hide for scaring the wits out of us, young lady." Then he smiled. "But I'm too glad to see you."

Sara shook hands with each of the *vaqueros* and spoke a few words with them. Her pain eased somewhat, knowing that she had so many friends who cared about her.

Doña Josefina interrupted the reunion with a complaint. "Must we stand around like peasants in the boiling sun? I need something to drink."

Sara turned to her. "We have a small house, señora. You could rest there."

The older woman's brows lifted. "We? Are you saying that you and Rafael are staying in the same house without a chaperone?"

Sara had forgotten how irritating Doña Josefina could be. She sighed. "I've been quite ill, if you'll remember. And we do have Felix with us. Come along, and I will see that you have some morning chocolate."

"You go ahead with Sara, Madre. I wish to say hello to Rafael before I join you." Estella didn't give her mother a chance to protest, but walked briskly away.

Sara wished she could approach Rafael that easily. She could hear the older woman muttering to herself as they made their way to the house. Sara sent Felix for refreshments, and offered Doña Josefina one of the two chairs in the front room.

She ignored the offer and sniffed as she walked about the room. "This is not much better than a hovel." She stopped and pulled back the blanket that covered the bedroom doorway and looked inside. "Did you sleep in here?" she asked and turned to pin Sara with her sharp eyes.

Sara nodded and clasped her hands behind her back to keep them still.

"And where did Rafael sleep?"

"I don't know," Sara said, uncomfortable with the

inquisition. "I would imagine he and Felix slept in here. I was unconscious when we arrived."

"But not the whole time?" the señora asked.

"No."

"I see," Doña Josefina said, taking note of the high color in Sara's cheeks. She lifted her black lace mantilla off the tortoiseshell comb on her head, and draped it across her shoulders. Sitting down in one of the chairs, she smiled almost pleasantly. "I am looking forward to my morning chocolate."

Sara felt the woman's change of attitude boded ill for her in some way. She was, however, glad the questioning was over.

Boone Keegan was a charming man, personable with a quick wit. The ladies loved him, not only for these qualities, but for his handsome, black-Irish looks. His hair was as dark as a raven's wing and his eyes were the color of midnight. He was of medium height, well muscled, and neat in his choice of clothes. He was also intelligent, observant, and deadly fast with his gun.

Today, he sat relaxed in Jonas Farber's ornate office at the bank. He didn't like the florid-faced banker, but liking his clients had nothing to do with business, he reminded himself. A professional bounty hunter dealt with low-life scum on both sides of the law.

Farber finally looked up from the report he had been reading, and removed his glasses. "Santa Fe? That's a long trip, if it turns out to be a wild-goose chase."

Keegan's left eyebrow rose a fraction. "There's very little speculation in this case, Mr. Farber. I wish all my investigations yielded this much information. However, if you'd like to hire someone else to cover the same ground, be my guest. My feelings won't be hurt, I assure you."

Kegan's self-assured attitude irritated Farber. He had been recommended as the best, and Farber was secretly pleased by the thorough job the man had done. He had merely been hoping to negotiate a smaller fee from the bounty hunter, for the services he was about to solicit from him. However, this case was too important to quibble over a few dollars. Swallowing his pride, he summoned up a weak smile. "That won't be necessary. I have to say that your idea of placing a darkie spy in the Clayton house was smart. The Clayton slaves are as close-mouthed as most darkies are gossipy. I couldn't get a thing out of them."

Keegan didn't return the smile, but studied the man across the desk who tried to bully everyone into submission. Keegan preferred alternative ways to gain his own ends whenever possible. "My man, Willy, said they were fiercely loyal to Miss Clayton. He also told me the cook's helper hinted that her mistress was afraid of you. Perhaps that's why they wouldn't talk to you."

Farber shifted his large bulk in the chair, and dabbed at the perspiration on his face with his handkerchief. He wondered what else the servants had told Willy. Keegan's dark, piercing eyes seemed to look through him as if to ferret out any secrets. Farber composed himself and met the other man's eyes once more. "Nonsense. You know how dramatic these darkies can be. Miss Clayton is a headstrong young woman, and running off like this proves it. When I informed her that her affairs were to be turned over to her uncle in Savannah—since she is not married yet—she threw a fit of temper. Wants to manage her own life, she told me in no uncertain terms."

Keegan had done his job. He'd found out where she'd gone. What happened between the banker and his ward was none of his business, but he didn't believe the man. From the information Willy had brought him, Sara Clayton had the temperament of an angel with a face to match. Shrugging, Keegan said, "I've never understood the female mind and probably never will. I believe our business will be finished, Mr. Farber, when you pay me."

Farber nodded and opened a drawer in his desk. He handed a bankdraft to the man, and watched as Keegan read it carefully before putting it in his pocket. "If you're interested, I have another job for you," he said casually.

Keegan stood up. "I have some new business already lined up." He didn't, but just talking with Farber left a bad taste in his mouth.

"I want you to go to Santa Fe and bring Miss Clayton back." Farber opened another drawer and pulled out a small portrait in an oval frame. He handed it across the desk.

Keegan was ready with a firm refusal, but took the picture out of curiosity. The young woman who stared back at him had an arresting face. However, it was the soft blue eyes that drew him in, giving him a glimpse of her soul. Farber had given him a description of her, but nothing prepared him for the visual impact. It would be a mistake to take this job, he told himself. "I suppose if the price is right, I might think about it," Keegan said slowly.

Long after Keegan left, Jonas Farber sat thinking about the Clayton situation. McLaird, his superior at the bank, was not at all pleased that Miss Clayton, the heiress to one of the largest fortunes in the city, had vanished. Her money and her welfare had been the responsibility of the bank, and as he saw it, Farber had been an incompetent fool. McLaird wanted her back, before any unfortunate publicity could taint the bank's reputation.

Jonas heaved himself up out of his chair and picked up a flat, silk fan from the desk. He fanned himself vigorously for a moment, and gazed out the second-story window at the heat waves shimmering on the street below. St. Louis in August was brutal. For a moment, he wished fervently that he could go after Sara himself. Just pack a few changes of clothes and go west to find freedom . . . and Sara. There were those who envied him, Farber thought with a disgusted snort. He was vice president of a bank, lived in a stately home, had a socially active wife and six healthy children. That was the picture everyone saw. The reality was quite different. McLaird, a dour Scotsman, made his life miserable with nit-picking complaints and a self-righteous attitude. The old bastard had found out about one of Farber's liaisons with a prostitute, and had been

227

watching him like a hawk ever since. McLaird was suspicious about Sara Clayton, but could prove nothing. And then there was his wife, Martha. She had firmly locked him out of her bedroom ten years ago, saying his sexual habits were disgusting. He wouldn't have turned to other women if Martha would have played the games he had tried to introduce in their marriage bed. He sighed, the fan still moving briskly, stirring a hot breeze. Much of their wealth had come from her family, so everything hinged on his wife and his boss. His children gave him no comfort either. They whined and complained incessantly. There was no peace in his life.

Although he had showed Keegan the portrait of Sara as a means of enticing him to take the job, Farber felt a stab of jealousy as he recalled the man's rapt expression. Sara was his, Farber thought fiercely. And he intended to have her, one way or another.

At her first sight of the city of Santa Fe, Sara had the strange feeling that she was coming home. Perhaps Max's descriptive letters made the place seem familiar, or maybe in a past life she had lived here. Sara didn't know the reason, but the feeling was strong. It would have been a happy homecoming, she mused to herself, if only Rafael was by her side.

He was, however, riding up ahead with the soldiers escorting the caravans. Sara's eyes caressed his dark head and broad shoulders, as he rode the black stallion. He was still angry with her, and she didn't blame him, but oh, how she missed the warmth of his smile. She turned her attention back to the sweeping panorama before her. The valley to the northwest was dotted with occasional groups of trees, skirted with corn and wheat fields. Here and there, square, blocklike adobes reared in the midst. In the background, the Sangre de Cristo mountains rose in snow-covered peaks, overlooking the verdant valley where the city of Santa Fe nestled.

"Well, señorita, what do you think of our city?" Señor Pina asked, watching the play of emotion on her expressive face as they rode along.

"It's more beautiful than I imagined, señor," she said, giving him a smile.

He nodded, pleased with her answer. *Sí,* he thought with satisfaction, she was going to make a wonderful wife for Rafael.

When they had descended the last mile of the table-plain, and the lively market town came into view, all traces of weariness left Sara. They entered the plaza's east side and crossed San Francisco Street. She caught a glimpse of the cathedral, before they turned toward the customhouse. This building was flanked by shops, as were the other sides of the public square, except where a street broke the continuous line. All the buildings were shaded by wide *portales,* or porch roof.

As their wagons rolled to a stop, a soldier approached Rafael, who was dismounting. Sara could not hear their exchange, but a moment later, the soldier saluted and walked away. Rafael moved in their direction and asked Pedro to take charge of the paperwork at the customhouse. He then turned to Sara. "The governor has requested that we take refreshments at his palace."

"That sounds lovely, Rafael, but you need not include me. I could perhaps be of some help to Señor Pino," she offered.

Rafael shook his head. "The invitation was not mine, señorita. Governor Chavez had reports about you from the couriers he dispatched to our caravan. I'm told he is anxious to meet you."

Sara pushed at some stray tendrils of hair that had escaped her braid. She wished she looked more presentable to meet the most important man in the territory. "I cannot imagine why he wishes to see me, but I will be happy to attend."

Rafael knew why as he gazed at her. Even with trail dust coating her, she was beautiful beyond compare. Despite the hat she wore religiously, her face had turned golden with the sun, while her hair was streaked with several shades of silver. He turned away before she read the longing in his eyes. "I will fetch Doña Josefina and Estella if you are ready?"

The four of them were soon crossing the plaza. Sara was fascinated by the bustle and unique sights that met her eyes. There was a man driving a strange-looking cart loaded with sacks of grain, while another short, swarthy man, dressed in white cotton pants and shirt, led a string of burros carrying firewood. Many of the shopkeepers had their brightly colored goods displayed in front of their stores in neat rows. In the northeast corner of the plaza, a stand of cottonwood trees provided shade for some little boys at play. Sara saw some mutton hanging from a tree limb, while round loaves of bread and various fruits were displayed on wool blankets on the ground. The sounds of the vendors, hawking their wares, blended with children's voices and gay fandango music from the cantinas. There was too much to be taken in all at once.

Sara was curious about the open ditch filled with water that flowed in front of the covered porch on the western side of the plaza, and Estella explained, "The water is brought from a nearby swamp for drinking and washing." Sara realized now that she hadn't seen a well in the center of the plaza, as there had been in San Miguel. She followed the two women across a wide wooden plank placed over the water, and past two soldiers who stood guard outside the door of the palace.

The exterior of the building looked no different than the rest of the buildings around the plaza, but inside she could see that the furnishings in the anteroom, along with the wool rugs on the floors, were elegant and of the finest quality. A soldier led them down a wide hallway to the governor's private apartments. In an undertone, Estella told her the palace also contained a prison, offices, a guard-room, and a large ballroom located on the upper floor.

Finally, the guard held open a heavily carved wooden door for them. Sara was impressed with the large *sala* they entered. It was richly furnished with velvet sofas and chairs, wool rugs, and dark wooden tables. On the far side of the room, a doorway opened onto a courtyard, and sun streamed in through two tall windows flanking the door.

Before Sara had time to comment on the lovely room to Estella, a middle-aged man in a uniform stepped into the room from the patio. His red coat, white pants, and black boots were immaculate, his smile cordial. *"Bievenido. Mi casa e su casa."* He came forward and took Doña Josefina's hand, kissing it. "I trust your journey was a good one, Señora Perez?"

Doña Josefina smiled almost coquettishly. *Sí*, your Excellency, but Estella and I are happy to be home."

Governor Chavez then took Estella's hand, placing a brief kiss on it. "You are looking well, señorita."

Sara noted that Estella dipped her head respectfully, and dropped a small curtsey as she murmured a reply. He moved to Sara then, and Rafael, who had stood by quietly, stepped forward and introduced her formally. "Your Excellency, may I present Señorita Sara Clayton. Señorita, his Excellency, Governor Jose Antonio Chavez."

Sara extended her hand and smiled. "It is an honor, your Excellency," she said, following Estella's example by dropping a curtsey.

"The honor and pleasure are mine, señorita," he said, his voice deep and robust. His eyes lit with admiration as he continued, "My men spoke of your great beauty, but they did not do you justice."

Sara blushed at his lavish praise, murmuring, *"Gracias.* You and your men are most kind to a stranger in your land."

His wide smile flashed in his dark face. "I hope you will not remain a stranger, Señorita Clayton.

You have brought sunshine to Santa Fe, and I hereby adopt you into our community."

Sara was completely charmed by his grand manners and warm welcome. Again she thanked him. He exchanged cordial greetings with Rafael, and then bade them sit. A servant woman entered the room with a tray and placed it on a low table next to the settee. The governor sat down beside Sara and nodded to the servant. The woman poured steaming chocolate from a silver pot into dainty china cups and began passing them to each guest.

Rafael asked for news. The governor shrugged and said that all had been fairly quiet since Rafael's departure.

"Your grandfather stopped in to visit two weeks ago, however, and told me there had been several more deaths among the mine workers," the older man said.

Rafale's eyebrows rose. "Was there an accident?"

"No. These men suffered from some sort of fever, the manager of the mine reported. It seems they died before a doctor could be summoned. Don Vicente is worried, for there were several deaths before, I believe."

Rafael nodded. "That's correct, Excellency. It is beginning to sound like an epidemic. I trust Don Vicente had called for a doctor to look into this."

"*Sí*. That was one of the reasons he came to town that day." The governor glanced at the ladies, who were quietly sipping their chocolate, and apologized. "Forgive me for bringing up such a subject in your presence. We will talk of more pleasant things, eh?" Turning to Sara, he said, "I was told that you are to teach the children on Hacienda Delgado."

"*Sí*, Excellency. I have been practicing my Spanish, so that I can understand my students."

"I think Don Vicente will be pleased with Don Rafael's choice of a teacher," he assured her graciously. "I am puzzled, though, as to why you traveled so far to take this post? If, that is, I am not being too personal?"

Sara smiled. "Not at all, sir. My brother spoke in such glowing terms of this area, that I longed to see it. He lived here for two years before he was killed in a mine accident."

The governor frowned for a moment. "It is no wonder the name sounded familiar to me! I remember now. I had just taken this post when the accident occurred, and the young *norteamericano* was killed. Please accept my sympathies, Señorita Clayton."

She nodded and took a sip of her chocolate, as the governor mentioned a mutual friend to Doña Josefina. As the conversation moved away from her, Sara breathed a sigh of relief. Her pleasure at arriving in Santa Fe was beginning to diminish. It was a strain to act normal in Rafael's presence, and the mention of Max had sent her spirits on a downward spiral.

She stole a glance from under her thick lashes at Rafael, sitting across from her. He was telling the governor what his caravan had brought back. The sound of his deep-timbred voice sent involuntary shivers over her skin. Never far from her thoughts was the pain of her loss. Her only hope was that she would not be in his company too much when they reached Hacienda Delgado. She didn't think she could bear to be near him.

After a while, Rafael stood up. "I regret that we must leave your gracious company, your Excellency, but we should be on the road if we are to reach home before dark."

The others stood up and thanked their host for his hospitality. The governor offered his arm to Doña Josefina as they walked toward the anteroom, which left Rafael to escort Sara and Estella. Sara's hand on his arm sent waves of longing through him, while her lavender scent brought unbidden images of her to play in his tortured mind. He struck down his desire, reminding himself that she was a shallow woman.

When they emerged into the sunlight, Sara quickly let go of Rafael's arm. She had felt him stiffen as she took his proffered arm, but propriety had forced them together. Touching him had been pleasure as well as pain.

Governor Chavez spoke a few polite words with each of them again, and parted with, "I am sending an escort of soldiers with both your parties. And please remember I am at your disposal, should you ever need me for anything."

As they crossed the plaza toward their wagons, Estella turned to Sara. "I have enjoyed our journey together, Sara, and will miss your company. When you have the opportunity, I would be pleased if you would pay me a visit."

She noticed that Doña Josefina didn't echo the invitation, but she smiled at Estella. "I, too, am glad we've become friends. I will certainly try to pay a call, and you must stop by to see me." They had reached the carriage, and the two young women hugged each other. In a hurried whisper, Sara said, "You must let me know how things go with Garth." Estella gave her friend a subtle nod.

Sara said a brief goodbye to Doña Josefina, and then turned away. Rafael had moved on to arrange details with his men, so Sara waited in the shade of the *portales*. Garth and Matt found her there.

"What are your plans now?" she asked the two of them.

Garth shrugged. "I'm taking up residence at one of the cantinas for now." He glanced briefly in Estella's direction. "Later, who knows?"

Matt pushed up his spectacles. "I'll be staying in town also. My fingers are itching to paint a dozen different things at once."

Sara laughed. "What about my portrait? I suppose I've already been forgotten?"

Unexpectedly, the artist leaned over and kissed her cheek. "My favorite subject? I haven't forgotten."

Sara was touched by his show of affection. Tears stung her eyes as she hugged and admonished the two of them to pay her a visit at the hacienda. They departed with promises to do just that, as Rafael approached.

"It is time to depart, señorita. Carlos has a horse ready for you, unless you would prefer riding in the wagon?" he asked, treating her with the formality that had marked the first days of their journey.

Sara followed his lead with a polite nod. "Thank you. I believe I will ride." She made her way to the *vaquero* and let him assist her into the saddle. She waited for two of their armed guards to take the lead beside Rafael, and then she fell in behind.

Once they left the town, they followed the road south to the region known as Río Abajo, or lower river area, Carlos explained. He rode beside her, and she suspected he had been ordered to do so as her personal guard. "How long will it take us to reach the hacienda," she asked him.

"Not more than two hours, señorita, but if you become tired, Don Rafael has ordered that we stop to rest."

Sara nodded and felt a painful twist in her stomach. Even though he was angry with her, he still worried over her well-being. She wanted to weep over their situation. Instead, she concentrated on the scenery to put it out of her mind. The rainy season, which started in July, Carlos told her, would be over by the end of October, just a month away. Due to the rains, there was much greenery and blooming wildflowers to be seen along the road, although very few trees. Brownish red patches of sand were interspersed with the vegetation, while a deep blue sky formed a brilliant canopy over the landscape. And everpresent were the majestic peaks of the Sangre de Cristo Mountains to the east. It was little wonder that Max had loved this area, Sara thought. It was wild and beautiful.

Occasionally they passed wheat fields that stretched as far as the eye could see, and Carlos explained that in such cases, a hacienda was close by. The Río del Norte meandered close to the road in some places, and then disappeared behind mesas or canyons at other points. Sara tried to keep her thoughts on these new sights, but her gaze rested on Rafael more than once.

One of the rear guards rode up next to Sara after an hour of travel, and introduced himself. "I am Capt. Mariano de Silva, señorita."

Sara smiled. "Sara Clayton, Captain. I'm pleased to meet you." She liked the friendly flash of his white smile beneath a thick mustache. She guessed him to be about Rafael's age.

"We will be stopping for a rest shortly, and I am at your disposal, should you need anything," he offered, his dark eyes resting warmly on her face.

"Why, thank you, Captain de Silva, I'll remember that. However, just having you and your men along makes me feel very safe." She gave him another smile, as he saluted and returned to the rear.

The party stopped alongside the river under a stand of cottonwoods. Carlos helped Sara down and took her horse to water. She walked idly down to the edge of the river and stooped to wash her hands.

"Allow me, Señorita Clayton," Captain de Silva said, reaching down to grasp her elbow. Helping her up, he then produced a clean handkerchief from his coat pocket and offered it.

Sara thanked him and dried her hands. When she tried to hand it back, he shook his head. "Keep it, *por favor*. You may have need of it before we reach the hacienda."

He walked back up the bank with her, asking her impressions of the trail and Santa Fe. Sara felt more at ease as they spoke of general topics. When it was time to move on, the captain helped Sara mount. Carlos fell in beside her as they moved off. Captain de Silva moved to her other side to continue their conversation. He remained thus until they arrived at the hacienda.

After they turned off the main track, it took a quarter hour to reach the small valley where the large quadrangle adobe structure sat like a king on a throne. Sara fell in love with Hacienda Delgado at first sight. The massive, red-brown walls rose from earth of the same color to dominate the surrounding meadows. Hazy hills climbed gracefully in the background, along with distant mesas that flattened out against the horizon in a brown line. The incline they traveled allowed her to see pointed towers on all four corners of the rectangle. In the late afternoon sun, the glint of something shiny flashed from one of the towers, and Sara commented to Captain de Silva about this.

"Most likely it was the sunlight reflecting off the guard's gun, señorita. The larger *ranchos* are rarely attacked, but it is because they take these precautions."

As they drew closer, Sara could see the tall iron gates with intricate designs in the walls abutting them. Off to the right, rolling down a winding track, was a line of wagons moving toward the hacienda, loaded with freshly harvested corn.

A guard in one of the front towers called down an order to open the gates. Their party passed through the thick-walled tunnel into an enormous courtyard. Sara was amazed to find it quite as large as the central plaza in Santa Fe. Servants came forward to take the horses. Captain de Silva dismounted and moved to help Sara down before Carlos had a chance, causing Sara to blush at his obvious attention. She stepped back and looked around at the bustling activity going on. It reminded her again of the city of Santa Fe. There was a kitchen and bakehouse, where many dark-skinned women moved to and fro. Several large dome-shaped ovens of clay sat in front of these buildings. Sara heard the clang of a blacksmith shop, and saw several Indian women spinning wool on a large wheel.

Rafael moved to her side and nodded to the captain. "We would be honored if you and your men would stay for refreshments."

Sara glanced up at Rafael in surprise when he took her arm possessively. He had been carefully avoiding her since San Miguel. She couldn't help but notice that while his words were correct and polite to the captain, they lacked warmth. She looked from one man to the other.

"*Gracias,* Don Rafael. We are pleased to accept," the captain said with a broad smile. His eyes rested on Sara for a moment before he turned to the soldiers and spoke rapidly.

Rafael took that opportunity to steer Sara toward a set of wooden double doors at the back of the rectangle. An Indian servant opened them as they approached, and to Sara's surprise, she saw that they were entering a smaller private courtyard. A stone fountain bubbled in the center, and several trees provided shade for the benches. Flower beds were filled with bright blooms, and pots hanging from the *portales* overflowed with flowers. This courtyard was quite large, with many ornately carved doors leading off it on the first floor, and the second floor as well. A set of steps in the northwest corner led up to the covered porch from the outside.

Rafael retained his hold on her arm. "The family apartments."

Sara looked up at him. "It's beautiful, Rafael. Everything here is so vastly different from home, so vivid and colorful. No wonder Max loved this area. He wrote the most descriptive letters to me. And I'm not a bit disappointed either."

The genuine pleasure that lit her beautiful face caught him off guard for a moment. He had a sudden urge to kiss her ripe mouth, to hold her close. Quelling that urge, he swallowed tightly. *"Gracias, Sara.* I am sure Don Vicente will be pleased that you like it," he replied in a neutral tone. Glancing over her head, he smiled. "Ah, Rosita! It is good to see you."

Sara turned to find a middle-aged Mexican woman coming toward them from the main doorway. Her dark hair was pulled back in a snug bun at the nape of her neck, and her smile was wide. She was wearing a white blouse and a full, red skirt with an apron at her waist.

The woman took Rafael's outstretched hand and pumped it happily, breaking into a torrent of Spanish. Sara followed her words for the most part as a welcome home speech. Rafael answered, and then pulled Sara forward. "Rosita, this is Señorita Sara Clayton, the new *profesora* for the children."

Sara smiled and held out her hand. "How do you do, Rosita?"

Shyly, the servant took her hand and nodded. "I am much pleased to meet you, señorita. Anything you need, please tell Rosita, eh?"

Sara's smile broadened. *"Sí, gracias."*

Captain de Silva and his men came though the gate at that moment, and Rafael led the way into the *sala*. It was cool and spacious. Sara noted a stone floor beneath her feet and scattered expensive wool rugs. The furniture was large, dark, and heavily carved in the Spanish style. The stark white walls were covered at the bottom with a brightly colored woven cloth. Sara had already learned in San Miguel that this practice was for keeping the sticky whitewash off the occupants in the household. However, it made a lovely decoration as well.

"Make yourselves comfortable, *por favor,*" Rafael said to his guests. "Rosita will bring refreshments."

Sara chose the settee facing the back wall, so that she could look at the paintings hanging there. Captain de Silva managed to sit beside her and received a frown from Rafael. "Hacienda Delgado is the most beautiful *rancho* in the Río Abajo, señorita. Perhaps I could take you for a tour of the area sometime," the captain said to her.

Before she could answer, Rafael spoke up. "Don Vincente will most likely want to do that, Captain." The smile he gave the officer did not reach his eyes.

Captain de Silva nodded respectfully. *"Sí.* I was not thinking."

Sara felt the tension between the two men beginning to build when a distinguished older man strode into the room. He possessed a presence that would dominate most rooms; however, Rafael was a match for him, Sara felt. He had steel gray hair, a hawklike nose, and green eyes beneath craggy brows. He was attractive despite his irregular features. He was thicker through the middle than Rafael, but managed to look neat in his black Spanish suit with silver trim.

Rafael rose, as did the other men in the room. "Don Vicente. You are looking well," he said.

The older man walked forward and held out his hand formally to his grandson. "And you also, Rafael." They shook hands, and the older man turned immediately to his guests. *"Bienvenido.* Forgive me for not being here when you arrived. I have been to the mine today, and just returned."

Captain de Silva gave a courtly bow. "We understand perfectly, Don Vicente. I was sorry to hear you were having trouble out there."

The older man waved his hand dismissively. "I will sort it out." He glanced in Sara's direction. She smiled tentatively and stood up, smoothing her skirt.

The older man made his way to her and bowed over the hand she extended. "Señorita Clayton, welcome to my household. Pedro sent word of your arrival days ago, and I have been very anxious to meet you."

Sara smiled and dropped a small curtsey. *"Gracias,* Señor Delgado. I am happy to be here."

Vicente was pleased with what he saw. Pedro had chosen very well. "You must be tired from the journey, señorita. Would you rather be shown to your room now, and have refreshments there?"

Sara shook her head. *"Gracias,* but no, I'm fine. Actually, I had several days of rest after my accident." She sat down and the men followed suit.

Don Vicente took the large chair across from her. His bushy eyebrow had risen in surprise and question.

"Señor Pino didn't tell you?" she said.

"No, señorita. His message was brief. Tell me about it, *por favor,*" Don Vicente encouraged.

Sara wished she hadn't mentioned it, for all eyes in the room were on her. As briefly as possible, she related the story and ended with, "Don Rafael saved my life with his medicines and excellent care, señor."

Don Vicente glanced at his grandson, and then back at Sara. The two of them avoided glancing at each other. "Rafael is very gifted with herbs. I am truly glad he was there when this happened."

Sara thought she saw a spark of pride in the older man's eyes, but he turned away, and she couldn't tell for sure.

Rosita brought in a pot of chocolate and some pastries. While they ate, Don Vicente kept the conversation flowing, asking questions about the trip, and also drawing the soldiers into the talk with comments about Santa Fe. Sara noticed that Rafael sat stiffly and said very little. After a while, Captain de Silva and the other soldiers rose to leave.

The captain made a grand show of kissing Sara's hand as he took leave of her. "Until we meet again, señorita," he murmured.

Don Vicente glanced at Rafael out of the corner of his eye, and noted the grim tightening in his grandson's mouth. A thoughtful smile curved his own mouth as he said, "When you find yourself in the area, stop in to see us, Captain."

The captain gave Sara's flushed countenance one

last lingering look. *"Gracias,* Señor Delgado. I will do just that."

When the men had gone, Vicente rang the bell for Rosita and turned to Sara. "I am sorry my sister Ines was not here to greet you. A friend of hers was taken very ill, and she was called to her bedside this morning. Also, my nephew Manolo stayed behind at the mine today, but should be here at the dinner hour."

"I understand, Don Vicente. Thank you once again for your hospitality," Sara said demurely and turned to Rafael. "I must thank you also, Don Rafael, for your many kindnesses on the journey."

Rafael nodded stiffly. *"De nada,* señorita. I was but doing my job."

Sara felt depressed all of a sudden, at the facade they were forced to maintain. It was almost as if they were strangers. She took her leave and followed Rosita out into the courtyard, and up the steps to the second floor.

Chapter 11

"I think we should move Juan to the Indio Plata mine, Don Manolo. He was acting strange today when Don Vicente was here." Sancho Valdez, a wiry man with graying, dark hair, sat down at the crude table with a fresh bottle of wine and two glasses.

"I noticed that also, but he said nothing. If he had, his tongue would not still be residing in his mouth tonight," Manolo Delgado said casually, accepting a glass of wine from the mine manager.

"He knows that, señor, but these men all reach a point when they no longer care. They come to realize that escape is impossible, and life in the mines is no longer bearable. I, too, would not care, eh." The older man wiped the sweat from his face with a dirty handkerchief, and drained his glass.

The one-room adobe where Sancho Valdez lived, in Manolo's opinion, was little better than the prison quarters across the compound, where the majority of the workers were kept when not working. Most of their men came from the prisons at Chihuahua. The government was happy to sell the excess of criminals to mine owners. Not only did they make a little money, but they were not responsible for feeding these men any longer. Don Vicente also employed a few Pueblo Indians, but they tended to come and go, and could not be depended upon. Manolo refilled his glass and took a sip. "Perhaps you are right. Move him tomorrow, and do not tell the other prisoners anything. If we report one more false death, Tío Vicente may just bring the authorities into the investigation."

"There are other ways of getting the labor we need," Valdez pointed out. "My men could raid another Indian village."

Manolo shook his head. "Not now. Even isolated kidnappings will be reported. We do not want anyone to put together the pieces and discover our operation. We must lay low, and use the manpower we have at the moment. My bastard cousin, Rafael, has returned, and I have no doubt that Tío Vicente will alert him to the deaths at the mine. That half-breed is as cunning as a fox."

"Very well, Don Manolo. But we could be taking out much more silver with more labor," Valdez pointed out.

Manolo rose and turned toward the door. "So we get rich a few months later, *amigo.* No one knows the existence of our mine except us, and the poor beggers we kidnapped to work it, so there is no hurry. And besides, that mine is not the only worry I have at the moment. Your job is to keep everything

247

running smoothly at Tío Vicente's mine and ours. I do not want anyone snooping around."

Manolo did not wait for an answer. Valdez knew it was a command, and Don Manolo expected obedience. Sancho had known the younger man for fifteen years. He had been a *vaquero* in the days when Don Manolo's father owned a large hacienda north of Mexico City. Three years ago, however, a shift in government officials brought ruin to that branch of Delgados. Don Cristobal Delgado had lost his lands, his hacienda, and his government seat. The old man and his son had survived only by selling their vast herds of cattle and moving to the town house they owned in Mexico City. Sancho had chosen to go with his patron, not particularly out of loyalty, but because the work would be lighter than that of a *vaquero* for the new owner.

His life had begun to look brighter though, when Don Manolo had gone to visit his Tío Vicente two years ago and procured a job as mine manager for him. Don Manolo's plan was to ingratiate himself with the old man in hopes of inheriting. But the most wonderful thing had happened. The location of a hidden silver mine was disclosed to Sancho by an old Pueblo Indian, who was on his deathbed. Between himself and Don Manolo, they had found it and begun secret operations. They took some of Don Vicente's workers and faked their deaths. And they had kidnapped a few Pueblo Indians. They even had a norteamericano slaving away, making them rich.

Sancho walked to the doorway to watch the setting sun. Across the compound, the guards were marching the workers back to the barracks for the night, and he shuddered at their pitiful appearance. No, he did not blame them for giving up. He would die if forced into such an existence.

Sara felt like a new woman as she turned before the tall mirror in the corner of her bedroom. She had slept for two hours in the large, soft bed. A warm, scented bath in a real tub had been prepared for her. Her personal maid, Pepita, had shampooed her hair, and dressed it in a simple bun at the nape of her neck when it dried. Her formal gowns had been aired, pressed, and hung in the wardrobe. In short, she felt like a princess instead of a paid employee.

The blue satin gown she was wearing matched her eyes, and she wondered if Rafael would notice. Pepita had said the whole family would be there for dinner, so naturally Sara assumed that meant Rafael also. She wandered over to the door that opened onto the upstairs balcony, and stepped out. The evening breeze was refreshing and carried a little nip to it, promising colder weather in the next month or so. She looked out over the top of the roof at the sprinkling of stars in the black velvet sky. Dinner was served at a very late hour in the New Mexican province; Señor Pino had already explained this to her. She would be glad when he finished his business in Santa Fe, and returned to the hacienda. He had been a friend to her, and she needed his moral support.

Reentering her room, she picked up her white

wool shawl and draped it over her shoulders. She took the steps down to the courtyard, where lanterns hung at each end to light the dark path to the dining room. As she made her way around the fountain, a dark shadow detached itself from the trunk of a cottonwood tree, causing her to gasp.

"Sara." Rafael's deep voice sent a shiver down her spine. "I wanted a private word with you."

She pulled the shawl tighter in an effort to still the trembling of her body. She wanted to walk into the warmth of his strong arms, and stay there forever. Instead, she swallowed past the lump in her throat, and said, "Haven't we said everything already?"

"No, we have not," he replied evenly. He swept his arm toward a nearby stone bench that sat in shadow. "Could we sit a *momento, por favor?*"

Sara had been drinking in the sight of him, so handsome in a snug jacket and pants of fine red wool that fit his body like a glove. The soft moonlight caught the blue-black highlights in his hair. Acquiescing, she moved to the bench and sat down, folding her hands in her lap.

Rafael sat beside her and gazed at her bent head for a moment. "I have been thinking about our situation, Sara. I cannot in good conscience leave things as they are, and go on with my life as if nothing happened between us."

Sara's heartbeat quickened, but she forced herself to remember why she turned down his proposal before. She squeezed her eyes shut against the pain. "You must, Rafael. Circumstances being what they are, our decision was the best one."

250

"It was your decision—not mine," he said harshly, trying to hold onto his temper. "What if there is a baby? Have you thought of that?"

Sara wished there had been, for that would have taken the decision out of her hands. She forced her gaze up and caught a hint of anguish in his expression. "There isn't. I have proof of it."

Any small hope he had died with her firm words. "I see . . . however, that fact does not absolve me of my duty."

"I won't be anyone's *duty,* Rafael. And I don't wish to discuss this again," she said, standing up. If he pressed her more, she was afraid she would give in. "Would you kindly escort me in to dinner now?"

Her flat tone of voice ended the discussion. There was nothing more he could do at the moment, so he stood and offered his arm. Sara blinked back the tears that filled her eyes as they moved to the dining room.

Don Vicente was standing next to the fireplace that took up one corner of the elegant room. A beautiful, black wrought-iron chandelier above the table was lit with many candles, while a cheery fire crackled in the grate, softly lighting the room. He and the two people with him turned as Rafael and Sara entered the room. They were all in formal dress. The young man had light brown hair and a handsome face. He was as tall as Rafael, but not as muscular. The woman's steel gray hair was pulled up in an elaborate coiffure, with a tortoiseshell comb securing it. Her black silk dress was matronly, yet stylish. When her eyes rested on Rafael, she smiled, her face growing softer with genuine affection.

"Buenas noches, Sara, Rafael," Don Vicente greeted them, and moved forward to take Sara's hand. He bowed over it and placed a brief kiss there, as Sara nodded and murmured a polite response. "Let me introduce you, señorita."

"This is my sister, Doña Ines Isabel Morales. And this young man is my nephew, Don Manolo Delgado. Señorita Sara Clayton, our new *profesora."*

"I am happy to meet both of you," she said, dropping a small curtsey.

Manolo's eyes lit with obvious admiration as he kissed her hand. "The pleasure is all mine, señorita. I only wish I was a *muchacho* again, so that I might attend your school."

Sara felt Rafael stiffen at her side as she smiled. "That could be risky, señor. I might be a very stern teacher."

"One who has the face of an angel would surely have the temperament as well," Manolo replied smoothly.

Rafael spoke up then. "I see my cousin has not lost his ability to charm the señoritas." He moved around Sara to kiss his aunt on the cheek. "I have missed you, Tía Ines. I trust you have been well?"

Sara noticed that the hint of sarcasm left Rafael's voice when he spoke to his aunt. The older woman gave his cheek a loving pat. "For an old woman, *sí.* And I have missed you."

Don Vicente offered his arm to Sara. "Shall we sit down now?" Sara smiled and allowed him to seat her at the long table. She was on his right side, and

252

Rafael seated his aunt on the left of her brother.

Polished silver, exquisite china, and fragile crystal graced the white linen tablecloth. Sara wondered if the formal setting was used every night, or tonight because it was a homecoming celebration. The New Mexicans, she had found, were very formal in their speech and manners. Don Vicente rang a small silver bell, and almost immediately, two servants appeared, one with a bottle of wine and the other with a cold soup.

Rafael, who was sitting beside his aunt, turned to her. "How is Doña Lucia, Tía?"

The older woman shook her head sadly. "I fear the end is near for her. The doctor said she will not last another week. Her heart has been bad for a long time, Rafael."

He nodded. "I will go see her tomorrow." Glancing over at Sara, he said, "Doña Lucia is Estella's grandmother. She is Señor Perez's madre."

"What a shame. Estella mentioned to me once that her grandmother lived with them, and wasn't well. The way she spoke, I believe she is quite fond of her."

Manolo changed the subject with a question for Sara about her home. Sara talked about St. Louis and her family, but then asked about the children she would be teaching.

Doña Ines was enthusiastic about the project. "My brother has provided two rooms for your use, and I had them cleaned thoroughly. However, we wanted to wait to furnish them, until we got some idea of what you want."

253

"That was very thoughtful of you. Perhaps you could show them to me tomorrow, and we could decide," Sara said with a smile. She was relieved that Doña Ines wanted to help with the school. Now she did not feel so alone.

"By all means, look over your classrooms, señorita," Don Vicente said. "However, take a few days to rest and see your surroundings before you begin serious work, eh?"

Sara smiled. "*Gracias,* señor. I would love to see your *rancho.* Everything is so beautiful here."

"I am at your disposal, señorita. When would you like to take a tour?" Manolo offered immediately.

"Since you are quite busy at the moment, Manolo, I will take her," Don Vicente said, and then smiled to soften his words.

Manolo gave a mock grimace. "As you wish, Tío. However, now that Rafael is back, the workload will be lightened. I am glad you made it before the fall roundup, cousin."

"It is a large undertaking, but one I look forward to," Rafael said. "By next week, the harvesting will be done. Everyone will then be free for the roundup."

Don Vicente turned to Sara. "I have been thinking that it would be better if you open the school after roundup is completed, señorita. The older children help during this time, and the younger ones enjoy the excitement."

"Whatever you wish. I was told about this event, señor, and I am looking forward to it."

"As Rafael said, it is a lot of work, but everyone

254

enjoys the fiesta that follows," Don Vicente said.

They were served several more courses, while conversation flowed lightly around the table. It was nearly midnight when they rose to retire.

At mid-morning, Sara found Doña Ines in the large *sala* doing needlework. "It's lovely. What is it for?" Sara asked, looking over the older woman's shoulder.

"It is an altar cloth for our small chapel here at the *rancho*. For most holy days, we try to travel into Santa Fe to hear mass, but it is not convenient to go there all the time." Doña Ines rose and moved her needlework frame next to the wall, and then took a seat beside Sara on the settee. "Rosita will be here any moment with my morning chocolate. Won't you join me?"

"*Sí.* I would love to. And then perhaps, we could take a look at the new schoolrooms," Sara suggested with a smile.

Rosita arrived with the refreshments and then withdrew. Sara and Doña Ines talked for a time about books, slates, and maps for the children. "My brother will send to Mexico City for whatever you need. Our store in town will provide some things to begin with."

"Do you know how many children there will be? Perhaps we could make a list," Sara suggested.

A short time later, the two women were looking over the two spacious rooms off the main courtyard, and making plans. Doña Ines commissioned one of

255

the servant boys who could read and write to visit each household on the hacienda, for a head count of all the children.

The two women then visited the carpenter's shop. Sara explained to him that she wanted several low tables built, and small stools. Visiting the *rancho* storeroom next, they found some heavy black and white wool rugs for the dirt floors. By the time they had seen them installed, it was time for the noon meal. After freshening up, Sara met the others in the dining room.

She was disappointed to find Rafael absent. Don Vicente rang the bell to begin. "I hear you have been very busy this morning," he said to Sara.

"*Sí*, señor. I think it's probably a good thing we are waiting until the roundup is over to begin. There is much to do, and books to be ordered," she replied enthusiastically.

"Do not hesitate to ask for anything you need. I want the children to have the proper supplies," he said.

As Manolo gave a brief account of the morning's labors, Sara watched Don Vicente from beneath her lashes. He was not the ogre she had expected. So far he had been charming, cordial, and generous. Yet, he did seem somewhat distant with Rafael. And she hadn't forgotten the story Rafael had told of his childhood. It was very hard to reconcile the two images of the man.

Rafael entered the dining room with apologies halfway through the meal. He took his place across from Sara, but refrained from looking at her. "Doña

256

Lucia passed away this morning, while I was there. The mass for her will be said in the family chapel the day after tomorrow."

Doña Ines's eyes misted, but she held her emotions in check. "I will miss her. For twenty years we have been friends."

"I'm glad Estella got home before she passed away. Would it be all right if I attended the funeral with you? I would like to offer my sympathies to Estella . . . and the rest of the family, of course," Sara asked.

Don Vicente assured her it was all right, and then asked, "Would you like to take a ride today after siesta? I was going to look over the fields that have been harvested."

"Thank you, yes," she agreed. Glancing at Rafael as she sipped her wine, she felt an acute sense of loss. Twice now, he had proposed marriage to her, and twice she had turned him down. Being noble had its disadvantages, she thought miserably.

Sara followed Don Vicente's lead as they galloped across the northern meadow toward the low hills. The sun was warm, but a cool breeze made the weather in the valley nearly perfect. The vegetation was green and thriving, but patchy. As they climbed farther into the hills, however, the growth became thicker, and the trees were more abundant.

The track they rode on was wide and well used. They soon reached a mesa that flattened out as far as the eye could see. Here were the corn fields, some harvested, some waiting to be cut. "There's so much of it," Sara said, shading her eyes as she gazed out over the vast area.

"Corn is a staple in our diet, señorita. It takes a lot to feed all my people, as well as the animals. I raise enough to sell in my store also," he explained.

Sara saw countless workers cutting the corn, while others loaded it onto wagons. Back at the hacienda, there were just as many people engaged in other tasks. "Taking care of so many people is a big responsibility, señor. Doesn't it ever make you nervous?"

He smiled and removed his hat, smoothing his hair back before he put it on again. "Not as long as there is plenty of rain for the crops, and there are no cases of disease that may wipe out my herds, or threats of Indian uprisings."

Sara chuckled. "In other words, yes, it does make you nervous at times. It was a silly question."

"It is not silly, señorita. Feel free to ask me anything you like. It's just that I have been doing this for so many years, it is second nature. I came here as a young man with my bride, all the way from Spain. Land grants were being given to those who could afford to make the journey and finance their own start in the new land. I was the youngest son in a family of six boys and four girls, so there was not much to be expected in the way of inheritance. My family did, however, finance our start here. The rest was up to me."

"I would say you didn't let them down, Don Vicente," she said.

He was gazing off into the distance in a distracted way. "But it made me a hard man. I have hurt those I love," he murmured, almost to himself.

If he realized this, Sara thought, he was most likely trying to make amends to Rafael by choosing a wife for him. If the old man didn't care, he wouldn't see his grandson's loneliness. "A weak man could not have survived, nor carved out a home in this land, Don Vicente," she pointed out.

He turned and gave her a grim smile. "You have a kind heart, to make such a generous excuse for me."

Sara shrugged. "It's the truth, señor, however, it is never too late to change. If you see a wrong, right it."

Don Vicente shook his head as if perplexed. "I do not know what has come over me, Señorita Clayton. I have never expressed such private thoughts to anyone, and here I am doing so to a stranger!"

Sara smiled. "It's not just you, señor. My tutor, Master Filbert, used to tell me that I have a sympathetic spirit, and people recognize that. They tell me secrets and confide in me, without any conscious encouragement on my part."

Don Vicente cleared his throat self-consciously. "Forgive my lapse in manners, *por favor?* We should get on with the tour."

Sara let the subject drop, and followed him down the track with mixed emotions. On the one hand, she was happy that Rafael and his grandfather might mend their fences . . . and on the other hand, she saw a bleak future for herself without the man she loved.

*   *   *

Doña Lucia was laid to rest in the family cemetery, with an abundance of family and friends attending the service. The governor was there with his military escort, and Sara was surprised to see Garth and Matt.

Estella wept silent tears, and Sara sensed that Garth wanted to comfort her, but didn't dare with her mother hovering about.

In the family courtyard, several tables were set up and filled with food for the mourners. Sara had stepped back unnoticed in the shade of a tree, while Don Vicente and the rest of the family were engaged in conversation with neighbors. She watched as Garth spoke briefly with Estella, and then made his way over to her. "Walk with me, Sara. I need to talk to you," he urged in an undertone.

She nodded and took his arm. "Of course. Let's get something to drink."

As they moved across the courtyard toward the wine table, Garth bent his head to whisper, "Estella and I want to elope, and you've got to help us."

Sara's eyebrows rose. "I thought you were going to approach her father about marrying her?"

He shook his head, but waited to answer until he had retrieved two glasses of wine for them and moved away from the table to a quiet spot. "It's too late for that, Sara. As soon as they got home, Estella's mother sent a letter to her betrothed, finalizing the marriage plans. When Estella asked her if I could call on her father, Doña Josefina told her what she'd done, and that the marriage would take place after the first of the year. Apparently,

Doña Josefina was shrewd enough to guess our intentions."

"I was hoping she had softened where you're concerned, but I should have known better. How can I help?" Sara said, giving a perfunctory smile to Captain de Silva, who was looking at her from across the courtyard.

"For a while, I'm afraid, Doña Josefina will be keeping a close eye on Estella, but I've told Estella to pretend to go along with her mother's plans. Sooner or later, the old lady will let her guard down, and Estella will be allowed to come visit you. When that happens, send word to me, *pronto,* and I will come spirit her away." He downed his wine in one gulp, and gave her a grim smile.

"What if Doña Josefina forbids her to visit me?" Sara asked skeptically.

"Perhaps you could ask Don Vicente or his sister to extend an invitation?" he asked, a desperate gleam in his eyes.

Sara took pity on him. "Rest easy, Garth. I'll work something out and send word to you. Now, I don't think we should let Doña Josefina see us together."

"I am staying at LaFonda Inn," he whispered.

With that, Sara walked away. Rafael intercepted her as she made her way toward his aunt.

"You collect admirers like flowers collect bees, Sara," he said in an undertone. "Captain de Silva has been waiting for you to finish with Prescott so that *he* could claim you, but I want a word first." He took her arm and steered her toward the open door to the *sala.*

261

Sara got a brief glimpse of the captain moving in their direction, as Rafael whisked her away. His actions were high-handed, to say the least, but his touch on her arm sent jolts of pleasure through her. She was also curious about what he wanted. "Where are we to go—"

"Some place private," he interrupted shortly. Sara refrained from snapping at him when she noticed that a few of the older people were taking advantage of the coolness in the dim room. She really couldn't bring herself to make a scene, especially on this solemn occasion.

He guided her through a doorway, down a long hallway and into a smaller *sala,* which was deserted. Sara turned to face him. "Now, will you tell me why you dragged me in here without my permission?"

"As long as you work for the Delgado family, señorita, you will not encourage these suitors without a chaperone," he said, his dark eyes flashing angrily.

Sara was stunned for a moment, her mind refusing to accept what her ears had just heard. "Wha . . . what are you saying, Rafael?"

"Señor Prescott and Captain de Silva. If you are not careful, Sara, they will be at each other's throats, or dueling over you," he said harshly.

"They are not my suitors! You know Garth is in love with Estella! And besides that, there were countless people around while I was talking to him," she protested, smarting from his attack.

"I have eyes, Sara. I saw the way both men looked at you—as if you were the only woman in the world," he ground out between clenched teeth.

He was jealous, Sara realized suddenly. It soothed her pride and cooled her building anger. Her expression softened, as she laid her hand on his arm. "I have no feelings for these men except friendship, Rafael. And if I've overstepped the bounds of propriety, I apologize."

Her soft apology melted his anger. He stared into her eyes for a moment, and then sighed heavily. Caressing her face with his fingertips, he said, "Forgive me, *por favor*. You have done nothing, sweet Sara. I am behaving like a jackass."

Sara's heartbeat quickened at his gentle touch. She could barely breathe as he slipped an arm around her waist and slowly pulled her close to his body. Their eyes were locked, and neither could remember why they should not be doing this. Rafael's mouth descended to Sara's, and her moist lips parted. There was a throbbing ache in the lower part of Rafael's body that soon became an intolerable pain.

Sara welcomed the warmth of his body against her own. The masculine smell that was Rafael filled her nostrils, making her dizzy with desire. His hands moved over her back and down to pull her hips closer to his, leaving her in no doubt as to how quickly he had become aroused.

The intensity of this brief contact shook both of them as the kiss ended. Sara broke away and stepped back to compose herself, smoothing her dress. "We mustn't—" she began in a shaky voice.

"*Sí*, Sara. You do not have to remind me that we

cannot touch each other," he cut in. "I forgot for a moment that I am not suitable for you."

Sara wanted to weep for the bitterness she heard in his voice. However, she couldn't tell him the truth, so she let it stand. Raising her eyes, she said softly, "You're a fine man, Rafael. Someday soon, there will be a woman who will appreciate you."

For a moment, Rafael was confused by the anguish he saw in her large blue eyes. She said one thing, and her eyes said another. Taking her arm, he escorted her back the way they had come. "Obviously, it will be someone with less exacting standards than yours, eh?"

Sara let that remark pass. When they reached the courtyard, Rafael left her with his aunt and made his way to Estella's side. Sara watched the two of them move to a stone bench against the wall for a private conversation.

Doña Ines was watching the couple also and commented, "I once thought they would make a perfect couple, but I suppose there is nothing more than friendship between them."

"I believe Rafael is still mourning his wife," Sara said.

"He loved her, sí. But Rafael is ready to love again, and it will only take the right woman to stir his heart. I have a feeling that will be soon," Doña Ines replied quietly.

Sara missed the speculative glance the older woman turned on her.

After a while, the mourners began to take their leave. Manolo and Captain de Silva both insisted on escorting Sara to her carriage. Manolo managed to maneuver himself into the position of helping Sara inside, while Captain de Silva was left to assist Doña Ines. *"Gracias,* Captain. Do not let us keep you. I see his Excellency is ready to depart," the older woman said, nodding to the approaching governor. Captain de Silva said goodbye to Sara and took his leave reluctantly. Doña Ines then turned to Manolo. "Could you see what is keeping Vicente, nephew?"

"Doña Josefina asked for a private word with him, Tía Ines. I am sure he will be along shortly," he answered, not wanting to leave Sara's side.

"Just tell him, *por favor,* that we are waiting in the carriage. You know how Doña Josefina can go on and on," she insisted.

Courtesy forbade him to refuse, so he sighed and left to do her bidding. When he was out of earshot, Doña Ines smiled. "I thought perhaps that you could use a rest from those two. Forgive me if I was wrong."

Sara laughed. "They are both charming, but, a little overwhelming." She sobered as Rafael came into sight on his horse. "I am not ready to be courted, señora."

Doña Ines saw the direction of Sara's gaze and hid a smile. "I know that you are absorbed with your plans for the little school right now, so if these ardent young *caballeros* become bothersome, let me know. I will cuff their ears."

Rafael followed the trail over the rise and down

into a lush green valley in the foothills of the Sandia Mountains. It was dusk, and he was home. Even in the dimming light, he could see the sprawling adobe *rancho* in the distance, a thin curl of smoke rising from the house. It was a welcome sight, and a soothing balm to his raw spirit.

He had been tortured by thoughts of Sara the whole night through. His body had ached for her since their encounter at the Perez hacienda. After a sleepless night, he had risen, packed some provisions, and left for his *rancho*. He had told his manservant to tell his grandfather where he was going.

He heard the dogs barking in the distance, and knew they had picked up his scent. As he rode down the lane that cut through the meadow in front of the *rancho,* he saw Blanca and Jayme emerge from the iron gate in the front wall of the house. They waved in recognition and ran to meet him. "Don Rafael! *Bienvenido!*" they called, almost in unison.

"Hola. It has been too long, my friends," Rafael said, a smile creasing his face, despite his mood. He dismounted and Jayme took the reins, while Blanca led the way back through the gate and then secured it. The courtyard was filled with beautiful flowers, some hanging in pots, some growing in barrels, all flourishing under Blanca's care.

Rafael headed for the kitchen, where light spilled out the doorway from several lamps. "Did the cattle arrive yet? Tell me about our crops this year, Jayme? Will there be enough hay for the winter?" Rafael sat down at the large trestle table, and smiled at Blanca as she placed a cup of coffee in front of him. *"Gracias,"* he murmured, taking a sip.

Jayme sat down across from his patron. *"Sí,* señor. Felix and Carlos arrived yesterday, and I sent them to the south pasture. It has been a very good year, Don Rafael. We harvested the hay last month during a short dry spell. And the corn crop as well as the other vegetables have been harvested."

"That is indeed good news, Jayme. I knew I could trust you and Blanca to take care of everything," Rafael said, accepting a plate of chicken stew and tortillas from Blanca. The two servants flushed with pleasure at the compliment, as Rafael continued, "Has my father's tribe arrived at their camp in the valley yet?"

"No, señor. I did not expect them until after the roundup. We did not expect to see you until then either, did we, Blanca?" Jayme glanced up at his wife, as she placed a plate of food in front of him.

Blanca's smile transformed her from plain to pretty. "No, Jayme. But I think Don Rafael is as anxious to see the little one as we are."

"Kahuu will not be so little this year, I think. She is twelve now. And *sí,* I am looking forward to having her here," Rafael said, and thought of Sara. He had wanted to bring Sara here to his *rancho* as his wife, and as a mother for Kahuu. The food in his mouth suddenly tasted like sand. Jayme brought him up to date on happenings on the *rancho,* while Rafael sipped his coffee. After a while, Rafael excused himself and retired to his bedroom.

Leaving the lamp burning, he crawled naked

beneath the red and blue wool blanket on his bed. His room, like the rest of the hacienda, was colorful and homey, due to Blanca's influence. Having no wife, he gave his housekeeper free rein to turn his house into a home. His arms crossed beneath his head, he glared at the whitewashed ceiling. He did not need the high and mighty Sara Clayton for a wife, he decided angrily. He would take Tuwikaa's sister as his wife. She had made it plain on many occasions that she desired him. And she was Kahuu's aunt, and had taken care of the little girl for years. It was really the best solution to his problems. He was weary of prostitutes and living alone. He wanted his daughter with him. He wanted to turn over his work at Hacienda Delgado to Manolo, and not have to deal with his arrogant grandfather any longer. He wanted to live here at his own *rancho. Sí*, he thought, *that is exactly what I will do. Once the roundup is over and The People arrive, I will put Sara out of my thoughts and my life forever.*

Leaning over, he blew out the lamp and settled back into bed, a determined, but unhappy man.

Chapter 12

Manolo strode across the main courtyard, weaving around empty *carretas* returning from the granary, where the corn had been unloaded. His silver spurs jingled musically as he walked, and he presented the perfect picture of a handsome young *caballero*. His brown jacket and pants were trimmed with black and silver braid, and his white shirt was as snowy as the peaks of the Sandia Mountains.

He was whistling a tune as he headed for the schoolrooms, where he hoped to find Sara. Life was good, he thought with satisfaction. He was growing richer every day with the output from the Indio Plata mine, he was planning to inherit Hacienda Delgado from his uncle, and he had found the perfect woman to be his wife. He had no doubts he could convince Sara, given time and care. His good looks and charm had won him many fair maidens.

As he stepped inside the room and let his eyes adjust to the dimness, he saw her in the other room, talking to Renato, the carpenter. They were bent over a low table, and Sara was holding her hand out, as if measuring something for the man.

For a moment, Manolo let his eyes roam over her hungrily. She was a beautiful creature, dainty, yet curving in all the right places. He felt himself grow hard just looking at her. He wanted to bury his face in her flowing silver hair, and he wanted to bury his manhood in her warm, sweet body. Shaking these thoughts, he stepped back outside to cool off, and saw his uncle walking toward him. *"Hola,* Tío Vicente, you are dressed for riding. Are you going to the mine today?"

The older man gave his nephew a half smile. "No. I need to go into Santa Fe. Perhaps I could ride in with you and Sara?"

Manolo's heart sank. "Of course. I was just going to fetch Sara."

"Good, we are ready then." Don Vicente turned toward the three saddled horses Julio was leading, while Manolo stepped inside the building.

Sara was adjusting the chin strap on her wide-brimmed hat as she came through the doorway. She smiled brightly at the older man and accepted his help in mounting her horse. *"Gracias.* I'm pleased you're joining us, Don Vicente. I would appreciate your help in choosing the supplies for the school."

"It will be my pleasure," he replied, as the three of them trotted toward the gates. One of the guards swung them wide so they could pass through.

The sun overhead was hot, but a glorious breeze moved across the valley from the river as they cantered down the wide track. After giving the horses a good run, the three riders settled down to a walk. "Pedro sent his regards to you in a message I received from him this morning, señorita," Don Vicente said.

Sara, riding between the two men, smiled. "How nice of him. He was very good to me on the journey. Will he be returning to Hacienda Delgado soon?"

"Most likely he will return with us today. His message was to let Rafael know that the official forms had been completed on our trade goods, and Rafael's signature was needed. However, my grandson left at dawn for his *rancho,* so I am obliged to see to the paperwork."

Sara's smile slipped a notch. She turned her attention back to the road ahead. "After a long absence, I suppose he wanted to check on everything."

"Perhaps, but I had progress reports for him to look over as soon as he got home," Don Vicente said with a shrug.

"Rafael probably did not mean to be thoughtless, Tío Vicente. Moreover, I could have done this paperwork for you. It would have saved you the long ride," Manolo said.

"*Gracias,* Manolo, but I am not decrepit yet. Besides, escorting a beautiful señorita is a pleasure, not a chore," Don Vicente said, a trace of amusement in his voice.

"I—I did not mean to imply—" Manolo began, his face flushed.

Don Vicente interrupted, "I am teasing, nephew. Now we should get moving, or it will take all day, eh?"

The trip was made in little over an hour without

the encumbrance of a wagon to slow them. Sara couldn't keep her thoughts away from Rafael, and her disappointment that he was gone. She wanted to ask when he would be returning, but didn't want to show undue interest. Contenting herself with the fact that he would return by roundup, she tried to take pleasure in the outing.

The church bells were pealing as they rode sedately down San Francisco Street. Small boys, playing in the dusty thoroughfare, darted in their path several times. Before they rounded the corner into the main plaza, Sara could hear the traces of guitar music coming from various cantinas. The plaza was busy with vendors and shopkeepers selling their wares to farmers and city dwellers alike. The smell of food cooking caused Sara's stomach to growl.

"I must pay my respects to the governor first," Don Vicente said. "Unless you would like to go with me, señorita, you could go to the LaFonda Inn with Manolo for refreshments."

"I do feel thirsty, señor," she agreed, not wanting to sit in on the boring business talk of her employer and the governor.

"It is settled then. Manolo, see that the señorita is made comfortable. I will meet you both at the store in an hour." The older man turned his horse toward the Governor's Palace.

Sara and Manolo moved on to the inn. Manolo gave a silver coin to a small boy to take their horses to the stable, and then escorted her inside the dim building.

It was a large room with many tables, but most

of those tables were unoccupied at the moment. Manolo motioned to a boy who was wiping glasses at the end of the bar. When the lad trotted over, he said, "Show the señorita where she can freshen up, Pepe." Manolo waited at a small table close to the long bar; before long, Sara was back. His mood was light, since he had ascertained that Juliana was not working this morning. The *puta* was growing possessive, and he didn't want her anywhere near Sara. He took the chair across from her and smiled.

"Tío Vicente will most likely take a meal with the governor, so I think we should eat. Are you hungry, Sara?"

"Yes, very. I'm a little embarrassed by my appetite since I arrived in Santa Fe. It seems I am always hungry," she told him with a laugh.

He loved the music of her voice. "It is our pure mountain air, Sara. It agrees with you. I think you have grown more beautiful since the first time I saw you . . . if that is possible."

Pepe appeared, saving Sara from replying to the flirtatious remark. She studied Manolo while he gave their order to the boy. Manolo was handsome, and he'd been very nice to her, but she honestly didn't want any more romantic entanglements. What had happened with Rafael was a painful lesson.

When they arrived at Don Vicente's store, he was there waiting for them. *"Hola.* The governor had many appointments this morning, so I got away early," he explained, and then held up a blue lace *rebozo*. "Give me your opinion, señorita. Would a young woman your age like this?"

273

Sara touched a delicate fold and smiled. "Well, señor, I can only speak for myself. I think it's beautiful."

He nodded and handed the shawl to his store-keeper, who was standing behind the counter. "Wrap that one up also, Manuel." Taking her arm, he urged her to move down the counter with him. "Would you mind helping me choose some other things? They are gifts for a young woman who will be a part of our family soon."

Sara's spirits plummeted as the meaning of his words sank in. He was surely talking about Rafael's wife. Her smile slid away, as she pointed out, "She may not share my tastes."

Don Vicente took note of Sara's sudden pallor with a certain satisfaction. He chuckled, "Your choices, however, will be far better than mine."

Reluctantly, Sara helped him pick out some tortoiseshell hair combs, an ivory fan, and a soft, blue wool shawl. "I hope she likes these things, señor," Sara said, as they waited for Manuel to wrap their choices.

"I am fairly certain she will. Now, if you will come with me to the storeroom, I will show you what I unearthed for the school while waiting for you and Manolo."

Looking through the books he'd found helped take her mind off Rafael and his intended bride. She chose several, and Don Vicente added these to the other things he was having sent out to the hacienda. Señor Pino arrived when they were ready to leave. He bowed low over Sara's hand, and gave her a warm smile. "I am very pleased to see you

274

again, señorita. I hope your new home was all that you expected?"

Sara returned the smile. "More, Señor Pino. I fully understand why my brother loved this area. Everyone at the hacienda has made me feel welcome."

"Good. I am happy to hear that." The older man offered his arm to her, as they left the store. Don Vicente and Manolo followed, and soon the four of them were galloping away from the city toward home.

Over the next few days, Señor Pino introduced Sara to his large family: wife, daughters, sons, in-laws, and grandchildren. Maria, his wife, took Sara under her wing, as if she belonged to the family. And Sara adored the children. They were bright, curious, dark-eyed sprites with ready smiles. Sara found herself wondering if she had a child with Rafael, what it would look like? Would it be dark or fair? A flash of loneliness stabbed at her when she realized that she wouldn't have the chance to find that out. And how could she bear to see Rafael with another woman?

"Señorita Sara, you are squeezing me too hard," Marta protested in a squeak.

Instantly, Sara relaxed her arms around the little girl. She had been sitting on a bench in the central courtyard, watching some of the Indian women weave cloth, when one of Señor Pino's granddaughters had climbed onto her lap. "I'm sorry, Marta. I must have been daydreaming, and thought

I was a big ole bear—gr-r-r-r!" Sara's growl sounded less than scary.

Marta giggled and wrapped her arms around Sara's neck, hugging her in return. "This bear will not be at our school, will it, señorita?"

Sara laughed. "I don't think so. But we will be learning about animals and plants and other interesting things."

Marta clapped her small hands. "Madre said you are beautiful as well as smart, and that we are very lucky to have you." Cocking her head to one side, she frowned. "She said it would not be long until a handsome *caballero* made you his wife and carried you away. I do not want you to leave, señorita."

Before an astonished Sara could give an answer, a shadow fell across the two of them. Sara looked up and met Rafael's gaze. His frown was a little more fierce than the child's. "Do not worry, little Marta. The señorita has assured me that marriage is not for her."

"Don Rafael!" Marta squealed and abandoned Sara's lap to hug his knees. He scooped her up and gave her a hug. Setting her back down on the ground, he asked, "Could you find your grandfather and tell him I am back, *por favor?*"

"*Sí. Adios,* señorita!" Marta called as she scampered away. Sara watched her go with trepidation. She now had to face Rafael alone. Her heart had begun to pound at the sound of his voice, while little shivers of excitement raced up and down her spine. She stood up and nervously smoothed her denim skirt. "I didn't expect you back until roundup," she said, glancing up. She caught a flash of hungry desire in his intense gaze, and felt liquid heat race through her veins.

"I could not stay away any longer," he said, watching the slow flush in her cheeks.

"I'm sure your grandfather needs your help," she said, hoping to steer the conversation into less personal channels.

Rafael smiled and reached out a strong, brown hand to stroke her loose hair. "That is not what I meant, Sara," he said, his tone as caressing as his hand. "Where is your hat? The cool breezes of autumn mask the heat of the sun."

Sara's breathing grew shallow, but she tried to remain still under his touch. "I will remember that."

His thumb strayed to her cheek, and made a path down her skin to her throat. "The sun has turned your skin golden," he mused, "like the warm color of gold before it is polished. Gold and silver . . ." he breathed, lifting a lock of her hair and winding it around his finger.

Sara's blue eyes locked with his dark ones, and she felt the heat of his desire all the way to her toes. For a moment, she swayed toward him before she realized what she was doing. Abruptly, she stepped back and broke eye contact. "I don't think you should say those things," she murmured. "I have to go freshen up for the noon meal." Without waiting for an answer, she walked away. He watched her go, and with an iron will, he struck down the desire that coursed through his blood. She was just a woman, he reminded himself angrily. Another woman would do just as well to warm his bed and take care of his child. Slowly, he followed in Sara's wake, heading toward his room.

After washing up, Rafael sought out his grandfather, finding him in the large *sala*. The older man was standing next to the fireplace, staring into his glass of Madeira.

"Buenos dias," Rafael said, standing in the doorway.

Don Vicente's brow rose as he said mildly, "So you have returned?"

"I wanted to see to my *rancho*." Rafael shrugged and walked over to the low cabinet to pour himself a glass of wine. "Is everything all right here?"

"Manolo has been taking care of the harvest. That is almost finished. However, there is an important matter I wish to discuss with you. I wanted to talk to you about this before, but you left." Don Vicente drained his glass and placed it carefully on the mantel.

Rafael mentally braced himself. He knew when his grandfather used that particular tone, it was something ominous. "Perhaps I should sit down," Rafael said, taking the nearest chair and leisurely stretching his long legs out in front of him.

"On the day of Doña Lucia's funeral, Doña Josefina spoke to me about a very important matter. It concerned Señorita Sara and you," he said, watching his grandson's face.

A new alertness stiffened Rafael's shoulders imperceptibly. "I can hardly wait to hear what she had to say," Rafael said, a vein of sarcasm in his quiet tone.

The older man picked up his glass and moved to fill it again, taking his time. He took a sip before he resumed. "She said that the señorita spent much time unchaperoned with you on the trail, and is no better than a prostitute."

Rafael was on his feet in an instant, a white-hot anger burning in his eyes. "That woman is a vicious old crow. *Por Dios!* What possessed her to say such a thing about Sara?"

Don Vicente's eyebrows rose. "I do not know . . . you tell me, Rafael."

The weight of Rafael's guilt bore down on him, even in his anger. This was his fault! He should have been more careful of Sara's reputation. He had always known Doña Josefina despised him, but he never once thought she would direct her venom in Sara's direction. Bringing his temper under control, Rafael focused once again on his grandfather. "She did not like Sara, but this accusation seems harsh, even for Doña Josefina. Perhaps she thinks Estella is still interested in me, and wishes to discredit me even more in her daughter's eyes." He flung his arm out in a disgusted gesture. "How should I know what sort of poison is in that old woman's mind?"

Don Vicente finished his wine and set his glass down. "If you did not spend any time in Sara's company, then there is nothing to worry about, eh? There are plenty of people in the caravan who will attest to her innocence in these charges."

Rafael sighed deeply and sat back down in his chair. "I did not say that," he said quietly. "I did compromise Sara's reputation—but she is innocent."

The older man studied his grandson critically. "I see. If you know this, why have you not done the honorable thing? Why did I have to hear about this from a gossiping old crone?"

Rafael raised contempt-filled eyes. "Sara, it seems, holds the opinion that a half-breed is not a suitable husband for her."

Don Vicente's eyes narrowed. "You asked her to marry you, and she refused?"

"*Sí*," Rafael bit off. "She used other excuses for refusing, like the fact that she has no dowry. And she also said I was still in love with my dead wife. However, I knew she was holding something back."

Don Vicente walked over to the open doorway and stared out into the courtyard. After the short time he'd had to observe his grandson and Sara, he was convinced they were attracted to each other. This was Pedro's opinion also. Rafael's grandfather almost smiled to himself over the way things were working out. Fixing a heavy frown on his face, Don Vicente turned. "Whatever her reasons are, she has two choices now. Either she marries you, or I will send her back to St. Louis. Her reputation and your honor are at stake."

Rafael scowled in return. "Let me know what she decides," he said, and stalked out of the room.

As the noon meal progressed, Don Vicente took note of the fact that Sara seemed preoccupied. She raised her head expectantly each time a servant came in with another course. He knew she was looking for Rafael, because the rest of the household was present at the meal. He also watched his great-nephew try to engage her in conversation. It was just as well that Rafael would be marrying Sara, for

280

Manolo had been casting an amorous eye in her direction.

"When we are finished, could I have a private word with you, señorita?" Don Vicente asked finally.

She murmured her agreement with barely a thought as to what he wanted. Once the meal was over, she took his arm, and they retired to the *sala*. "I will not keep you from your siesta very long, señorita," he promised with a smile.

"I'm not tired anyway," she assured him despondently.

As they seated themselves, he said, "Forgive me for mentioning this, but you have been looking *very* tired. There are dark circles under those beautiful blue eyes."

"I suppose it's the adjustment to a new place, a different climate," she hedged.

He nodded and cleared his throat. "I have a very disagreeable duty. There is no way to say it politely, so I will get to the point." At her puzzled look, he stood up and walked to the open doorway. "Some very disturbing information has come to me, señorita, and I am afraid I cannot ignore it. Doña Josefina has told me that my grandson compromised your reputation during the journey here. I have no choice but to insist that the two of you marry."

That snapped Sara out of her lethargic mood. She stared at his back for several seconds, before she gasped, "What did you say?"

Don Vicente turned to see some color in her cheeks. "I am truly sorry. Rafael has already been informed of this, and has agreed to wed for your sake."

Sara shook her head as if to clear her mind. For a brief moment, joy flooded her at the thought. However, cold reason crowded in when she realized what he'd said—Don Vicente's plans were ruined, and he was sorry. And Rafael was agreeing for *her* sake? She couldn't let this happen. "No!" she said, standing up abruptly. "How can you let a mean-tempered old woman change the course of all our lives?"

Don Vicente rose from his seat and took her hand gently. "If you do not marry, her gossip will have an effect on our lives anyway. Do you wish to see my grandson lose face and honor over this?"

"But . . . but you had a wife picked out for him. I know, Señor Pino told me. I don't want to ruin your plans," she said, tears welling up in her large blue eyes. "I'm sorry."

Don Vicente put his arm around her, and she laid her head on his chest. "Plans can change, señorita. I am not displeased by the way things have turned out. Our only other choice would be to send you home. Do you wish to do that?"

Sara thought about never seeing Rafael again. She also thought about Jonas Farber. "No," she whispered. "I will marry Rafael. I won't have his honor besmirched because of me." Did she have any choice? Wiping her eyes, she looked up at him. "When, señor? When would we . . . do this?"

He frowned for a moment. "The day after tomorrow. As soon as possible. It would be better to give Doña Josefina a wedding to talk about, rather

282

than a scandal, eh?"

"Two days?" Sara whispered, awed by the rapid changes that were taking place.

Giving her a fatherly pat on the shoulder, he offered, "Do not worry about a thing. I will send Doña Ines to your room after siesta. She will help you plan for the event."

"Gracias," she murmured. Making her way to her room, Sara felt bewildered, guilty, and happy all at once.

The following day, Sara tried in vain to see Rafael. She desperately wanted to talk to him, but he was not available. He had ridden to Santa Fe that morning to speak to the priest, she was told. And that evening when he returned, he departed almost immediately on another errand, before Sara knew he was there.

Sara pushed her food around her plate at dinner, frustrated by the fact that Rafael was evading her. He was angry, she knew, or else he would have sought her out. It was punishment, she decided. He wanted her to suffer the uncertainty of his mood. He had asked her to marry him before, out of need and duty. Now he was being *forced* to take her as his wife. Sara cringed at the ominous beginning of their marriage. How could they possibly be happy?

"Try not to be too nervous, my dear," Doña Ines said kindly. "The ceremony will be short, and the guests, few."

Sara looked up and tried to smile. Manolo plunked down his fork with a clatter. "I do not understand why this is happening at all! I have heard no gossip, and surely Doña Josefina could be discouraged by you, Tío Vicente, from starting any rumors? Why should Sara be punished for something she has not done?"

"We know Sara is blameless, however, I can tell you that Doña Josefina will not let this rest. Would you have Sara's reputation in ruins, and your cousin's honor sullied?" Don Vicente frowned at his nephew.

Manolo's face flushed. "I do not see my esteemed cousin here to protect his betrothed. If he does not wish to take Sara to wife, I will do so gladly!"

At the mention of Rafael's absence, Sara burst into tears. She hid her face in her napkin and sobbed, hurt and embarrassed at the same time.

"See what you have caused, Manolo!" Don Vincente growled. He motioned to his sister, and she went to Sara and helped her up and away from the table.

When the women had gone, Don Vincente turned his grim expression on his nephew. "We will speak of this no more. It is settled."

Manolo bit his tongue and nodded his assent. He did not wish to anger his uncle, but he had wanted Sara for his own. Thinking of his half-breed cousin having her nearly made him sick. Short of Rafael's dying suddenly, there was no way around this situation. Getting a grip on his emotions, he raised his head. "Forgive me, Tío Vicente, for my outburst. I will apologize to Sara as well. My only excuse is that she seemed so forlorn, I got angry."

"I understand, Manolo. I feel very protective of her myself. She's a woman who makes a man feel like a man. Rafael is very lucky," Don Vicente said.

Manolo bit back the sharp reply on his tongue. "*Sí*, very lucky."

Rafael sat on the grassy bank of a small lake in the hills above Hacienda Delgado. The air was cold, but he hardly noticed as he gazed at the moonlight patterns on the dark water. His back rested against the trunk of a piñon tree, while his knees were drawn up in front of him. When he needed to think or just be alone, he came to this spot. Tonight, he was wrestling with his pride. He was in love with Sara, and tomorrow, he would marry her. It was not as simple as that though. Why was he destined, he wondered fiercely, to feel great love for those who would not return it? First there had been his grandfather, and now Sara. Many years ago, he had erected a wall around his heart to protect it from Don Vicente's barbs. But how would he keep Sara from tearing his soul and his pride to shreds? He trembled when she was near, he ached for her touch. Despite his worries, however, his spirit felt lighter than it had in weeks. The howl of a great wolf in the distance rent the air, as Rafael mounted his horse to return. It was a good omen, and it pleased him.

Sara and Rafael stood before Father Mendoza in the small chapel of Hacienda Delgado at mid-morning. She stole a sidelong glance at his handsome face. It seemed to be carved out of stone on this occasion, but her heart pounded in anticipation just the same. They had repeated their vows, and the priest was droning on about marriage obligations. Sara let his voice flow over her as she wondered how she looked to Rafael today. She had chosen a cornflower blue dress after Don Vicente had gifted her with the blue lace rebozo she had helped him choose at his store. She had left her hair down on her shoulders, the way Rafael liked it. He might look stern and forbidding at the moment, but she had seen a spark of admiration in his eyes when she walked toward him down the aisle. It was the one thing that had kept her from quaking in her shoes through the ceremony.

Finally, it was over, and Father Mendoza was urging Rafael to kiss his bride. Sara lifted her face as he lowered his head, but his lips barely brushed hers. Despite his cool attitude, Sara was happy. She smiled shyly at the blur of faces as they passed down the aisle. Everyone who lived and worked at Hacienda Delgado had been given the day off to attend the nuptials.

Rafael was silent as they stood outside in the courtyard, waiting to receive their guests as they filed out. Sara tilted her head up to look at him. "I wanted to talk to you yesterday . . ."

He glanced down at her and then away. "What was there to say? Unless, of course, you wished to return to St. Louis and not go through with this. Knowing how you really feel about me, I am surprised you did not do just that."

Sara cringed at the underlying bitterness in his tone. "Please, Rafael, I must confess—"

Just then, Father Mendoza stepped through the door of the chapel with Don Vicente. "Ah! What a handsome couple you make," Don Vicente said, shaking his grandson's hand and kissing Sara's cheek. "Welcome to the family, Sara," he whispered.

Sara pasted a smile on her face, and murmured the appropriate responses to everyone as they passed through the line. What she really wanted was some time alone with Rafael to clear up the misunderstanding, but instead, they were urged into a cart decorated with flowers and paraded around the courtyard several times. The guests and musicians with guitars followed, shouting and singing. Sara fell against Rafael once as the wheel hit a hole, and he put his arms around her for the remainder of the ride. "We must make this look good," he explained in a low tone.

Sara shivered, loving the feel of his strong body pressed against hers, and the masculine scent that assailed her nostrils. It was hard to mantain her feelings of guilt over this forced marriage, when her spirits soared at his touch.

Finally, the cart stopped at the gates of the private family courtyard, where the bride and groom were helped to alight. Rafael held Sara's arm as they were swept through the gates with the crowd. Large tables had been set up and were laden with food. The musicians began a romantic ballad, while several of the *vaqueros* called for the groom to dance with the bride.

Sara blushed, wondering if Rafael would refuse to accommodate the crowd. When she felt his arm slide around her waist, she sighed with relief. Tucking her hand into his, Sara glanced up at Rafael's face. He smiled, but the smile did not reach his eyes. "We must not disappoint our guests, eh?" he murmured.

Sara suddenly wanted to weep. Rafael hated her, and Don Vicente's plans were ruined. Would they ever forgive her? She felt more alone at that moment than when her parents had died. She went through the motions of dancing, following Rafael with ease. He moved effortlessly and with a natural grace. After a few moments, Sara said, "I believe we could settle our differences, if we talk about this reasonably."

Rafael allowed himself to look into her soulful eyes, and immediately regretted it. There was raw pain reflected there, and it tore at him. He hardened his heart. "There is nothing to settle, Sara. We have married and satisfied all the proprieties, but you will have your life, and I will have mine. We need not concern ourselves with each other."

Sara was taken aback by his blunt pronouncement. "But that's not a marriage! I love you, Rafael . . . don't you feel anything for me? I once thought you did," she whispered, her voice growing husky with tears.

Rafael had to remind himself that she had taken him in once before with a declaration of love. He gazed at her beautiful face for a moment, before measuring his words. "Once the roundup is over, I will go to live at my *rancho* in the mountains. I will have no need of you there, for Tuwikka's sister will care for my daughter. You may do whatever you wish about companionship, as long as you are discreet."

Sara felt as if her heart was breaking in pieces. She stared at his stony face as if he were a stranger. "How.

can you say—" she began, holding back the tears.

"I do not wish to discuss it any further," he interrupted, looking away from her distress. The song ended and he dropped his arms, bowing formally to her.

Manolo stepped up and took Sara's arm. "May I have the next dance with the beautiful bride, cousin? You must share her a little at the party, eh?"

Rafael gave a brief nod, and without a word, turned away to ask his aunt to dance. The music began again, and Sara, in shock, followed Manolo into the dance.

"*Por Dios,* what is wrong!" he asked in a low tone, gazing down into her stricken face. "I saw your expression when you were talking to Rafael. What did he say?"

Sara swallowed the lump in her throat and squared her shoulders. "It was nothing, Manolo. We've just had our first disagreement as man and wife, that's all," she said, trying to smile.

Manolo felt something akin to elation. "Rafael is a fool for disagreeing with you about anything, Sara. If you were my wife, I would never give you a cross word," he said in a light tone.

"Your wife will be a very lucky woman, Manolo," she told him.

"Just remember, Sara, that we are now cousins, and you can come to me with anything. I am a very good listener," he offered.

"*Gracias,*" she murmured. Soon the dance ended. Rafael was beside her before she could wonder where he was. She was composed now, though, and let him take her arm. He led her to one of the tables, and filled a plate for her and then one for himself. She followed him to the table under the *portales,* set up especially for them. Don Vicente, Doña Ines, and Manolo joined them, and toasts were made. Sara smiled until her face hurt. She talked and even laughed at one of Manolo's funny stories, but there was a brittle edge to it. It all seemed like a play to Sara, and each of them was acting out a part. The celebration ended at siesta time. Rafael stood up and held out a hand to her. "Come, Sara. We should get changed and get started."

Taking his hand, she looked puzzled. "Where are we going?"

Don Vicente chuckled. "Ah, so you saved the trip as a surprise for her, eh?"

Rafael helped her to her feet. *"Sí.* We are going to spend a few days in Santa Fe—a honeymoon of sorts. I cannot spare more than that at roundup time."

Sara dropped her gaze from the stony look in his eyes. "I see . . . but I have nothing packed."

Rafael urged her toward the stairs to the second floor. "I told Pepita to do that for you."

"Another little surprise?" she asked, growing angry at his attitude.

He didn't bother to answer. Sara pulled free of his helping hand and moved ahead of him up the stairs, her spine stiff with irritation. At this point, she didn't care if everyone watching realized that there was something wrong.

When Sara arrived at her room, Pepita was just laying out a traveling dress. "Oh, Señora Delgado! You were the most beautiful bride I ever saw!" the

290

servant said, her smile wide.

Sara forced herself to return the young woman's smile. Why spoil Pepita's happiness, she thought. *"Gracias,"* she murmured, as the servant helped her undress. When the change was completed, Sara stood before her mirror and pulled her hair severely back into a bun at the nape of her neck, securing it with pins. Pepita sighed. "Your hair is so beautiful, when it is down your back, señora! And Don Rafael likes it that way. I have seen him staring with much admiration."

Sara reached for the hat that matched her dark blue dress, and put it on. "I know, but the wind will tangle it on the journey," she explained vaguely. In truth, she didn't care if she ever did anything to please her husband again.

"I will tell Jose to fetch your trunk now," Pepita offered, and Sara followed her downstairs.

The courtyard was empty of guests, but a few servants were cleaning up the food tables. Sara decided to wait in the *sala,* and stepped inside the door. She could hear muffled voices coming from Don Vicente's office in the next room. Recognizing Rafael's voice, she moved closer to the closed door, and then felt ashamed for eavesdropping. She started to step back when she heard her name mentioned. Her curiosity got the better of her. "I think you would have been better off with a Spanish girl of good family, but Sara will make you a suitable wife," Don Vicente said evenly.

"I do not know why you interfered at all, if you feel that way. Sara did not want to marry me. And I have been seriously considering Tuwikaa's sister,

Little Dove, as a wife. She has cared for my daughter all these years, and would be hardworking and obedient."

Don Vicente laughed harshly. "Is that what you want? Hardworking and obedient? It sounds rather dull to me, Rafael. Besides, she is an Indian, and could never move in your social circles."

"I do not care about social circles! However, Sara does and will fit into your household very neatly. After roundup, I will be moving to my *rancho* permanently. You have Manolo and Pedro to help you here," Rafael ground out.

Sara heard his booted feet coming toward the door and she moved to sit in one of the chairs. When Rafael came through the door and spotted her, he barked, "Are you ready?"

Sara fumed at his arrogant manner, but held her tongue. She intended to let him know just what she thought about his behavior, but wanted to do so in private. This honeymoon trip would be perfect.

Chapter 13

Sara had to be patient, for Rafael placed her in a carriage for the trip, while he rode his stallion. She had hoped they could begin their discussion on the way there, but it was not to be.

For two hours, Sara glared at the back of his head. So, he was thinking of taking his sister-in-law as a wife! Well, he just couldn't do that, she fumed. She was his wife, and there was no way she would put up with the humiliation! She would go back and face Jonas Farber first!

When the carriage stopped in front of LaFonda Inn, Sara stepped out before Carlos or Rafael could reach her. Rafael's eyebrows rose as she swept past him, ignoring his proffered arm. He followed, a slow smile curving his lips. Bernadino came around the bar and bowed courteously to them. "Welcome, Señor and Señora Delgado! I give you my felicitations on your marriage. I will show you to your room myself."

Rafael murmured, *"Gracias."* He waited for Sara

293

to proceed him up the steps, and then followed. Carlos came behind him with Sara's trunk and Rafael's bag.

Sara walked out onto the balcony and rested her hands on the balustrade. Inside, she was shaking with anger, as well as uncertainty. She wished now that she'd agreed to go back to Missouri. Although kind to her, Don Vicente had said a Spanish girl would have made a better wife for Rafael . . . and her new husband wanted to take an Indian concubine! Two tears slipped down her cheeks, and then two more. She couldn't stop them. She dug in her pockets for a handkerchief as she sniffled, trying to get hold of her emotions.

"Here, Sara," Rafael said, holding his handkerchief in front of her.

She hadn't heard him come up behind her, and now she was embarrassed. Jerking the piece of cloth from his hand, she blew her nose and wiped her eyes angrily. "Our marriage was a big mistake, Rafael. We must talk," she said.

He looked away, afraid his feelings would show. "There is nothing to talk about, Sara. We are married in the eyes of God, and nothing will change that except death."

His harsh tone wounded her further. "Would God approve of you leaving me behind and taking a second wife to live with?" she blurted out before she could stop herself. "Yes, I know your plans already . . . I heard you telling your grandfather."

Rafael heard the thread of pain in her voice, and wondered for the first time if she cared about him. He had no intention of living with the Indian woman, but the idea of it seemed to make Sara jealous. Perhaps he shouldn't enlighten her just yet. "We will speak of this later. For now, I have to take care of some important business," he said, ignoring her pointed question.

Sara glanced up at his granitelike profile. "More important than our marriage?" she asked, stung by his uncaring attitude.

"No," he said, finally glancing down at her wide, blue eyes. "Not more important, perhaps, but more urgent at the moment."

Sara's hands fisted at her sides, and she stamped her foot. "Oh-h-h! Then I *won't* be here when you decide you have time to talk, Rafael!"

He moved from her side and started through the doorway. "Do not leave the room. When I return, we will discuss this like adults."

Fresh tears poured down her cheeks: tears of anger. She hated being an adult! It seemed that each day there was some new, conflicting emotion that had to be dealt with, and she had no one to confide in about her feelings. When she heard the outer door close behind Rafael, she wiped at the tears and blew her nose. Squaring her shoulders, she thought, *Fine! If I am an adult, I will make my own decisions!* Pouring water into the bowl on the chest in the bedroom, she washed her face and smoothed her hair in front of the mirror. She picked up her reticule and left the room.

Her steps slowed, however, as she reached the common room below. There were some dusty *vaqueros* occupying the tables, and two painted señoritas at the bar. Bernadino was busy pouring drinks, and did not look her way as she crossed the room toward the door.

An arm snaked out before she could reach it, and she gasped as the man hauled her unceremoniously onto his lap. He and his companion laughed at her startled look. "Where are you going in such a hurry, my dove? I have not seen you before, are you a new girl?" he asked, his hand roaming freely over her leg.

"Let me go, you lout! Stop that or I'll—" Sara's threat was interrupted with a squeal, as he laughed and slipped his fingers in the low-cut bodice of her dress.

"If you value your life, you will let the lady go," a voice behind them said quietly.

Sara felt a wash of relief, as she twisted her head around to see Garth standing there with his derringer touching the back of the Mexican's head. Casually, he pulled his pistol from its holster at his side, and pointed it at the other *vaquero* who sat across the table. "Put the knife on the table. We don't want any bloodshed if possible."

The man did as Garth said, moving his hand into view with the deadly-looking knife clutched there. He placed it on the table and shrugged, looking at his companion. "We don't want no trouble, eh, Francisco?"

Bernadino had hurried over as soon as he saw the trouble, and stood wringing a towel in his hands. "They will leave, Señor Prescott, just let them go, *por favor?* You, Francisco, unhand Señora Delgado, *pronto!* Don Rafael will have your liver for dinner, if he finds out about this!"

At the mention of Rafael's name, the *vaquero*

stood Sara on her feet, his whole attitude changing. "Please forgive me, señora? I did not know you are of the Delgado family! I am a stupid man!"

Sara stepped into the protection of Garth's arm, and glared at the man. "It really doesn't matter what family I am from—no means *no!* If you promise to remember that, I won't tell my husband about this."

The man regained some color in his pale face, and nodded briskly. "You are such a kind lady! On my madre's grave, I give you my word."

Bernadino gave the man a shove. "Go now, make tracks, you hombres."

The two men glanced at Garth, who was putting his gun back in its holster, and they needed no further urging. They were out the door like a small whirlwind.

Sara started to shake with delayed reaction, and Garth helped her to sit down. "Bring some wine, Bernadino," he ordered, sitting down across from her, but holding onto her hand. "It's all right now. He didn't hurt you, did he?"

She shook her head. "No-o-o, just scared me. Oh, Garth, I don't know what would have happened, if you hadn't come along. Rafael told me to stay in our room, but I was so angry, I didn't, and look what happened. Oh-h-h-h dear. When he finds out, he'll be so angry!"

Garth gave her hand a gentle squeeze. "Calm down, Sara. In the first place, we won't tell him, all right?" Wide-eyed, she nodded. He turned toward the bar and said in a loud voice for all to hear. "Bernadino, I don't think Don Rafael needs to know of this, do you?"

The bartender hurried over with their bottle and two glasses. "No, señor. It is forgotten. It never happened, eh?" He shrugged and walked back to his post.

"Good," Garth said, and turned back to Sara. "Now, if I heard correctly, you are now Señora Delgado? Rafael's wife? When did this happen, pray tell?"

Sara's eyes filled with tears. "This morning . . . and it's all Doña Josefina's fault!"

Garth let out a sigh. "Not that I am surprised that the woman has caused you a problem, but perhaps you'd better tell me the whole story, so I can understand how it happened."

When Sara finished her telling, Garth nodded slowly, his expression bland. "So what you're saying is, that this vindictive old woman's gossip caused Don Vicente to force Rafael to marry you? It's strange, but Rafael does not seem the sort of man you could force into anything."

Sara had finished with her tears, and was once again in control of herself. "These people value honor and obligation above most things. I went along with the marriage, because I didn't want Rafael to lose face in any way. He's had enough censure in his life."

"That was quite a sacrifice for you to make, Sara," he commented with raised eyebrows.

Sara dropped her gaze to her wineglass, and swirled the red liquid around for a moment before answering. "Oh, Garth, I'm not that unselfish. I'm in love with Rafael."

Garth chuckled and drained his glass. "I knew

that already. However, where is the bridegroom, and why does the bride look so unhappy on her wedding day?"

Sara swallowed the lump in her throat and vowed silently not to cry again. She raised her chin stubbornly. "He had important business to conduct, and I'm not unhappy. I don't know where you got such a notion."

Garth stood up and reached for her hand. "All right, Sara, I'll mind my own business. Let's take a walk, and drop in on Matt for a visit. He's been talking about you."

Glad for the change of subject, Sara allowed him to pull her to her feet. "I would love to see Matt."

Garth stopped at the bar on the way out, and told Bernadino where they were going. "I'm playing poker with some of the governor's guards later, but we have time for a short visit with Matt," he explained to her as they stepped out into the late afternoon sunshine.

Sara was just glad to escape from the gloomy confines of the hotel for a while. Taking his arm, she asked, "Have you had any word from Estella since the funeral?"

They crossed the wide plaza and started down San Francisco Street. "No. I was just about to ask you that. I thought you were going to invite her to Hacienda Delgado?"

Sara shook her head. "I'm sorry, Garth. I was, but things have been happening to me rather fast lately. However, I promise to do that just as soon as we return home."

"Maybe she's had a change of heart, and doesn't

299

want to elope with me now," he said suddenly, stopping in midstride.

It was Sara's turn to smile. "Don't borrow trouble. Besides, I've just had an idea. Why don't you come out to the hacienda for the roundup? Stay a week or so. Matt could come with you. Yes, it's a wonderful idea. Then you'll be there when Estella arrives."

He glanced down at her expectant face. "What would Rafael and his grandfather say about us just dropping in like that?"

"I invited you, didn't I? In case you've forgotten, I'm the lady of the house now—a Delgado," she said in a light tone. "Besides, they've invited many people to stay during roundup. It's a tradition."

He smiled. "All right. But you must help me persuade Matt as well." They resumed walking, and at the end of the street, he stopped. "Here it is."

Garth knocked, waited a minute or so, and then knocked again, more loudly. After another wait, Matt jerked the door open. "I'm trying to create some—"

Garth chuckled when his irritable friend noticed Sara standing just behind him. "We could come back later, you cranky old bear! Sara, I'm sure, wouldn't want to interrupt your work."

Matt pulled Sara into his arms and hugged her soundly. "You, Garth, are an interruption, but Sara—never! Come in," he said, tugging on Sara's hand.

Sara laughed, following his lead. The room was sparsely furnished with a cot, a table, and two chairs. Matt led them through a doorway into another room, where sunshine poured through the windows. Canvases and paint supplies littered the floor. Through an open doorway leading out onto a small courtyard, Sara could see a canvas set up on an easel. She followed Matt outside, and they waited while he covered the canvas with an oilcloth. "Sit, sit," he commanded, sweeping his arm toward the stone bench against one wall. "I have a bottle of wine—"

Sara interrupted him. "Thank you, Matt, but no wine for me. Garth and I just had some, and we can't stay long anyway."

"That's right, *amigo*," Garth put in. "I have to get Sara back to the hotel before her husband returns."

Matt's owlish eyes popped open even wider than usual. "Husband?"

"Rafael and I were married this morning at the hacienda," she explained, giving Garth a reproving look.

"Well, well, well! Wasn't that rather sudden? And I didn't get an invitation to the wedding," he accused.

"Garth will explain it all to you later. For now, I wanted to say hello and invite you to come out to the hacienda for roundup. There will be all sorts of guests coming and going, a rodeo, and a fiesta. There could be some unusual subjects for you to sketch," she urged.

His eyes narrowed. "If you married Rafael this morning, what are you doing with Garth this afternoon? Something is wrong here," he persisted.

"Nothing is wrong, Matt. And I really don't have time to get into all the details, but please come out to

301

the hacienda?" she pleaded.

His eyebrows rose. "All right, but only because I want to make sure you're being well treated."

Sara smiled at his protective attitude. "For whatever reason, I will be glad to have you. Now, enough about me, what have *you* been doing?"

He shrugged and glanced at the oilcloth-covered painting on the easel. "Mostly, I've been painting from the sketches I made on the trail. That one is your portrait, but you can't see it yet."

"Punishing me for not telling you about my sudden marriage?" she asked, smiling mischievously.

He chuckled. "No, but I don't want you to see it before it's finished."

"We had better go, Sara. I want to show you the church, before we go back to the hotel," Garth said.

Sara gave Matt a parting hug, and they left.

Rafael hurried back down the stairs at the hotel to confront Bernadino. "Where is my wife?" he demanded, startling the older man from his task of polishing glasses.

Bernadino cringed under Rafael's fierce glare. "I—I—she left with Señor Prescott to visit the painter . . . uh, Señor Harrigan."

Though still angry, he was relieved. She had not run away or been abducted as he had feared when he saw the empty room. "Where does he live?" Rafael demanded.

He was on his way as soon as the bartender gave him directions. By the time he reached the artist's house, he was fuming again. Matt answered the loud pounding on his door with a dour expression. "What is it!"

Rafael returned his glare. "I have come for my wife," he said formally.

Curiosity got the better of Matt's irritation. "Come in, Señor Delgado. Sara is not here, but could I offer you a glass of wine?"

Rafael hesitated, then moved inside. *"Gracias,* but no. She has been here, I see, or you would have been surprised to hear that Sara is now my wife."

Matt took a seat at the table and swept his hand in the direction of the other chair. "She was here, yes . . . with Garth Prescott. But they've gone. Please sit down a moment."

Good manners made Rafael comply stiffly. "Do you know where they were going?"

Matt nodded. "Garth was going to show her the church on their way back to the hotel, I think. They're just friends, you know—she and Garth. I can see the jealousy in your eyes señor, and there is no need for it."

Rafael stared hard at the little man for a moment, and then relaxed. "I know that."

Matt smiled for the first time. "Well, what you don't know is that Sara invited Garth and myself out to your hacienda for the roundup festivities. Since you're here, I'll just ask if you have any objections?"

Rafael couldn't help the smile that curved his mouth. "Absolutely none, *amigo.* I would be pleased if the two of you would honor us with a visit." Sara amazed him sometimes. She wouldn't be like an Indian wife, or a Spanish one either. She took hold of life in her own quiet, determined way, and made things happen. Perhaps that was the quality that drew him to her, and also made him so angry at times.

"Good enough," Matt said. "I'd like to show you something."

Rafael followed the man out to the courtyard. When Matt removed the oilcloth from the painting on the easel, Rafael stared at the picture of Sara for several minutes without saying a word. Matt had captured her beauty, the sweet expression in her eyes, and the smile that caused the blood to pump furiously through his veins. He fell in love with her all over again. "I will buy this from you, Señor Harrigan. What is your price?"

Matt had been watching the younger man's face, and was satisfied with what he saw. "It's not for sale. However, when it's finished, it will be my wedding gift to you and Sara."

Rafael turned his gaze on the artist. "I would gladly pay—"

Matt interrupted him with an impatient wave of his hand. "I, sir, will have the last word on this, and no arguments."

Upon his return to LaFonda, Rafael looked inquiringly at Bernadino, but the man shook his head in a negative gesture. Making his way to a table in the corner, Rafael sat down to wait.

After waiting on a table of soldiers, Juliana moved to his side. "Would you like a drink, Don Rafael? Or perhaps some company?"

He glanced up at her absently. "Bring a bottle of your best wine, Juliana. And then you could perhaps have a drink with me, eh?" His mood had darkened again at not finding Sara at the hotel. He was trying to be patient, but it was difficult.

Juliana returned and poured each of them a glass. "I haven't seen Don Manolo around lately. Is he very busy at the hacienda?"

Rafael sipped his wine, pushing his disquieting thoughts away for the moment. "He has had a lot to do with the roundup. Before that, it was harvest. I'm afraid I've been less than helpful since I got back." He studied the young woman's face. Her interest was more than casual, he thought. He'd had reports that Manolo had been seeing her for quite some time, and that she saved all her favors for him. For a prostitute, that was serious business. Either Manolo was paying enough to sustain her, or she thought herself in love with him. For Juliana's sake, he hoped it was the former.

She nodded, hope flickering in her dark eyes. "I was sure it was something like that, señor. If you would give him my regards, *por favor?*"

Rafael reached over and gave her hand a reassuring pat. "Of course, Juliana."

Sara caught her breath, as she watched Rafael look affectionately at the beautiful girl sitting with him. And when he touched her hand, Sara cringed as hurt washed over her. Sara turned to Garth and leaned up on tiptoe to kiss his cheek. In surprise, he automatically put his arms around her. When he met Rafael's eyes across the room, he pleaded for understanding. "I believe I should make myself scarce for now, Sara. Your husband doesn't look happy."

Sara's blue eyes gleamed with malicious satisfaction. "Good. See you later."

Garth made his way to the bar, and Sara marched determinedly across the room and up the stairs, ignoring Rafael.

With unhurried movements, Rafael stood, picked up the bottle of wine and his glass, and followed her, forgetting Juliana's presence.

Sara was removing her hat in front of the mirror, when he kicked the door open and walked in. She flinched, but did not turn to acknowledge him.

He pushed the door closed. "My wife does not traipse all over the city with another man," he said, his tone angry.

Sara placed her hat on the chest and turned slowly to glare at him. "So far, you have not treated me like a wife, nor do you even want me for one. You have made that abundantly clear. And besides, don't you remember giving me permission to find other companionship?"

Rafael remembered his rash words very well. He hadn't meant them, and he had certainly found out he didn't like seeing Sara with anyone else. "I do not call what you did discreet, Sara," he growled.

Sara shrugged and turned her back to him, peeling off her gloves. A secret smile curved her lips. He was jealous, she realized. She fixed a serious expression on her face, before she turned back. "Perhaps we should discuss exactly what I may and may not do, Rafael. Why don't you order our dinner sent up here, so that we can have some privacy?"

He frowned at her, and then turned and left the room without another word. Sara chuckled, her earlier anger forgotten. If Rafael was jealous, he must care a little, she reasoned. The thought made her supremely happy. Humming to herself, she stepped outside the room and called to the boy who swept up the bar. When he reached her side, she instructed him to have a bath sent up to the room as soon as possible. Laying out her prettiest silk chemise, she decided that her wedding night might possibly be salvaged after all.

Rafael returned to their room an hour later, to find Sara relaxing in a brass tub filled with fragrant bubbles. The alluring picture she presented took his breath away.

He felt his loins grow tight as he growled, "Pardon, Sara . . . I did not know . . ." Tearing his gaze away from her flushed face, he moved out onto the balcony. *Por Dios!* he thought savagely. Why did she have to be so appealing? He wanted to ignore her, to leave her behind when he went to his rancho to live. How was he going to do that, when he quivered like a young buck in her presence?

Sara shivered as she thought of the raw desire she'd glimpsed in Rafael's gaze. Wasn't that what she'd wanted? It did, however, make her nervous. What if she seduced him, and he still left her behind? After all, she knew practically nothing about men and their feelings. Closing her eyes, she leaned her head back on the tub for a few moments to gather her courage. Taking a deep breath, she called out, "Rafael? Could you get my towel, *por favor?* The maid left it on the bed."

Rafael's knuckles were white where he gripped the

balustrade, before he turned and walked into the room. He picked up the towel from the bed, and his eye fell on the silky undergarment beside it. He swallowed tightly as he walked over to the tub. Sara looked up and smiled. *"Gracias,* Rafael," she murmured, and reached for the towel.

Instead of giving it to her, he held it open and offered in a low tone, "Let me help you."

Sara's heart was hammering so hard, she could hardly breathe. It was what she'd wanted, but she was scared all the same. She stood up slowly, the water and bubbles glistening on her satiny skin in the lamplight, as she held his fierce gaze. When his eyes dropped to her breasts, it felt like a physical touch, and her skin tingled. His heated gaze burned a path down her body, before he wrapped the towel around her. His arms stayed to lift her from the tub and hold her close.

Sara let her head rest on his chest, and gripped his shoulders to keep her knees from buckling. She murmured his name, her voice husky.

Rafael's mouth was dry and his breath a hard knot in his throat, as a sea of emotions washed over him. Her lavender scent assailed his nostrils, while the heat of her soft body pressed against him. One hand slid inside the towel to caress the silk of her skin. It was the plea of her voice that sent him over the edge though. He tipped her chin up to take her mouth, pushing his tongue inside with her eager encouragement. His kiss was soft, yet strong, demanding, yet giving. It sent the pit of her stomach into a wild swirl.

The caress of her mouth on his set his body aflame. He trembled violently with the need to possess her. Abruptly breaking the kiss, he swept her into his arms and strode to the door, setting the bolt. Turning, he carried her to the bed and placed her gently on it. His eyes burned with the fierce light of passion, as he began to undress. "I promised myself I would not do this, but I cannot help it," he growled, shedding his clothes.

Sara lay naked, reveling in the desire she saw in his eyes. "Why would you make such a rash promise . . . I'm your wife," she whispered, reaching for him as he lowered himself to the bed beside her.

Rafael pulled the pins from her hair and smoothed it across the pillow. "We are from different worlds . . . and involvement will bring pain," he said quietly and then buried his face in her fragrant hair.

Sara wrapped her arms around his neck and pressed closer to him, loving the feel of his muscled body. "Oh, Rafael, we could overcome those differences, if we try," she whispered, her breathing becoming more ragged by the second.

His lips seared a path down her throat to the tip of one breast. Taking the rosy peak in his mouth, he sucked gently until the bud hardened, and then moved to lave the other peak with his tongue. Sara moaned deep in her throat, her hands gripping his shoulders, pressing him closer. "I can't think when you do that," she protested weakly.

He moved up to brush her lips with his, while his hand slipped down between her thighs to caress her with tantalizing strokes. "There is no need for thinking at the moment, *cara mia,* only feeling," he breathed against her mouth.

A soft gasp escaped her lips, as his fingers wrought

new and wonderful sensations in her body. Wanting to give him as much pleasure as he was giving her, she slid her hand between them and caressed his swollen manhood. His body quivered at her sensuous touch, and he took her mouth fiercely in a deep drugging kiss. Abruptly, he broke the kiss, growling, "You cannot continue that, *niña.*" He raised up and brushed her hand away. Sliding his knee between her thighs, he spread her legs and gazed for a moment at her eyes, deep, smoky blue with heavy passion. "Now, Rafael . . . take me now," she pleaded. He lowered himself and guided his shaft deep inside her warmth. Fleetingly, he worried over the fact that she was so small, but her moans of pleasure quieted his fears. Sara rose to meet his demanding rhythm with a fierceness that kindled Rafael's passion. Their cries of release mingled, as waves of ecstasy washed over the two of them. For several moments, they lay spent, not moving. Then, with reluctance, Rafael shifted to lie beside her. Caressing her delicate jawline with his finger, he breathed, "You are so tiny and fragile-looking, I forget sometimes how much woman you are in bed . . . you were wonderful."

She smiled lazily. "You're not terribly sorry it happened then?"

He gazed at her warmly. "At the moment, I am a happy man, *niña.*"

Sara's expression turned serious. "Is that all we'll ever have, Rafael—moments? Perhaps we could talk now . . . about our future? Do you really plan to leave me behind when you move to your *rancho?*"

Sara's reminder of what they faced brought sharp

memories to mind of her prejudices. He wanted her, but he was half-Indian, and wanted her to accept that. "I cannot change what I am or how I feel, Sara," he said, brushing the hair back from her face absently.

Sara closed her eyes to hide the pain. In his gentle way, he was trying to say he didn't love her. Perhaps he cared, but that was not love, she thought miserably. And maybe he loved this Indian girl, just as he had his wife, but if that was true, how could he make love to her as he just had? The thought cut through her like a knife. Opening her eyes, she gazed at his handsome face, her heart breaking. "I suppose this marriage was a mistake, but when we're together like this, I have trouble seeing it that way."

Rafael sat up and draped his arms loosely over his raised knees. He was unwilling to let her see how her words had cut. "Remember on the trail, when I told you how some men and women are attracted to each other in a special way? We are like that, Sara. Our lust for each other becomes more than we can bear sometimes."

Sara raised up on one elbow and let her fingers trail over Rafael's bare back. "Perhaps that's enough to start with. Maybe love will follow, if we give it a chance," she suggested quietly, forgetting her pride.

"Physical attraction is a powerful thing, Sara, but more important than love is respect. We cannot have anything without that," he said flatly.

Sara sat up and laid her cheek on his back, wrapping her arms around him. "I know you still think I can't accept the fact that you're half-Indian, but believe me, Rafael, that has never been the case."

A tiny bud of hope grew inside him. "Then why did you refuse to marry me before?"

Sara sighed. She couldn't tell him about his grandfather's plans. It might break the fragile bond between the two of them. "It was just as I told you—I have no dowry, and I really needed to do something on my own."

His slender hope withered with her guarded tone. "Perhaps we could start over. Take this slowly, until we know how we feel?" he suggested, unable to put her completely out of his life.

It was better than nothing, Sara decided. However, she intended to fight with every weapon at her disposal. She let one hand slide down his stomach to encircle him. "I think that's a wonderful idea, Rafael. Is this slow enough?" She gently caressed the shaft that was growing by the second. Kissing the corded muscles of his neck, she murmured, "Or maybe you meant we shouldn't do this at all?"

Turning in her arms, he pinned her to the bed and growled, "I will show you, my little vixen, what I meant by slowly." He proceeded to tease every inch of her body with his tongue and fingers, until she writhed in an agony of pleasure. She pleaded and moaned for the release he held just out of her reach. When he finally entered her, she whimpered with relief. Sated and exhausted, they slept, never hearing the knock on the door announcing the arrival of their dinner.

Sara felt like a widow as she walked about the large bedroom, absently touching Rafael's possessions. His extra hat lay on the ornately carved chest, several formal suits hung in the wardrobe, and a fancy, braided lariat hung on a peg on the wall. His masculine smell permeated everything in the room, especially the bed that Sara had slept in by herself for the past five nights.

As soon as they returned from Santa Fe, Rafael had left with all the young men on the hacienda to gather the cattle from the mountain pastures. It would be only a few more days until the herd was gathered on a common range, but Sara felt it was a lifetime.

A knock on the door brought her back to the present. She called permission to enter, and Rosita came in. "Doña Ines asked if you will meet with her in the large *sala,* señora."

Sara nodded. *"Gracias,* Rosita. Tell her I will be down in a few minutes." When the woman had gone, Sara went to the mirror to brush her hair. Picking up her light shawl from the chair by the door, she let herself out and onto the balcony. The weather was growing cooler, and Sara was dreading the loss of freedom that winter always brought. Descending the steps to the courtyard, she idly wondered what Doña Ines wanted. They usually spent their mornings together, with the older woman teaching Sara the different aspects of running a household this large. Each evening they met before dinner in the large *sala.* Dinner, however, was still a few hours away.

When Sara entered the *sala,* she stopped short at the scene that greeted her. A young Indian woman, who looked to be her own age, was standing with a young girl next to the fireplace. Both of them were wearing long dresses made of deerskin. Their long sleeves were trimmed with buckskin fringe, while beads in a geometric pattern decorated the front of the dresses. Their feet were encased in soft buckskin moccasins. Doña Ines rose from her chair, a guarded look on her face. "Sara, please come and meet Rafael's daughter, Kahuu. And this is her aunt, Little Dove."

Sara regained her composure and smiled, moving forward to stand in front of their guests. "I'm very pleased to meet both of you. I'm sure Doña Ines has already welcomed you to Hacienda Delgado."

The young woman nodded in confirmation of Sara's assumption, while the little girl stared in fascination at Sara's hair. Doña Ines intervened. "This is Rafael's new wife . . . Kahuu, your step-mother—Sara."

Little Dove was taken aback, and could not hide the surprise in her expression. "We did not know . . . Blanca and Jayme did not tell us of Rafael's marriage. We were told only that Rafael wished us to join him here, when we arrived at his *rancho.*"

It was Sara's turn to be taken aback. When, she wondered, had he issued that order? This was the Indian woman, Sara was sure, who was Rafael's choice of a wife. Sara felt a painful twist of jealousy. In one so young, Little Dove had great poise, and there was the delicate beauty of her face.

Doña Ines intervened once again. "They decided rather suddenly to marry, so there was not time to send out word. However, I am happy you are here. When Rafael and Vicente return, the whole family

314

will be together."

Kahuu shyly took the hand that Doña Ines held out. "I am also happy to be here, Tía Ines." She gave Sara a tentative smile, and Sara smiled in return.

"Come. I have had your things taken to your rooms. Perhaps you would like to rest before dinner?" Doña Ines offered.

Little Dove gave a brief nod and spared a fleeting glance at Sara, before she and Kahuu left the room with a servant.

When they were gone, Sara turned to Doña Ines. "I didn't seem cold, did I? It was such a surprise, that I didn't know how to react."

The older woman smiled and touched Sara's shoulder affectionately. "I don't think you could ever be cold, *niña*. Forgive me, though, for plunging you into this situation without warning. I just wanted you to meet Rafael's daughter as soon as possible. And after all, the mistress of the house should be consulted first about everything that goes on."

Sara gave her a wry smile. "I don't feel like the mistress of the house, and I certainly don't want to take your place, Doña Ines."

Clucking her tongue, Doña Ines corrected her. "Tía Ines, Sara. I am your aunt now. Moreover, I am happy to relinquish the household duties to you, for it is much work, and I am not growing any younger."

Sara looked relieved. "Do you think Kahuu was upset, because her father married again?"

Doña Ines shook her head. "I don't think so, *niña*, but time will tell. I'm sure when she gets to know

315

you, she will love you as we do."

An hour later, Señor Pino happened upon Sara in the large courtyard. She was sitting on a stool outside the schoolroom in deep thought. "Ah, *niña* . . . or should I say Señora Delgado?" he said, a smile on his weathered face.

When she looked up, she gave a cry of delight and stood up to hug his thin, dusty frame. "You're back! Does this mean Rafael is back also?" she asked eagerly.

He shook his head. "No, he is still with the herd. I returned to alert Juan that his cook-wagon and his services are needed now. We are ready to begin the cutting and branding."

Sara looked crestfallen as she nodded. "Is everything going well?"

The old man hid a smile. The little *niña* looked as lonely as Rafael did. It was a very good sign. *"Sí.* The men are anxious to get the work done, so the rodeo can begin. How are things here at the hacienda?"

Sara's eyes widened suddenly. "Oh my, I almost forgot! Rafael's daughter, Kahuu, arrived today with her aunt. It seems Rafael is expecting them."

Pedro smiled. "He will be glad to see his *hija."*

"I didn't realize he'd sent for her until she arrived," Sara admitted, trying not to sound hurt.

"Don Rafael wanted to surprise you. As a matter of fact, he asked me personally to deliver the message to his *rancho,* before I joined him at the roundup," Pedro said with a laugh.

Sara's heart was pounding as she asked, "So he planned this after we returned from Santa Fe?"

"*Sí*, I have never seen him so anxious over anything."

Sara blinked at the sudden tears that stung her eyes, as she made up an excuse to return to her room. After the closeness they had shared on their honeymoon, Sara couldn't believe that Rafael would want another woman! However, Little Dove was here—sent for by him, and Pedro had said he was very anxious. During siesta that afternoon, Sara was unable to sleep. Instead, she was tortured by thoughts of Rafael and Little Dove together.

Chapter 14

Despite the cool water Sara had splashed on her eyes, they were still slightly puffy from crying. She went through the motions of a good hostess at the dinner table with Doña Ines, Little Dove, and Kahuu, but her heart was not in it. Every time Sara glanced at Little Dove, the Indian woman was watching her with a knowing expression in her eyes. Perversely, that helped to strengthen Sara's backbone. When Señor Pino entered the dining room at the end of the meal, he bowed formally to the women, and then addressed Sara. "Forgive me for interrupting, Doña Sara, but I thought that since Kahuu has not seen her father in a long while, I could escort all of you out to the herd tomorrow. It is only an hour's ride from here, and I am sure Don Rafael would be happy to see you."

A moment of happy anticipation gripped Sara, before she glanced at her guests and saw a brief smile cross Little Dove's face. Still, she nodded. "That is very kind of you, Pedro. I would enjoy that, if

Kahuu . . . and Little Dove would like to go." She turned to Doña Ines with a questioning glance.

The older woman shook her head. "I will stay here where my comforts are near, my dear, but you young people go along."

Kahuu looked to her aunt for an answer, and Sara could see the excitement in the child's eyes. Little Dove nodded. *"Gracias,* we will go."

Sara and Pedro discussed what time the following day they would depart, before he left them to drink their coffee.

The thin man's head hung in defeat, as the two guards dragged him down the hillside and back to the lean-to next to the entrance of the mine. He had been a trifle weak before his attempt to escape, but failing in his attempt robbed him of the remainder of his strength. Carefully, they lowered him onto a wool blanket on the dirt floor. One of the men stepped out and brought back a skin filled with water, and offered the prisoner a drink. "Max, *amigo!* Is this how you repay our kindness?" the short, swarthy Mexican guard asked, shaking his head. "Don Manolo would gut us like fish, if we let you escape."

Max took a long, slow swallow, and then glanced at the guard who had spoken. "Forgive me, Rodrigo. I guess I forgot for a moment how good I have it here in this hellhole," he said dryly.

Rodrigo clucked his tongue. "We cannot help it, if you are a prisoner, eh, Arturo?"

The other guard shrugged. "This is true, *amigo.*

We only follow orders; our families have to eat."

Max closed his eyes for a moment. "I know, but you can't blame me for trying." He opened one eye and asked, "Are you going to tell Delgado about this?"

Arturo's long mustache drooped at the corners and he looked away. *"Sí,* Max . . . we must." Glancing up at the lone guard who stood sentry at the top of the hill overlooking the mine, he added, "Gomez will inform Don Manolo about this. Of that we can be sure. He is a bootlicker."

"Por Dios! You are lucky Gomez did not shoot you in the back, when you ran for that hill," Rodrigo said. "He was half-asleep, or he would have."

Max grimaced. "Since it's your job, why didn't either of you shoot me?"

The two Mexicans looked puzzled by his question. "We like you," Arturo said. "You are an amusing fellow."

Sara spread the brightly colored blanket under a piñon tree, and then took the picnic basket from Pedro. She put it down and turned toward the creek, where she could see Rafael walking with Kahuu and Little Dove. Sara had purposely hung back when he suggested a walk, giving him time with his daughter. It rankled though, that Little Dove had joined the two of them.

Pedro was watching them also. "They are alike, father and daughter, eh?"

Sara sighed. "Yes. She's as beautiful as he is handsome. Her mother must have been very pretty."

"*Sí*. I saw her once . . . Little Dove looks like her," Pedro commented, turning to glance at a rider galloping toward them.

Sara tried to ignore the sinking feeling that information gave her. She shaded her eyes with her hand, and recognized Manolo on the horse. He turned the horse with a flourish before reaching them, and jumped gracefully from the animal's back. He swept his hat from his head and smiled at Sara. "I was told the most beautiful woman in the province arrived a while ago," he said, taking her hand and bowing low over it.

Sara's face grew pink with pleasure. "It's not true, but it's so nice of you to say it."

His grin became cheeky. "You must not argue with me, cousin. It is not considered polite." Then he glanced at Pedro, who had moved a respectful distance away. "Pedro, Rafael has asked me to escort the ladies back to the hacienda this afternoon, so you can go back to your duties."

The older man looked up for a moment and then nodded. "*Sí*. If I can be of service to you before you go, Señora Delgado, let me know," he said in a level tone.

As he walked away, Sara wondered at his change of attitude. It almost seemed that he didn't like Manolo, but the younger man was always polite to Pedro. Sara sat down on the blanket, and said, "I hope this is not an inconvenience, Manolo."

He leaned one shoulder against the piñon tree. "It is a pleasure, I assure you. As a matter of fact, I will be stopping at the Santa Pilar mine at my uncle's request. That is the main reason Rafael asked me.

I will be killing two birds with one stone, eh?"

Sara had been watching the three people coming toward them from the creek. She felt unsure of herself and needed moral support. Hastily, she glanced at Manolo and asked, "Would you share our picnic with us? The cook packed enough to feed an army."

Manolo read the desperation in her eyes and rightly guessed the reason. This is an opportunity, he thought, too good to pass up. "*Gracias,* Sara. I would love it."

She breathed a sigh of relief and began unpacking the basket. Manolo stooped down to help her place the many dishes across the blanket, as the others strode up. Pasting a bright smile on her face, Sara looked up at them. "I hope you're hungry."

Rafael held out a hand to her. "I would like to speak with you privately for a moment, Sara? The others could start without us."

Sara's glance slid away from the serious expression in his eyes, as she took his hand. "Of course," she murmured as he helped her up. They walked a good distance away from the others, before he spoke. "Are you upset that I sent for my daughter without telling you?"

Sara shook her head. "No. Why should you consult me on such matters? It's your daughter and your home," she said evenly.

"Then it is Little Dove who causes the problem," he said with more sureness. "I know what I said before, but I do not intend to take her for a wife."

Stung, Sara asked, "Then why did you send for her as soon as we returned from Santa Fe?"

Rafael sighed. "I sent for Kahuu. I did not know Little Dove would bring her. Sara, you must know that I would not be so callous."

Sara wanted desperately to believe him, but the other woman's presence had shaken her faith. They had moved into a stand of evergreens, out of sight and earshot of the others. Sara stopped and leaned back warily against a tree. "I couldn't swear to it, but I'm almost sure Little Dove is expecting something from you. Did you ever speak to her about marriage?" she asked.

Rafael tipped her chin up, so her gaze would meet his. "No, but in all honesty, Little Dove has never made a secret of her feelings for me. I believe she always expected me to marry her someday."

"And you were considering it . . ." Sara murmured.

He leaned forward and brushed his lips across hers. "Perhaps I was, but we are married now, and it no longer matters." He took her lips then in a slow, numbing kiss, while Sara clung to him, angry at herself for her weakness.

When he finally drew back, Sara persisted. "She acts as if there has been no marriage between us."

"The Comanche do not recognize any ceremonies but their own. However, she understands what has happened between us," he explained, an impatient edge in his tone.

A stubborn light appeared in her eyes. She did not intend to be put off any longer. "Will she be staying with us for a while, or will you send her back to her people?"

Rafael sighed in exasperation, and turned to stare

at the mesa rising in the distance. "For Kahuu's sake, I cannot just send her away. The child has not been away from her aunt since her mother died."

"I understand that, Rafael. My heart is not made of stone, but with Little Dove here, I don't know that there's a chance for us." With that, Sara walked away and Rafael sighed, not knowing what else to say.

They returned to the picnic and settled down to eat. Manolo paid Sara extravagant compliments, and directed most of his conversation to her. She noticed Rafael's dour looks as the meal progressed, but ignored him. Before they left to return to the hacienda, Rafael and Manolo escorted the ladies around the valley, where they watched crews of *vaqueros* cutting out steers and branding new calves.

The sun was setting as Manolo rode into the isolated canyon, where his secret mine was located. He pulled his stallion to a halt, as Gomez made his way down from the hill where he kept watch. After speaking with the swarthy little man a few moments, Manolo continued on to the clearing where two adobe buildings flanked the mine opening. Arturo sat in front of the guard's house. Otherwise, the place looked deserted. Manolo knew that the men were still down in the shaft working, along with two guards to watch them. It was a small operation, but their returns had been considerable already, what with the high grade of pure silver they had found.

Arturo, who had been half-dozing, his sombrero covering his face, gave a start at the jingle of

Manolo's spurs. Scrambling to his feet, he gave a sheepish grin to his boss. *"Hola,* Señor Delgado! What a pleasant surprise."

Manolo dismounted and handed the reins to the guard with a scowl. "A surprise, I am sure, but pleasant, no. Gomez told me about the attempted escape."

Arturo gave an exaggeráted shrug. "A small problem, no more. The *norteamericano* is very clever, señor, but he did not even get out of the compound, before we caught him. And we punished him."

"If the guards down in the shaft were doing their job, an escape of this sort would not be possible. All of you are lucky the man did not get away," Manolo said, his voice soft, but deadly. "Now, fetch some wine and bring the *norteamericano* to me."

Arturo nodded, knowing Manolo did not want to hear his feeble excuses. He tied the horse to a rail and hurried inside the guardhouse to fetch the refreshment, wiping the sweat from his clammy face.

In a quarter of an hour, Max Clayton stood in front of Manolo in the guardhouse. They eyed each other across the table with equal amounts of suspicion. Manolo took a leisurely sip of his wine, and then gave the thin, ragged man a friendly smile. "This interview can be dealt with quickly, I think. I want your word that you will not try to escape again."

Max's brows rose in surprise, and a hoarse bark of laughter passed his lips. He was so tired and weak, he had to make a conscious effort to keep from falling, but pride kept him upright. "Of course,

325

Señor Delgado. I give it to you from one honorable gentleman to another . . . now, is that all you want?"

The look in Manolo's eyes hardened. "You are not showing me the proper respect, but I will overlook that for the moment. Until I am a rich man, I do not want the existence of this mine known. Now, if you were to escape, you would go straight to the authorities, and I would be in a little trouble, eh?"

Max nodded. "I think that is a fair assessment of the situation, yes."

"Well, then you and I will strike a deal. I will not harm your sister, Sara, if you promise to behave. And perhaps someday, I will release all of you . . . that is, when I have enough money to leave the country as a wealthy man."

It took a moment for Manolo's matter-of-fact statement to sink in, but when it did, Max blinked in confusion. "Sara? What do you know about her? Sara is not—"

Manolo interrupted, "*Sí*, Clayton. Sara is residing at Hacienda Delgado . . . as a matter of fact, she is now married to my cousin, Rafael. Of course, I do not approve of that at all. He is a half-breed, and not good enough for a treasure like Sara, but I could not stop the marriage, so . . ." He gave an elaborate shrug.

Max shook his head to clear his chaotic thoughts. "My sister is here . . . in Santa Fe? What do you mean—harm her?" His voice rose on his last question.

Manolo smiled. "If you cooperate, I will have no need even to think about arranging an accident . . . like the one I arranged for your nosy partner, John

326

Edgar. He asked too many questions about your disappearance, and it made me nervous."

The man's calm admission of murder sent a new weakness through Max, that had nothing to do with hunger and deprivation. "I won't try to escape again, I promise you," Max whispered.

Manolo slapped the table abruptly and grinned. "I knew you were a reasonable man, *amigo.*"

Arturo led Max to the prisoner quarters and locked him in. He headed for the shaft to help herd the other prisoners out for the night. Max lay down on his filthy cot, and a newer, stronger purpose fired his blood. His eyes glowed with the plans for escape he was already forming in his mind. Delgado was as mad as a hatter if he thought Max would keep the absurd promise. Now he had more to think about than himself, and he felt new strength flowing through his tired body.

"I would appreciate it if you would invite Estella to visit, Tía Ines," Sara said, as they sat in the *sala* having their morning chocolate.

Although her nephew's wife looked bright and crisp in her flocked cotton day dress, the young woman's attitude had been lackluster for a few days. Smiling, Ines said, "Of course, I will invite her. That is a small request, and one I can easily grant. The poor child has probably been grieving for her grandmother, and the visit would do her good. I think it would do you good as well, *niña,* to have a younger woman to talk to."

Impulsively, Sara got up and gave the older

woman a hug. "That's not my purpose for asking, Tía Ines. I love spending time with you. To tell you the truth, I have grown very fond of you in the short time I've been here."

Doña Ines blinked back the tears that stung her eyes, and smiled. "God has been very good to me, giving me Rafael to love, and now you, *niña*. I could not have children of my own, you know, and then my husband died, leaving me alone. However, Vicente offered me a home when Rafael was a boy, and I have been happy here."

Sara returned to her seat. "I, too, have been lucky. Not too many months ago, I had no one in the world to call my own, and now I have a husband and a family—even a stepdaughter."

"Do you think Kahuu is beginning to accept you?" the older woman asked. She knew Sara and Rafael were having some sort of difficulty, and hoped it had nothing to do with the child. She was praying that their problems could be worked out with time.

Sara smiled. "I think so. Yesterday, I noticed that she admired the ribbon I had in my hair, so I gave her one as a gift last night. I suppose you noticed she wore it to dinner?"

"*Sí*. She's a beautiful child. If only the aunt . . ."

Sara's gaze dropped. "Little Dove doesn't like me, I know. It's despicable of me, but I wish she would go back to her people. Kahuu and I could get to know each other if Little Dove didn't hover over her all the time."

Doña Ines nodded. "You are her stepmother now, and it's only natural to want to take your rightful place with the child. Perhaps we could let her help us with the preparations for the rodeo and fiesta?"

Sara perked up. "That's a good idea, Tía Ines. I'll ask her at lunch."

For the next two days, Kahuu became Sara's shadow. The child seemed delighted to help Sara organize the menus, and plan the decorations for the fiesta. On a bright sunny morning, Sara and Kahuu sat together at a table in the family courtyard, cutting strips of colored paper into streamers. Kahuu brushed her dark, straight hair over her shoulders, as she bent over her task. Sara glanced at her fondly, and was happy that for once Little Dove had left them alone. "We could hang several colors from each lantern and some in the trees. What do you say?" Sara asked.

"Sí, and maybe drape some along the *portales.* Last year Rosita and I did that. It looked very beautiful," Kahuu said shyly.

"Oh, yes!" Sara agreed enthusiastically. "When I was growing up, my mother decorated our house with fresh flowers for summer parties, and evergreen for winter ones. We never had pretty colored paper like this."

"I like the customs of my father's people," Kahuu admitted. "This is my favorite time of year. I get to see my father and the rodeo."

Sara laughed. "I think this will be my favorite time of the year as well. I'm anxious to help Rosita make the *piñatas,* aren't you?"

Kahuu giggled. *"Sí.* Tomorrow is a long time to wait."

Garth and Matt arrived the following day to find Sara, Kahuu, and Rosita busily working on the *piñatas*. Sara jumped up and gave her friends a hug, and then introduced them. "I was hoping you would arrive before everyone returned, so that we could catch up," she said with a laugh.

Kahuu's eyes had grown rounder when the men embraced her stepmother. An uneasy feeling washed over her as she realized that her father had not shown this much affection toward Sara, and she was his wife.

"I'll show you to your rooms myself. Lunch will be served shortly, but I'm afraid the men are all gone for the day at least. Don Vicente and Manolo rode out to the mine, and Rafael is with the herd. However, we expect them all back tomorrow. The rodeo will begin in just a couple of days," she said, leading them toward the stairs.

"We have you to entertain us," Garth said.

"And I can do some sketches of the hacienda. It's a beautiful example of architecture. I've found the colors and structures made out of natural materials to be very pleasing to the eye," Matt enthused.

Sara laughed. "I knew I wouldn't have to worry about the two of you." She touched Kahuu on the shoulder. "This lovely young lady is my stepdaughter, Kahuu. Meet my good friends, Señor Prescott and Señor Harrigan."

"Buenos dias," the girl said shyly, and then ducked her head back to her work.

As they made their way around the balcony on the second story, Garth dropped his voice suddenly, asking, "Have you talked to Estella?"

Sara nodded. "Tía Ines sent her a special invitation to visit. She'll be arriving tomorrow . . . without her mother. Her note said that Doña Josefina would not attend the festivities this year."

Garth looked relieved. "I can't believe the news is this good!"

Sara opened two doors, side by side. "If you need anything before lunch, just ring the bell. I'll send a servant up with water for you."

Matt stepped inside his room, but Garth bent to kiss her cheek before she walked away. "Thanks for everything, Sara," he whispered.

On the western side of the hacienda wall, the large corral fence had been prepared for the rodeo events. Anticipation crackled in the air, as the men who were left behind set up stalls for the events and benches for the spectators. A canvas lean-to had been erected for the women of the household to sit under. Their delicate complexions had to be preserved, even though the sun had lost much of its strength this late in the year. The women had been cooking for a week, preparing enough food to feed everyone at the fiesta.

Rafael leaned against the wooden fence, gazing toward the smaller corrals, where the horses, cows, and bulls were being kept until the events began. He'd arrived at the hacienda an hour ago, anxious to see Sara, only to find that she'd gone for a morning ride with Manolo and Garth Prescott. He clamped down on the disappointment and jealousy he felt. It didn't matter that he'd vowed to himself to keep an emotional distance from Sara, those raw feelings ripped through him every time another man looked at her, or showed undue interest. Garth Prescott, he knew, was no more than a friend to Sara, but Manolo was a different story. His cousin barely hid his attraction.

The bawling of the cattle and snorting of the bulls, along with the friendly banter of the *vaqueros* at work around him, masked Little Dove's approach. He gave a small start when she touched his arm and spoke. "I've been anxious to talk to you, Rafael. It's been a long time," she said, her voice edged with hurt.

He turned to face her and his expression softened. "Forgive my manners, Little Dove. I intended to come see you, as soon as I finished here."

The young Comanche woman gazed at him, her heart in her eyes, and nodded. "Kahuu is out riding with your . . . wife."

Rafael cringed inside at the pain he heard in her voice. She was beautiful—just as Tuwikaa had been—and he appreciated the care and devotion she'd given his daughter, but he didn't love her . . . he loved Sara. "Thank you for bringing her to me, Little Dove. I have always been able to count on you."

Little Dove turned away from the pity she saw in his eyes. She leaned her arms on the fence and gazed at the high-spirited horses that pranced around the corral. "Kahuu has been like a daughter to me. Each year, she is shy when she first arrives here to visit . . . my presence makes it easier for her."

Rafael sighed. He knew she had too much pride to

listen to an explanation of why he married Sara, instead of approaching her as she had always expected. Instead, he changed the subject. "How is Running Fox? Does he still petition your father for your hand, or has he given up?"

One of her pencil-thin eyebrows rose. "He called on my father again not long ago. Just before we crossed the mountains." She swallowed the lump in her throat, and then lied, "I am considering his offer this time. I think he would make a good husband."

"He is a brave warrior and a good man. He loves you very much," Rafael said quietly, knowing she must save face.

For a few moments, Little Dove struggled with her emotions, and then said, "Kahuu knows you wish for her to live with you permanently, and she wants this also. I think it is time father and daughter are reunited."

"I have missed her, but you will feel the loss more than anyone. You know, Little Dove, that you are welcome to come visit us anytime. I want you to feel that my home is your home . . . and Sara will agree with me, I am sure."

Resolutely, Little Dove turned to look at Rafael. "Your Sara . . . she is a good woman. One woman knows this about another. I think she will be a good mother to Kahuu, and so I am not worried. All I ask is that you try to make a happy home for my sister's child."

Rafael smiled. "I gladly make that promise."

Sara's heart pounded with excitement, as she left

Estella's room after lunch and made her way to her own. Once inside, she hurried to the wardrobe and extracted her riding habit. As she turned to lay it on the bed, she gasped in surprise. Rafael was watching her lazily, his back propped against the headboard. "Who is taking you riding this time? One of your admirers, perhaps?"

Sara's gaze swept hungrily over his handsome face and muscular body. It seemed like years instead of days since she'd seen him. Just how much she'd missed him struck her forcefully. "Rafael . . . I . . . where were you at lunch? Don Vicente said you were back," she stammered, feeling unsure of herself under his penetrating gaze.

He drew one leg up to rest his arm on, and shrugged. "I had much to see to. But, *niña,* you did not answer my question."

Sara realized that she was clutching her riding clothes tightly to her bosom and relaxed her grip, laying them on the end of the bed. "I have no admirers. That's nonsense," she said, avoiding his gaze. She didn't want him to see the guilt in her eyes and mistake the reason. The excitement she had felt a few minutes ago changed to anxiety. Trying to calm her shaking hands, she smoothed the wrinkles in the green material of her coat.

In a quick, graceful motion, Rafael stood up and walked around to where she stood. He lifted her chin with his finger, and slid his other hand behind her neck, under her hair. "You do not seem overjoyed to see your husband. As a matter of fact, you seem very nervous, *mi alma.* What is wrong?"

Sara could barely think when Rafael stood this

close to her. She trembled as she gazed into his dark eyes, and rested her hands on his chest to steady herself. She felt his heart pounding rapidly in time with her own. "I am happy to see you, Rafael," she whispered, her large, blue eyes dropping to his wide, sensuous mouth. All thought of what she was supposed to be doing flew from her mind, as he caressed her neck with strong, yet gentle fingers.

Rafael felt another hot surge of jealousy at her evasiveness. He wondered who had been keeping her company, while he was away . . . and why she'd been in such a hurry to change and go riding. "Then give me a welcome-home kiss and show me," he urged, his voice growing husky.

Mesmerized by the kindling desire in his eyes, Sara reached up and pulled his head down to hers, touching her lips to his. Instant passion ignited between them, and he pulled her roughly to his body, his mouth opening to take her tongue inside. Sara moaned as the kiss deepened, and she melted against his heat.

Rafael's body burned everywhere she touched him, and his senses reeled from the contact. He hadn't meant for this to happen. He'd been angry and had wanted to keep his distance, but a mere touch from her had him shaking with desire. Abruptly, he broke the kiss and glared fiercely into her passion-glazed eyes. "You were in a hurry, Sara," he rasped. "Let me help you, before this gets out of hand." Taking her shoulders, he turned her around, even as she protested hoarsely. "I will unhook your dress, and there will be no need to call the maid."

"Rafael, please," she whispered, trembling in reaction to his kiss. "Why are you angry with me? Just talk to me!"

He ignored her plea and unhooked the back of her gown. When it fell open, he swallowed tightly at the sight of her slender back encased in a silk chemise. The soft curve of her buttocks was his undoing. He slipped his arms around her waist, and pulled her back against him. Pushing her hair aside, he kissed her bare shoulder and murmured, "I cannot stay angry with you, *cara mia*. I have missed you too much, and talk is not what I want at this moment." His hands slid her dress off her shoulders.

Sara sighed with frustration, but closed her eyes and took pleasure in his exciting touch. She wanted him, no matter what problems they shared. "We must talk later . . ." she breathed, as his kisses continued up the slim column of her throat, and one of his hands found its way under her chemise between her legs. He stroked her gently and caressed one breast, causing her to arch her back and groan with pleasure. Suddenly, she was lifted into the cradle of his arms and carried to the bed. He left her there to bolt the door. Sara watched him undress from under heavy lids, and then welcomed him into her arms. The heat of his strong muscular body covered hers, and she opened her mouth for his hungry kiss.

Sara's hands moved feverishly over his sun-browned skin, as he slid down to tease a dusky pink nipple through the silky chemise. Before her moan of pleasure had passed her lips, he had moved down her taut stomach to the apex of her thighs, where he kissed her gently. Sara gasped and arched her back, as his mouth loved her until waves of ecstasy throbbed through her. "Oh, Rafael, I need you inside me . . . please love me . . ." she whimpered.

He raised up and slid his throbbing manhood into her in one swift movement. Whispering broken words of passion in her ear, he loved her with his hard body, building a fierce rhythm that she had no trouble following. The hot tide of passion that raged through both of them soon exploded in fiery sensations. Afterwards, they lay panting, unable to speak.

Finally, Rafael rolled to one side and gazed tenderly at her flushed face. "There, *cara mia,* was that not better than a gallop through the valley?" he teased.

Sara's eyes widened, and she sat up abruptly, "Oh no, I forgot!"

As she tried to scramble off the bed, he caught her around the waist and pulled her back against him. "What, my little vixen, did you forget? You're not going to seduce me and then run away."

Sara leaned over his chest and brushed her lips against his. "It's a secret, but I'll tell you *if* you promise not to tell anyone?"

She looked so beautiful—her cheeks flushed with his lovemaking, and her silver hair in wild disarray—that he was loath to let her up. "I promise," he said solemnly, his eyes twinkling.

Her eyes softened. She loved it when he let his guard down enough to be playful and trust her. "Garth and Estella are going to elope, and I'm helping them," she confided. "We're going for a ride,

337

but I'll be coming back alone."

Rafael's brows rose. "So, you are playing cupid, eh? That is all right, little one, but I am coming with you. It is not safe for you to be out alone."

"You don't disapprove? I was afraid you might, so—"

He pulled her up with him and swatted playfully at her bare backside. "So you were going to leave me out of all the fun, eh?"

Sara giggled as she scrambled for her clothes. "I didn't know how you would feel about it, but I'm so glad you're going along. We must hurry though. I promised to be at the stable a while ago. Garth and Estella are probably at their wits' end."

As Rafael dressed, his spirits felt lighter than they had in a long time. Sara had not planned an assignation with another man after all, and he was very happy about that.

Rafael and Sara said *adios* and good luck to Garth and Estella, on the road that led to Chihuahua. The young couple planned to travel from that city to the coastal town of Matamoras, where they could take a ship to New Orleans.

Sara was tearful as she watched them ride away. "I'm happy for them, but we've lost two dear friends," she said, wiping at the tears that rolled down her cheeks.

Rafael leaned over and kissed her gently. "Perhaps they will return someday to visit."

Sara smiled. "Not soon, I hope. I have a feeling that Doña Josefina will be angry for years."

Rafael chuckled. "If she ever finds out we had a part in this, our heads will roll as well."

"Then we will act as surprised as everyone else, when the maid finds Estella's note on her pillow, eh?" she said, laughing, her youthful exuberance returning.

Rafael turned his horse eastward. "I think, perhaps, we should not return until dark. Do you remember when you were ill, and I talked to you of a pueblo called Pecos?"

Sara nodded. "The place where the ancient fire is kept burning?"

"*Sí.* Would you like to go there?" he asked.

Sara's mouth curved into a smile. "You did promise to take me, remember?"

For a while, they galloped over the well-worn track, letting the horses have their heads. When they slowed, Rafael gave names to the native flowers, distant hills, and mesas they passed. Occasionally, they met travellers on the road, dark, swarthy men dressed in rough cotton pants and shirts, with wide-brimmed sombreros shading their dark heads. Most rode or led mules laden with supplies or firewood. Rafael told her everyone in the lowlands had to gather the piñon wood in the mountains for their fires.

When they arrived at the pueblo, Sara was amazed at the size of the huge quadrangle. It was easy to see that it had once been like a fortress, several stories high. Now it was crumbling in many places. As they rode through an archway in the high wall, Sara saw Rafael salute an Indian man who was standing guard atop the wall. "They are accustomed to visitors occasionally. He mainly watches for renegade warriors from the plains, that seek to attack or do them harm. There are only about twenty-five of this tribe living here now."

Sara looked around at the interior plaza, silent and nearly empty. She tried to imagine what it was like when hundreds of people lived here. Whether ghostly imaginings or a trick of the wind, Sara could hear for a moment the sounds of a busy town—children laughing, mules braying, peddlers hawking their wares. Cocking her head to one side, she strained to hold onto the strange sensation, but it was quickly gone. "Do you think they'll mind, if we look around? I would very much like to visit the sacred fire, if it's allowed," she said, her voice taking on a reverent tone.

Rafael dismounted and helped her down, tying their horses to a rail. "*Sí*, I am acquainted with the priest, and he will be happy to meet you."

As they walked across the dusty plaza, Sara saw a young Indian woman with a child in tow, leaving the church. She nodded politely to them, but said nothing as she moved on. As they climbed the four steps and stood between twin adobe arches, Rafael told her, "This mission church was first built by the Franciscans in the early 1600's, only to be destroyed during the Revolt of 1680. Indians all over the New Mexican territory rose up and drove out their cruel Spanish conquerors at that time. It took the Spanish twelve years to reconquer what they had lost, but after they did, they were much kinder masters."

Sara ran her hand lightly over the grainy arch, trying to imagine the bloody battle that had taken place here so many years ago. "I suppose they had learned their lesson," she commented.

He nodded. "My ancestors understood only the sword, but we have become more civilized since then, more humane, I hope. Anyway, the church was rebuilt on site of the original Aztec temple. The Spanish priests allowed the Indians to retain some of their own ceremonial rites, along with the new Catholic beliefs. Hence, the sacred fire that still burns."

Sara shook her head in wonder. "Fascinating. I can feel the vibrations in this place . . . it is a place where the spirit endures."

They entered the cool, quiet sanctuary, where paintings of saints adorned the front of the high altar, and carved, wooden *santos* rested piously in recessed niches in the walls. Rafael stopped just inside the door and crossed himself.

A dark, wizened little man in a brown robe came through a doorway to the right of the altar, carrying a silver candelabrum. He smiled when he saw them advancing down the aisle. "Don Rafael, it is so good to see you again! And you have brought a friend," he said, placing the candelabrum on a table and coming forward to meet them.

"Father Narbona, I have brought my wife, Sara," Rafael said, returning his smile.

The priest took her hand and gazed intently into her eyes for a moment, before he nodded in satisfaction. "Señora Delgado, we are honored to have you visit our humble village."

Sara felt almost as if she had just passed some sort of test. For one so old, his grip was surprisingly firm, and she saw wisdom, knowledge, and kindness in his eyes. *"Gracias,* Father. I am honored to be here," she said quietly.

He released her hand and offered her his arm. "You wish to see the sacred fire . . . I knew you were coming."

Sara took his arm and nodded slowly. Somehow, she was not surprised by his pronouncement. He was a man who had achieved a realm of understanding that most mortals did not know existed. She felt this with every fiber of her being. Master Filbert's teachings came back to her with clarity in this holy place; this man and this temple were at one with nature.

He took them through a doorway on the left of the altar, and down two flights of steps into the subterranean vaults, where the kiva was located. Small recessed shelves in the walls held candles that threw off a flickering light in the dim rooms they passed through. Sara shivered a little at the drop in temperature on this level, as well as the eerieness of the ancient aura.

Finally, Father Narbona stopped inside a room that was different from the others. In the center was a stone basin. Thin wisps of smoke rose from the silent, smoldering fire beneath a layer of protective ashes. There was a young Indian man sitting cross-legged at the head of the rectangular pit, his countenance solemn. The priest nodded toward the young man. "Toltema guards the holy fire of Montezuma. He is a warrior whose ancestors have lived here for hundreds of years. We have so few left in our village, that each of us must take the watch by turns each week."

342

Rafael glanced at Sara, and then asked, "Would you say a blessing over us, Father?"

"Of course, my children," he responded. Closing his eyes, he lifted his hands to touch each of them on their bowed heads. Sara remembered what Rafael had said about the Indian legend: wishes were granted to those blessed in this temple. She wished with all her heart that her life with Rafael would be happy. As the priest chanted an ancient blessing in a language she didn't understand, Sara wondered fleetingly what Rafael's wish was.

Before they left the pueblo, they took a glass of wine with Father Narbona in his tiny apartment next to the church. As they rode out of the quadrangle, the sepulchral silence of the place was disturbed only by the barking of a dog on a distant hill.

For several miles, they gave the rested horses a good run. When the track wove through a rocky canyon, however, they slowed their pace. Sara wanted to ask Rafael about his wish, but was afraid of his answer. Instead, she said, "I believe Kahuu is enjoying her visit. She's really looking forward to the rodeo and fiesta."

Rafael smiled. "I will wager she did not tell you what a superb horsewoman she is, did she? There is an event each year for trick-riders, and she has entered it for the last three years."

"No, I didn't know that. I suppose she's modest like her father," Sara said. "Pedro and Juan both told me how wonderful you are with horses."

"I'm no better than the others," he said with a shrug. Changing the subject, he said, "Little Dove has told me that Kahuu wants to live with me permanently."

Sara swallowed the lump that formed in her throat. She wondered where Little Dove fit into this situation. "That's wonderful, Rafael. I know it will make you happy to have your daughter with you."

Rafael nodded. "I am ready now to make a real home for her, Sara. For so many years, I was hurt and bitter over her mother's death. Deep down, I knew I was not fit company for the child."

"And Don Vicente dotes on her," Sara said, reining her horse around a protruding cactus plant.

Rafael's head snapped up. "That's not possible, with the way he feels about the Comanche."

One pencil-thin brow rose, as she replied, "Perhaps he's changed, and you just didn't realize it. I've seen them together."

For a few minutes, Rafael was silent as they let their horses pick their way across the rough canyon floor. His grandfather *had* seemed more tolerant of late. The old Don Vicente had disapproved of everything . . . the new one seemed to take most things with a smile. What had happened to the old man, Rafael wondered? "I thought he just tolerated Kahuu, as he does me, but if it is as you say, I am glad. I don't want my daughter to feel the sting of prejudice and rejection."

The trail was winding up a hill, toward a brushy thicket edged with yucca plants. Out of the corner of her eye, Sara caught the flash of something glinting in the sunlight, just before she heard the explosion of a gun. Rafael made a strange sound and pitched sideways, falling from his horse. Sara screamed his

344

name, quickly slid from her mount, and squatted beside him. "Keep your head down, Sara," he hissed, looking her over to make sure she was all right.

Sara's worried gaze alighted on the blood-soaked rip across the shoulder of Rafael's coat. "Let me look at the wound, Rafael. Do you think it's bad?" she asked anxiously.

He shook his head, gazing intently up the hill for signs of his attacker. "Not now, Sara. I just need something to stop the flow of blood. We've got to find better cover than this."

Sara ripped the bottom ruffle from her petticoat, and folded it hastily into a square. Gently, she slipped it inside his shirt. Rafael used one hand to apply pressure. "All right—now what?" she asked.

"Help me to stand, but we must keep our heads down, until we know it is safe. We will walk behind our horses around the hill at an angle, until we reach the mesa," he instructed quietly. When he was upright, he slipped his pistol from the holster at his side and cocked it. They crouched behind their mounts, and started off.

Sara was a bundle of nerves by the time they reached the top of the mesa, and found themselves alone. Breathing a ragged sigh, she made Rafael let her look at the wound and bind it tightly, before they mounted up and rode for the hacienda.

Chapter 15

Sara's heart was in her throat, as she sat under the lean-to watching Rafael ride a wild horse around the rodeo ring. He had mastered the bucking, but the stallion's eyes were still wild with confusion at having the unaccustomed weight on his back. He pranced sideways suddenly, trying to rake Rafael against the fence, and Sara gasped.

Doña Ines reached over and patted Sara's hand. "He will be fine, *niña*. It was just a flesh wound, and Rosita did a beautiful job of stitching it up."

Kahuu, sitting on the other side of Sara, said, "If you are nervous now, wait until you see my papa fight the bull."

Sara closed her eyes. "That will surely make me faint," she predicted. It can't frighten me much more than Rafael's getting shot, though, she thought grimly. He had insisted that it was most likely a stray bullet from a hunter, or even perhaps a renegade Indian, but Sara had an uneasy feeling. Nothing she could put her finger on, but still a foreboding.

When Rafael had the horse properly subdued, he dismounted and rubbed the horse's nose, until he could step closer and breathe into the animal's nostrils. After that, Rafael led the animal out of the ring amid shouts and whistles from the audience. Sara clapped her hands as long and loud as the rest.

"That is the Comanche way to tame a horse. Now the animal will know the master's scent," Kahuu explained to Sara, when the noise died down.

Next up was Manolo, but his showing was a little less skilled than his cousin's. He took his bows, his expression pinched. Making his way over to the lean-to, he forced himself to smile at Rafael, who stood behind Sara's chair. "As usual, cousin, you have made the grandest showing. Congratulations."

Rafael held out a hand to his cousin. *"Gracias,* Manolo. But I believe our little Kahuu won the most applause today with her trick riding."

Doña Ines and Sara were adding their praise, when Don Vicente joined them. "Rafael should not have entered any of the events today with that shoulder," the old man said gruffly. "Hacienda Delgado and its people will be your responsibility someday. The *patrón* has to take care of himself!"

Stunned by his grandfather's statement, Rafael stared at the old man, who had stooped down beside Kahuu's chair to talk to her. Don Vicente had never before said that he would leave his holdings to his grandson. As a matter of fact, Rafael had assumed that the old man had sent for Manolo to groom him for the position. After all, Manolo was a blood relative, and his blood was pure Castilian. After a moment, Rafael cleared his throat. "I have withdrawn from the bullfighting event."

Kahuu protested, "That is my favorite event, Papa. And you look so brave and handsome waving the red cape!"

"Your father's shoulder is stiff today, *muchacha*. You would not want the bull to have a better chance than your papa, would you?" Don Vicente chided the child gently.

Manolo had been listening to the conversation with growing anger. He had been sure that the old man would name him heir to his estates, instead of Rafael. Manolo turned and walked away, afraid the rage would show in his eyes. It wasn't fair, he railed silently. Rafael had everything that he himself wanted—respect from everyone, a child who adored him, a beautiful wife . . . and now he would inherit what should rightfully be Manolo's. He made his way back inside the hacienda walls, and ordered a passing servant to fetch a bottle of wine to his room. If only his bullet had found its mark yesterday, he wouldn't have to work out a new plan. Before today, he had intended to get rid of Rafael so that he could have Sara. Now, however, Tío Vicente's surprising revelation made the stakes even higher.

After the servant brought his wine, Manolo sprawled in a chair and tipped the bottle frequently, thinking coldly and furiously about how he could have it all.

Dinner that night was a festive occasion. Everyone seemed to be in high spirits, due to the exciting day of rodeo, as well as anticipation of the fiesta the following day. Doña Ines had presented Kahuu with a beautiful, red silk dress and matching lace mantilla. She looked like a Spanish princess. In an expansive mood, Don Vicente had given Sara a diamond necklace and matching eardrops that had been in the Delgado family for five generations. "I gave these to my beloved Pilar on our wedding day, and now they should belong to my grandson's wife," he said, admiring the way the diamonds sparkled to life in the glow of hundreds of candles in the dining room.

Doña Ines, sitting next to Rafael, leaned over and whispered, "Your grandfather is very pleased with your wife."

"My grandfather is a different man since I have returned from my trip, Tía Ines. He no longer seems . . . cold and hard. What has changed him?" Rafael asked quietly.

Doñ Ines glanced down the table toward her brother, seeing how happy he looked as he talked animatedly with Sara and Kahuu. "While you were gone, he was very ill for a while. After he collapsed in the courtyard, I sent for the *médico* in Santa Fe to see him. It is his heart. He was lucky to regain his strength, the doctor said, but he is supposed to take it very easy—which he does not do. Anyway, while he was ill, he talked to me as he had never done before, baring the secrets of his soul."

Rafael looked at his grandfather closely for a moment, and asked, "I had not noticed, but he does look more frail. Will he be all right now?"

Doña Ines shrugged. "He is an old man, Rafael, just as I am an old woman. God wills when it is our time to die. However, what I want you to know is this—Vicente loves you, he has always loved you. But, in the beginning, after your mother died and then your grandmother, he was bitter and lonely. For a time, he saw only the Comanche in you, and the Comanche had caused all of his troubles. He told me that as you grew up, he realized how much he loved you, but pride kept him from showing it."

Rafael was thoughtful for a moment. "I am glad he's forgotten his bitterness, and that he accepts Kahuu . . . but I don't know that I can forget."

Doña Ines touched his cheek affectionately. "All we can do in this life is try."

Manolo could barely keep up with what Matt Harrigan was saying. He nodded periodically, but his gaze kept straying to Sara. She looked more beautiful tonight than he had ever seen her. The royal blue satin gown brought out the blue in her eyes, while her hair floated like a silver cloud around her shoulders. She was perfection. She would be his after tomorrow.

Rafael watched from the sidelines, as Kahuu and Sara participated in the games. The children of the hacienda squealed with delight, as Sara was blindfolded and spun around before she swung her stick, looking for the *piñata*. Rafael smiled fondly as the younger children raced into the circle, guiding her aim by tugging on her skirt. Kahuu and the older children shouted encouragement, as Sara got closer and closer. When she hit her target and the broken *piñata* spilled its wonderful contents, Sara pulled the blindfold off and watched as the children scrambled for the candy and small trinkets. Moving back out of the way, Sara stepped right into Rafael's waiting arms. She turned her face up and smiled into his dark eyes. "What fun fiesta is! I've loved it all—the music, the dancing, the food, and the games, even when I lost," she said, laughing.

Rafael felt happiness swell up inside of him like a great wave on the ocean. This woman had crept into his heart, and given him hope for a bright future that he'd never dreamed possible. "If it makes you this happy, perhaps we should have fiesta every day," he teased, his eyes caressing her face.

"We wouldn't get a lot of work done that way," she teased him back, seeing a new emotion in his gaze that she hoped was love. She prayed that her patience was paying off.

"No, but we would be happy," he said, drawing her closer.

"We could be happy anyway, if we try," she said softly, her tone becoming serious.

"Sara . . . I—" he began, but broke off when Don Vicente appeared at their side.

"Come along, you two. The target shooting is about to begin, and Rafael must start it off."

As they made their way through the crowd of people, Sara wondered what Rafael had been about to say. By the look in his eye, it had been important. She clamped down on her frustration, telling herself that they would have time later to talk.

She moved to stand under the *portales* to watch, for the late afternoon sun had grown very warm. A man she'd never seen before was leaning against a

351

post nearby, and gave her a polite nod. She nodded in return and he stepped closer, his voice low when he spoke. "You are Sara Clayton?"

She blinked and turned to face him, nodding. "Yes, well, that was my name before I married."

"I have a message for you from your brother Max," he said quietly.

Sara caught her breath as myriad emotions washed over her. "Th—that can't be . . . my brother—Max died," she stammered, confusion in her eyes.

He met her gaze steadily. "He is not dead, señora, he is a prisoner—a slave to a heartless master. I will take you to him, if you wish."

His astounding revelation was almost more than she could absorb in a moment's notice. "Who are you? I think you should tell my husband—"

The man's dark eyes grew guarded. "I work for Don Vicente at his silver mine. And I would not advise telling Don Rafael about this, señora . . . he is the man who holds your brother and many others prisoner."

Sara felt as if the wind had been knocked out of her, as she stared at him, speechless for a moment. "But . . . but that can't be so!" she whispered, a sharp pain slicing her midsection. Rafael was not a cruel person . . . was he? What did she really know about him? This whole scenario was so bizarre, that she strained to get a grip on reality. "I don't know you, and I can't just take your word for something as important as this. Explain what this is all about," she said.

He looked furtively around, making sure that no one could hear their quiet conversation, and that

352

Rafael was engaged in target shooting for the moment. "A few years ago, a Pueblo Indian in your husband's employ told him of a hidden silver mine in the mountains of Tome, near the village of Manzano. Don Rafael did not wish to share this with his grandfather, for they were ever at odds. He began to secretly work the mine himself, but soon found he needed help. That is when some of the workers from Don Vicente's mine began to disappear, as well as an occasional farmer and shepherd."

Sara didn't want to believe the horror of this, but why, she asked herself, would this man make up such a story? "And how would *you* know all of this, if it was so secret?" she asked suspiciously.

"Two days ago, an Indian staggered into my camp at the Santa Pilar. He was near death, but managed to tell me of his existence as a prisoner at Don Rafael's secret mine. He also mentioned a *norteamericano* by the name of Clayton. I remembered the story of the man's death, as well as the disappearance of his partner. I made him describe the location, and went to check it out myself before I told anyone. I watched the camp all day yesterday. There are four guards and ten prisoners. I believe one of them is your brother."

"Why haven't you told Don Vicente about this?" she questioned, still not ready to accept his story.

"I am afraid for my job, señora. It is possible Don Vicente would try to cover his grandson's crimes. And I considered also the possibility that Don Rafael, if confronted, might get rid of these prisoners to protect himself."

Sara's eyes widened, and fear rose up in her

breast. What if the man was telling the truth? What if Max was really alive, and she had misjudged Rafael? She knew he had carried a lot of bitterness and hate in his soul for years. Finally, she asked, "Why are you telling me this, and what do you want me to do?"

A brief look of relief flickered in his eyes. "If you would come with me, señora, and see for yourself that your brother is alive, you could go to the governor, and he would help you." The man looked pained as he added, "I feel such pity for these creatures who are being worked to death."

A picture of her young, vibrant brother flashed through her mind, and she knew that if there was a chance that he was alive, she had to help him. "Where is this place, and when could we go there?"

"It is less than an hour's ride from here. We can go now," he replied without hesitation.

Sara glanced at Rafael, who was engrossed in the shooting competition. There was a painful twist in her stomach, when she thought about what she'd been told just now. She had to find out the truth—no matter what that truth might be. "I will meet you at the west gate in a quarter hour," she promised, and headed for her room to change.

When the two riders left the hacienda behind and Sara could no longer see the familiar structure, she grew a bit uneasy. Glancing at her companion, she assured herself that all would be well. He had been polite and respectful. They rode as hard as the trail allowed, and slowly only when the track grew rough in spots. After a half hour, Sancho—as he had introduced himself—veered off the main road. She followed him through a small canyon and then up onto a mesa, dotted with yucca and greasewood. They were climbing gradually into the hills, and the air was growing cooler. Sara was glad of her riding coat and gloves. When they reached a small stream that ran down from the mountains, they stopped to water their mounts and refresh themselves. "Is it much farther?" she asked anxiously.

"No, señora. Just a short way now. I hope the ride has not been too taxing?" he asked.

Sara relaxed at the note of concern in his voice. "No. I'm fine," she assured him. Taking the canteen from her saddle, she drank, then filled it.

Sancho put his sombrero back on his head, and pulled the chin string to tighten it. "I marked the way last night, so that I could find my way back again," he said, pointing out some thin bent twigs on a piñon tree beside the stream. "Since it was growing dark when I left there, I was afraid to take a chance."

As they remounted, she asked, "Is the place that hard to find?"

"It is off the track, señora. I am sure that is why no one has stumbled on it before."

Manolo relished the look of fear that leapt into Rafael's eyes when he imparted his news. Of course, he was careful not to show his pleasure.

"Why would Sara ride away with Sancho Valdez? Where is the *vaquero* who told you this?" Rafael demanded.

Manolo had found his cousin at one of the refreshment tables lining the *portales*. He was sipping a glass of wine and scanning the crowd, no doubt looking for his wife. Manolo turned and motioned to a young man who was standing a few feet away respectfully holding his hat in his hands. "Come here, Pico. Tell Don Rafael what you know."

The young man dropped his eyes under Rafael's fierce glare. "Señor Valdez ordered me to saddle two horses, Don Rafael, and tie them up outside the west gate. I did as I was told, and when I went back to secure the gate, I saw them riding away in the distance. When I could not find you, I told Don Manolo."

"How long ago, and which way did they go?" Rafael snapped.

Pico glanced up fearfully. "They rode due west, señor. It has been about a quarter hour."

"Bring my horse to the west gate as fast as you can," he ordered. When the *vaquero* departed, Rafael turned to Manolo. "What do you make of this? You know Valdez better than I."

Manolo looked puzzled. "I don't know, Rafael. Sancho has always been quiet—a good manager. I will come with you, though, and we will soon find out."

"I cannot wait for you, but you can inform grandfather and follow if you wish," Rafael said, already walking away.

Manolo smiled to himself. Pico had played his part perfectly, and deserved the bribe he had been promised. Manolo had no intention of telling his uncle of this, for he wanted no interference when he killed Rafael. If all went well, Manolo would be rid of his cousin, *and* would succeed in making Sara believe he had saved her from a husband who would have killed her to keep his secret.

He made his way slowly to the west gate, and watched Rafael gallop off into the distance. Turning, he dropped some coins into Pico's hand. "When I am master here, Pico, you will hold an important position. Now, fetch my horse and do not mention a word of this to anyone, eh?"

Manolo made sure Rafael was following the trail Sancho had left, before he took a different track that would put him ahead of his cousin. When he arrived at the prearranged spot, not far from the hidden mine, he spotted Sancho and Sara. He had instructed his henchman to slow their progress at this spot. Carefully concealing himself behind a boulder, Manolo fired a couple of shots over their heads.

Sara gasped at the unexpected attack. She and Sancho quickly dismounted, running to the trees for cover. "Your husband must have followed us," Sancho whispered, crouching beside her with his pistol drawn.

"We don't know who's out there," she protested in a shaky voice, holding onto a slim hope. That hope died, however, when she heard Rafael calling.

Rafael had just arrived on the scene, and quickly took cover as he heard the shots. As he slid between some boulders, he caught a glimpse of Sara's silver hair in a stand of trees. "Sara . . . I'm here!"

The sharp pain of betrayal ripped through her at the sound of his voice. She had loved him; how could she have been so wrong?

Manolo fired another shot in their direction, and fear gripped Sara. Rafael's voice had sounded reassuring, but maybe he was just trying to lull her fears. How would they get away from him, she wondered frantically? His years with the Comanche—along with superior intelligence—would give him an edge over Sancho. And what would happen to Max? Her heart plummeted when she thought of her dear, dear brother. Oh, what a cruel fate to have discovered he lived, only to die herself before they could be reunited.

Rafael willed himself to remain calm and assess the situation. He was puzzled. The shots had not been fired in his direction. Was Sancho firing wildly, not knowing his position? Some sixth sense warned him to lie low, until he understood what was going on. Fear for Sara caused his heart to pound rapidly. What would he do if something happened to her? His life had had very little meaning until she came along, and now when the three of them could be a family, she was in danger . . . and out of his reach.

When Manolo heard Rafael call out to Sara, he ascertained his cousin's exact location. Excitement rose up in him, as he visualized Rafael's dead body sprawled in the dust. There would be no one to refute the story he had fabricated for Sancho to tell her, for he intended to kill the prisoners and pay off the guards at the Indio Plata mine. Sara would be his, Hacienda Delgado would be his, and the Santa Pilar mine . . . all his. Tío Vicente could not live much longer.

Creeping from his hiding place, Manolo moved stealthily toward the spot where Rafael had taken cover. Cupping his hands around his mouth, he imitated the bark of a coyote, a prearranged signal to Sancho. As if on cue, his accomplice fired in Rafael's direction to draw his attention. Manolo moved on, and during the next exchange of shots, he was near enough to hear his cousin's faint cry. Elated, Manolo sped closer, hoping a wounded Rafael would be an easier target. As Manolo reached the edge of the concealing boulders, a shadow leapt from behind a piñon tree and landed on him before he could turn. Silently, the two men rolled on the ground, each vying for the upper hand. Manolo's gun had been knocked from his grasp, but Rafael's pistol was between them.

Rafael had been stunned when he jumped his attacker and saw his cousin's face. The two men hit the ground with a thud, and for a split second, Rafael stared into green, hate-filled eyes. An instinct for self-preservation took over, however, and he fought with all his strength to keep his gun from being turned on himself. "You should have died the last time I shot you, cousin," Manolo breathed with a raspy voice. Abruptly, he landed a vicious chop to Rafael's injured shoulder with his left hand, while his right hand retained his hold on the gun barrel. Rafael twisted his body at the force of the blow, as a sickening pain caused his stomach to lurch. Gritting his teeth, Rafael called on all his strength and rolled over on top of Manolo. Beads of sweat stood out on his forehead, as the two strained to gain control of the pistol. Manolo gave a great heave, trying to dislodge Rafael from his body, but Rafael pressed his momentary advantage, forcing the barrel forward. He squeezed the trigger, and Manolo stared in surprise at him for a moment, before his body went slack.

Rafael checked Manolo's throat for a pulse, but felt none. A twinge of regret touched him, as he closed the sightless eyes of his cousin and crossed himself.

Rafael's shoulder throbbed in an agony of pain, and he could feel the sticky wetness of blood soaking his shirt, where the wound had been opened. Manolo must have followed him and Sara that day at Pecos! If he hadn't been so absorbed with Sara, he would have picked up on the warning signs. Why had Manolo hated him? And for what reason had his cousin planned to commit murder? For the moment, Rafael pushed these disturbing thoughts from his mind, and turned to the situation at hand. He had to get Sara away from Sancho. It was obvious now that Valdez and his cousin had been working together, and that this had been yet another ambush.

Rafael studied his options, but didn't like any of them. He was afraid of rushing the man, for fear he would kill Sara. And coming up behind Sancho was risky, for the man most likely had her close to his side. She could get hurt in a scuffle. If only he could draw Sancho out of his hiding place. Rafael had faked an injured cry to fool Manolo and make him careless, but what would bring Sancho out into the open? The answer came to him then, crystal clear. He'd heard Manolo bark like a coyote, just seconds before Sancho began firing on him. It had been a signal between the two. He had often used signals such as that with his Comanche brothers. Cupping his hands around his mouth, he imitated the call he'd heard his cousin use, and then waited.

Sancho heard the gunshot. He leaned around the tree far enough to survey the area, but nothing moved. Holding tightly to Sara's arm, he felt as if time stood still. A chill crept up his spine, as he waited for the signal that all had gone according to plan. He didn't relish facing Don Rafael's wrath, if something went wrong. Then the coyote bark came, and a small hiss of relief escaped his parted lips.

Sara was trembling from reaction to the situation. She felt as if her heart had been ripped into pieces. Was it only that morning when she had been entertaining hopes for a bright future for the three of them? It seemed a lifetime ago. Poor Kahuu, she thought with despair. The child loved her father more than anything in the world. It would crush her young spirit if she ever found out what her father had done.

When Sancho turned to her, Sara returned his gaze listlessly. "Stay here, señora," he ordered in a whisper. "I am going to try to circle behind him. It is our only chance."

She nodded and slid to the ground, as he let her arm go. There was no strength left in her legs. Her eyes pooled with tears as she watched Sancho move away. He was going to try to kill Rafael . . . a rational voice in her mind told her. Even though she knew it was kill or be killed, she couldn't bear the thought of Rafael's death. On the heels of that thought came a sudden surge of strength to her limbs. Through her mind flashed pictures of the Rafael she knew—of the kindness and depth of feeling he was capable of. Hadn't he mourned a dead wife for years, and revered her memory? Hadn't he returned to Hacienda Delgado to help his aging grandfather, who had never shown him love? And hadn't he married her to save her reputation? A cold-blooded killer did not possess honor and a selfless love for others. Sara sprang to her feet and followed Sancho. Somehow, everything seemed clearer to her now. She didn't know why Sancho had lied, but her heart told her Rafael was not guilty of the things he had accused him of.

Quietly, she moved from one boulder to another, from one tree to the next, her head down, her ears alert to any sound. She reached inside her coat pocket, and closed her fingers around the small derringer that she'd had the presence of mind to bring.

As she slowly made a circle of the area, she began to despair of finding Rafael. All was silent, not even the squawk of a startled bird gave her a clue. The underbrush was becoming more dense, and her anxiety for Rafael grew with each measured step. What if Sancho caught him off guard? What if she was too late to help?

Biting her lip, she strove to maintain her composure. She could see a small clearing through the trees, and caught her breath when she saw Sancho dart across it, his gun drawn, his gaze riveted on the rock formations ahead of him. "Don Manolo?" he called softly.

Manolo? What part did he play in all of this? she wondered. Keeping her gaze pinned on Sancho, and creeping closer, Sara didn't see the hole until her foot slipped in and twisted painfully. She gasped aloud before she could stop herself, as she grabbed for a tree. She caught her balance, but had also alerted Sancho to her presence. He turned in her direction and was moving toward her, a black scowl on his face.

Knowing there was nothing to lose now, she breathlessly called out Rafael's name and tried to run. A white hot pain shot up her leg with the effort. She slipped to the ground in defeat.

Sancho crossed the distance quickly and reached down to grab her arm. "Your husband is dead, señora, and calling his name will not bring him back to life," he said harshly.

Sara jerked free of his grasp. "Don't touch me! You were lying about Rafael, and I want to know why!"

Sancho stepped back and glanced around, as if reassuring himself that no one was there. Sara slipped her hand back into her pocket, and let her fingers curl around the gun once more. He turned back. "I had to tell you something to get you away from the hacienda. I am going to hold you for ransom. Don Vicente will pay much for you, I think."

Sara could tell he was lying again. It showed in his actions, and the way his eyes would not meet hers. Manolo was mixed up in this, but she didn't know how. He put his gun back in its holster, as if he knew he wouldn't need it for her . . . or Rafael. That frightening realization caused her stomach to lurch. Where was Rafael? And where was Manolo? Sancho had called to him as if he knew that he was close by.

Swallowing the fear that had lodged in her throat, Sara said, "So the story you told about my brother was a lie? You're not only a criminal, Sancho, you're a cruel man."

Sancho shrugged. "It worked. Now get up, señora. We have to travel."

Before he could reach down to help her, she pulled the derringer from her pocket and pointed it at him. "I think we have more talking to do, and then we're going back to the hacienda. Only you'll be my prisoner, instead of the other way around," she said, determination sparking in her blue eyes.

Sancho's eyes widened as he stared down the barrel of the tiny gun. At close range, there was no chance she would miss, he thought. Swallowing tightly, he nodded. *"Si."*

On the surface, Sara looked confident, but inside she was quaking. How the devil would she get this man—who was twice her size—back to the *rancho?* Her ankle was throbbing painfully now, without any pressure on it. And it was going to be dark soon. None of her apprehension showed, however, as she asked point-blank, "What does Manolo have to do with this, Sancho? I heard you calling to him."

A flicker of surprise lit his eyes for a moment. "You are mistaken, señora," he said evenly. His eyes darted around, as if looking for someone.

"Well, no matter. Don Vicente will get it out of you," she said briskly. Raising herself carefully to her knees, she decided she couldn't sit there all evening. If she could just get him to their horses, she could tie his hands and at least have a chance.

He watched her just as intently as she watched

him, looking for an opening. When she managed to stand on her good foot, she balanced herself with the bad one, and cried out at the slight pressure. As swift as a flash of lightning, Sancho slapped the gun from her hand and grabbed her around the waist. Sara screamed, as fresh, jagged pain ran up her leg from the ankle.

"Let her go or you die right here," Rafael said, appearing suddenly behind him.

Sancho whipped around, dread clutching at his heart. "I will kill her, Don Rafael, if you come one step closer," he threatened, his free arm moving swiftly to her throat. "She is so fragile, señor, I could crush her windpipe before you fire a shot, eh?"

Rafael's gun was pointed at them, but he was afraid to fire while Sancho held her. If the man moved, the bullet might hit Sara . . . and then there was Sancho's threat.

"You might as well let her go. Manolo cannot help you, if that is what you are thinking. He is dead," Rafael told him calmly.

Sancho sucked in his breath, and turned so that Sara's body was between him and Rafael. "I don't need his help, señor. Now throw down your gun," he said, a muscle twitching nervously in his jaw.

Rafael assessed the situation, reading the message in the other man's eyes, he decided to comply. Sancho was desperate. He would kill Sara. Rafael dropped his gun and backed up a step.

Sancho visibly relaxed and drew Sara backwards with him. She went deathly pale, as she was forced to put pressure on her bad ankle. Rafael sent her a reassuring message with his eyes.

"When I am safely away, I will let her go," Sancho called to Rafael, the metallic taste of fear still in his mouth.

Rafael stood rigid, and watched until they were out of sight. When he picked up his gun, he spotted Sara's derringer and retrieved it as well. He ran to where his horse was tied, and turned in the direction Sancho and Sara had gone.

Sancho reached the hidden mine as darkness began to settle. He was alone, and the sentry nodded to him as he passed by, leading an extra horse. Sancho couldn't resist looking over his shoulder every few minutes, fearing Rafael would be there. By the time he'd gotten Sara to where their horses were tied, she had passed out from the pain. He was afraid to take the time to tie her onto her horse, so he left her there on the ground, took the two horses, and rode as hard as he could ride. He knew Rafael would find her, and it would surely slow him down. That was all Sancho needed. He intended to retrieve his bags of hidden silver, and leave the country.

Sancho tied the horses outside the guardhouse and turned to Arturo, who was stirring a pot of beans over a fire at the end of the adobe. "Brush my horses down and give them some feed. I will be leaving shortly," he barked without preamble.

When he entered the house, Rodrigo was sitting at the table, drinking wine from the bottle. The guard rose unsteadily to his feet. "Señor Sancho, *buenas no—*"

"Go help Arturo with my horses. I'm in a hurry,"

he ordered, giving the half-drunken man a hard stare.

Rodrigo blinked and set the bottle down. He got up and moved unsteadily out the door, closing it behind him.

Sancho moved swiftly to the window opening, and pulled back the canvas that covered it. Seeing that the two guards were doing his bidding, he dropped the flap and moved to a large wooden box that held picks and shovels. Pulling it away from the wall, he lifted a loose board from the floor, revealing a hole dug in the earth. There were four bags inside, and he took them out, stuffing them into his shirt. He carefully replaced the board and the box, knowing he could not trust his men if they suspected he carried this much silver.

When he stepped outside, the two guards were just putting the saddles back on the animals. Taking a silver dollar from his pocket, he flipped it to Arturo. "Fetch a bottle of your wine for me, and some corn cakes, if you have any." The guard glanced at Rodrigo, and after he finished cinching the strap on the horse's belly, he made his way inside.

In less than five minutes, Sancho was on his way south, and away from the wrath of Rafael.

When Sara awoke, it was dark, except for the flickering light of a campfire close by, and she was cradled in Rafael's arms. He smiled down into her eyes, when he saw that her gaze held a residue of fear. "You are all right, *mi alma*. Sancho is gone, and he left you behind," he said, stroking the hair back

367

from her face tenderly. "That was a very wise thing for him to do."

Sara freed her hands from the blanket he had wrapped around her, and clasped his hand in hers. "Oh, Rafael . . . it was a nightmare," she whispered. "He told me a horrible story about you, about how you were operating a secret mine, and that my brother Max was alive, little more than a slave at that mine."

Rafael felt a surge of anger at the man for hurting her that way. He bent his head and kissed her hair. "He and my cousin were in this together. I'm sure Manolo came up with the story about your brother, because he knew it would take something important to get your attention."

Sara wiped at her eyes. "But it was so cruel. Why did they do this at all? I just don't understand, Rafael."

"When I catch up with Sancho, I will make him talk, but until then, all I can do is guess at the reasons. Over the years whenever Manolo and his father came to visit Hacienda Delgado, my cousin never failed to taunt me about the condition of my birth. He would tell me that he, a true Delgado, would inherit my grandfather's lands someday. And I truly think he believed that, until the other day when my grandfather said that I would be *patrón* someday." Rafael paused for a moment, his silence speaking of deep emotions. He shifted his weight and leaned back against the tree once more. "We are not too far from the Santa Pilar mine, *niña*. At first light I'll take you there. After the shock you've had, you need some coffee and food, before we set out for the *rancho.*"

"Is Manolo really dead?" she asked.

"*Sí.* We struggled, and I killed him," he said flatly.

Sara saw the flicker of remorse in Rafael's eyes. After all that his cousin had done, Rafael still felt regret over killing him. "You had to defend yourself, and you also saved my life," she pointed out softly.

"I think you were part of the prize Manolo was working for, Sara. I was very jealous of the way he looked at you," he said, gazing into the fire.

Her heart picked up speed at this admission. "I didn't think you cared, Rafael. After all, you married me because you felt duty-bound."

"I married you, because I love you," he admitted, his voice growing husky.

Sara sat up straighter. "Oh, Rafael," she breathed. "Why didn't you tell me before?"

He laced his fingers with hers and stared for a moment at their joined hands. "I was . . . afraid. Afraid that you didn't love me—afraid to love someone as much as I loved you. I cared for my grandfather, and he ignored me . . . and then I loved Tuwikka, and she died. It has been hard for me to show my feelings, Sara. But when I nearly lost you, I realized how foolish I had been."

"Oh, Rafael! You were not the only foolish one. I've loved you from the first, but I let silly doubts and fears come between us. Pedro told me your grandfather had chosen a wife for you, so I bowed out. I didn't want to come between the two of you, just when it looked like you would heal the breach."

Rafael felt the load fall from his shoulders at her confession. "I thought you shied away from the fact that I was half-Comanche."

Sara stroked his face tenderly, tears in her eyes. "Forgive me, Rafael, I let you believe that. If you were angry with me, I knew you would fall in with Don Vicente's plans. It nearly killed me."

He shook his head in confusion. "I know nothing about any wife my grandfather had in mind. As a matter of fact, he told me himself how pleased he was by our marriage."

Sara frowned. "He has seemed very happy about it, hasn't he? Well, we will speak to him when we return."

"*Sí*. He and Pedro have some questions to answer," he agreed firmly. "For now, though, we will forget them. We are alone, and I want to kiss my wife . . . the woman I love . . ." His mouth descended to hers, and Sara wound her arms around his neck. She felt as if she had finally come home. She felt loved, cherished, and protected. The loneliness inside her melted away, as the kiss deepened. Without spoken words, he promised her a life of love and happiness, and she gave him the same promise, holding back nothing. They touched, whispered, and held each other for a long while, before they slept.

"Are you sure you're feeling all right, Sara?" Rafael asked, as they followed the visible signs of Sancho's trail.

"I feel wonderful," she said, laying her cheek against his back as they rode double on his horse. "Since you wrapped it this morning, my ankle doesn't even hurt. And we should follow Sancho's trail while it's fresh."

Absently, he scanned the ridge they were climbing, and patted her arm wound around his waist. "I do not think we will find him, but I was curious as to why he traveled this way. It is off the regular trail, which would have been more logical for him to follow."

When they reached the mesa, Rafael's eyes narrowed as he spotted a thin plume of smoke in the canyon beyond. The trees were dense, so he could see little else. "Perhaps we should check on that fire," he suggested, reaching into his pocket. Pulling out her small derringer, he passed it back to her. "You may need this."

Sara put the gun in her coat pocket and sat up straighter, putting her hat back on her head. The sun was climbing above the horizon, and she didn't want her silver hair to become a target, in case they found Sancho.

As they silently followed the winding trail Sancho had left, Sara felt the strangest sensation wash over her. It was almost like happy anticipation. When they neared the bottom of the canyon floor, Sara felt Rafael stiffen. "What is it?" she whispered.

"On that rise to the right—I see someone," he whispered back, reining their horse behind a thicket. He dismounted and handed the reins to her, then he peered around a piñon tree. After a moment, he stepped back to her side. "It is a guard, but he seems to be sleeping. I want you to stay here, while I circle around for a better look," he said in a hushed tone. Noting the anxious expression in her eyes, he

371

touched her hand. "I won't take any chances, *niña,* but if you hear shots, ride back the way we came and follow the road until you come to the Santa Pilar. It's not far from here."

"Maybe we should go there first and get some help," she suggested, her voice edged with fear.

"Try not to worry, Sara," he said, giving her a smile before he slipped away through the woods.

Sara would have followed him, if her ankle hadn't been such a problem. Instead, she concentrated on keeping the stallion quiet by rubbing his neck and whispering softly to him. It kept her mind off what might be happening across the canyon. She did wonder, though, what the man was guarding. There was no *rancho* nearby; Rafael had said this area was deserted. To keep the awful anxiety at bay, Sara let her mind drift back to the night before, when Rafael had held her in his arms and told her he loved her. Just thinking about it made shivers of excitement race over her skin. She felt that finally they had a chance for happiness. That thought brought her back to the present. Why hadn't Rafael returned yet? Slipping her hand into her pocket, she felt for the derringer, the smooth, hard surface of the barrel reassuring her. If he didn't return soon, she would go after him, she promised herself.

"It's Rafael, Sara," he said, coming up quietly behind her.

Sara gasped sharply, not having heard the slightest sound of his approach. "Oh, Rafael! What happened?"

He swung up in the saddle in front of her, and urged the horse in the direction from which he had just come. "I tapped the lookout guard on the head, so he will sleep a little longer, and then tied and gagged him. Sancho's story about the hidden mine was true. From up there, you can see the mine entrance, as well as two adobes. We arrived at just the right time, *niña,* for four guards were transferring about ten men from one of the houses to the mine for their workday. The prisoners had wrist chains on. I stayed long enough to see them go into the mine, along with two of the guards. The other two stayed at ground level."

Sara's heart had begun to beat furiously. "Do you think one of them is Max? Oh, Rafael! It would be so wonderful, if that part of his story was true as well."

"I couldn't tell, Sara. They were all dirty and in rags. They barely looked human. Don't get your hopes up, *por favor,"* he cautioned gently.

"What are we going to do now? And what about the man you tied up?" she asked anxiously.

"I moved him away to a safe spot, until we return. We're going to the Santa Pilar for help. I don't want you getting hurt," he told her firmly.

Sara didn't argue, but held onto the slim hope that Max might be one of the prisoners.

A short ride brought them to his grandfather's mine site, and a half hour later, Rafael led four men back to the hidden mine. Sara waited until they were just out of sight, and then hobbled to a donkey that stood patiently outside the guardhouse. She had told Renato, the young man who was supposed to be watching over her, that she needed a few moments alone out back. He had blushed—catching her meaning—and nodded vigorously. Sara smiled to herself, as she lifted her bad leg over the small animal's back and settled into place astride. Grabbing the reins, she turned him toward the road. By the time Renato discovered that she and the donkey were missing, she would be long gone.

The little mule was docile and followed her commands. Sara would have felt lucky, except for the fact that the ride jolted her ankle with each step. Gritting her teeth, she continued, refusing to be left out of the rescue. If Max was there, he might need her, she reasoned.

The sun was high over the mountains when she recognized the entrance to the small canyon. Silence reigned, and she felt unsure for the first time. What if something had gone wrong? Urging the donkey off the trail, she wove her way through the concealing wooded area. When she came to the clearing where the mine site was, she tied her mount to a tree, and hobbled to the back of the guardhouse. As quietly as she could, she made her way around the adobe building and peered around the corner. There was not a soul in sight, but Rafael's horse, along with several others, was tied to the hitching post in front. She sighed with relief. Everything must be all right, she reasoned. Perhaps the men were in the guard-house, or maybe they had descended into the mine shaft to rescue the prisoners. Just as she was about to step away from the building, the front door was flung open, and a dark, swarthy man stepped out and moved toward the mine entrance. She didn't recognize him as one of the guards who had accompanied Rafael from the Santa Pilar. Hastily, she stepped back and flattened herself against the wall. Her heart began to pound. Where was Rafael? Chancing a peek around the corner again, she watched the man enter the dark hole in the side of the hill. She needed a look inside the building, she thought. Making her way back to the end of the adobe, she circled around, hoping there was a window on the other side. Luck was with her. Carefully, she crept along the wall, glancing every now and then toward the mine opening, to make sure the man didn't return. When she reached the window, she breathed a sigh of relief. The shutters were open, and she could hear Rafael's voice inside. "If we are not back very shortly, someone will come looking for us," he was saying.

Sara edged closer until she could see inside. Swiftly, her gaze took in the room. Rafael and his men were tied, hand and foot, and sitting with their backs against the opposite wall. She couldn't see how many men held them captive, but guessed it was only one. When she had left with Rafael earlier, there had been two guards above ground, and one of them had just gone down into the shaft—that left one. While these thoughts raced through her mind, Rafael's gaze caught a flicker of movement at the window, and his heart nearly stopped. There was no mistaking her silver hair.

Sara caught Rafael's eye and gave him a questioning look. In silent communication, he tipped his head slightly to the right, and then turned in that direction as the guard spoke. "We will be gone soon, Señor Delgado. We do not own this little operation, and to tell the truth, *amigo,* we don't want no trouble with you, eh? If what you say is true, your people will find you here," Arturo said calmly, almost apologetically. "When Rodrigo returns with our other two *compadres,* we will have to borrow your horses and bid you *adios.*"

Maybe the man meant what he said, and maybe he didn't. Sara knew there wasn't much time. She hobbled around to the front, and pulled her gun from her pocket. She boldly opened the door. The guard, holding the gun on Rafael and the others, was resting one hip on the table with his back to her. "Ah, here's my *amigo* now—" he said, turning toward the door. His mouth dropped open at the sight of Sara pointing her derringer at his face.

"Throw your gun on the floor, and do it now," she ordered in a no-nonsense tone. She was steadying the derringer with both hands, and did not intend to be tricked again.

Arturo started to say something, but he thought better of it as he heard her cock the small weapon. Dropping his gun, he raised his hands in a gesture of surrender.

"Kick it across to me, and then untie Rafael . . . and you'd better hurry. If I hear your friend returning, I'm going to have to shoot you. I'd hate to do it, but I don't think I can manage two of you, *comprender?*" she said calmly, moving to kick the door shut with her heel. She appeared to be composed, even though her insides were quaking. If the man knew how scared she was, he would try something. Her heart slowed down as he moved to do her bidding.

Rafael's eyes glinted with admiration, as he watched Sara handle the situation with aplomb. When Arturo had him untied, he immediately set about tying the man's hands behind his back. "The worm has turned, eh, Arturo?" he said, pushing him down to sit on the floor. Crossing the room in quick strides, he retrieved Arturo's gun and took Sara's from her hands. "You are wonderful, *cara mia*," he whispered, for her ears only. "Can you untie my men, while I watch for the other guard?"

Her hands trembled, as he caressed her with his eyes. She gave a shaky laugh. "You aren't angry with me for following you?"

He stroked her arm gently. "Very angry. But I am also very proud of you, *mi alma*."

Sara set about her task, her heart warmed by Rafael's praise. One by one, she untied the men, and then moved to her husband's side again. They didn't have long to wait, before he spotted the other three guards coming from the mouth of the mine shaft. Turning from the window toward the door, he waited with his men, guns drawn.

There was no fight. When the three walked in the door, it was too late for them to do anything. They were soon tied up, and questioned about the prisoners who had been left down in the shaft. Rafael sent one of his men to fetch them, and before long, the sad-looking troop marched out of the dark hole in the ground. Sara and Rafael were waiting near the entrance. One of the men broke the line when he spotted her. "Sara!" he breathed, walking unsteadily toward her.

Her eyes filled with tears of joy, as she and Rafael

moved forward to grasp him by the arms. "Oh, Maxwell . . . my dearest brother, I thought you were dead," she said tenderly, hugging his thin frame.

The gaunt-faced young man rested his head on hers, as tears slipped down his dirty cheeks. "My baby sister," he whispered.

The love that flowed between brother and sister was a tangible thing, and Rafael was torn by conflicting emotions. He was happy that Sara had found her brother, but at the same time, he didn't want her to love anyone more than she did him. Then she reached out and clasped his hand in hers, drawing him into their circle. Rafael's world fell into place. They were a family now.

Chapter 16

Sara awoke from her siesta and stretched like a feline on the soft bed. The room was dim, and she realized with a start that she had slept for hours. It was dusk outside, and it would soon be time to dress for dinner. She rolled off the bed and shivered a little, as she padded in bare feet across the cold wooden floor to the window. Pulling aside the curtain, she gazed out at the dark shape of the fountain in the courtyard. She moved away from the window, lit a lamp next to the bed, and placed a log on the red embers in the fireplace.

After washing, she slipped into a warm robe and sat down at her dressing table to brush her hair. Smiling at her reflection in the mirror, she marveled at the happy events that had taken place in her life in the last few weeks. Finding Max had been an extraordinary gift. He was growing stronger every day, with rest and proper food to fill out his thin frame.

When they had returned to the hacienda from the

hidden mine that day, a man named Boone Keegan was waiting to talk to her. She had nearly fainted when he said he worked for Jonas Farber. Rafael had unraveled the whole story from her explanations and Keegan's account of his mission. Sara smiled to herself. It was a good thing Farber was so far away, for Rafael had been murderously angry at him for what he'd done to Sara. After hearing Sara's story, Boone decided he could not accept the bank's money for this job; he felt no loyalty to a man as unscrupulous as Farber. Max and Boone held several conferences and decided they would wait until spring and travel back to St. Louis to straighten out the Clayton affairs . . . and also deal with Farber. They had all taken a liking to Boone, and Rafael invited him to stay the winter and work on the hacienda.

When the bedroom door opened, she turned. A happy glow of confidence lit her eyes. Finding that Rafael loved her deeply, had given her life the meaning she'd always searched for. She moved to meet him halfway across the room, and stepped into his waiting arms. "You're not ill, are you, *mi alma?* I just returned from Santa Fe, and Rosita said you had been asleep all afternoon," he murmured, kissing the top of her head.

Sara leaned against his chest, feeling the strong beat of his heart under her hand. "No, my love, I'm not sick, but I do have something to tell you."

Old doubts and fears clutched at his heart for a moment, and then he relaxed, stroking her silver hair. She loved him, and he knew that now. "So many unexpected things have happened in my life since I met you, I'm almost afraid to ask what it is."

She could hear the smile in his voice, and chuckled. "This is not an ambush or a murder attempt, or even a kidnapping. It's good news . . . anyway, I think it is," she said, leaning back to see his face. "We're going to have a baby."

For a moment, he stared at her blankly, and then his gaze grew warm and tender. He leaned down and kissed her. "A baby," he breathed softly against her lips.

Sara wound her arms around his neck and pressed closer to him. "Are you . . . happy about it, Rafael?" she asked.

"I could not be happier, Sara," he growled, his voice thick with emotion. "You have given me more than any man deserves in this life . . . and now you're giving me another child to love."

Closing her eyes with a satisfied sigh, Sara threaded her fingers in his thick, dark hair. "Oh, Rafael, everything is so wonderful in my life, sometimes I'm afraid fate will snatch it all away. I have you and Kahuu, and a whole new family now. And I want this baby so much, it frightens me," she said, her voice growing husky.

He rubbed his rough cheek against her soft one, and stroked her back. "Do not let fear steal your happiness, *cara mia*. Believe in our love and our future," he urged.

Sara felt a sense of peace wash over her as he spoke. The visit they had made to the village of Pecos flashed through her mind, and she smiled. In the sacred temple, her wish had been for a happy family. Didn't she have that now? she asked herself.

Even Max had been returned to her.

Rafael gently put her away from him, and reached into his coat pocket. "I have something here you might want to see," he said, smiling. "It's a letter from Garth."

Sara took the envelope and pulled out the note, scanning it quickly. A wide smile lit her face. "So they're married . . . and happy. That doesn't surprise me. I'm glad he let us know they'll definitely be settling in New Orleans. Do you think we could visit them sometime?"

"We can do anything you want, my love. However, not until the baby is older, I think," he promised.

Sara chuckled. "I wasn't thinking of going now." She replaced the note inside the envelope, and dropped it on the end of the bed. Turning back to Rafael, she reached for his coat to help him off with it. "You have time for a hot bath before dinner. I'll wash your back like a good and obedient wife," she said archly, tossing the coat onto the bed and turning to unbutton his shirt.

A slow smile curved his mouth at her seductive ministrations. He reached for her robe and opened the front, to gaze at her beautiful body clad in the revealing chemise. "Obedient, eh? Would you obey, if I ordered you into the tub with me?"

His deep voice, simmering with passion, made her pulse skitter wildly. When his hands settled on her waist and he drew her against him, she could feel his arousal. A delightful shiver of wanting ran through her at his exciting proposal. Cocking her head to the side, she asked in a teasing tone, "What will we do while Rosita heats the water? I'm too cold to stand here naked."

A laugh rumbled low in his chest, as he scooped her up into his arms and deposited her on the bed. He grinned at the mock-innocent look she gave him as he finished undressing. "Slide under the covers, and we will think of something, eh?"

Always a voracious reader, Sandy discovered at a very early age that she also wanted to be a writer. To her, a good book was a magical place where exciting people set out on adventures that took them all over the world and beyond, a place where dreams came true, and a happy ending was a given. Sandy attempted several novels, from her first at age twelve, to her first published romance at age thirty-eight.

Combining her love of history and romance, she's sold seven Heartfire historicals to Zebra. Previous releases are: *Deception's Fire*, *Rapture's Reward*, and *Restless Passions*.

Sandy lives in St. Louis, Missouri with her husband of twenty-four years, has one daughter and twin granddaughters. She enjoys hearing from readers: 2683 S. Big Bend, Suite #15, St. Louis, Missouri 63143.